Jack Sheffield was born in 1945 and grew up in the tough environment of Gipton Estate, in north-east Leeds. After a job as a 'pitch boy', repairing roofs, he became a Corona Pop Man before going to St John's College, York, and training to be a teacher. In the late seventies and eighties, he was a headteacher of two schools in North Yorkshire before becoming Senior Lecturer in Primary Education at Bretton Hall near Wakefield. It was at this time that he began to record his many amusing stories of village life portrayed in *Teacher, Teacher!* and *Mister Teacher*. He lives in York and Hampshire.

Visit his website at www.jacksheffield.com

DEAR TEACHER

The Alternative School Logbook 1979–1980

Jack Sheffield

BANTAM PRESS

LONDON · TORONTO · SYDNEY · AUCKLAND · JOHANNESBURG

TRANSWORLD PUBLISHERS
61–63 Uxbridge Road, London W5 5SA
A Random House Group Company
www.rbooks.co.uk

First published in Great Britain
in 2009 by Bantam Press
an imprint of Transworld Publishers

Chapter 8 was first published as *An Angel Called Harold* in 2008

A CIP catalogue record for this book
is available from the British Library.

ISBN 9780593061503

Addresses for Random House Group Ltd companies outside the UK
can be found at: www.randomhouse.co.uk
The Random House Group Ltd Reg. No. 954009

The Random House Group Limited supports The Forest Stewardship
Council (FSC), the leading international forest certification organization.
All our titles that are printed on Greenpeace-approved FSC-certified paper
carry the FSC logo. Our paper procurement policy can be found at
www.rbooks.co.uk/environment

Typeset in 11/15pt Palatino by
Kestrel Data, Exeter, Devon.
Printed and bound in Great Britain by
Clays Ltd, Bungay, Suffolk.

2 4 6 8 10 9 7 5 3

Mixed Sources
Product group from well-managed
forests and other controlled sources
www.fsc.org Cert no. TT-COC-2139
© 1996 Forest Stewardship Council
FSC

For my brother Roy

Acknowledgements

I am deeply indebted to my ever-patient and hugely supportive editor, Linda Evans; the dynamic publicity team of Stina Smemo and Lynsey Dalladay and all at Transworld for their support, particularly Katie Espiner, Nick Robinson, Sophie Holmes and fellow 'Old Roundhegian' Martin Myers. Also, thanks go to my hardworking agent, Philip Patterson of Marjacq Scripts, for his good humour and vast knowledge of world trivia.

I am grateful to all those who assisted in the research for this novel – in particular: Sarah Barrett, school nurse, Hampshire; Janina Bywater, nurse and lecturer in psychology, Cornwall; Marie Cragg, director, PHASE Charity, South Yorkshire; Mary Cragg, adviser, Citizens' Advice Bureau, Hampshire; Dr Bill Inness, dentist, York; Julie Kenny, managing director, Pyronix, Sheffield; Sue Matthews, primary-school teacher, York; Caroline Stockdale, librarian, York Central Library; Christine Swann, radio presenter, York Hospital Radio, and Roy Turgoose, retired military pilot, York.

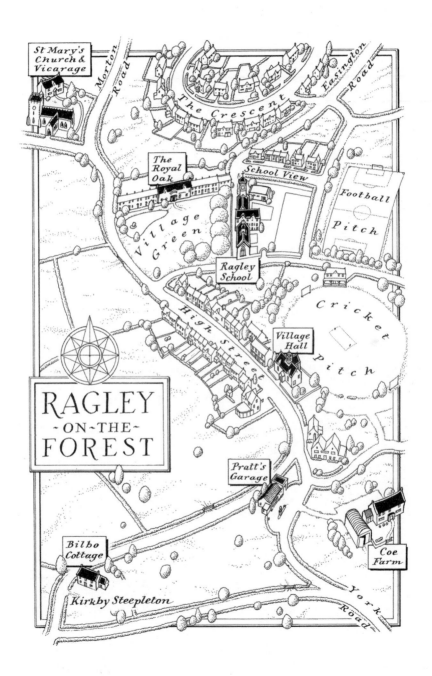

Prologue

Three people . . . two sisters . . . one problem.

Ragley School was still and silent on this late-summer day. A shaft of early-morning amber sunlight streamed in through the high arched Victorian windows and lit up my old oak headmaster's desk.

Propped against a brass paperweight was a photograph of three people, captured at a moment in time. I was in the centre, smiling at the camera, the July sunshine glinting on my Buddy Holly spectacles. My arms were wrapped round the slim waists of two beautiful women.

To my left, Laura Henderson was glancing up at me with soft green eyes. She was wearing a forget-me-not-blue dress and her long brown hair hung free over her suntanned shoulders. To my right was Beth Henderson and, once again, I felt that familiar ache in my heart. There was a time I had hoped I might spend the rest of my life with her but it appeared it was not to be.

I tilted the photograph towards the light and examined it more closely. Beth looked stunning in a cream suit and matching wide-brimmed hat. Her honey-blonde hair caressed her high cheekbones and I sighed at the memory of the day. I noticed she was staring curiously at her sister.

On the back of the photograph was a message that read: '*Dear Jack, a reminder of a lovely day. See you on 3 September, Jo and Dan.*'

Jo Hunter, the class teacher of the older infant children, had married our local police constable at the end of the summer term. After the wedding everyone had gathered in the village hall for a party that gradually broke up when the happy couple had driven off into the sunset.

Once more I stared at the photograph and remembered that day six weeks ago. Laura had invited me back to her flat in York. 'I'm having a relaxing night in, tonight, Jack. I was hoping you might like to join me for a meal,' she said before driving away.

Minutes later, to my surprise, Beth made the same offer. 'It would be good to see you tonight, if you want to come back to Morton,' she said. 'We've got some catching-up to do.' Then she stretched up and kissed me gently on the lips. It was so unexpected. Earlier in the year, Beth had made it clear that she didn't want any permanent commitment.

Her words were still etched in my mind.

So, that evening, with hope in my heart, I had driven to Beth's house in Morton village. As I opened my car door, she walked down the path to meet me. Her reception was cautious. 'I've just had a call from my little sister,' she said, 'and she says she's expecting you.' Beth looked sad. Then she stretched up and kissed me lightly on the cheek. When she walked away she didn't look back.

Feeling confused, I drove to York, where Laura had prepared a lovely meal and, though I tried to be attentive, my thoughts were elsewhere. Weeks passed and, as the summer holiday progressed, I saw more of Laura and less of Beth. Eventually, August came to an end and I turned my attention back to my work and the new school year ahead.

It was Saturday, 1 September 1979. My third year as headmaster of Ragley-on-the-Forest Church of England Primary School in North Yorkshire was about to begin. I unlocked the bottom drawer of my desk and slid the photograph inside for safekeeping. Then I took out the large, leather-bound school logbook and opened it to the next clean page. I filled my fountain pen with black Quink ink, wrote the date and stared at the empty page. The record of another school year was about to begin.

Two years ago, the retiring headmaster, John Pruett, had told me how to fill in the official school logbook. 'Just keep it simple,' he said. 'Whatever you do, don't say what really happens, because no one will believe you!'

So the real stories were written in my 'Alternative School Logbook'. And this is it!

Chapter One

Beatrix Potter and the Pest Controller

86 children were registered on roll on the first day of the school year. Following a Health & Safety directive from County Hall, Star Wars *light sabres were banned. The Pest Control Officer visited school.*
Extract from the Ragley School Logbook:
Tuesday, 4 September 1979

'So where's our Damian's light sabre, Mr Sheffield?'

It occurred to me that the beginning of another school year just wouldn't be the same without the pit-bull presence of our least favourite parent, Mrs Winifred Brown.

'I haven't seen it, Mrs Brown; what does it look like?'

'It's three foot long an' it glows blue in t'dark . . . at least, it would if my Eddie got off 'is backside an' put t'batt'ries in.'

I removed my Buddy Holly spectacles and began to

polish them to give me thinking time. 'And when did it go missing?'

"E brought it t'school jus' afore all you teachers went off on y'cushy six-week 'oliday.' Next to her, five-year-old Damian lifted his sinister Darth Vader mask, dispelled all thoughts of Empire domination and proceeded to pick his nose.

'I'm sorry, Mrs Brown. I'll ask Mrs Grainger to look in her Lost Property box.'

'Y'better do that 'cause it cos' me a fortune.'

With that I retreated quickly and shut the office door.

'An' ah'll be back at quarter t'three,' she shouted. 'Our Damian needs some shoes from t'Co-Op,' and she stormed out.

It was just after 8.30 a.m. on Tuesday, 4 September 1979 and my third year as headmaster of Ragley Church of England Primary School in North Yorkshire had begun.

Anne Grainger, the deputy headmistress, walked into the office from the staff-room clutching a copy of Beatrix Potter's *The Tale of Mrs Tittlemouse*.

'May the force be with you, Jack,' said Anne with a grin.

Anne, a tall, slim brunette in her mid-forties, was always a reassuring presence. Her patience was legendary and she certainly needed it as our Reception Class teacher.

'Force?'

'Yes, you know, as in *Star Wars*.'

A distant memory of sitting next to Beth Henderson in the Odeon cinema in York, watching *Star Wars IV, A New Hope*, flickered across my mind. I recalled that Beth had asked me why the film had begun at episode IV but all I could think about was how lucky I was to be sitting next to such a beautiful woman.

Anne shook her head in mock dismay and grabbed my arm. 'Come on,' she said, 'Vera's giving out the new registers,' and we walked out of the office, past the little cloakroom area and into the staff-room.

Miss Vera Evans, our fifty-seven-year-old secretary, looked imperiously over her steel-rimmed spectacles. 'May I remind you all to mark your pupils present in black and the ones who are absent in red.' Then she handed out the new attendance registers.

'Your word is our command, Vera,' said Sally Pringle.

A tall, freckle-faced thirty-eight-year-old with bright ginger hair, Sally taught the younger junior children and her lively dress sense was a world away from Vera's immaculate Marks & Spencer's pin-striped business suit. Vera frowned and glanced at Sally, who was picking absent-mindedly at the hand-stitching on the pockets of her voluminous tie-dyed tangerine dress. She never fully understood Sally's humour.

'Thanks, Vera,' said Jo Hunter.

Jo was a diminutive, athletic twenty-four-year-old with long jet-black hair who taught the older infants. She looked thoughtfully at her name on the front cover of her class register, written by Vera in neat copperplate handwriting. After being Jo Maddison all her life, her new married name still intrigued her.

'And you will recall,' continued Vera, 'that last year County Hall banned skateboards in school . . . Well, this year they've banned something called a "light sabre", which I understand is a toy that resembles a broomstick.'

'Quite right, Vera,' I said, recalling my conversation with Mrs Brown.

Anne gave me a knowing look, picked up her new register and hurried off to check her Lost Property box. Jo gathered together a collection of posters on 'The Seashore' and set off back to her classroom, where she stood on a chair to write the date on the top of her chalkboard. Meanwhile Sally put her new register in her hippy, open-weave shoulder bag, selected a garibaldi from the biscuit tin and walked out of the staff-room – but, noticeably, without her usual enthusiasm.

Vera smoothed her beautifully permed greying hair and passed me a cup of milky coffee. 'Here's to another good year, Mr Sheffield.'

I smiled as Vera continued to call me 'Mr Sheffield'. She had always insisted this was the proper manner to address the headmaster.

'Thank you, Vera.' I looked at my watch. 'Almost time for the bell.' With a spring in my step I pushed open the giant oak entrance door and walked down the worn steps under the archway of Yorkshire stone. In the playground, a group of mothers clung on to their new starters, while the other children removed the embarrassment of their new school shoes by scraping them against the Victorian school wall, discussed the merits of Chopper bikes and swapped magazine photos of David Cassidy and Donny Osmond.

As I walked towards the school gates a few mothers looked over their shoulders at the arrival of Mrs Dudley-Palmer in her distinctive Oxford Blue 1975 Rolls-Royce Silver Shadow. She got out of her car and approached me, clutching seven-year-old Elisabeth Amelia and five-year-old Victoria Alice.

'Good morning, Mr Sheffield,' she said with a polite smile. Mrs Dudley-Palmer was a short, plump thirty-five-year-old who thought of herself as a cut above the rest. She was wearing a stylish light-grey coat with a mink-fur collar. 'I've brought my Elisabeth Amelia back to your charming little school but I have an appointment at a private school in York this afternoon. I'll call in later today to let you know my decision whether or not to send her there.' Mrs Dudley-Palmer had made it clear that when Elisabeth Amelia reached the age of eight she would switch to private education. However, it was often difficult to take Mrs Dudley-Palmer seriously as she seemed to live in a world of her own and her distinctive wide-eyed stare gave her a surprisingly startled look.

Leaning against the school wall, Mrs Margery Ackroyd, mother of Tony, Theresa and Charlotte, nodded towards Mrs Dudley-Palmer. 'All fur coat 'n' no knickers,' she whispered to her friends. They all laughed. 'Off y'go, Tony,' she said. 'Look after y'sisters an' keep that lid on y'shoebox.'

Meanwhile, at the school gates, seven-year-old Jimmy Poole, a small, sturdy boy with a mop of curly ginger hair and a distinct lisp, was staring up towards the heavens.

Curious, I walked up to him. 'Hello, Jimmy. What are you looking at?'

'Mith Maddithon thaid you can tell the time by looking at the thun,' said Jimmy, still squinting up at the sky.

'Your teacher's called Mrs Hunter now, Jimmy.'

'It's that big polithman'th fault,' said Jimmy knowingly.

I glanced up at the sun. 'So what time is it, Jimmy?'

He shook his head mournfully. 'With I knew, Mr Theffield, but I can't thee the numberth.' Celestial mysteries quickly forgotten, he wandered off to play conkers with Tony Ackroyd, who put down his shoebox and took out a conker threaded on to a length of baling twine.

As I walked through the throng of excited children, I glanced up at the silent bell in the tall, incongruous bell-tower. It was the highest point of our Victorian school building with its steeply sloping grey-slate roof and high arched windows. In the entrance hall I checked my wristwatch and, on the stroke of nine o'clock, I pulled the ancient bell rope to announce the beginning of another school year.

It was the early autumn of 1979. Mrs Thatcher was settling into her new job as prime minister, Cliff Richard was top of the pops with 'We Don't Talk Any More' and Larry Hagman, as the scheming JR Ewing in *Dallas*, was about to become television's greatest villain of all time. Suddenly denim jeans were no longer flared: instead, they were straight, and stone-washed or paint-splattered. Stephen Hawking, regarded as the greatest scientist since

Einstein and a cruel victim of an incurable disease of the nervous system, bravely announced there were 'black holes' in space. Back on earth, some things didn't change and Yorkshire's Geoffrey Boycott continued to grind out his runs in the Test Match against India at the Oval.

As I rang the bell I looked through the open entrance door and watched the late-comers scurry through the gates and dash up the cobbled driveway. Beyond the wrought-iron railings Ragley village was coming to life. On the village green, outside The Royal Oak, old Tommy Piercy was sitting on the bench next to the duck pond and feeding the ducks. All the shops on the High Street – the Post Office, Diane's Hair Salon, Nora's Coffee Shop, Pratt's Hardware Emporium, the Village Pharmacy, Piercy's Butcher's Shop and Prudence Golightly's General Stores & Newsagent – had opened their doors. Early-morning shoppers with their wickerwork baskets walked down the High Street, which was flanked by pretty terraced cottages with reddish-brown pantile roofs and tall chimney stacks. Only the occasional noisy farm tractor disturbed the peace of this picturesque Yorkshire village.

I walked into my classroom, sat at my desk and surveyed the twenty-three expectant faces in front of me. This was my third class of upper juniors in Ragley School and it was heart-warming to see their excitement at their new tins of Lakeland crayons, pristine exercise books, new HB pencils and a Reading Record Card complete with their name on the top.

A new boy, ten-year-old Darrell Topper, had put a note

on my desk. I opened it and smiled; it was one for the collection. It read: 'Please excuse our Darrell from PE as his big sister took his shorts for hot pants.'

After registration I checked each child's reading age using the Schonell Graded Word Reading Test while they completed some simple comprehension exercises. Sadly, eleven-year-old Jodie Cuthbertson seemed to have regressed during the school summer holiday. In answer to the question 'How many seconds in a year?' Jodie had written: 'January 2nd, February 2nd, March 2nd . . .'

When the bell rang for morning assembly, I felt that familiar sense of history. For over a hundred years the headteacher had gathered all the children of Ragley village together to begin another school year. My theme this morning was 'Friendship' and I spoke about how we should look after one another – especially the youngest children, who had just begun full-time education. I tried to encourage the new starters to speak.

Benjamin Roberts, a confident four-year-old in Anne's class, raised his hand. 'My name is Ben,' he said. He frowned. '"Cept when I'm naughty,' he added as an after-thought; 'then my mummy calls me Benjamin.'

'So, Ben, what did you want to say about friendship?' I asked.

'Well, my uncle Ted is my best friend and we went fishing at Scarborough,' said Ben.

'And what happened?' I asked.

''E sat in 'is little boat all day and came back with crabs.'

Anne gave me her wide-eyed 'Well, you did ask' look

from the back of the hall and I moved on to Tony Ackroyd, who wasn't looking his usual cheerful self.

'What about you, Tony?' I asked.

'M'best friend is Petula an' . . . ah think she's gone for ever.'

'I'm really sorry to hear that, Tony,' I said and, not wishing to dwell on the loss of a family member, I moved on to the next child. After Jimmy Poole had described the antisocial antics of his Yorkshire terrier, Scargill, – or, as Jimmy called him, 'Thcargill' – I said, 'So, boys and girls, we must all be friends.'

Suddenly, the twins, six-year-old Rowena and Katrina Buttle, waved their hands in the air simultaneously. 'Our mummy says we're like different-coloured crayons . . .' said Rowena.

'. . . But we all live in the same tin,' said Katrina.

At times like these I realized why I loved being a teacher. I might not have the best-paid job in the world but it did have its rewards.

'Time for t'bell,' announced Jodie Cuthbertson, our new bell monitor.

It was half past ten and I had volunteered to do the first playground duty. I collected my coffee from Vera and walked on to the school field, where Jimmy Poole was standing all alone.

'Hello, Jimmy. Why are you standing here while all your friends are playing with a ball at the other end of the field?' I asked.

'Becauth I'm the goalkeeper, Mithter Theffield,' said Jimmy simply.

Nearby, five-year-old Terry Earnshaw was taking his role of Luke Skywalker very seriously and he eventually defeated five-year-old Damian Brown, the nose-picking Darth Vader, by flicking the elastic on his mask on to his ears. Meanwhile, the Buttle twins, as the two androids, C3PO and R2D2, tried valiantly to save Jimmy Poole as the lisping Obi-Wan Kenobi. Finally, with a pragmatism that resided somewhere between the Communist Party and the local Co-Op, seven-year old Heathcliffe Earnshaw said pacifically, 'OK, let's all rule t'G'lactic Empire.'

At the end of playtime I looked into Jo's classroom, where a group of children had resumed their paintings as part of their 'Seaside' project. Six-year-old Hazel Smith was painting blue stripes across the top of her A3 piece of sugar paper.

'Is that the sky?' I asked cheerfully.

She looked at me with a puzzled expression. 'No, Mr Sheffield, jus' paint.'

'Ah, yes, of course,' I said, feeling suitably reprimanded.

'An' this is Mary the Mermaid,' explained Hazel. 'She's got a lady top 'alf an' a fish bottom 'alf. She's a good swimmer an' she won't get pregnant.' It occurred to me that children seemed to grow up faster these days.

On a nearby table, Elisabeth Amelia Dudley-Palmer seemed to prove the point. She was busy trying to complete her School Mathematics Project card concerning long multiplication. Jo walked in, glanced at her exercise book and frowned.

'You need to work hard at your mathematics so you will be good at sums,' said Jo.

'Don't worry, Miss,' said Elisabeth Amelia. 'Daddy has an excellent accountant.'

At twelve o'clock Jodie rang the dinner bell and I walked into the school office as Vera was checking Anne and Jo's dinner registers.

'What's for lunch?' I said. Anne Grainger leaned out of the doorway and sniffed the air. Her sense of smell was renowned. She could recognize a damp gabardine raincoat at fifty yards. Today, however, it was the unmistakable smell of damp cabbage. Anne, with the experience of twenty-five years of school dinners behind her, sniffed the air like a French wine taster. The merest hint of the subtle bouquet of Spam fritter reached her sensitive nostrils and she nodded in recognition. 'Spam fritters, mashed potato and cabbage,' she said confidently.

While the sweet pear-drop smell of the aerosol fixative, used to prevent pastel drawings from smudging, was obvious to the rest of us, the higher echelon of school odours had really only been mastered by Anne and Vera.

'Correct,' agreed Vera, half closing her eyes in deep concentration, 'with perhaps the merest possibility of diced carrots.'

Jo stared in awe at this exhibition of advanced sensory perception, folded up her wall chart of 'Seaside Shells', and walked into the school hall to join the queue for her first school dinner of the year.

I followed her and saw Heathcliffe Earnshaw pushing into the front of the queue. 'Go to the back of the line, Heathcliffe,' I said.

'But there's somebody there already, Mr Sheffield,' replied Heathcliffe, quick as a flash.

Just behind me, Anne Grainger turned away to stifle her laughter while I scrutinized the cheerful face of the ex-Barnsley boy. There was definitely something about him that you couldn't help but like.

After lunch, back in the staff-room, Vera was reading the front page of her *Daily Telegraph* and shaking her head in dismay. Mr Mark Carlisle, the education secretary, was considering the introduction of a Continental-style school day starting at 8.00 a.m. and closing at 2.00 p.m. as part of the government cuts of £600 million per year. Also, the Yorkshire Ripper had claimed his twelfth victim in Bradford and had sent a tape recording to George Oldfield, head of the CID in West Yorkshire, taunting the police in a Wearside accent.

'What a world we live in,' said Vera in despair. 'It can't get worse.'

But at that moment it suddenly did . . . much worse!

Anne came into the staff-room, white as a sheet. 'Jack . . . everybody . . . I've just seen a mouse . . . a big mouse!'

Jo and Sally immediately lifted their feet off the floor and Vera leapt towards her metal filing cabinet and pulled out her 'Telephone in emergencies' folder.

'Where was it?' I asked.

'Walking bold as brass into Ruby the caretaker's cupboard, so I slammed the door and locked it,' said Anne.

'We need to ring the pest controller at County Hall immediately, Mr Sheffield,' said Vera.

I nodded and smiled grimly. Vera was wonderful in emergencies. 'Thanks, Vera. We'll do it now.'

Thirty minutes later a dirty green, rusty old van pulled up in the school car park. The words 'Maurice Ackroyd, PEST CONTROLLER' were crudely painted on the side of the van. I walked out to meet him.

''Ow do,' said Maurice. 'Ah'm Maurice the Mouseman from Pest Control.' His huge front teeth and wispy moustache reinforced my belief that Maurice was born for this vocation. He was a small, unshaven, wiry man wearing a battered flat cap, in spite of the hot weather, and a filthy collarless long-sleeved shirt with the cuffs firmly double-buttoned. His baggy cord trousers were held up with a length of baling twine and his trouser-leg bottoms were tucked firmly into his socks. A pair of shabby steel-toe-capped builder's boots completed the ensemble.

'Hello, er, Maurice,' I said. 'Thanks for coming. I think we've got a mouse.'

Maurice sucked air through his teeth and then shook his head. ''Owd on, 'owd on, not so 'asty, Mr Sheffield. It could be rats, tha knaws,' he said with a hopeful glint in his eye.

'Rats! I hope not,' I said in alarm.

'Rats is everywhere, Mr Sheffield – y'never far from a rat,' said Maurice, nodding in a very knowing way.

'But we should have to close the school . . . and it's the

27

first day of term.' I could already see the headline in the *Easington Herald & Pioneer*.

'Don't fret, Mr Sheffield: 'elp is at 'and,' said Maurice with false modesty, while stroking the words 'PEST CONTROLLER' on the side of his van with obvious affection. Then he leaned back and surveyed the school building like Clint Eastwood before a gunfight. 'Ah allus start by giving it two coats o' lookin' over. Y'gotta think like t'little buggers afore y'catch 'em.'

'Yes, I suppose so,' I said.

'Ah come from a long line o' rodent-catchers, tha knaws. Rodents 'ave allus run in our family,' said Maurice proudly.

'Oh, that's good,' I said unconvincingly.

He wrinkled up his pointed nose and sniffed the air. 'We use t'psychol'gy,' he added proudly.

'I see,' I said . . . but I didn't.

Afternoon lessons were haunted by the thought that I would have to shut the school and it was a gloomy group of teachers who assembled in the staff-room at afternoon playtime to hear the verdict of Maurice the Mouseman.

'It's norra rat,' proclaimed Maurice.

'That's a relief,' said Anne. 'So I presume it's a mouse.'

'It's a mouse, all reight,' he said. 'Ah caught a glimpse of it in t'caretaker's cupboard.'

Suddenly Tony Ackroyd appeared at the staff-room door. He looked nervous.

'Hello, Tony,' I said. 'What's wrong?'

Tony looked up at Maurice. ''Ello, Uncle Maurice,' he said.

I looked in surprise at Maurice. 'So Tony is your nephew?'

'That's reight, Mr Sheffield. 'E's our Margery's eldest.'

'Oh, I see,' I said. 'So what is it, Tony?'

Tony's cheeks flushed. 'Mr Sheffield, ah'm reight sorry, ah should've told y'sooner,' said Tony, 'but then ah saw Uncle Maurice's van.'

'Told me what, Tony?' I said.

'Ah brought Petula this morning t'show you, but then she went missing,' he said. 'Ah told yer in assembly.'

'Petula?'

'Yes, Mr Sheffield: m'pet mouse.'

'You have a mouse called Petula?'

'Yes, Mr Sheffield,' replied Tony, as if it was entirely logical. 'Me mam named 'er after Mrs Dudley-Palmer, 'cause me mouse 'as staring eyes.'

'Oh, I see,' I said, trying not to smile.

'An' ah thought me uncle Maurice might kill 'er if 'e didn't know it were Petula.'

'Well, I'm glad you've told me, Tony, but you should have let me know straight away. We've been very worried.'

'Ah'm reight sorry, Mr Sheffield,' said Tony forlornly.

Maurice looked down at his little nephew and then up at me.

'Don't worry, ah'll use psychol'gy,' he said, stroking the side of his nose with a gnarled forefinger. 'Ah've got jus t'thing in t'van.' He scurried off eagerly and returned moments later. ''Ere it is . . . carbolic soap. Petula will love it,' he said, holding up a large bar of potent-smelling soap that would have stopped a clock at ten paces.

'Can ah tek Tony to 'elp me?' said Maurice.

'Er, yes, of course, but be careful, Tony,' I said.

With that, uncle and nephew trotted out into the entrance hall and carefully opened Ruby's cupboard. We could hear their raised voices.

'Use that broom 'andle, Tony, t'coax 'er out,' shouted Maurice, 'an' ah'll get me wire basket ready.'

At that moment, Vera walked through the little corridor that linked the school office to the staff-room. 'Excuse me, Mr Sheffield, but Mrs Dudley-Palmer is in the office and would like a word.'

Mrs Dudley-Palmer was standing next to the open office door. 'Oh, hello, er . . . Mrs Dudley-Palmer, what can I do to help?'

'Well, Mr Sheffield,' she said, taking out an expensive-looking school prospectus, 'you will recall I have a difficult decision to make about Elisabeth Amelia's future as she will be eight at the end of this school year.'

'Ah, yes,' I said. 'It would be a shame to lose such a delightful girl from our school.'

Petula Dudley-Palmer studied me for a moment. 'It's kind of you to say so, Mr Sheffield. However, I've just returned from York and the school is very appealing.'

'I'm sure it is,' I said, looking at the impressive coat of arms above some Latin script on the prospectus.

'And then I shall have to decide what to do with Victoria Alice as she would eventually follow her sister.'

'I understand,' I said, 'and we should be sorry to lose

Victoria Alice as well. She's such a happy and well-behaved little girl.'

'Yes, she's the one who takes after me, of course,' said Mrs Dudley-Palmer with a self-satisfied smile.

Suddenly, five-year-old Victoria Alice ran in from the playground and stopped outside the door. 'Hello, Mummy. I've just kissed Terry Earnshaw,' she said proudly.

Mrs Dudley-Palmer was rooted to the spot. 'How did that happen?' she asked in horror.

'It was difficult, Mummy. Molly Paxton had to help me catch him.' Then she ran off and into class.

'Oh dear,' said Mrs Dudley-Palmer. She stepped into the office and looked down at the prospectus as if she had finally made up her mind. It suddenly appeared as if Ragley School did not come up to expectations. As she was pondering what to say next, the silence was broken suddenly by loud voices from the staff-room.

'Is everything OK now?' asked Vera anxiously.

''Tis now,' said Maurice.

Little Tony, with a big smile on his face, propped the broom handle in the staff-room doorway and set off back to the classroom.

'I'm pleased to hear that,' said Vera.

Mrs Dudley-Palmer and I could hear every word but the speakers were out of sight.

'All t'better for seeing Petula,' said Maurice, holding up the caged mouse in triumph.

Petula Dudley-Palmer stiffened slightly.

'Well, I'm sure you have an expert eye,' said Vera.

'Petula's allus been such a 'andsome creature,' said

Maurice, pushing a piece of carbolic soap towards the tiny mouse.

Mrs Dudley-Palmer smiled and I stepped forward quickly and shut the door between the office and the corridor to the staff-room.

'Well, must be on m'way,' said Maurice and he strode out towards the car park.

In the office, Mrs Dudley-Palmer gave a beatific smile and replaced the prospectus in her leather handbag. 'Do you know, Mr Sheffield, that was most fortuitous.'

'Really?' I said.

'Yes, it's always nice to know that one is held in such high regard in the village.'

'Er, yes,' I said. 'I agree.'

'Perhaps my darling little girls should stay at Ragley after all.'

'Well, er, that would be good news,' I said and we walked out into the entrance hall, where Vera was standing next to the open staff-room door. The smell of strong soap filled the air.

'Oh, carbolic soap, Miss Evans,' said Mrs Dudley-Palmer, sniffing appreciatively. 'That takes me back to when I was young. I've always had an attraction to carbolic soap.'

Vera smiled and looked to the heavens as Mrs Dudley-Palmer walked out to her Rolls-Royce.

'An eventful day, Mr Sheffield,' said Vera.

I glanced at my watch. I should have been back in my classroom. 'I'll tell you about it at the end of school,' I said.

There was a sudden banging on the office door. 'Oh

dear,' I groaned, 'whatever next?' I picked up the strange-looking broom handle and opened the door.

Mrs Winifred Brown was standing there, clutching little Damian Brown's hand. 'Ah'm tekking 'im now,' she said and then looked down at the broom handle in my hand. 'Oh, y'found it, then,' and she grabbed it.

'Pardon?'

'Y'found 'is light sabre, then?'

The penny dropped. Ruby's spare broom handle was in fact Damian Brown's *Star Wars* weapon. I was speechless.

Jo Hunter, who had been standing quietly behind me, stepped forward. 'I would appreciate it, Mrs Brown,' she said very firmly, 'if you would try to avoid Damian missing school. This is not the best start to the term for him to miss the last lesson of his first day.'

Mrs Brown looked down at the slight, quietly spoken infant teacher and sneered. 'Prob'ly jus' as well. Ah saw t'pest controller's van 'ere an' ah shouldn't be s'prised to 'ear from our Damian that y'riddled wi' vermin.'

Jo Hunter stepped forward and raised herself to her full five-feet-three-inches and stared up at Mrs Brown. 'Let's have an understanding, Mrs Brown,' said Jo in a determined voice. Winifred Brown took a step back. 'If you promise not to believe everything Damian says happens in school, I'll promise not to believe everything he says happens at home.' Jo had clearly struck a nerve. The colour drained from Mrs Brown's face and she retreated quickly. Jo closed the door and muttered, 'I'll give her vermin!'

Anne and Vera both clapped in appreciation. 'Well said, Jo,' said Vera.

'And now it's time for another little mouse,' said Anne as she held up her Beatrix Potter book. I walked back to class with her and watched as she sat down with her children in the carpeted Book Corner. Anne surveyed the expectant little faces of the four- and five-year-olds at her feet. Then she held up the picture on the front cover of the book and said slowly and clearly, 'Our first story of the year, boys and girls, is *The Tale of Mrs Tittlemouse*,' and she winked in my direction. I nodded as I recalled the classic story of the little wood-mouse who strove to keep her house in order in spite of numerous unwanted visitors.

As I walked back to my classroom, with the end of our first day of school approaching, it occurred to me that Beatrix Potter definitely knew what she was talking about.

Chapter Two

The Gateway to Harmony

County Hall authorized the replacement of the school gates. The Revd Joseph Evans took his weekly RE lesson.
Extract from the Ragley School Logbook:
Tuesday, 25 September 1979

'Peace and harmony,' said Vera triumphantly. She opened her elegant Marks & Spencer's leather handbag and held up a sheaf of carefully typed notes entitled 'The Gateway to Harmony – 30 days to a harmonious life'. It was Tuesday, 25 September, and we had all gathered in the office at the end of the school day. 'Would you like to hear it?' asked Vera expectantly. She stood up behind her desk and smoothed the creases from the seat of her immaculate two-piece charcoal-grey suit. Everyone stood around, feeling awkward.

'Of course, Vera,' said Anne quickly and with slightly too much enthusiasm, 'but . . . er, perhaps tomorrow lunchtime when we can fully appreciate it.'

'And it will give you one more night to practise it,' added Sally, both helpfully and hopefully.

'Perhaps you're right,' said Vera, looking slightly deflated. 'The first section, "Day One – Harmony Through Inner Peace", probably requires a little fine tuning.' She carefully folded her life-changing speech and returned it to her handbag.

As president of the Ragley and Morton Women's Institute, Vera was anxious to make her mark and the following evening she was to deliver a lecture at their monthly meeting in the village hall. The special guest was Lady Alexandra Denham from Harrogate, author of *A Woman's Guide to Happy Living*, and one of the most influential ladies in the Women's Institute movement in the north of England.

Suddenly there was a knock on the staff-room door and Vera opened it. 'Oh, Mr Trump,' she said, looking disdainfully at the little man clutching a paint-splattered clipboard. 'I don't think we were expecting you.'

Cecil Trump, the school maintenance officer, stiffened slightly and removed a pink maintenance slip from his clipboard with a theatrical flourish. 'We're painting y'school gates tomorrow,' he announced proudly, 'so sign 'ere.'

Vera studied the form. 'Yes, I reported the poor state of the gates last term but County Hall said they would be replaced,' she said.

'Don't know nowt about that,' said Mr Trump defiantly. 'Ah'm just 'ere t'mek sure they're painted.'

'And what colour are you painting them?' asked Vera.

Mr Trump coughed affectedly. 'It's one of our more subtle blends of Sienna Amber an' Rustic Redwood,' he announced with the confidence of a man who misguidedly believed he understood the mysteries of colour coordination better than a woman did. With a smirk of satisfaction he pointed to his dog-eared Crown paint colour chart.

'You mean brown,' stated Vera dispassionately.

Undeterred, Mr Trump pressed on. 'They'll be 'ere at t'end of school an' finished afore it gets dark,' he said. Vera signed and he thrust the carbon copy into her hand, turned on his heel and drove away in his little white van.

Vera opened her grey metal filing cabinet and filed the sheet under 'Maintenance'. Once again I reflected what a wonderful servant she was to Ragley School. I would have been lost without her ability to organize the day-to-day administration and finances. Vera and her brother, the Revd Joseph Evans, lived in the elegant and beautifully furnished vicarage in the grounds of St Mary's Church on the Morton Road and each day she brought order into our lives. Occasionally, however, she did get a little irritated.

'I really have no confidence in that little man,' she said as she walked out to collect her coat.

'Peace and harmony, Vera,' called Anne after her in a singsong voice.

'Mmmm, yes,' said Vera, with a tight-lipped smile.

Suddenly the telephone rang on Vera's desk. I picked it up.

'Ragley School,' I said, automatically.

'Hello, Jack.'

My heart skipped a beat. It was Beth . . . or was it?

'Hello . . . er . . . how are you?' I stuttered, stalling for time. It was almost impossible to tell whether it was Beth or Laura. The two sisters sounded so alike on the telephone.

'Jack, I'm ringing from Liberty's. I thought I'd stay in York tonight for a bite to eat and then go to the Odeon to see *Kramer vs Kramer*. I wondered if you wanted to come along.'

'Oh, hello, Laura,' I said. Laura had moved up from London earlier in the year to take charge of Liberty's ladies' fashion department and had bought a flat in York.

'We could meet outside the cinema at seven thirty,' she said with her usual confidence.

Around me was a human tableau. Vera had stopped buttoning her coat, Anne and Sally suddenly showed interest in the noticeboard and Jo stared out of the window. It was as if time had stood still.

'Fine. I'll see you there,' I said hurriedly.

''Bye,' said Laura and rang off.

As I returned the telephone to its cradle, everyone switched back into life but no one mentioned the phone call.

That evening, I walked out to my emerald-green Morris Minor Traveller with its ash-wood frame and brightly polished chromium grill. As I set off towards York, I was uncomfortably aware that I smelled like a perfume factory. I had just invested in a bottle of Brut aftershave. The boxer Henry Cooper, the motorcycle ace Barry Sheen and the international footballer Kevin Keegan, on a never-ending stream of television advertisements, had urged me to 'splash it on'. I had done just that and reflected on the power of advertising.

I parked my car and walked under the archway of Micklegate Bar, one of York's four ancient gateways to the city, and on to the cinema. Laura was already there, slim and attractive with her long warm brown hair loose round her shoulders. She looked stunning in her chic little Jean Allen suit that was soft to the touch. The jacket was a flowing black bolero and the skirt was panelled in emerald and she drew admiring glances from everyone around her.

She smiled and kissed me on the cheek and her green eyes reminded me of Beth.

'Sorry,' I said, looking at my watch. 'I hope you haven't been waiting long.'

'No, Jack, it's not far from Liberty's and it's a lovely evening. I've enjoyed the fresh air.' Her smooth skin glowed with health and the merest hint of rouge emphasized her high cheekbones. 'Come on – my treat,' she said, tugging my sleeve, and we joined the queue.

I glanced down at my sports jacket and sighed. The leather cuffs were frayed and the patches on my elbows were worn.

'Nice tie, Jack,' said Laura encouragingly.

'Er, thanks.' Beth had bought it for me a year ago. 'You look wonderful,' I said quickly.

Laura smiled and took my arm as we found two seats next to an aisle where I could stretch out my six-feet-one-inch gangling frame. Then we sat through the best film of 1979, *Kramer vs Kramer*, and watched the Oscar-winning stars, Dustin Hoffman and Meryl Streep, unravel their tangled web of emotions.

At the end, Laura was wiping away a tear with her handkerchief. 'Isn't life complicated, Jack?' she said, squeezing my hand.

I enjoyed being with Laura. She was dynamic, positive and always full of fun. It was just that when I looked at her I couldn't help but think of Beth and the times we spent together. I wondered what she was doing on this autumn night, but, sadly, those days were gone now. I walked Laura back to her car and kissed her briefly. As I drove home I wondered if the old adage of time being a great healer would work for me. September, with its mellow reflections of happy times under a distant sun, would soon be over.

I drove back to Kirkby Steepleton, walked into the silence of Bilbo Cottage and switched on my television set. ITV had started transmitting in colour but for me, on a teacher's salary, the rental was difficult to afford. I settled down to watch *Kojak* on BBC 1 but when the bald-headed, lolly-sucking New York cop said, 'Who loves you, baby?' I switched off. In my case the answer was nobody.

Early on Friday morning I picked up a steaming mug of tea, walked out into my lovely garden and sat on the old garden seat. The scent of the yellow floribunda roses was fragrant in my nostrils. Autumn was advancing. Teardrop cobwebs hung heavy in the branches and shivered in the brittle wind. Beneath my feet bright summer had gone. Russet leaves, like dying embers, bared their skeletal souls. Now only the lace filigree remained – a tracery of what once had been.

I climbed into my car and set off towards Ragley village as the early-morning sun broke through and lit up the fields round me. It was a joy to live in this beautiful part of God's Own Country and I pulled in under the shade of a copse of sycamores and drank in the clean air. I stood for a while watching the sinuous motion of the ripe corn, the last field of the harvest, the end of another season. It was a field of swaying, living rhythm, a field of burnished gold, a field of dreams. As I stood there I wondered what this term held in store for me.

In Ragley High Street I stopped outside the General Stores & Newsagent to buy my newspaper. A sudden frenetic bark made me stop in my tracks.

'Thtop it, Thcargill,' shouted Jimmy Poole. Scargill was appropriately named. He had a very loud bark, a huge following of equally angry canine supporters, and enjoyed biting anyone in authority. His particular favourites, however, were the local policeman, the postman and me.

'Good morning, Jimmy,' I said, walking quickly towards the shop door.

'Hello, Mithter Theffield,' said Jimmy. 'I've jutht thlipped on my knee.'

'Oh dear,' I said. 'Show it to your mother when you get home and then tell Mrs Hunter when you get to school.'

'OK, Mithter Theffield. I'll tell 'er 'ow much it thtingth,' he added with a brave smile.

As I turned right at the village green towards the school, the warm red, brown and amber of the Yorkshire stone wall that surrounded the playground reflected the sun's rays like new honey. Above it, at waist height, the cast-iron railings, painted black as Whitby jet, cast long morning shadows across the tarmac. The pointed fleur-de-lis at the top of every rail gave the impression of Victorian order and permanence. However, the wrought-iron school gates, fitted in 1948 after the original gates had been removed to support the war effort, now showed the effects of time. Thirty years of children swinging on them had finally twisted the flimsy bars and loosened the giant hinges. It was time for them to be replaced, but at least we were to have them painted. They creaked noisily as Ruby the caretaker pushed them back to begin another school day.

"Morning, Ruby,' I shouted as I drove past.

"Mornin', Mr Sheffield, an' a reight good un it is an' all,' shouted Ruby.

Vera and Joseph pulled into the car park behind me in their spotless Austin A40. Vera got out and stared hard at the school gates before walking into the office. The Revd Joseph Evans, meanwhile, trudged in gloomily. He always found his weekly Religious Education lesson an ordeal and today was not destined to be different.

Everyone gathered in the staff-room before morning

school and Vera spread out her life-changing speech on the coffee table.

'Big night tonight, Vera,' I said.

'Yes, Mr Sheffield, and the village hall is likely to be full with Lady Denham attending.'

'How's the speech, Vera?' asked Anne.

'Well, Joseph thought it was rather good,' said Vera, glancing up at her younger brother. 'Didn't you, Joseph?'

Joseph nodded timidly. He was a tall, angular, slightly nervous fifty-five-year-old with thinning grey hair, and this week Class 2, Jo Hunter's class, was to be the recipient of one of Joseph's Bible stories.

'Er, yes . . . it was . . . er, uplifting,' mumbled Joseph, casting a look to the heavens as if requesting forgiveness. Joseph had heard Vera's motivational lecture three times the previous evening and the thought of hearing it yet again was almost too much to bear. Even her three cats, Treacle, Jess and Maggie, the latter named after her political heroine, had nodded off halfway through.

'So what's it about, Vera?' I asked, eager to show interest.

'Peace and harmony, Mr Sheffield,' she replied with a Mother Teresa smile. 'After all, a harmonious life is a happy one,' recited Vera.

'Impressive,' said Sally.

Jo looked up from writing her netball team notice. 'I agree,' she said with enthusiasm, having just realized that, thanks to Joseph, she was about to get a free period.

'Sounds good,' said Anne.

'Thank you,' said Vera. 'I do appreciate your support and it's so important for me to set a good example, particularly as Lady Denham is attending. By the way, she's calling to collect me at the end of school today.'

It was a quiet morning, except for Class 2, where Joseph was struggling.

'Why did they all 'ave mucky feet in t'Bible?' asked Heathcliffe Earnshaw. 'Jesus seemed t'spend a lot o' time washing other people's feet.'

The Revd Joseph Evans, vicar of the parish and chairman of the school governors, pressed his long thin fingers against his furrowed brow while he strove for an answer. As we were a Church of England primary school, Joseph came in each week to take a Religious Education lesson and once again he was thinking that he preferred communicating with his parishioners rather than with a class of inquisitive seven-year-olds.

Joseph had asked all the children to draw a picture of something from the Bible and had just approached the table where Heathcliffe Earnshaw appeared to be drawing Father Christmas. 'What's your name again?' he asked politely. Joseph had a terrible memory for children's names even though it was now two years since Heathcliffe had arrived at Ragley from Barnsley in South Yorkshire.

''Eathcliffe,' replied Heathcliffe curtly, concentrating on his drawing.

'Heathcliffe?' said Joseph in surprise.

Heathcliffe was used to this reaction. 'Yeah, 'Eathcliffe,' he retorted, shading the long beard with a white crayon.

'Oh, yes, I remember now . . . er . . . well, Heathcliffe,' said Joseph, 'that's a lovely drawing.' Heathcliffe didn't look up. He just reached for the purple wax crayon from the collection in the upturned shoe-box lid in front of him. 'And what is it, exactly . . . er, that you're drawing?' asked Joseph, wondering who in the Bible wore bright purple gloves. He was unaware that Heathcliffe knew for a fact that it was very cold in heaven and essential clothing included a warm jumper and a pair of gloves.

'Ah'm drawing God,' he said, emphatically. Heathcliffe didn't do things by halves.

'God?' questioned Joseph.

'Yeah, God,' said Heathcliffe.

'So, you're actually drawing a picture of God?' said Joseph, still slightly perplexed at the young Michelangelo with the snotty nose and the confidence of childhood.

'Yeah, ah'm drawing God,' said Heathcliffe, sketching in a pair of National Health spectacles, just like his grand-dad's.

'But nobody really knows what God looks like,' said Joseph anxiously.

Heathcliffe didn't flinch. Nor did he raise his head. He just reached for another crayon and added the finishing touches to God's red and white York City bobble hat. 'Well, they will in a minute!' said Heathcliffe emphatically while adding a bolt of lightning for dramatic effect.

'Oh, well . . . er . . . that's very good,' said Joseph. 'Have you finished now?'

Heathcliffe had perfected a sound that could be interpreted as 'Yes' or 'No'. He achieved this while moving his head in a diagonal direction so it constituted neither nodding nor shaking.

Joseph was utterly fooled. He picked up the drawing and showed it to the rest of the class. 'Now, who is this meant to represent?' asked Joseph enthusiastically. A wall of silence descended. 'It's a very important person,' he added. No one moved. Finally a nervous hand went up at the back of the class. 'Yes?' said Joseph, feeling relieved.

'It's Heathcliffe's granddad,' said Elisabeth Amelia Dudley-Palmer.

'No, this man saves souls,' Joseph implored.

'So does Heathcliffe's granddad,' said Elisabeth Amelia. 'He mends shoes.'

It was a relief when the bell rang for morning playtime and we all gathered in the staff-room.

'How did it go, Joseph?' asked Vera, as she stirred the pan of hot milk in preparation for our milky coffees.

'I'm not sure,' muttered Joseph.

Vera looked up quickly at her younger brother and decided to add an extra spoonful of sugar before handing him his coffee. Joseph proceeded to stir it vigorously with his pencil as if in a trance.

In the corner, Sally had picked up my copy of *The Times* from the coffee table and scanned the headline, which read, HESELTINE PREPARES WAY FOR MORE CUTS − LOCAL COUNCILS TO HAVE FREEDOM TO MAKE BIG CUTS IN SPENDING. She groaned, tossed it back on the table and rummaged in the biscuit tin for a custard cream.

Jo rushed in and Vera handed her a mug of coffee. 'What a lovely day for playground duty,' said Jo cheerfully as she skipped out.

'Married life seems to be suiting Jo,' said Sally glumly, pulling the biscuit tin a little closer.

We all sat deep in our own thoughts until the silence was shattered by the ringing telephone.

'Good morning. Ragley School,' said Vera, then she listened intently with a furrowed brow. 'Well, that's good news so long as someone in your department communicates with the painters.' There was another pause. 'Yes, they're due to be painted today.' Vera looked up and shook her head. 'Very well. Thank you for calling.'

'What is it, Vera?' asked Sally.

Vera replaced the receiver thoughtfully. 'The school gates are going to be replaced at last. That was the school buildings office to say they're coming on Monday.'

'Good news,' I said.

Vera stood up as the bell rang. 'So when would you all like to hear my speech?'

'Lunchtime,' I mumbled and we all trooped out to our classrooms.

Joseph was in Sally's class during the second half of the morning. Again, he was concerned that the religious messages of previous lessons had been misconstrued when he read in one notebook, 'Last night I baptized my budgie.'

Meanwhile, Sally was in the staff-room, pasting children's writing into a huge sugar-paper folder entitled

'Class 3 Newspaper'. She picked up eight-year-old Sarah Louise Tait's article and smiled. Sarah had written, 'Mrs Thatcher has the power to appoint and disappoint the members of her cabinet,' and Sally gleefully pasted it on the front page.

At twelve thirty everyone in the staff-room sat spellbound. Vera had reached the triumphal conclusion. 'Together, ladies, we shall walk through the gateway to harmony.' She looked up from her script for a reaction and fingered her Victorian brooch nervously. 'So let us show sympathy and compassion towards one another,' continued Vera, 'for a harmonious life is a happy life.'

'Sympathy,' murmured Sally thoughtfully.

'Compassion,' agreed Joseph with an encouraging nod.

'Harmony,' said Anne as if in a trance.

I found myself staring out of the window. On the school field, children with suntanned faces ran and skipped and, in the window boxes, the fiery flowers of geraniums were vivid in the autumn sunshine.

'A stunning speech,' said Sally.

'Almost evangelical,' said Joseph.

'What do you think, Jack?' asked Anne.

Everyone turned to look at me. I knew that hesitation would be fatal. 'Er, yes, I agree,' I said. 'Er . . . harmony,' I added.

Vera scanned the rest of her speech and then picked up her free copy of Miss Denham's motivational book. She was determined to put her philosophy into practice.

'I really must show all the women in the Institute that we should avoid conflict and find inner peace,' she continued, sitting down again at her desk and shuffling her pages back into order.

'Well said, Vera,' said Anne.

'Also,' said Vera, glancing quickly at Sally, 'I thought I would use the vision of Margaret Thatcher for a happy and prosperous nation.'

Sally spluttered into her coffee. It was widely known that Sally's politics resided closer to Arthur Scargill's than our new prime minister's. 'You mean Thatcher the milk-snatcher,' grumbled Sally, who had never forgiven Margaret Thatcher for her controversial decision in October 1970, as education secretary in Ted Heath's government, to abolish free school milk for children over seven. Anne gave Sally a 'This is neither the time nor place' look.

'Sorry, Vera,' said Sally. 'It's a wonderful speech.'

Vera folded her speech neatly and replaced it carefully in her handbag.

'Well done,' said Joseph and, looking slightly relieved, walked out to the car park to drive back to Morton.

'It will be excellent,' said Anne reassuringly.

'Avoid conflict,' said Sally.

'Inner peace,' said Jo.

'I'm sure it will go well for you, Vera,' I said.

Vera responded with a slightly nervous smile and settled down at her desk once again. She put a sheet of carbon paper between two sheets of white typing paper, fed them into her Royal typewriter and began to

49

hammer out the title 'Replacement of School Gates'.

At the end of school the children sauntered down the drive, groups of mothers wandered over to Nora's Coffee Shop and slowly the school became silent once again. I sat down at my desk and had just written in the school logbook 'County Hall authorized the replacement of the school gates' when Anne, Sally and Jo suddenly burst into the office.

'You had better come and see this, Jack,' said Anne.

We all walked out of school and down the driveway towards the sound of raised voices.

'But it's on t'list,' insisted Mr Trump. His little white van was parked under the horse-chestnut trees at the front of the school and his colleague, dressed in white overalls, was attempting to paint the school gates.

'What is the point of painting these gates, only to re-place them on Monday?' shouted Vera.

'If it's on t'list it 'as t'be done,' persisted Mr Trump.

'Never mind your list, what about common sense?' said Vera.

Ruby the caretaker had left her cleaning and joined us on the school drive.

'You tell 'im, Miss Evans,' yelled Ruby, waving her broom.

'You will pack up immediately and stop wasting tax payers' money,' shouted Vera.

'Hear, hear!' shouted Jo and Sally.

'But it's on t'list,' said Mr Trump nervously waving his clipboard.

Vera finally snapped. 'You stupid little man,' she shouted. I had never seen her so angry. Then she grabbed his clipboard, ripped off the pink maintenance sheet and tore it up before his eyes. 'Now it's not on the list any more, is it?' She stuffed the torn pieces in the bib pocket of his overalls and walked back up the drive.

Mr Trump and his friend jumped back into the van and roared off while Ruby and Sally cheered.

At that moment a smart, top-of-the-range Land-Rover turned into the school gates and drove smoothly up the drive. The distinctive figure of Lady Alexandra Denham wound down her car window and slowed up alongside the president of the Ragley and Morton Women's Institute. Vera was striding, red-faced with fury, towards the school entrance.

'Good afternoon, Vera,' said Lady Denham.

'Oh, good afternoon, Lady Denham,' said Vera, quickly trying to regain composure.

'Looking forward to this evening?' said Lady Denham.

'Of course, Lady Denham,' said Vera, a little breathlessly.

'Just remind me, Vera,' said Lady Denham as she stepped out of the Land-Rover, 'what's your subject for tonight?'

'Peace and harmony, Lady Denham,' said Vera, her fury gradually subsiding.

'Jolly good show, Vera,' said Her Ladyship with a grin. 'You can't beat a bit of peace and harmony.'

Chapter Three

Jimmy Savile Cleans Our Windows

*Following the new window-cleaning contract from County
Hall, Witherspoons Window Cleaners of Easington cleaned
the school windows today and will return each month.*
Extract from the Ragley School Logbook:
Monday, 1 October 1979

It was 8.30 a.m. on the first day of October and, outside
the staff-room window, the season was changing. The
hammock webs of busy spiders glistened in the morning sunlight and in the hedgerow the red hips of dog
roses heralded darker days. Robins and wrens sang their
autumn songs to claim their territory, while goldfinches
plundered the seeds of the tall teasels.

Meanwhile, Ruby the caretaker pushed her galvanized
bucket to one side and leaned on the staff-room door. It
was clear that the wonders of nature were not uppermost
in her mind.

'Ah want t'look like 'er in Abba,' said Ruby.

Ruby Smith weighed twenty stones and, in her extra-large double X, bright-orange overall, she looked a long way from a Swedish superstar.

'Which one?' I asked politely.

'Not that blonde lass,' said Ruby – 't'other one.'

It was unusual for Ruby to be so late in putting away her mop and bucket. Her cheeks were brightly flushed with the exertion of mopping the wood-block floor.

'She's called Anni Frid,' said Jo, glancing up from her *Nuffield Book of Science Experiments*.

'That's a funny name,' said Ruby.

Sally put down her *Cosmopolitan* magazine. Her knowledge of pop music was generally regarded as second to none. 'Jo's right, Ruby, and the blonde one is called Agnetha,' agreed Sally. 'Originally they were called 'Bjorn and Benny, Agnetha and Anni', but that was a bit of a mouthful, so they decided on the acronym ABBA.'

Ruby looked puzzled. She thought acronyms worked in a circus.

Vera walked into the staff-room from the school office and handed out the attendance registers. She had heard the conversation and was puzzled by Ruby's sudden interest in new hairstyles. With six children and an unemployed husband, Ruby rarely had enough spare cash to have a hair-do. However, Vera had taken Ruby under her wing and always took an interest in the somewhat dysfunctional life of our cheerful caretaker.

'So what is it about this singer that you like, Ruby?' asked Vera.

'It's 'er fancy perm, Miss Evans,' said Ruby. 'It's reight smart an' Jimmy says mine's same colour. So ah'm thinking of going t'Diane's 'Air Salon.'

'Good idea, Ruby,' said Vera. 'Diane made a lovely job of Nora Pratt's hair when you won that singing competition.'

Ruby smiled with happy memories of a special day in her life.

'By the way, who's Jimmy?' I asked.

Ruby's cheeks flushed even more. 'Jimmy Witherspoon, Mr Sheffield – that new window cleaner from Easington.' She pointed out of the window at a grubby white van in the car park. The words JIMMY THE SHINE were printed in large letters on the side.

''E says 'e's got t'contract t'clean them big windows outside 'cause o' that new union rule,' said Ruby breathlessly.

Vera selected an official-looking letter from her desk and frowned. 'It's all here, Mr Sheffield,' she said stonily. 'The union representative, a certain Miss Plumtree, has written to inform us that caretakers must not clean windows above six feet in height.'

I vaguely remembered the spate of recent circulars from County Hall that explained the new Health and Safety rules relating to caretakers. The rules were so complicated I had left Vera to make sense of them. I decided to go outside and meet our new window cleaner.

Jimmy Witherspoon was a short, wiry man with a Status Quo T-shirt, grubby denim jacket, skin-tight blue jeans and battered Kicker boots with an incongruous red-leather, flower-shaped cut-out attached to his boot-lace. Around his neck he wore a tarnished chain with a large shiny pendant on which the word *Jimmy* was inscribed.

He was roping a large extendable wooden ladder to the roof rack of his van and, as I approached, he shook his incredibly long hair in an affected way. Dyed platinum blond and parted down the centre, it hung in cascading waves round his shoulders. A large white towelling headband proclaiming in bright-red letters LOVE MACHINE completed the ensemble.

'Now then, now then, now then,' said Jimmy cheerfully with a brown-toothed smile.

'Pardon?'

''Ow's about that, then?' said Jimmy, nodding towards the windows.

He reminded me of someone but I couldn't place him. 'Oh, yes, er, thank you, Jimmy,' I said. 'I'm sure Ruby will be very grateful.'

'Y'not wrong,' said Jimmy with an evil leer. He tapped the side of his nose with a nicotine-stained finger.

Puzzled, I just stared at him. He seemed to be speaking another language. Then the penny dropped. He was trying to imitate Jimmy Savile, the Leeds-born disc jockey. 'Now then, now then, now then,' was one of Jimmy Savile's catchphrases. Quite frankly, though, if you took away Jimmy Witherspoon's long, flowing hair he was really nothing like the Yorkshire icon.

'Is there anything to sign, Jimmy?' I asked, eager to get back inside.

'Jus' m'pink sheet, Mr Sheffield, an' then ah jus' need a quick word wi' Ruby afore ah go.'

I signed his sheet and left him looking at his reflection in the van window while he stroked his flowing locks.

Ruby glanced at him as she hurried out of school.

Jimmy leaned casually against his van and shouted across the car park: 'Ah'll be in T'Royal Oak tonight, Ruby.'

'If ah go, it'll be wi' my Ronnie,' retorted Ruby.

'Ah'll buy y'one o' them fancy cocktails,' yelled Jimmy with a nonchalant flick of his hair. 'An' ah'll mek sure it 'as a humbrella in it.'

As Ruby trotted down the cobbled drive she reflected that in all her married life Ronnie had never bought her a cocktail. At the school gates she paused and looked back at Jimmy, who was adjusting his headband in his rear-view mirror, and she smiled to herself. When she finally arrived at her cramped little council house at number 7, School View, she stopped to look at the overgrown garden and shook her head in despair. The unkempt lawn was littered with old motorcycle parts. Ronnie had promised to tidy the garden three years ago but always managed to find an excuse.

Ruby's husband, Ronnie Smith, was one of the country's two million unemployed and she had given up hope that he would ever get a job. Apart from pigeon-racing, his only hobbies included managing the Ragley Rovers football team and drinking large quantities of Tetley's bitter.

Thirty years ago, in 1949, as a slim, attractive sixteen-year-old, Ruby had fallen in love with Yorkshire's unlikeliest soldier. National Service awaited the country's eighteen-year-olds and Ronnie, as a new conscript, was about to earn twenty-eight shillings a week. Although the average wage at the time was eight pounds, eight shillings and sixpence, this amount was a fortune for the habitually unemployed Ronnie.

When Ronnie left the army he had learned little of any use. His frequent punishments had included whitewashing lumps of coal, cutting a lawn with a pair of scissors and scrubbing the cookhouse floor with a toothbrush. As Ruby sat at her kitchen table and drank tea from a chipped Robertson's Golly mug, she thought about her children.

Her eldest son, twenty-eight-year-old Andy, was a corporal in the army and twenty-six-year-old Racquel, a chocolate-box packer at the Joseph Rowntree factory, lived in York with her husband. Her other four children still lived with Ruby in their council house. Duggie, a twenty-four-year-old undertaker's assistant with the nickname 'Deadly', loved his mother's cooking so much he vowed he would never leave home. Nineteen-year-old Sharon was going steady with the local milkman; seventeen-year-old Natasha had recently left Easington School and started work as an assistant in Diane's Hair Salon; and the baby of the family, six-year-old Hazel, was a rosy-cheeked happy little girl in Jo Hunter's class. Ruby loved them all and looked round the silent kitchen. She remembered the happy days of her life when they were growing up around her and she missed all their tears and tantrums.

She also wondered what it would be like to meet Jimmy Witherspoon in The Royal Oak and run her fingers through his gorgeous hair. It really was spectacular. Then she glanced at Ronnie's spare Leeds United bobble hat hanging on the coat peg on the kitchen door and sighed deeply. As she walked into her cluttered kitchen to clear up the breakfast bowls she began to sing 'I am sixteen, going on seventeen' from her favourite musical, *The Sound of Music*.

Back in school, after I had collected the children's dinner money my morning lessons went well and I was delighted that, even though Jodie Cuthbertson's comprehension still left a lot to be desired, her spelling had finally improved. She was beginning to use her dictionary at last.

'There y'are, Mr Sheffield,' said Jodie as she put her English comprehension notebook on top of the pile on my desk. She had written: 'Lots of mummies used to live in Ancient Egypt. They wrote in a funny language called hydraulics.' When the bell went for morning playtime, I was ready for my morning coffee, particularly after Tony Ackroyd had written: 'One horsepower is the amount of energy needed to pull one horse.'

Vera had prepared five mugs of hot milky coffee and was showing Anne the front page of her *Daily Telegraph* when I walked into the staff-room. 'Doesn't she look wonderful in that scarf?' she said in admiration. The front-page photograph showed a confident-looking Mrs Thatcher standing alongside Herr Schmidt, the West German chancellor, while reviewing a guard of honour in Bonn.

'She could do with being back at home to sort out this ITV strike,' said Sally grumpily. ITV workers wanted a 5 to 10 per cent pay rise to end their seven-week strike but there seemed little hope of a resolution.

Vera ignored the perceived criticism of her political heroine and changed the subject. 'And Miss Henderson rang, Mr Sheffield.' She glanced at her spiral-bound notebook. 'She said she would be in The Royal Oak at seven thirty.'

I looked up. 'Laura?'

'Yes, Mr Sheffield,' replied Vera with the merest hint of disapproval.

Anne, Sally and Jo suddenly seemed to find the view out of the staff-room window of particular interest. For the rest of the school day thoughts of the two sisters, Beth and Laura, kept flicking across my mind.

At a quarter past seven I pulled up near the duck pond outside The Royal Oak. The bar was crowded when I walked in as the members of the Ragley Rovers football team were eager to quench their thirst after a brief training session. Their manager, Ronnie Smith, was already on his second pint of Tetley's bitter and Ruby was sitting at the bench seat under the dartboard with her son Duggie. In the far corner, the familiar click-click of a domino game could be heard as four old farmers, all of them wealthy enough to purchase The Royal Oak, battled fiercely to win the five-pence stake, or 'one shilling' as they called it, in their weekly game of threes-and-fives.

In the taproom Don Bradshaw, the landlord, was standing on a chair behind the bar, fixing a shelf bracket to the wall. Don was an ex-wrestler and the electric drill looked tiny in his giant fist. His wife, the buxom Sheila, was bending over to hold the chair steady. Meanwhile, Ragley's favourite bin men, Dave Robinson, the Ragley Rovers captain, and his cousin, Malcolm Robinson, were staring in utter confusion at this DIY project. As Dave was a six-feet-four-inch goalkeeper and Malcolm was a five-feet-four-inch midfield maestro, they viewed this dramatic change in their familiar surroundings from a different perspective.

'What's goin' on, Don? Y'can't 'ave a telly in our tap-room,' said Big Dave. 'It'll be an extraction.'

'Y'reight there, Dave,' said Little Malcolm, who always agreed with his cousin. 'It'll be a big extraction.'

'Distraction,' corrected Stevie 'Supersub' Coleclough and then wished he hadn't.

Stevie, the frail number 12 who rarely got a game, was the only member of the football team with any sort of academic qualification and regarded himself as the brains of the group. Unfortunately his intellect was not immediately evident from his latest multicoloured tank top, yet another gift from his colour-blind Aunty Maureen from Pontefract. She had certainly exceeded herself on this occasion with a startling red, white and blue horizontal-striped creation. Maureen had attempted to integrate large letters into the pattern across the chest. However, instead of the intended word STRIKER, after difficulty with the letter K, it finally looked like STRIPPER.

'Shurrup, y'big soft stripper!' shouted Big Dave.

Stevie's cheeks glowed bright red, clashing horribly with his freckles and red hair. He glanced down forlornly at his chest and shut up.

'Pubs in London 'ave tellies,' shouted Sheila Bradshaw from the other end of the bar. She looked in admiration at Don. ''E's not backwards in coming forwards is my Don.' Sheila leaned over the bar once again in her low-cut blouse to reveal her astonishing cleavage and, momentarily, the footballers were distracted.

Big Dave was the first to regain his composure. 'Well, they can keep 'em. What do we want t'be like London for?' he said, banging his giant fist on the bar.

'Y'reight there, Dave,' said Little Malcolm.

'They even 'ave warm beer down there,' persisted Big Dave.

'Y'definitely reight there, Dave,' said Little Malcolm.

'An' our dad sez they're all southern softies,' added Clint Ramsbottom.

Clint was dressed in a brand-new Rod Stewart shiny synthetic shellsuit in lurid green with yellow piping. Although it squeaked like a demented budgerigar every time he moved, he was proud of his new image as the dawn of the eighties approached.

'They're soft all reight,' growled Clint's big brother, Shane Ramsbottom. He clenched his right fist, upon which the letters H-A-R-D were tattooed on the knuckles.

Shane was a skinhead with all the charm of a short-tempered Rottweiler. He ruffled his younger brother's recently coiffured, David Bowie feather-cut. 'Ain't that reight, Nancy?'

Clint knew when to be silent and this was one of those occasions. Ever since he had begun to frequent Diane's Hair Salon, his big brother had taken to calling him Nancy. While he could cope with having a father called Deke who sang cowboy songs for beer money, being called Nancy really got under his skin.

Clint's father, Derek 'Deke' Ramsbottom, the local farmhand and occasional snow-plough driver, looked up, nodded in agreement, absent-mindedly polished his sheriff's badge on his leather waistcoat, and returned to his dominoes game.

'Yeah, they're all soft,' mumbled Clint, while carefully rearranging his hair and praying the subtle highlights had not been disturbed.

''Cept f'Chopper 'Arris,' said Norman 'Nutter' Neilson, the psychopathic fullback. There was a moment's pause as everyone considered this possible exception to what was a well-known fact.

'Ah'll give y'that, Nutter,' agreed Big Dave: ''Cept f'Chopper.'

Everyone nodded in agreement. Chelsea Football Club was in Division Two of the Football League and Chopper Harris was their notoriously tough defender.

'It said in t'paper they beat Cambridge one–nil, Chopper were booked an' fifteen spectators got arrested,' added Stevie authoritatively, trying to restore his reputation.

'Sounds like a good game,' said Chris 'Kojak' Wojciechowski, the Bald-Headed Ball Wizard.

At that moment Laura, wearing a beautifully tailored narrow skirt, a checked blouse and a fashionable 'Sherpa' woollen quilted waistcoat, walked into the lounge bar. She looked as if she had just stepped from the cover of *Cosmopolitan*.

'Hello, Jack,' she said and kissed me on the cheek before she sat down. 'What a day!' She slipped off her waistcoat, stretched and massaged her neck. 'Liberty's was heaving today,' she said, 'but at least my business plan is working.'

'Business plan?' I queried.

'Yes. Nothing to worry your head about, Jack: it's just a few sales strategies of mine to increase profits. Desmond from head office in London rang me today to say he was impressed.'

'I'm pleased it's going well,' I said. 'So what would you like to drink?'

'I need a G and T.' She took a pound note from her sleek leather purse and offered it to me.

'No, it's my turn,' I said and walked to the bar.

Sheila moved swiftly to serve me and made sure I had a good view of her cleavage. 'What can ah do for you, Mr Sheffield?' she said, leaning forward and fluttering her huge false eyelashes.

'Just a G and T and a half of Chestnut, please, Sheila.'

As she pulled on the hand pump she glanced across at Laura. 'Ah see you're with y'girlfriend, then.'

'She's just a friend, Sheila.'

'Looks a bit young f'you, Mr Sheffield. You'd be better off wi' a more experienced woman . . . if y'get me meaning.'

I glanced nervously from Sheila to the bulging biceps of her husband Don at the other end of the bar and beat a hasty retreat to Laura. She sipped her drink and began to twirl her hair round her finger and thumb in the same way that Beth used to do.

'What's all the fuss in the other bar?' asked Laura.

'They're installing a television set,' I said, 'and the locals don't like change.'

'It's part of the London scene now, Jack,' said Laura. 'You must let me show it to you some time.'

'Well, I love the theatres and museums.'

'So do I . . . We could plan a visit.'

'Sounds a good idea, Laura . . . Perhaps later.'

'I'll hold you to that,' she said with a mischievous smile and downed her drink quickly.

'Another?' I said.

Laura nodded. 'Just an orange – I'm driving.'

Half an hour later Laura glanced at her watch. 'Sorry, Jack, but I've got an early start tomorrow. I had better get back to York.'

I walked her back to her car.

'Thanks, Jack. It was good to see you.'

'My pleasure, Laura.'

She kissed me on the cheek. 'Let's do it again soon,' she said and disappeared into the night.

When I wandered back into the bar a loud cheer rattled the walls. Don had fixed the television in place. 'There y'are. Job's a good 'un,' he said.

'Guess we'll 'ave t'ope for t'best,' grumbled Big Dave.

'Y'reight there, Dave,' said Little Malcolm.

I attracted Sheila's attention. 'Another half of Chestnut Mild, please, Sheila.'

Sheila fluttered her false eyelashes. 'Comin' up, Mr Sheffield. Anything f'you.'

'Ruby seems to be enjoying herself,' I said.

'That's Jimmy Savile. 'E cleans our winders,' said Sheila, 'an' 'e's a bit of a lady's man.'

While Ronnie was in the Gents, Jimmy had moved in for the kill and slipped into the bench seat next to Ruby. ''Ow about that cocktail, Ruby?' said Jimmy.

'Ah'd better not, Jimmy. My Ronnie might get vexed,' said Ruby.

'Nay, Ruby, when ah were in t'army wi' Ronnie we 'ad some fun,' said Jimmy, slipping his arm round Ruby's shoulders.

'Mebbe y'did but my Ronnie used t'write t'me regular,' said Ruby.

'Ah used t'write t'dozens o' girls,' boasted Jimmy.

''E once wrote SWALK on one of 'is letters,' said Ruby dreamily.

'Ah used t'write NORWICH on mine,' said Jimmy, with a knowing look.

'Norwich?' said Ruby, looking puzzled.

'Aye,' said Jimmy: 'Nickers Off Ready When I Come Home!'

'Oooh, Jimmy, you are a one,' said Ruby, her cheeks red with embarrassment.

'That's f'me t'know an' you t'find out,' said Jimmy, suggestively stroking the letters on his headband. 'Y'should've come away wi' me instead o' marrying Ronnie. 'E were never gonna mek owt of 'imself . . . not like me.'

'Y'blow yer own trumpet, Jimmy,' said Ruby.

'Ah've allus fancied you summat rotten, Ruby, so 'ow about lettin' me walk yer 'ome? Your Ronnie's a waste o' space.'

But, unfortunately for Jimmy, Ronnie's son Duggie had heard this conversation and hurried away to whisper in his father's ear. Jimmy, finally rebuffed by Ruby, wandered out to his van and Ronnie followed close behind with the Ragley Rovers football team in close attendance. Ruby, sensing trouble, hurried after them.

Outside in the darkness, Ronnie grabbed Jimmy's shoulder and swung him round. 'You leave my Ruby alone, y'big, long-'aired jessie,' he shouted angrily.

Jimmy, a born coward, stepped back in alarm and stumbled on the steep slope of the grass bank. To his horror he fell backwards with a huge splash into the duck pond. Ruby screamed; Ronnie ran down the bank in alarm and grabbed Jimmy's flailing arm. But it was too late.

'Oh no!' shouted Jimmy as he splashed frantically in the water. All the football team had gathered behind Ronnie and stared in amazement as Jimmy stood up in the muddy water.

'Bloody 'ell, jus' look at that,' shouted Ronnie and the crowd began to laugh. The Jimmy that emerged from the water was very different from the Jimmy that had fallen in. Jimmy was completely bald and his blond wig, like a fluorescent lily pad in the moonlight, was floating away.

''E's no 'air!' exclaimed Big Dave.

'Y'reight there, Dave,' agreed Little Malcolm.

With his image shattered for ever, Jimmy ran to his van and drove off up the Easington Road.

Ruby walked over to Ronnie and put her arm round his waist. ''E were a reight flash 'Arry,' she said.

'Forget 'im, Ruby,' said Ronnie.

Ruby didn't reply but looked wistful.

'You'll allus be my Ruby,' said Ronnie as he leaned over and pecked her lightly on the cheek.

'Oh, Ronnie,' spluttered Ruby, 'y'mekkin' me feel all unnecessary.'

The first hint of alarm bells began to ring in Ronnie's head. 'Anyway,' he added, taking a step back, 'ah allus thought y'were beautiful.'

'Oh, Ronnie,' said Ruby, almost overcome with emotion.

'An' yur 'air is a lovely colour,' said Ronnie a little desperately. 'It's just like Cleopatra.'

'Y'mean when Elizabeth Taylor were that Queen of Egypt?'

Ronnie looked confused. He thought Elizabeth Taylor was a film star. 'No,' he said. 'Ah mean Jodie Cuthbertson's talking parrot.'

'A parrot!' said Ruby. 'Y'mean my 'air looks like a parrot?'

'But it's a smashing colour,' said Ronnie hastily. 'It won a prize at las' year's show.'

'Oh, ah see,' said Ruby.

'Anyway, Ruby, y'know 'ow ah feel about you,' whispered Ronnie.

'Tell me, then,' said Ruby.

'Ah don't like. One o' t'lads might 'ear us.'

'Y'used t'tell me when ah were a girl,' said Ruby softly.

Ronnie looked around furtively to make sure no one was in earshot and then he spoke softly in Ruby's ear, 'Ah love you, Ruby.'

Ruby stared at Ronnie and put her dumpy hands on either side of his Leeds United bobble hat. 'Come 'ere, y'soft ha'porth,' she said.

She pulled his head into her prodigious bosom, kissed the top of his bobble hat and held him there lovingly. Twenty years of mopping floors had given Ruby a grip like a steam shovel. Ronnie was slowly asphyxiating but he knew there was no escape. When he was finally allowed up for air, Ruby let go of his head and wrapped her arms round him in a loving bear hug. Ronnie thought he heard two of his ribs crack as he desperately tried to breathe.

'An' ah love you, Ronnie,' whispered Ruby.

'So, y'don't fancy that Jimmy Witherspoon?' wheezed Ronnie.

'No, ah don't,' said Ruby.

Ronnie looked relieved. 'So are y'coming?' he said.

'Not yet, Ronnie. You walk on 'ome, put t'kettle on an' ah'll wait f'our Duggie.'

Ronnie set off to the council estate and Ruby walked to

the bench by the duck pond and sat down. She stared at Jimmy Witherspoon's platinum-blond wig with its bright red LOVE MACHINE headband as it sank for the third and final time into the murky depths.

Then Ruby reflected on happier times and thought about one of her favourite scenes from *The Sound of Music*. She recalled Julie Andrews in the summer house singing with Christopher Plummer and then wearing the most magnificent wedding dress. When the ripples in the pond had settled and the village green was silent, Ruby leaned back on the bench and looked up at the graceful canopy of branches of the weeping-willow tree. In the strange silence she looked round and remembered a summer's day long ago when she had sat on this very spot. The young slim Ruby had looked beautiful in her borrowed wedding dress and the scent of her bouquet of wild roses was still vivid.

Suddenly the bright full moon reappeared from behind a cloud, bathing the village green in a mysterious white light. Ruby held up her work-red hand to shield her eyes from the reflection of the moonlight on the surface of the pond. As she began to hum 'How Do You Solve a Problem Like Maria', the bright shafts of light flickered through her fingers.

And, in that moment, Ruby wondered if, one day, it would ever be her turn to hold a moonbeam in her hand.

Chapter Four

Rita's Revolution

Miss Evans, School Secretary, left today for three days of compassionate leave to attend a funeral. A temporary secretary will be provided by County Hall until Miss Evans returns.

Extract from the Ragley School Logbook:
Monday, 15 October 1979

'Absence makes the 'eart grow fonder, Miss Evans,' said Ruby in a singsong voice.

'It's only three days, Ruby,' said Vera. 'Joseph and I will be on the train to Truro tomorrow, the funeral is on Wednesday and we return to Yorkshire on Thursday. So I'll see you all again on Friday.'

The sad news of the death of Vera's favourite aunt in Cornwall had caused a flurry of activity. It was the end of the school day on Monday, 15 October, and all the staff had gathered in the school entrance hall to say goodbye.

'Ruby's right,' said Anne: 'we shall all miss you.'

Vera gave her a tired smile and squeezed her hand.

'Best wishes, Vera,' said Sally, and gave her a hug.

'And have a safe journey,' added Jo anxiously.

Vera glanced round at our concerned faces and handed me the keys to her precious filing cabinet. It was a symbolic gesture and everyone recognized it as such.

'Thank you, Vera,' I said quietly.

'Don't worry, Mr Sheffield,' said Vera. 'Everything will be fine.'

There was a moment's silence as we all looked at one another. I noticed that Anne looked decidedly nervous. 'I'm sure it will,' she said a little uncertainly. 'The temporary secretary arrives tomorrow.'

'Well, there's the list of all the jobs I would have done,' said Vera. She pointed to a neatly typed list on a single sheet of paper in the exact centre of her immaculately tidy desk. 'And I'll see you all soon.'

'Come on, Vera,' I said. 'Let's walk you out to your car.'

We all processed out to the car park and watched as Vera climbed into her car. She drove slowly down the cobbled school drive and we waved goodbye. Above our heads, pale amber sunlight caressed the autumn leaves as they fell gently on to the village green, soon to form a shroud for the sleeping earth. I stared at her car and realized just how much I relied on her. For the first time since I had become headmaster of Ragley, Vera's reassuring presence would not be in the school office. I breathed in the clean Yorkshire air and sighed.

Vera drove past The Royal Oak and pulled up at the junction. Beneath a sky of wheeling swallows we watched her turn right up the Morton Road and head north. Then, as we walked back into school, a chill breeze swept through the branches of the horse-chestnut trees above our heads. We can survive three days without Vera, I thought to myself without conviction. I should have known that life is never that simple.

The following morning I looked out of the leaded pane windows of Bilbo Cottage. The dew, like untouched diamonds, sparkled in the morning sunlight. In the far corner of the garden, harvest mice were weaving their nests of grass and in the hedgerow the red hips of dog roses were providing valuable food for hungry voles. The nights were drawing in now and the earth was cooling but it was a fine autumn day.

As I walked out of my front door I glanced up at the porch where spiders were making their webs and beads of moisture, trapped on the silken threads, were glistening in the sunlight. It felt good to be alive on this bracing Yorkshire morning, until a thought crossed my mind. The new secretary was due to start work today.

According to the telephone call from County Hall, Rita Plumtree had attended the North of England Higher Secretarial College in Leeds and had emerged with a host of Pitman's shorthand and typing qualifications. So everything appeared to be fine and I was relaxed as I drove into the dappled sunlight of Ragley High Street and pulled up outside Prudence Golightly's

General Stores & Newsagent to buy my copy of *The Times*. Outside the shop window, the usual morning rush of children had gathered with what was left of their pocket money. There were difficult decisions to make about the conflicting merits of aniseed balls, bull's-eyes, gobstoppers, sherbet dips, coconut lumps, treacle toffee and liquorice laces.

The High Street was filling with cars and Mrs Dudley-Palmer had pulled up in her Rolls-Royce after dropping off her daughters earlier than usual. She was on her way to Harrogate to order a kidney-shaped swimming pool, an indoor sauna and a spa bath.

Just before nine o'clock the sound of a misfiring car engine shattered the silence of the school office and I looked out of the window. Our new temporary secretary had finally arrived. A battered royal-blue 1968 Renault 4, with sliding windows on runners, pulled up in the No Parking area immediately outside the boilerhouse doors. From it emerged a tall lady wearing green cord trousers, sturdy brown shoes and a shapeless Arran sweater. She walked round to the strange tin-can bonnet, undid the catch and tipped it forward. Then, after stooping to stare at the engine, she shook her head in disgust, slammed down the bonnet and strode confidently towards the school entrance in a determined manner.

She walked into the school office without knocking. At six-feet-one-inch tall she gave me a level stare. 'Good morning. I'm Rita Plumtree,' she said. Her slate-grey eyes were unblinking.

'Oh, hello, Miss Plumtree,' I said. 'Thank you for helping us out this week.'

'Ms,' said Rita.

'Pardon?'

'It's Ms Plumtree, not Miss,' said Rita.

'Oh, er . . . sorry. Well . . . er, Miss Evans has left a list of
jobs for you . . . er, Ms Plumtree, so if there's anything you
need please ask,' I said hesitantly.

Anne stepped forward. 'I'm Anne,' she said cautiously,
'and I'll show you round if you wish. The cloakroom and
staff-room are this way.'

Rita gave Anne an enigmatic smile and they both
headed off. Relieved, I made a quick exit.

At half past ten I was ready for my morning coffee. After
reading Frankie Kershaw's English comprehension
exercise I needed a pick-me-up. In answer to the question
'Why do birds fly south in winter?' Frankie had written,
'Because it's too far to walk!'

However, when I walked into the staff-room, there was
no sign of the usual pan of hot milk simmering merrily on
our single-ring primitive cooker. Nor were our individual
mugs lined up as they usually were. Instead Rita Plumtree
was pouring a steaming-hot milky drink from a flask into
a large plastic mug, which left a damp, unsightly ring on
Vera's shiny desk top in amongst an untidy pile of mail
from County Hall.

'We usually have coffee at half past ten,' I said.

'So do I,' replied Rita, not looking up.

'Vera usually makes hot milky coffee for us,' I added.

'Did you know that seventy-seven per cent of teachers in primary schools are women?' asked Rita.

'Pardon?'

'It's a statistical fact,' said Rita, picking up my copy of *The Times* and scanning the front page.

'Er . . . no, I didn't,' I said. 'Is it important?'

'It is when you consider that the National Union of Teachers has only four women on its forty-four-member executive. It's just another breach of the Sex Discrimination Act,' said Rita forcefully.

I took a deep breath. 'I'll prepare the coffee today, Ms Plumtree. Perhaps you would be kind enough to do it in future.'

Sally and Anne walked in as the telephone rang. Rita continued to drink her coffee. Anne gave her a stare and picked up the phone. 'Oh, hello, Beth,' she said with a quick grin in my direction. 'Good to hear from you. How's the new headship?' There was a pause. 'Yes, I expect it is. Anyway, Jack's here,' said Anne and passed me the receiver.

'Hello, Beth. How are you?' I said. Suddenly my heart was beating fast.

'Fine, thanks, Jack. It's a bit hectic here.'

Beth had just begun her new headship of Hartingdale Primary School near Thirkby in North Yorkshire. It was an exciting time in her professional life and I could tell she was in a hurry.

'So how can I help?' I said.

'Well, I've got a governors' meeting tomorrow night, Jack, and we really need to introduce a new maths scheme.

I know you're pleased with your School Mathematics Project with all the coloured boxes and graded workcards and I wondered if you had any brochures or samples you could let me have.'

'Of course. Shall I drop them in at your house?' I said hopefully.

'That would be lovely,' she said. 'I should be home by six thirty.'

'Fine. See you then.'

''Bye, Jack.'

''Bye.'

I stared out of the staff-room window. If only for a short while, Beth was back in my life.

'Coffee, Jack?' asked Anne. As she passed the mug of coffee I noticed she and Sally were looking at me with broad smiles on their faces.

After school and before going to Beth's I called into Nora's Coffee Shop in the High Street. As I walked in, the Buggles' new number 1 hit 'Video Killed the Radio Star' was blasting out on the jukebox. Dorothy Humpleby, the Coffee Shop assistant and would-be model, was carefully painting her nails behind the counter. At five-feet-eleven-inches tall and with peroxide-blonde hair and a micro miniskirt, Dorothy was popular among the menfolk of Ragley, especially her current boyfriend, Malcolm Robinson, the five-feet-four-inch bin man.

Dorothy was sitting on a stool and Malcolm, standing on tiptoe at the counter and peering over a pyramid of two-day-old Eccles cakes, was staring intently at the love of his life. 'What y'doing, Dorothy?' he asked.

'She's painting 'er nails, y'soft ha'porth,' shouted Dave Robinson, his six-feet-four-inch cousin, from a nearby table. The two cousins, both in their thirties, had been inseparable since childhood and Big Dave disapproved of Little Malcolm's new liaison. He gave Little Malcolm his 'big girl's blouse' look and returned to his rock-hard pork pie and mug of sweet tea.

'It's 'Ot Passion Pink, Malcolm,' said Dorothy, glancing up with a flutter of her false eyelashes.

'It goes wi' yer eyes, Dorothy,' said Malcolm, who had recently read in the *Sun* that it was important to tell a woman that she had beautiful eyes, lovely hair and a small bum.

'But my eyes aren't pink, Malcolm,' said Dorothy, perplexed.

'No. Ah mean all that stuff on yer eyelids,' said Malcolm a little desperately.

'Oh, that's m'Mary Quant Raving-Pink eye gloss,' said Dorothy. 'It's reight subtle.'

'An' y've got lovely 'air,' said Malcolm.

'No. Ah need m'roots seeing to,' said Dorothy, pulling at a tangle of her backcombed Blondie hairstyle.

Malcolm leaned forward between the Eccles cakes and the cream horns. 'An' you've gorra small bum,' he whispered.

'Oooh, Malcolm, y'say t'most wonderful things,' swooned Dorothy as she swatted a large fly from the topmost cream horn. 'Here y'are: 'ave a cream 'orn.'

Malcolm blushed and his thick neck, sticking out of his council donkey jacket, went bright red.

Nora Pratt, the owner of Nora's Coffee Shop, put down her chamois leather on top of the jukebox. 'Dowothy,' she shouted, "as Little Malcolm paid for 'is cweam 'orn?' Nora had difficulty saying the letter 'r', which, fortunately, had never deterred her from getting the star part in the annual Ragley pantomime.

Malcolm blushed again. He didn't like being called 'Little' by someone two inches shorter than he was and he slapped a ten-pence piece on the counter.

"Urry up, Romeo,' shouted Big Dave.

'Ah won't be long,' replied Little Malcolm, slightly irritated.

Dorothy leaned over the counter and looked earnestly at Malcolm. 'Ah've been 'aving lots o' strange dreams since ah started going out wi' you,' she said.

'Oh 'eck,' said Little Malcolm, unsure whether this was good news or not.

'Ah keep dreaming ah'm flying away wi' a super 'ero and ah'm frightened o' falling.'

'Ah wunt let y'fall, Dorothy,' said Little Malcolm, holding his mug of tea in one hand and his cream horn, like an Olympic torch, in the other.

'Oooh, Malcolm,' said Dorothy, adding another spoonful of sugar into Malcolm's tea and stirring it thoughtfully.

Nora suddenly showed interest and, while much of Dorothy's world remained a mystery to her, this revelation had struck a chord. 'That's intewesting, Dowothy,' said Nora. She stopped polishing the plastic window of the jukebox and stared thoughtfully into space. 'I 'ave a weoccuwing dweam as well.' She propped her expansive bottom on the jukebox. 'An' in it ah'm a weincawnation of Queen Cleopatwa.'

Dorothy wondered briefly what Queen Cleopatra had to do with a can of evaporated milk but decided not to bother asking.

Half an hour later I was standing outside Beth's front door, holding a box of mathematics booklets and cards. Beth looked tired when she answered her door. She was still in her two-piece business suit and white blouse but she had kicked off her shoes.

'This is so kind of you,' she said, tucking a few strands of her honey-blonde hair behind her ears.

I stood on the doorstep, wondering whether to go in or not. 'All this stuff should help. I've put a copy of the teacher's book in as well so that you can show your staff.'

'Thanks, Jack,' she said and looked up at me. Her green eyes were just as I remembered them.

'Well, er, I don't want to hold you up, Beth. I know life must be very busy. I'll just put these in the hall, shall I?' Beth stood back and I put the box on the hall table, next to her briefcase and a huge pile of folders of schemes of work.

'I do appreciate your help, Jack,' she said.

'Good luck with the governors' meeting,' I said, stepping back through the door, 'and if I can do anything more to help just let me know.'

'I will, Jack.'

There was an awkward pause as I walked out on to the path and Beth closed the door. I stood there for a moment. Next to me was a beautiful climbing rose, a thornless Zephirine Drouhin in its final flush of carmine-pink blooms, and I remembered that Beth had put one in my buttonhole at Jo and Dan's wedding. I breathed in its wonderful fragrance and remembered happier times. Then, deep in thought, I drove back to Kirkby Steepleton past gardens filled with the autumn harvest and the sour flame of fallen apples.

The next morning the weather had changed. Through the bedroom window of Bilbo Cottage, the steepled bulk of distant villages formed a sharp partition against the grey October sky. Beneath the gossip of starlings I walked hurriedly out to my car and, as the wind turned in its groove, I arrived at school within an arrow-shower of steel rain.

At nine o'clock I was about to begin registration, when I heard raised voices in the entrance hall. I went to investigate and found Mrs Earnshaw, mother of Heathcliffe and Terry, standing at the office door, engaged in animated conversation with Rita Plumtree.

'We don't administer medicines here,' said Rita firmly. 'That's your job.'

'It's jus' for our Terry's cough,' said Mrs Earnshaw.

'It's union rules,' said Rita finally and closed the door.

'Well, thanks f'nothing!' exclaimed Mrs Earnshaw. Then she saw me. "Ello, Mr Sheffield. Ah don't think much of 'er,' she said. 'When's Miss Evans coming back?'

'Very soon, Mrs Earnshaw,' I said. I looked at the bottle of cough syrup. 'And if you leave this with me I'll pass it on to Mrs Grainger and she'll make sure Terry's all right.'

'Thanks, Mr Sheffield,' she said. She looked flushed and was breathing heavily. 'Mebbe y'can keep an eye on 'em? Ah think they're coming down wi' summat.'

Both boys immediately rushed off to their classes and I smiled. The Earnshaw boys, as always, looked among the fittest children in school – regularly grubby and frequently standing in puddles, but never ill.

'Of course, Mrs Earnshaw. I'll tell Mrs Grainger and Mrs Hunter. But what about you? Would you like to sit down for a moment?

'Don't worry about me, Mr Sheffield. As y'can see, ah've fallen again.'

'Oh, I'm sorry to hear that, Mrs Earnshaw. Where did it happen? I hope it wasn't in school.'

It was her turn to look puzzled. Then Mrs Earnshaw chuckled to herself and opened her overcoat and put both hands on her tummy. 'No, what ah meant was ah'm 'aving another baby and it's due soon.' She pointed to the huge bulge bursting out of her outsize Lycra jogging trousers. I glanced down a little self-consciously. A piece of thick elastic stretched from the button hole to the button. 'Ah'm 'oping for a little sister for our Heathcliffe an' Terry.'

'Oh, well, I wish you luck,' I said. 'Have you decided on a name?'

'Well, if it's a girl ah want Dallas.'

'Dallas?'

'That's reight, Mr Sheffield. We both love *Dallas*. It's our favourite programme.'

'And what if it's a boy?'

'My Eric wants JR.'

'JR?'

'That's reight – jus' t'letters JR.'

'I see,' I said hesitantly.

'You've not met my 'usband Eric, 'ave you, Mr Sheffield?'

'No, I haven't.'

"E's not a bad lad,' said Mrs Earnshaw, leaning back on the table to take the weight off her feet. "E's very caring is my Eric. 'E got one o' them new doo-vays cheap an', cos 'e knows ah don't like cold feet, 'e allus keeps 'is socks on in bed. Ah tell y', 'e's a martyr is my Eric.'

'I'm sure he is, Mrs Earnshaw, and, er . . . if you'll excuse me, I'll have to get into class.'

'All reight, ah'll be on m'way,' she said and wandered off.

I popped my head round the office door. 'If someone turns up with medicine for their children, please can you let me know,' I said.

Rita looked up at me from behind her cluttered desk. 'We need to talk about official procedure,' she said curtly.

'We're a village school,' I said, 'a sort of extended family, so we don't always follow the rules you talk about.' I closed the door and hurried back to class.

* * *

The rain stopped and I was on playground duty. Tony Ackroyd, ever the entrepreneur, was using fallen leaves as currency and taking bets on snail-racing on the damp playground. 'Three to one on t'littlest,' he cried as I walked by. Meanwhile, in the staff-room, Sally, Anne and Jo stared open-mouthed as Rita fished a dog-eared photograph out of her shoulder bag. It showed her carrying a banner at the women's march through Birmingham in 1978 stating 'Men Are the Enemy'. She told them she was a revolutionary feminist and, much to Jo and Sally's interest, she declared she did not wear high heels or a bra and would never read a book written by a man.

In an attempt to change the subject, Anne said, 'Have an apple.' Shirley had put half a dozen in a bowl and left it on the staff-room coffee table.

Rita held one up to the light and studied it. 'I do not support oppression in South Africa,' she declared.

'Pardon?' said Anne.

'This could be a Cape apple,' said Rita, replacing it in the bowl.

'They're from Mary Hardisty's garden on the Morton Road, Rita,' said Anne.

Sally gave Anne a wide-eyed look and returned to her packet of Monster Munch pickled-onion corn snack.

By Thursday morning we had all had enough. The school office looked as if it had been ransacked. Vera's precious photograph of her three cats was under a pile of unopened brown manila envelopes. Rita kept telling us she wanted to end women's pain and we had all become tired of the constant lectures.

'Did you know that fifty per cent of men are on the lowest two pay scales compared with eighty per cent of women?' she announced.

Meanwhile, Anne was trying to pacify Sue Phillips, our school nurse and a guiding light in the Parent–Teacher Association.

'Your new secretary's making up rules on the hoof,' said Sue, holding the hand of her five-year-old daughter Dawn. 'She's just told me not to bring Dawn back until next week and she's only got a cold. I tried to explain to her I was the school nurse but all she did was wave a rule book in my face.'

At a quarter to four we all gathered in the school office as Rita took her leave. 'Call me if your secretary's ever off again,' said Rita. Then she gave me that intimidating look and walked out. With a crunch of gears she roared off down the drive and took a coat of paint off our new school gates.

'Good riddance!' said Sally and we all sat down and laughed, mostly with relief.

'Just look at this mess!' said Anne, surveying the state of the office.

'I think I'll stay behind to clear up,' said Jo.

'Me too,' said Sally.

'Count me in,' said Anne.

'You're right,' I said. 'We can't let Vera see this.'

Two hours later Anne was tidying the filing cabinet, Sally was polishing Vera's desk, Jo was washing up all the crockery and Ruby the caretaker was helping me to drag black bags of rubbish into the entrance hall. We finally stood back to admire our handiwork. 'Oh, one final thing,' said Sally and she picked up the photograph frame on Vera's desk and polished the glass with her sleeve. Once again Vera's three cats were back in their rightful place.

On Friday morning when Vera walked into school we all stood in a line in the entrance hall as a welcoming committee.

'Hello again,' said Vera. 'It's good to be back.'

'Welcome back, Vera,' I said.

'We've all missed you,' said Anne.

Jo gave Vera a hug and Sally surprisingly produced a bunch of dahlias from her garden. 'For you, Vera,' she said.

'Thank you so much, Sally,' said Vera and went into the office.

'Oh, I'm so pleased Miss Plumtree kept everything just so, Mr Sheffield,' said Vera scanning the beautifully tidy office. 'What was she like?'

Everyone went quiet until Ruby clattered into view with her galvanized bucket and mop. ''Ello, Miss Evans,' shouted Ruby. 'They all believe me now.'

'What's that, Ruby?' said Vera.

'Absence makes the 'eart grow fonder.'

Vera smiled and hung up her coat. 'I'm sure you didn't miss me really!' Then she made a minute adjustment to the positioning of the photograph of her cats and gave out the dinner registers.

Chapter Five

Gunpowder, Treason and Pratt

County Hall sent a 'rationalization' document to all schools in the Easington area explaining that the high costs of maintaining small schools may result in some having to close. Preparations were made for the PTA School Bonfire.
Extract from the Ragley School Logbook:
Thursday, 1 November 1979

'Remember, remember the fifth of November, gunpowder, treason and plot,' read the Standard Fireworks poster on the doorway of Timothy Pratt's Hardware Emporium. Timothy, or Tidy Tim as he was known in the village, owing to his obsessively fastidious nature, had used a spirit level to ensure the correct alignment of the poster. Timothy liked horizontal posters.

It was lunchtime on Thursday, 1 November, and I had called into Pratt's Hardware Emporium on the High Street to buy a roll of chicken wire for Jo Hunter's afternoon craft lesson. As I walked in, a heated argument was going on.

'Y'don't know what y'talking about,' snarled Stan Coe, the local landowner.

'But we've always 'ad a village bonfire in t'big field at t'back of t'school,' protested Timothy.

'Not if y'tresspassin', y'not,' growled Stan, his face red with anger. He buttoned up his bright-yellow waistcoat underneath his oilskin jacket. The buttons looked about to burst under the strain.

''Ow can we be tresspassin' on public land?' asked Timothy.

'You'll soon find out, Pratt,' sneered Stan, grabbing the new sledge-hammer he had just purchased. Then he stormed out, pausing to give me an evil stare.

'Judgement Day, Sheffield,' he growled as he passed me in the doorway.

I watched him as he stormed out to his mud-splattered Land-Rover. Stanley Coe, local bully and pig farmer, always seemed to be up to no good. Our paths had crossed in the past and we held each other in mutual contempt.

Albert Jenkins, local councillor and school governor, was selecting a set of brass hinges in the far corner of the store and had heard the conversation. He walked over to join me by the front door. 'He's up to something, Jack,' said Albert, 'so watch yourself.'

'I don't trust him, Albert,' I said, 'particularly when he looks so pleased with himself.'

We both peered thoughtfully through the window

as Stan Coe's Land-Rover thundered off up the High Street.

'He's always been envious of other people, Jack . . . "O! beware, my lord, of jealousy",' quoted Albert in a sonorous tone.

It was well known that Albert loved his Shakespeare. '*Othello*?' I asked.

'Well done,' said Albert with a wry grin. 'Act III, scene iii.'

'Anyway, I'm here for a roll of chicken wire,' I announced and walked towards the counter.

Albert returned to his brass hinges and Timothy hurried into the back store.

'Here y'are, Mr Sheffield,' said Timothy. 'Is it f'model-making?'

'Yes, Timothy. The children in Mrs Hunter's class are making their guy for the annual bonfire on Saturday.'

'Yes, ah'm looking forward to it,' said Timothy. 'Ah were jus' saying, y'can't beat tradition.'

For the past one hundred years the Ragley village bonfire had taken place on the spare ground between the school and the football field and, each year, the children had made a guy to sit on the top. Excitement was growing as the big day drew near. On my way back to school with the roll of chicken wire under my arm, I paused for a moment beside the village green to reflect upon the ribbon of shops in the High Street that were the life-blood of the village. All the needs of the villagers from a jar of Vic decongestant to a left-handed potato peeler could be purchased here.

Meanwhile, Tidy Tim walked into the storeroom at the back of his emporium and stared lovingly at the carefully labelled shelves. Then, from the top shelf, he took down the faded red cardboard box that contained his old Meccano set and recalled that Christmas morning in 1953 when, as a thirteen-year-old boy, he had found it at the foot of his bed. The picture on the box cover of an enthusiastic little boy playing with his working model of a crane had fascinated the young Timothy.

He remembered the excitement of opening it for the first time and seeing the red and green perforated metal pieces; the rods, tyres and wheels; the nuts, bolts, screws and spanners. The manual had advertised extra girders, swivel bearings and driving bands and, throughout the early months of 1954, he had saved his pocket money. Eventually, he had enough parts to construct a miniature, working lawnmower and, finally, his *tour de force* . . . a working elevator using a mechanical motor. On the day his mother had bought him his first pair of long trousers, he knew that his journey towards owning his own hardware emporium had begun.

Timothy had been an avid reader of *Meccano Magazine* and a member of the Meccano Guild, the Brotherhood of Boys. He had worn his little triangular badge with pride. But in the 1960s, the golden age of construction kits had ended for Timothy. His beloved Meccano had been replaced by cheaper plastic alternatives such as Fischer Technic and K'nex. For Timothy it was the end of traditional construction toys and, after all these years, it still tortured his organized soul.

So, with a sigh, Timothy replaced his Meccano set neatly on the shelf next to his Airfix Modeller's Kit and his John Bull Printing Set and, with loving care, rearranged the boxes so that the labels were neatly aligned. Only then did he close the door with a sense of satisfaction. Tidy Tim liked organized cupboards.

Back in the staff-room, a heated debate was going on. 'It's a disgrace,' said Vera, pointing to the front page of her *Daily Telegraph*. 'The Post Office made a profit of £375 million last year, yet they're still putting up the price of a first-class stamp to 12p.'

'What about second-class?' asked Sally.

'That's going up from 8p to 10p,' recited Vera while scanning the text, 'and they're blaming it on the postmen who have just had a sixteen per cent pay rise.' She shook her head in dismay and passed the newspaper to Anne.

'And prescription charges are going up as well, from 45p to 70p,' said Anne. 'Where will it all end?' She passed the newspaper to me and I glanced at the front page.

'Oh dear,' I said.

'What is it, Jack?' asked Sally.

I read the headline. 'SELLING OFF SCHOOL BUILDINGS AND LAND COULD BE THE KEY TO REORGANIZATION.'

'Sounds ominous,' said Anne.

'It gets worse,' I said. 'It says, "The cuts in local authority spending mean twenty-one thousand fewer teachers and the closure of small, uneconomical schools."'

'That might mean some in the Easington area,' said Sally with a look of concern. With inflation running at

17 per cent and entrepreneurs buying up school land, the future looked ominous.

'That reminds me,' said Vera, taking a smart spiral-bound booklet from a large County Hall brown manila envelope. 'This has just arrived.' The title, *The Rationalization of Small Schools in North Yorkshire*, sent a chill down my spine. That evening it was still on my mind until seven thirty, when I was faced with the choice of *Top of the Pops* with Mike Reed on BBC 1 or *Charlie's Angels* on ITV. It was no contest. I settled down with a large mug of black tea for an evening with Farrah Fawcett.

Next morning I called in for petrol at Victor Pratt's garage. A liquid rainbow reflected in the dark pools of oil and rainwater on the forecourt as I pulled up beside the single pump and rummaged in my pocket for a ten-pound note. Victor was the elder brother of Timothy Pratt, and renowned for his lack of humour and constantly untidy state. Beneath the smears of grease and engine oil, his stubbly face was set in its customary scowl.

'Good morning, Victor. Fill her up, please.'

'Ah've got that trellis elbow again,' said Victor as he unscrewed my filler cap.

I winced as he put a greasy handprint on my recently polished rear window.

'I'm sorry to hear that, Victor,' I said, trying to sound suitably concerned.

'All this cold an' wet, it sets off m'pneumatics.'

'Are you coming to the bonfire?' I said, trying to move on to something more positive.

'Never miss it, Mr Sheffield,' he said gruffly. 'Ah allus 'elp our Timothy wi' t'fireworks. Me an' Timothy an' John Grainger 'ave done it f'years. It's tradition.'

School was a hive of activity when I arrived. Jo Hunter was working in the hall with her husband, Police Constable Dan Hunter. Dan was taking assembly on the theme of the firework code and Jo was helping him mount some large posters. They were hoping to move out of their rented flat in Easington and had just begun to search for a home of their own, but with average house prices leaping to £17,000 they were finding it difficult. Dan was a huge six-feet-four-inch rugby player and, as always, he looked very smart in his navy-blue uniform with a small coat of arms on each collar.

'Thanks, Dan,' I said. 'This is really important for the children.'

'A pleasure, Jack, especially as I can be on duty and spend time with my lovely wife.'

Jo grinned and looked up, full of admiration for her handsome husband. With his fashionable long sideburns and droopy seventies moustache, he resembled one of the mean lawmen chasing Robert Redford and Paul Newman in *The Sting*.

The assembly went well and Dan answered all the children's questions in his relaxed style. He was drinking coffee in the staff-room when he looked out of the window at the spare ground beyond our school field. 'That's strange,' he said. 'Isn't that supposed to be common land?'

Two workmen were hammering large posts into the

ground. Alongside was a muddy Land-Rover and in the trailer behind was a roll of chainlink fencing.

'It always has been,' said Vera, looking concerned.

'And that's exactly where the PTA will be building the bonfire tomorrow,' said Anne.

'I'd better check this out,' said Dan and he walked out to his little grey van and drove off. Ten minutes later he was back, looking puzzled. 'You've got a problem, Jack,' he said. 'Stan Coe says there's an old statute that entitles him to the land and he's fencing it off. I'll get back to the station and let them know what's going on.' Dan drove off and Vera stared out of the window with grim determination on her face.

'Don't worry, Mr Sheffield,' said Vera calmly. 'I know just the person who will sort this out.'

At twelve o'clock a large shiny, chauffeur-driven, classic black Bentley purred into the school car park and a tall athletic sixty-one-year-old man leapt out of the back seat and strode confidently into school. Major Rupert Forbes-Kitchener, as usual, looked the immaculate country gent in his tweed sports jacket, lovat-green waistcoat, regimental tie, cavalry-twill trousers with knife-edge creases and sturdy brown brogues polished to a military shine. He tapped on the office door, walked in and placed his brass-topped walking cane on the high Victorian window ledge.

'Good morning, Jack,' he said and shook my hand in a crushingly firm grip. The major had replaced Stan Coe as a school governor.

'Good morning, Major,' I said. 'Thank you for coming in at such short notice.'

He looked at Vera, bowed slightly, and his steel-blue eyes noticeably softened. 'Good morning, Vera,' he said. 'You're well, I hope . . . what?'

Vera blushed slightly. 'Yes, thank you, Rupert. I do hope you can help us in our hour of need.'

The major glanced out of the window at the distant field where the two workmen had fixed the chain-link fencing to the wooden stakes. Then they climbed back in the Land-Rover and drove away. 'So what's that ruffian Coe up to now?' he said.

'He told PC Hunter that he was taking advantage of an old statute,' said Vera.

'Sounds jolly underhand, what?' said the major.

'It certainly does,' I said.

'Rupert, we can't let this man get away with this,' said Vera in a determined voice.

The major's keen eyes narrowed as he walked to the door. 'Jack, let's investigate.'

Minutes later we both leaned on the school fence and surveyed the fenced-off land. Attached to one of the posts was a sign that read PRIVATE LAND.

'The blighter!' exclaimed the major, 'and, by the way, Jack, the next field up the Easington Road belongs to me.' He pointed to a distant gateway in the hedge. 'My daughter Virginia keeps a few of her horses there.' Next to a sturdy five-barred gate I could just make out a tall white post with a sign attached but it was too far away to read.

We returned to the staff-room and the major moved smoothly into operations mode. 'With your permission, Jack, and of course yours, Vera, we'll make this office the command centre.' Vera smiled and I nodded. 'Good. Now let's get to it, what?' He sat at my desk, picked up the telephone and dialled a well-rehearsed number. 'Torquil, old chap,' said the major, 'I need a favour.'

Ten miles away in the County Council Planning Office, Torquil Lovejoy carefully unrolled an ancient tithe map of 1841 on his beautifully polished desk and focused his attention on the area, known as 'The Strays'. A few months short of his fortieth birthday, Torquil was at the peak of his career. He was renowned for his brilliant mind and his attention to detail was second to none. Within a matter of minutes he had found exactly what he was looking for and dialled the number given to him by the major.

'This is it, Major,' said Torquil. 'In 1965 the Government passed an Act of Parliament making provision for a "Register of Commons".'

'Jolly good, Torquil old chap . . . but what does it mean?'

Torquil traced a beautifully manicured finger towards a green shaded area on the map of Ragley. 'If a sufficient number of individuals register their right of access within five years, this claim is overturned.'

'And what's "a sufficient number", Torquil?'

'Possibly ten or fifteen, I suggest, Major,' said Torquil.

'You mean a protest march, what?'

'Something like that. Maybe tomorrow morning before Coe puts any livestock in the enclosure. Perhaps I should come along, Major.'

'Well done, old chap. See you at the Manor at nine hundred hours.'

'I'll be there, Major.'

'Good show, Torquil.'

The major replaced the receiver and stood up. 'Jack, my boy,' he said, 'it's time for *esprit de corps*.' Before leaving, the major put Vera in charge of communications and Jo was told exactly what to say to PC Dan Hunter.

A few minutes later the chauffeur-driven Bentley pulled up outside Pratt's Hardware Emporium. When the major walked in, Timothy immediately stood to attention and puffed out his chest. His army cadets training of twenty-five years ago was still a vivid memory.

'At ease, Timothy,' commanded the major with a wry smile. 'Now, tell me this. Have you got any broom handles?'

'Ah've just 'ad a delivery o' fifty, Major,' said Tidy Tim.

'Excellent. Now, there's something I need you to do.'

Timothy listened carefully to his instructions and knew immediately that he was the perfect man for the job.

Saturday morning dawned bright but bitterly cold and I arrived at school just before nine o'clock. With the last sighs of autumn a flurry of golden brown leaves swept across the cobbled driveway and came to rest under the creaking eaves of the cycle shed. Like tired tumbleweed, they had made their final journey. As they settled in a patchwork quilt of reds, browns, ochres and yellows the wind became sharp and cold. I stepped out of my car, fastened the top toggle of my duffel coat and wrapped my old college scarf a little tighter. Over the school field a grey mist was slowly clearing and a dusting of frost had coated the petals of the bright dahlias outside Anne Grainger's classroom. With seamless transition autumn had departed and winter had arrived.

A mile away, the major looked out of the window of Old Morton Manor House and surveyed his estates. In the elegant lounge his daughter Virginia was serving coffee to Torquil Lovejoy, who smiled with satisfaction at the detailed official document he had brought from the County Planning Office. 'All in order, Major,' he said and replaced it in his briefcase. Alongside him, Vera Evans put a final tick against her neatly typed list of villagers. The grandfather clock chimed. 'It's time,' said the major.

Meanwhile, in Pratt's Hardware Emporium, Timothy and Nora Pratt had been working since dawn. Tidy Tim had nailed an A3 sheet of stiff card precisely two and a quarter inches from the top of each broomstick, while his sister Nora had painted the words SAVE OUR FIELD in neat letters.

Their elder brother Victor had also made an early start. He was in his shed at the back of his garage applying some red-oxide primer to his 1908 Aveling and Porter tandem steam-driven road roller. The top of the funnel stood ten feet above the ground and was rimmed with a gleaming brass collar. He had bought it from a scrap yard many years ago and it was his pride and joy. Victor stood back to admire his handiwork and looked at his oil-smeared wristwatch. He smiled grimly. It was time.

By nine thirty, the school was a hive of activity. Jo and Dan Hunter, significantly not in uniform, were in the staff-room with Anne and Sally. Meanwhile, Anne's husband, John Grainger, was outside Pratt's Hardware Emporium stacking the broomsticks and placards into the back of his rusty Cortina Estate. In the school kitchen, Shirley the cook and Mrs Critchley were making Yorkshire parkin. Into the large mixing bowl she added black treacle, soft brown sugar, oatmeal and ginger. 'Ginger's f'warming y'blood, Mr Sheffield,' said Shirley knowingly.

Ruby the caretaker was watching closely. 'That's reight,' she added. 'My mam calls it "cut-an'-come-again cake".'

In the last house in the village, Geoffrey Dudley-Palmer picked up his car keys from the hall table and sighed deeply. He didn't like protest marches but Miss Evans had been persuasive. Also, following Petula's latest spending spree in Leeds, she had insisted they wore matching his and hers Daks Charisma raincoats in camel beige with a brightly checked lining. Petula Dudley-Palmer said that at £169 each they were a bargain and made them look a cut above the rest of the villagers: 'Image is everything, dear.' But when Geoffrey looked at their reflection in the windows of their Rolls-Royce, he secretly believed they looked like Swedish porn stars.

At precisely nine forty-five, Torquil Lovejoy collected Timothy Pratt from his Hardware Emporium and they drove down the High Street to Coe Farm. An apoplectic Stan Coe stared in astonishment at the County Planning Office letter presented to him by Torquil. Minutes later Stan had donned an oilskin coat and his wellington boots and roared off in his Land-Rover.

Nigel and Felicity Miles-Humphreys were running late.

Nigel, the stuttering bank clerk, looked at the carriage clock on the mantelpiece. 'H-h-hurry up, F-Felicity. M-Miss Evans said t-ten o'clock.'

'But I want to look my best,' shouted Felicity from upstairs as she rummaged through her selection of kaftans.

Felicity was the producer of the Ragley Amateur Dramatic Society and had just returned from West Scrafton, a beautiful, unspoilt village in the Yorkshire Dales. She had been an extra during the filming of the third series of *All Creatures Great and Small*. When Christopher Timothy and Carol Drinkwater had driven through the centre of the village in their Morris 8 Tourer, Felicity had been told to walk out of a barn and watch them go by with a long-suffering expression. Fortunately, after living with Nigel for twenty years, she had perfected long-suffering expressions. When they arrived in the school car park, Nora Pratt gave them a broomstick-placard and they joined the throng. It seemed the whole village was on the march.

Major Rupert Forbes-Kitchener was standing in the bon-fire field, flanked by his trusty lieutenants, Timothy Pratt, Torquil Lovejoy, Vera Evans and myself. He checked his pocket watch. 'Ten hundred hours,' said the major. Then he pointed his brass-topped cane towards the far end of the field. 'First the heavy armour.'

With an ear-splitting hoot of his steam-whistle, Victor led the way into the field on his magnificent road-roller. This was his finest hour and, at a sedate pace, he calmly crushed Stan Coe's fencing as if he was driving a Crusader tank. Stan Coe stared goggle-eyed through the dirty windscreen of his Land-Rover and hurriedly sought reverse gear.

Close behind Victor, on his old tractor and waving his Stetson hat, was Derek 'Deke' Ramsbottom, complete with cowboy boots and sheriff's badge. Behind the tractor was a flat-bed trailer full of timber from the many broken outbuildings of Ragley village and sitting on the trailer were his three sons, Shane, Clint and Wayne. They had come to build a bonfire and no one was going to stop them.

Next in line came Big Dave and Little Malcolm in their bin wagon. On the bench seat, wedged in between them, and much to Big Dave's disgust, was Dorothy Humpleby, wearing her Suzie Quatro denim outfit and her bright-red Wonder Woman boots. It was a day to be noticed and she was not going to waste the opportunity.

Dorothy was impressed when she saw Torquil standing next to Timothy Pratt. 'Ooh, look at 'im,' she said. ''E looks jus' like Donny Osmond.'

Little Malcolm simply grunted, while Big Dave thought Dorothy had more lip than Mick Jagger.

'Now the cavalry,' said the major.

Virginia Anastasia Forbes-Kitchener, in skin-tight jodhpurs, and accompanied by members of her riding school, rode into the arena through the gateway from her training field as if it was the three-day equestrian event at the forthcoming Moscow Olympics.

'Finally the infantry,' said the major.

Nora Pratt, holding her protest banner, led a mixed assortment of villagers on to the field. As Nora came to stand beside us she looked at her two brothers and said, 'Once a Pwatt, allus a Pwatt.'

'Well done, Nora,' I shouted.

'It's times like these, Mr Sheffield, that I'm weally pwoud to be a Pwatt,' she replied as she marched towards Stan Coe's Land-Rover.

Stan was in a state of panic. He reversed his Land-Rover wildly towards the nearest gateway and slewed round in a wheel-spinning arc, until there was a loud crack. Next to the gate, the tall white post, with a sign that read HORSE MANURE – HELP YOURSELF, slowly toppled. Alarmed, Stan opened his driver's door and leapt out of his seat. He landed with a squelch into something very slippery and promptly fell on his large backside.

'Oh, no, what the 'ell's this?' yelled Stan. To make matters worse the broken post fell across his chest. ''Elp me up, somebody,' screamed Stan, but there were no takers.

Dan Hunter appeared. 'Officer,' yelled Stan, 'arrest 'em.'

'Looks like you've caused some criminal damage here, Mr Coe,' said Dan with a smile, lifting up the broken signpost.

The crowd gathered and watched Stan trying to stand up in the steaming pile of Yorkshire's finest horse dung. Each time he tried he fell down again and every time he got up he wiped his hands on his bright-yellow waistcoat.

Albert Jenkins whispered in my ear, 'The soul of this man is his clothes. Trust him not in the manner of heavy consequence.'

'Shakespeare?'

'*All's Well That Ends Well,*' said Albert with a grin.

Finally, Stan Coe extricated himself from the dung heap, leapt into his Land-Rover and roared off, accompanied by the cheers of the crowd.

Timothy Pratt saluted the major. 'Mission accomplished, Major.'

'An' good widdance t'bad wubbish,' said Nora.

'Well done, everybody,' said the major.

'How about a nice cup of tea?' said Vera, and we all followed her into school.

That afternoon the Ramsbottoms, assisted by members of the PTA, completed the building of the bonfire and Torquil helped Timothy Pratt to retrieve all his broomsticks and returned with him to his Hardware Emporium. When Timothy led Torquil into the back room, Torquil's eyes widened in appreciation at the Meccano set.

'I've got an original Subbuteo Table Football game, Timothy,' said Torquil modestly.

"Ave you really?' asked Tidy Tim, his eyes wide in amazement.

'Yes. It's the real thing, made by Waddington's in Leeds.'

'Did you know it's named after a hunting bird, the Falcon Subbuteo?' said Tidy Tim, moving swiftly into his familiar *Mastermind* mode.

'Really?' said Torquil.

'So, would you like to see my Meccano set, Torquil?' asked Timothy.

Torquil looked at his new friend in sheer wonderment and they settled down together to build a working crane.

That evening, with the bonfire roaring and fireworks exploding in the air, I approached Timothy.

'Thank you, Timothy,' I said. 'We couldn't have had our bonfire without you.'

'Like ah said, Mr Sheffield,' replied Timothy, 'tradition . . . y'can't beat tradition.'

Chapter Six

Sorry Seems to be the Hardest Word

The weekly staff meeting was cancelled owing to Mr Sheffield's toothache (A. Grainger, Deputy Headteacher).
Extract from the Ragley School Logbook:
Friday, 30 November 1979

'Sorry, Miss Henderson,' said Vera rather sharply. 'Mr Sheffield is unable to speak to you.' I looked up from my desk in the school office. A few murmurings could be heard from Vera's telephone. 'No, you don't understand,' cut in Vera. 'Mr Sheffield actually *can't* speak to you. In fact, he hasn't been able to speak to anyone. He has severe toothache.'

I nodded in agreement and then stopped quickly. My head felt like a football and nodding made it worse.

The conversation continued until Vera said, 'I can pass on your request if you wish.' The message seemed to take an age. Vera scribbled a note in her immaculate shorthand

and said, 'Thank you, Miss Henderson. Goodbye.' She replaced the receiver on its cradle and looked sternly at me. 'That was Miss Henderson . . . Miss *Laura* Henderson.' Vera emphasized the word 'Laura' with the merest hint of disapproval and then glanced at her notepad. 'She says would you like to meet her outside Liberty's at six thirty, tomorrow evening.'

'Ank-oo, Ve-agh,' I mumbled and then winced.

It was the last day of November and somehow I had survived to the end of the school week. My toothache had begun with a slight twinge during the middle of the month but had gradually worsened. Finally, by lunchtime, I could no longer communicate, so the staff had rallied round. Vera had volunteered to do my paperwork, Anne had cancelled the weekly staff meeting and Sally had taken my class as well as her own into the school hall for an afternoon of drama and music.

It was slightly irritating to me that the school continued to run perfectly and I didn't seem to be missed. Also, it didn't help when Jodie Cuthbertson waved goodbye at the end of school and shouted, 'That were a great afternoon, Mr Sheffield. Can we do it every week?'

As I gathered my coat, scarf and old leather briefcase, everyone crowded into the office to take a last sympathetic look at my swollen face. I felt like a specimen in the Natural History Museum.

'Looks dreadful,' said Jo. 'Shame you haven't got teeth like my Dan. He never has toothache.'

Anne and Vera gave Jo a sharp stare. They could see this was help I didn't need. 'Take some aspirin, Jack, and try to get some rest,' said Anne as she draped my college scarf carefully across my swollen jaw in a motherly way.

'And gargle with hot, salty water,' added Vera.

Ruby had arrived at the staff-room door with a familiar clatter of her mop and bucket. 'My aunty Gladys swears by cloves, Mr Sheffield,' she said. 'Jus' put a couple nex' t'your tooth and keep y'mouth shut . . . if y'get m'meanin'.'

'Ank-oo, Ooo-bee.' I was beginning to sound like Bill and Ben the Flowerpot Men.

'Whisky, Jack,' said Sally, finally. 'That'll take y'mind off it.'

That evening I took Sally's advice and called into The Royal Oak and pointed to a small bottle of malt whisky. 'Is that all, Mr Sheffield?' said Sheila, slapping the bottle on the counter. 'Y'don't look y'self.'

I pointed to my swollen jaw and winced visibly.

'Oh, you've got toothache?' said Sheila. 'Wait there. Ah'll get y'summat.' She hurried into the back room muttering, 'Men! They're only good f'one thing, an' most of 'em are useless at that!'

I sat on a bar stool and looked round. The usual crowd of footballers were at the far end of the bar and they were all staring at Clint Ramsbottom. Clint had gone to a lot of trouble to create his new image and the transformation was considerable. Up to quite recently Clint had been a seventies man with a Kevin Keegan bubble perm, flared trousers and skin-tight shirt. Today, after a visit to Diane's Hair Salon, he was sporting his new David Bowie feather-cut with subtle bronze and crimson highlights. His jeans were tight stonewashed denim and, from the waist down, with his Doc Marten boots, he looked like Mickey Mouse. However, the *pièce de resistance* was his huge white shirt with a lacy collar and baggy sleeves. Clint looked as if he had just auditioned for *The Three Musketeers*.

'What's all this, then?' shouted Big Dave across the taproom. 'Y'look like Errol Flynn in *Sinbad*.'

'Y'reight there, Dave,' added Little Malcolm. ''E looks like a big, soft pirate.'

'It's m'new look,' said Clint proudly. 'Ah'm gonna be an eighties man.'

'New look?' queried Kojak.

'Yeah, it's New Wave,' said Clint proudly.

'New Wave?' said Big Dave.

'Ah'd wave it bye-bye if ah were you, Nancy,' said Shane unsympathetically.

Clint looked in annoyance at his big brother but, wisely, said nothing.

Sheila came back with two pink tablets and a small glass of dark rum. 'Get this down yer, Mr Sheffield.'

'Ank-oo, She-agh,' I said and stared at the tablets, undecided.

'Bloody men!' said Sheila. 'Y'don't know what pain is. Gerrit down yer.'

I took the tablets and swigged down the rum. My eyes watered.

'You'll be all reight wi' them tablets, Mr Sheffield. They do wonders fur all me women's troubles.'

Not entirely reassured, I drove home very carefully.

Then, with a tumbler of malt whisky, I settled down to watch Angela Rippon read the news. She said that Prime Minister Margaret Thatcher was beginning to take a dim view of the antics of a certain Mr Arthur Scargill. When my telephone rang I could only answer it with what sounded like fluent Japanese.

'Aah-loh?'

'Hi, Jack. Just confirming tomorrow night.' It was Laura, in her usual hurry.

'Aah-loh, Lor-aah,' I said as tears sprang from my eyes with the effort.

'Didn't quite catch that but see you at six thirty outside Liberty's. Thought we could call in to the wine-tasting evening at the Assembly Rooms,' she said. 'Anyway, must rush. 'Bye.'

I stared at the receiver, sipped my whisky and stared round my empty room with only Angela Rippon and toothache for company. I was feeling sorry for myself but I remembered that Laura was a wonderful, attractive and dynamic companion. It was just that talking to her might be a problem.

Saturday morning was freezing cold and the sharp air made my jaw ache even more. A robin, perched on a spade handle, was quietly reciting its cheerful song of whispers and stared at me unblinkingly as I tottered towards the driveway. I scraped the ice from the windscreen of my car, blew on my key before I inserted it into the door lock and soon I was driving through Ragley village and then up the Easington Road.

In the market town of Easington, stalls were already doing early-morning business as I parked in the cobbled main square next to one selling fresh pheasants. The dentist's surgery was above the chemist's shop and I walked down a narrow alley to the back entrance. Next to a warped wooden door with peeling blue paint was a tarnished brass plate and on it was engraved *H. Nelson, BDS*.

Horatio Nelson, a portly fifty-five-year-old, humourless Bradfordian, had never forgiven his father, a lover of famous sea-battles, for christening him after England's greatest admiral. To make matters worse he had stopped growing at five feet and a half-inch tall. Inevitably, on his first day as a student at Leeds University, he had been given the nickname 'Half-Nelson' and it had stayed with him throughout his career.

The doorway opened on to a shabby, musty and poorly lit staircase covered in threadbare carpet. I climbed unsteadily up the stairs to another door on the first-floor landing. The dentist's opening hours were displayed on a card that had once been white and now had curled grey edges.

I walked into a dingy waiting room lined with hard-backed chairs. In the centre of the room a dusty, hardboard coffee table was piled high with old copies of *Horse and Hound*. An elderly, bald-headed man, with an uncanny resemblance to Popeye the Sailorman, was sitting there and he held a set of his dentures in each hand and clicked them together like castanets. He looked up with a toothless grin as I surveyed the room.

On the walls, posters of happy, smiling, suntanned people with sparkling white teeth beamed down from a pain-free world, devoid of crime, cloudy skies and, especially, toothache. After living on soup and soft foods for a week I took an instant dislike to the image of the smug man in the loudly checked sports jacket who was eating his steak and chips with the confidence of someone who could light up a medium-sized shopping precinct with a single smile.

Off to my right, one wall was partitioned off with a doorway, a counter and a sliding, frosted-glass window. In front of it was a small bell. I rang it and a shadowy figure appeared behind the glass. The sliding window opened and a grey-haired woman peered over her half-moon spectacles at me. It was Mrs Elsie Crapper, church organist and wife of Ernest Crapper, Ragley's finest and only encyclopaedia salesman. Elsie had just taken a Valium tablet and looked reasonably composed.

'Hello, Mr Sheffield . . . Oh dear, you look like death warmed up.'

'Aagh gor too-ayhk,' I said.

Years of practice provided her with an instant translation. 'So, you've got toothache?'

'Yaagh,' I replied.

'Very well, we'll try to fit you in. Come back at half past ten.'

'Ank-oo, Mithith Clap-ha.'

She shut the screen with a thump.

I looked at my watch. Two hours to kill. I was doing a passable imitation of 'The Scream' by Edvard Munch, so I set off back to the first-floor landing to find the toilet.

Beneath an antique cistern with a rusty chain was a cracked washbasin. The hot tap didn't work and the block of coal-tar soap resisted the capacity to produce lather under the tiny trickle from the cold-water tap. The smooth and shiny toilet paper in the unused box had anti-absorption qualities that would have interested the designers of space shuttles. On a rolling pin attached to the wall, the damp roller towel, which was actually a tea towel sewn into a loop, held little attraction so I returned to the waiting room after flushing the toilet. This was a mistake as it sounded like the contents of an iron-monger's shop going over Niagara Falls.

When I returned, a well-dressed lady and her daughter had arrived. The girl looked about eleven years old, had blonde pigtails and was wearing a bright-blue public-school jacket with a gold-stitched coat of arms on the breast pocket. The Latin motto under the badge, roughly translated, read, 'We seek a virtuous life.'

'I *don't* want *no* beastly injections, Mummy,' she said.

Her mother sighed, shook her head and gave me a 'What do they teach them in schools these days?' look.

'Darling, I've told you before. A double negative in English turns it into a positive. Even though in Russian a double negative can form a positive, you must realize that there is no language where a double positive forms a negative.'

'Yeah . . . right,' said the girl and returned to drooling

over a full-page colour photograph of Fonzie, *aka* Henry Winkler, in her *Jackie Annual*.

Her mother looked at her curiously for a moment. Then she picked up a copy of *Yorkshire Life* and murmured in appreciation at the photograph of all the fine red-coated huntsmen of the Middleton Hunt leaving Garrowby Hall.

The fortunate people with appointments came and went. A laboratory technician came down from the attic to collect both sets of Popeye's false teeth for repair and, occasionally, screams from the surgery caused a flurry of concern in the waiting room. Finally ten thirty arrived and, once again, I was face to face with Elsie Crapper. She selected a brown, dog-eared National Health Service envelope from the teeming files on the shelf behind her and directed me to the surgery.

I walked into the condemned cell.

'Cilla, put a bib on Mr Sheffield,' said Horatio without looking up. As he washed his hands in the small sink in the corner I noticed the familiar roller towel was there but his hot tap was working.

Cilla, the leggy dental assistant in a short white overall that didn't quite cover her miniskirt, selected the least damp of the two bibs on the radiator, directed me towards an ancient black leather dentist's chair in the centre of the room and attached the Velcro tabs of the bib round my neck.

When Horatio examined me, the overpowering smell of Brut aftershave momentarily made me forget my discomfort. He peered over his round-lens, John Lennon spectacles and put two fingers in my mouth, one on either side of the swollen gum, and his thumb under my jawbone. This was the era before surgical gloves and I could taste the soap. Then he squeezed with a vice-like grip and I nearly passed out. Silent screams were now my speciality.

Cilla reached up to the Contiboard shelving unit attached to the wall and increased the volume on the Bush radio, presumably to drown my attempt at a scream. Joan Baez's rendition of 'Help Me Make it Through the Night', now at full volume, seemed somehow appropriate. Meanwhile, Horatio, undeterred, merely gripped tighter. Next to the radio was a huge photograph of the diminutive dentist holding a silver trophy on which the inscription read, *Winner of the Dentists' Annual Golf Tournament at Moortown Golf Club, Leeds, 1979*. This tended to confirm the little-known fact that all dentists have a good grip.

After extricating his fingers Horatio shook his head mournfully as if someone had died. 'X-ray, please, Cilla.' She rummaged in a drawer and produced a tiny white envelope. Horatio took out a small X-ray slide and with great ceremony he held it up to the harsh single light bulb above my head. 'Oh dear, oh dear,' he said. Then he grinned and replaced the slide. 'Sorry.'

'Saarh-ee?'

'Yes, Mr Sheffield. Sorry – it'll have to come out.'

'Aah.'

'You'll pay cash, I presume?'

'Yaah.'

Horatio seemed pleased. He received a bigger fee for extractions and a cash payment need not go through the books. A good lunch at the Pig and Ferret beckoned.

'We'll numb it off for you,' he said.

Cilla passed the syringe and then returned to the radio, her hand poised over the volume control. Horatio's gorilla fingers were inside my mouth once more as he injected both the inside and the outside of the infected gum. Tears sprang from my eyes as Ian Dury and the Blockheads sang 'Reasons to be Cheerful'.

Then to my horror Horatio called out, 'Another cartridge of Lignocaine, please, Cilla. We'd better make sure with this one.' My whole body went rigid as he repeated the procedure. Finally he said, 'Rinse out and come back in half an hour.'

The glass tumbler was chipped and scratched and I washed away mouthfuls of blood and spit. Cilla removed the soaked bib and hung it next to its partner on the radiator.

Back in the waiting room more patients had arrived. It felt like an audition for the Chamber of Horrors as we all groaned and squirmed. Thirty minutes went by as my face gradually took on the appearance of a giant hamster. At last, Elsie summoned me once again.

When I walked in Cilla was standing by the sink and yawning. The sixth vodka and blackcurrant she had drunk the previous evening at the Pig and Ferret had tasted like Brasso polish and another heavy night's drinking with her boyfriend was in store. She was looking forward to getting home for an afternoon's rest. Above her, the hot-water boiler hissed as she washed the instruments. The theory was to sterilize them but the truth was she was merely giving the bacteria a warm and luxurious bath. She approached the black chair with a tray of chisel-like instruments while Horatio prodded my gum with something that resembled a broken coat hanger.

'Can you feel anything?' he asked.

I tried to press my toes through the soles of my shoes. 'Yaah.' I realized I was doing my Bill and Ben the Flower-pot Men impression again.

Then he forced a mini-crowbar between my back teeth. There followed terrible crunching sounds and I thought my jaw was about to break.

Horatio shook his head in disappointment. 'Sorry, Mr Sheffield. Things aren't going to plan.'

'Whaah?'

'Cilla, get out the surgical kit and tell Mrs Nelson I'll be late for lunch. We've got a long haul with this one.'

On her way out Cilla turned up the volume once again. Elton John began to sing his 1976 classic, 'Sorry Seems to be the Hardest Word'.

'I'm going to cut the gum and drill out the bone before the fractured tooth can be removed,' he said.

I didn't feel him slice open the inside of my mouth but I did smell burning bone as his red-hot drill bored into my aching jaw. Cilla used her pistol-like syringe to cool things down but, as her boyfriend Darren had recently bought her an Elton John LP, she swayed to the music and occasionally squirted up my left nostril.

Finally, at about the time I was wishing I was trapped

in a locked room with Sigourney Weaver's *Alien* or, worse still, on the front row of a Sex Pistols concert, Horatio finally breathed a sigh of relief. 'Well, it was touch and go but I've sutured it now,' he said in triumph as he walked out. 'Clean him up, please, Cilla, and then Mr Sheffield can pay Mrs Crapper.'

Cilla removed my bib, threw it over the radiator and handed me a tumbler of water. ''Ave a spit,' she said. Then she surveyed me dispassionately. 'S'gonna 'urt summat rotten is that.'

In the chemist's shop I joined the queue. Horatio had given me a prescription for a powerful painkiller. Ragley's oldest resident was being served.

'It begins with "s", ah think,' shouted ninety-three-year-old Ada Cade from her wheelchair. Her granddaughter looked puzzled and sighed. Bringing her grandmother to the weekly market was a labour of love but she knew it was the highlight of Ada's week. The assistant surveyed the hundreds of creams and potions on the shelves. 'They're advertised on telly,' shouted Ada, who, once again, had refused to wear her hearing aid.

Everyone in the queue began to look for anything that began with 's'.

'Shampoo?' said the grumpy old man who was behind Ada in the queue and was fiercely clutching his prescription for piles cream.

'Sterodent?' queried the teenage girl holding her weekly ration of Aqua Manda hairspray and a bottle of Pagan Man aftershave for her latest fourteen-year-old

117

boyfriend who had just begun to shave the fluff from above his top lip.

I noticed a pair of surgical stockings but hoped someone else would offer this suggestion.

'Or it might be "n",' said Ada.

Everyone groaned and began a new search.

'What's it for?' shouted her granddaughter.

'A bit o'comfort, tha knaws, when ah sit down,' replied Ada in a deafening voice.

The gentleman with the prescription for piles cream began to show more interest and he scanned the shelves with greater purpose.

'Ah've remembered,' yelled Ada. Everyone sighed with relief. 'It's them Snugglers nappies.'

The assistant looked surprised and Ada's granddaughter flushed crimson.

'Nappies?' said the white-coated young lady.

'That's reight. Ah turn 'em inside out an' stuff a couple down me pants. It meks it real comfy when ah watch *Emmerdale.*'

Ada was pushed hurriedly towards the door, clutching her precious box of nappies. The door jingled once again and normal service was resumed.

'Teks all sorts,' said the assistant. 'Now then, sir, what can I do f'you?'

'A tube o' this, please . . . an' a box o' them nappies.'

On Saturday evening just after six o'clock I parked my Morris Minor Traveller near Whip-Ma-Whop-Ma-Gate in the city centre. It was ironic that York's shortest street had one of the longest names. I needed a walk to clear my throbbing head and I paused on Ouse Bridge and stared at the moonlit river travelling silently through one of England's finest cities and the jewel in Yorkshire's crown. Within the medieval walls, the population had slumbered through the Reformation and the English Civil War and, unscathed, York had retained its timeless majesty. The arrival of the railway and the chocolate industry had breathed new life into the city but, happily, its elegance had remained untouched.

I walked back into the city and under the Christmas lights on Parliament Street to Liberty's and arrived as Laura came out of the store. She was wearing a fashionable black leather coat and, with her long brown hair piled high in stylish plaits, she looked simply stunning.

'Hello, Jack,' she said, and then she saw my face under the sharp neon lights. 'Oh dear, you are in a state,' she added and stretched up to kiss me on my swollen cheek.

Automatically I drew back and then realized what I had done. The message from my brain said, 'Sorry.' The actual sound that came out said, 'Saarh-ee.' Raquel Welch in the film *One Million Years BC* would have understood immediately but, sadly, Laura had not seen the film.

'Pardon?' she said.

'Saarh-ee,' I repeated, imploringly.

'You definitely need some TLC,' said Laura as we walked towards the Assembly Rooms.

The wine-tasting was fun and Laura appeared to have a remarkable knowledge of the various wines of the world. Vintages from Australia, South Africa and France seemed to taste the same to me, but Laura explained the subtle differences. Also, with my swollen jaw, it was helpful that she did all the talking.

It was late when I walked Laura back to her flat near the Museum Gardens and stopped outside her door. We stood there under a perfect clear, cold night sky and above our heads the Milky Way shone bright like eternal stardust. Laura had never looked more attractive. She touched my swollen cheek gently.

'Would you like to come in for a coffee, Jack?' she asked.

'Saarh-ee,' I said.

'Is that a yes or a no?'

I shook my head and pointed to my jaw.

'Pity,' said Laura. She looked disappointed. 'I could have probably taken your mind off it,' and, with a mischievous smile, she brushed her lips against mine and in a moment she was gone.

As I drove home I switched on the car radio. Elton John was singing 'Sorry Seems to be the Hardest Word'. It occurred to me that he probably had toothache when he wrote it.

Chapter Seven

The Thinnest Father Christmas in the World

Rehearsals began for the School Christmas concert.
Extract from the Ragley School Logbook:
Friday, 7 December 1979

'It's the Hartingdale School Christmas fair tomorrow, Jack,' said Beth, 'and I was hoping you might be able to come along. It's the usual stuff . . . a few stalls, coffee and mince pies, a brass band, even Santa's grotto.'

It was the first call from Beth for several weeks and I was excited to hear her voice.

'Of course, Beth. I'd love to come. What time should I get there?'

'It starts at two o'clock but there's a lovely pub here in the village, Jack – the Golden Hart. Perhaps we could meet there and have a bite of lunch first if you like; say, about midday?'

'Fine. I'll see you then.'

''Bye.'

The line went dead and I stared at the receiver. It was Friday morning, 9 December, and my spirits lifted. When I glanced up again, Anne, Jo and Sally had stopped compiling their list of costumes for our annual Christmas concert and were exchanging knowing glances. It was obvious they had listened to my conversation. Vera, on the other hand, appeared preoccupied. 'It's time to cool down, Mr Sheffield,' she announced from the other side of the office.

'Pardon?' I looked up a little self-consciously and Anne chuckled over her coffee.

Vera was looking at a sheaf of papers from County Hall. 'We've been commanded to officially cool down,' she announced. 'The government says all offices should reduce their minimum permitted temperature to sixty degrees Fahrenheit and the top temperature should be no more than sixty-six.'

Sally slammed shut her *Carol, Gaily Carol* teachers' song book and snorted. 'Rubbish! My classroom's on the north side of the school and it's like Siberia in there.' Then, in defiance, she walked through to the staff-room and turned up the gas fire. It was noticeable that Sally was getting more and more irritated by the slightest problem and her usual sunny nature was fast disappearing.

Jo picked up her register and leaned over Vera's desk to read the headline on her *Daily Telegraph*. 'Mortgages are due to rise by fifteen per cent,' said Jo mournfully. 'Dan and I will never have a place of our own.' She looked disconsolate and followed Sally into the staff-room to get warm by the gas fire.

Anne looked sadly after Jo. 'It must be difficult for young couples,' she said. 'One day a decent house might cost more than £20,000 the way things are going.' She, too, collected her register and made for the warmth of the staff-room.

Vera looked out of the window at the children arriving for school. They appeared completely impervious to the cold with their rosy cheeks glowing on this cold winter's day. 'Well, at least the children don't seem to feel it,' she said quietly to herself. Then she picked up her coffee and newspaper and joined Sally and Jo in the staff-room, where she settled to admire the front-page photograph of Angela Rippon. The BBC's prettiest newsgirl had been picked to compete at Olympia against Prince Charles's all-star showjumping squad in order to raise money for the British Equestrian Olympic Fund.

'Pity she's too old for Charles,' murmured Vera as she sipped her coffee. 'He really needs a beautiful, innocent young girl.'

'Innocent!' exclaimed Sally.

'I think Vera means someone fitting to be our future queen,' said Anne quickly, ever the peacemaker.

'Well, his latest girlfriend sounds a bit of a tearaway,' said Sally. 'Apparently her nickname's "Whiplash Wallace",' she added pointedly.

'Whiplash!' exclaimed Vera. 'Oh dear, how very common.'

'He's certainly had a few interesting companions,' mused Anne.

'I liked Lady Jane Wellesley,' said Vera. 'She would have been perfect, but he was too young then,' she added.

'Better than that Fiona Watson,' said Jo.

'I don't remember her,' said Anne.

'Her nickname was "Yum-yum",' said Jo, 'and I think she posed for *Playboy*.'

'Oh dear,' said Vera, 'what must his mother think?'

'Mind you, every time he needs a shoulder to cry on, he goes back to that Camilla what's-her-name,' said Anne.

'Parker-Bowles,' said Vera with authority. 'Yes, that was a pity. I read he was heartbroken when she got married.'

'And then there was Skippy, that bubbly Australian blonde,' added Anne.

'Kanga, not Skippy,' said Jo. 'Skippy's that intelligent kangaroo.'

'You're probably right,' said Anne with a grin.

'Maybe he secretly fancies one of the Three Degrees,' said Sally mischievously. 'He did invite them to sing at his thirtieth-birthday party last year.'

'That reminds me, everybody,' said Vera: 'we'd better turn the gas fire down.'

Grumbling under their breath, Anne, Sally and Jo walked back to their draughty classrooms, while, for me, the thought of Beth's phone call meant that the cold weather was no longer important.

In the entrance hall I passed Mr and Mrs Dudley-Palmer deep in conversation. Mrs Dudley-Palmer was having Victoria Alice's costume for the nativity play professionally made in York and had called in to discuss the correct shade of blue for Mary's headscarf. In preparation for the big event, Geoffrey Dudley-Palmer had bought an Olympus Trip 35mm camera for his wife. 'It will fit neatly into your handbag, dear,' said Geoffrey persuasively. 'And, apart from the birth of Jesus, you can photograph pieces of furniture before you buy them.' Geoffrey was a past master at appealing to Petula's baser instincts. Sadly, although this was a tactful strategy, the state-of-the-art, cutting-edge technology was completely lost on Petula. Her first photographic results were destined to comprise twenty-four perfectly focused close-ups of her right ear against a variety of backgrounds.

Just before the end of school Deke Ramsbottom arrived on his tractor and unloaded the school Christmas tree. Immediately, a throng of children from Anne's reception class gathered in the corner of the hall to watch Ruby and me erect it in a half-barrel plant tub. As we stood back to admire our handiwork a host of little faces shone with excitement and I recalled once again the magic of Christmas for our four- and five-year-olds. 'Santa's coming soon,' whispered five-year-old Victoria Alice to the Buttle twins, Rowena and Katrina. They both nodded in perfect unison and dreamed of Tressy dolls with their stylish hair and Mary Quant's fashionably dressed Daisy dolls. They were also determined to discuss the possibility of a pet goat when they next met Santa in his grotto.

I left school earlier than usual and settled down in my cosy lounge with a cup of tea and switched on the television. It was just before five o'clock and Ed Stewart was encouraging his youthful audience to join in the fun of *Crackerjack*. I felt slightly guilty watching such a youthful programme and switched to ITV. A young female with legs that went up to her armpits was telling me that she was sick of stubble-rash but fortunately her life would now be complete with a new Ladies' Remington Shaver. I wished my life was as simple. When *Better Badminton* came on at seven o'clock I switched off, unwilling to watch fit, athletic men in tight shorts and headbands knocking the feathers off a shuttlecock.

After looking in my empty cupboards and at the lonely slice of cheese in my fridge, I decided to go into Ragley for a drink and enjoy one of Sheila Bradshaw's famous 'Belly Buster' mince and onion pies.

When I arrived, The Royal Oak was filling up with its usual Friday night crowd and topics that were in the news were being discussed.

'A Channel tunnel?' exclaimed Big Dave.

'That's reight, Dave,' confirmed Little Malcolm: 'a tunnel under t'English Channel.'

'It were in t'paper this morning,' said Stevie 'Supersub' Coleclough with authority. Stevie, as the only member of the football team with any academic qualifications, was proud of his superior knowledge. 'A Member o' Parliament called Norman Fowler said so.'

'Norman Fowler? Who's 'e when 'e's at 'ome?' asked Don the barman.

"E'll be some southerner wantin' cheap 'olidays in France,' said Chris 'Kojak' Wojciechowski, the Bald-Headed Ball Wizard.

'Y'reight there, Kojak,' agreed Little Malcolm. 'Warm beer an' cheap 'olidays – y'can't trust southerners.'

''Ow they gonna dig it?' asked Big Dave.

'Frenchies will be diggin' from their side an' we're gonna dig from ours,' said Stevie.

'But 'ow will they meet in t'middle?' said Kojak. 'Couple o' degrees out an' they'll miss each other.'

'Then you'll 'ave two tunnels,' said Norman 'Nutter' Neilson. While Norman was not regarded as the sharpest knife in the drawer, everyone agreed he had made a good point.

'An' we'll get that disease that meks dogs foam at t'mouth,' said Don the barman, putting down his tea towel.

Big Dave laughed. 'Nay, we already get that from your beer.'

'Ah've seen them mad dogs on telly,' said Clint Ramsbottom.

'Rabbis,' said Shane.

'Rabbis!' said Stevie. 'No, y'mean . . .' and then stopped in mid-sentence when he saw Shane's look.

As I walked from the bar with my steaming hot mince and onion pie and a half of Chestnut Mild I glanced at Shane's bulging muscles. It wasn't wise to correct a skinhead with psychopathic tendencies.

On Saturday morning in the bright pale December sunshine I gave my car a quick polish before I left Bilbo Cottage and then drove out of Kirkby Steepleton, through Ragley village and on to the Easington Road towards the winding country roads of the Hambleton hills. Hartingdale was an unspoilt market town amid the heather-covered moors and picturesque dales and a scenic drive stretched out before me.

After half an hour I pulled up on the crest of a wind-swept hill and stepped out on to the grassy verge. The clean air of the high moors filled my lungs and I surveyed the valley before me and the hills beyond. Creation had blessed this windswept land. When I was a boy, my father had brought me to a place such as this and said, 'Son, this is God's Own Country.' As I stood on this lonely hillside with the eternal rocks beneath my feet I remembered his words and understood their meaning.

Around me, the dense forests had lost their autumn colour and the red and ochre leaves were now form-ing dense piles of leaf mould round the gnarled trunks. Up ahead, in the distant valley below, was the beautiful North Yorkshire village of Hartingdale with its church spire, Victorian school building, village green and a cluster of cottages with reddish-brown pantile roofs. It looked as it always did, steadfast and untouched by the passing of time.

Standing there, I thought of Beth. She would be busy in her school, a headteacher immersed in her work at the centre of her village community, as I tried to be in mine. I remembered the sadness of our parting after Dan and Jo's wedding. While her sister Laura had filled a void in my life it was Beth that I missed most of all. Like a circle ripped at the seams, I had tried to let her go. I took one last long look at the Victorian rooftop of the village school and remembered our times together. After all these months, I still remembered that first kiss, etched in the stillness of time. The sharp wind whipped at my duffel coat and tears of cold filled my eyes. It was time to drive on.

I climbed back in my car and began the winding descent down the steep hill. Hartingdale village settled neatly into the wild moorland valley through which a pretty river wound its way over scattered shale through bracken, peat and moss. In the distance I heard the sound of grouse chattering their familiar warning cry 'go-back, go-back'. Undeterred, I drove down the hill into the village.

Hartingdale had become popular with tourists but, thanks to prudent planning, the town never seemed overcrowded and had retained its character. The cobbled main street stretched out before me, flanked by wide grassy mounds. On either side the terraced cottages looked impregnable, with solid walls that were two feet thick and with deep-set, tiny windows. These were homes that were snug and warm in winter and cool in summer. Around the village green some of the older properties had thatched roofs made of wheat straw, where the deserted nests of long-gone sparrows gradually untangled themselves in the winter breeze.

Long before the Industrial Revolution, the weavers of Hartingdale were famous across the North of England for the quality of their linen and woollen fabrics. When the day had arrived when they could no longer compete with the huge factories of the great cities of Yorkshire, the town returned to farming and tourism. With its clean air and attractive blend of Georgian and Elizabethan houses, the market square was a popular stopping-off place for bus-loads of city dwellers.

I spotted Beth's pale-blue Volkswagen Beetle outside the school and I parked in the square. Then I walked across the cobbles to the welcoming sight of the Golden Hart, its brightly coloured pub sign swinging in the breeze. It had a façade of Victorian permanence and, in 1838, it had become Hartingdale's principal coaching inn when a stagecoach known as the Hartingdale Flyer ran from York to Hartingdale and on to Kirkbymoorside. William Wordsworth had stayed here and history was my companion as I walked in.

Beth was already there, sitting alone at a table in the bay window and staring through the leaded panes, lost in her own thoughts. The lounge bar was beautifully furnished with relics of the past and the original oak beams had been left exposed. A pair of carver chairs, in the Chippendale style, flanked the huge local stone fireplace.

She stood up to meet me, elegant in a beautifully tailored dark business suit and a cream collarless blouse. Even though she looked stunning with her slim figure and proud, high cheekbones, today her green eyes were tired and stray wisps of long honey-blonde hair fell round her face. She tucked the loose strands back behind her ears in that familiar way I loved so much and then beckoned me to sit down at the table with her.

'Thanks for coming, Jack,' she said. 'You've no idea how much I needed your help today.'

My heart beat faster in expectation. 'Good to see you, Beth.' I smiled. 'Would you like a drink?'

'Yes, please,' said Beth. 'A white wine would be lovely.'

I walked over to the Tudor bar, ordered two glasses of white wine, and the waitress brought them over to us and set them down on the sturdy oak table. Its rugged surface, shaped with an adze, bore the carved mouse trademark of Robert Thompson, 'the Mouseman of Kilburn'. We ordered the 'Golden Hart Traditional Yorkshire Lunch', a £3.25 special comprising a giant Yorkshire pudding filled with beef stew and onion gravy. When the waitress walked away I could tell there was something troubling Beth.

'What is it?' I asked. 'Is something wrong?'

Her green eyes lingered on me for a precious moment. Cocooned in our private space and intoxicated by sweet-smelling cinnamon, we faced each other. She sipped her wine as if searching for the right words.

'There is something . . . but that can wait.' It was as if she had changed her mind mid-sentence. Then she put down her wine glass and smiled. 'Remember last New Year's Eve when you asked me to help you build a snow-man?'

'How could I forget?'

'It's a bit like that.'

'I give in.'

She tugged at a tiny green earring. 'Well, it's like this, Jack,' she said at last. 'I'm short of a Father Christmas and I'm desperate.' She gave me that familiar determined stare. 'I'm sorry to drop this on you but I've been let down at the last minute by my chairman of governors and I don't know who to turn to.'

'Oh, I see,' I said, struggling to take it all in. I tried to hide my disappointment.

'My chairman of governors is Whylbert Peach, the local artist,' explained Beth. 'That's one of his.' She pointed to a huge picture over the mantelpiece. It was a dramatic water-colour painting of Lake Gormire, near Sutton-under-Whitestone Cliff. The lakeside was studded with bulrushes and surrounded by deer and great-crested grebes. In the background reared the steep buttress of Sutton Bank, formed by glacial action and a popular launchpad for the local gliding club. Whylbert had used artistic licence and included the famous White Horse of Kilburn, carved out on the face of Roulston Scar in 1857.

I nodded in appreciation. 'So he was supposed to be Father Christmas?'

'Yes, Jack, but he's had one of his famous panic attacks. He's a bit of an oddball, to be truthful. My deputy, Simon, would have done it, but everyone here knows him too well.' The penny was dropping slowly. 'The children will be so disappointed if Santa doesn't make an appearance. So can you help?'

I shook my head. 'Beth, look at me!' I said. 'I'm six-feet-one-inch tall. I weigh thirteen stones four pounds and I've got a thirty-four-inch waist. I'm just not your usual build for Father Christmas.'

'There's no else I can think of, Jack.'

The steaming Yorkshire puddings arrived and I sighed and took off my spectacles to clean the lenses with my handkerchief. 'Also, Father Christmas doesn't wear Buddy Holly spectacles,' I added for good measure.

'Well, you'll just have to take them off,' said Beth firmly.

'But without them, I can't see a thing!' I yelled in despair.

'You'll be perfect, Jack, trust me.' And she gave me that look and I knew resistance was pointless.

An hour later I was sitting behind the curtain in the hall. The PE store had been cleared out and two staff-room chairs had been provided. On the wall behind me, on a panel of black sugar paper, a child's painting of a reindeer had been mounted to give the impression I was sitting in the Arctic Circle. My huge bright-red Father Christmas costume hung on me like an oversize tent, the ticklish white beard made me want to sneeze and the black boots were too small.

Next to me were two girls from Beth's top class. They were dressed as a fairy and an elf and were sitting on a bale of hay and looking bored.

'What are you getting f'Christmas, Shelley?' asked the fairy.

'Ah'm gettin' a record player an' a Donny Osmond record,' said the elf.

'Donny Osmond? Ah don't like 'im,' said the fairy disdainfully. 'Why don't y'get summat decent like Johnny Rotten?'

'Ah can't change me mind now,' said the elf. ''E's proper brassed off is me dad. 'E sez 'e 'ates Christmas.'

So, full of seasonal spirit, we welcomed our first customer. A little blonde-haired girl walked in, dragging her reluctant elder sister behind her. Reassured, I moved smoothly into Father Christmas mode. 'Ho-ho-ho, hello, little girl,' I said in a deep booming voice. The elf and the fairy looked at me as if I should be taken away by men in white coats.

'Hello, Father Christmas. I'm Lucy, I'm six, an' this is my sister, Emily, she's nine.'

I smiled at Lucy, while Emily gave me a knowing look. 'So, what would you like for Christmas?' I asked, immediately forsaking the booming voice.

'I'd like a *Doctor Who Annual*, please, and a Talking K-9 so I can share it with my sister 'cause she likes Tom Baker,' said the little girl.

'That's very kind of you to think of your sister,' I said.

'Well, I love my sister 'cause she gives me all her old clothes an' she 'as t'go out an' buy new ones.'

Her big sister grinned.

'I see,' I said. 'Well, I'll tell my little elves and we'll do our best.'

'Thank you, Father Christmas,' said Lucy and she walked out of the grotto through the narrow gap in the curtains.

As they disappeared from sight, Emily turned round and gave me a thumbs-up.

The elf turned to the fairy. 'An' what are you getting f'Christmas?'

'A Starsky an' 'Utch shoulder 'olster an' a fibre-optic lamp,' said the fairy.

There was a pause while the elf considered this modest collection of presents. 'Is that all?' asked the elf.

The curtains fluttered again and a mother came in with a pushchair and a five-year-old girl who was eating a Curlywurly.

'Go on, then,' said the mother, 'ask Santa for what ah sed.'

'Please can ah 'ave an Abba doll an' a skateboard,' recited the little girl.

Her mother nodded at me furiously.

'And have you been a good girl this year?' I asked.

'Yes, she 'as,' said the mother indignantly, 'and she'll be leaving y'usual mince pie an' a glass o' port.'

'Oh, well, er . . . thank you and I'll tell my little elves. Happy Christmas and a ho-ho-ho.'

The mother gave me a disparaging look. I thought the line about elves was rather good but decided to drop the ho-ho-ho.

The next customers came thick and fast until, an hour later, the final little girl asked for Kermit the Frog, Miss Piggy and a Muppet Show Board Game. The moustache went up my nose and I sneezed and her mother rushed her out quickly.

Then, followed by the elf and the fairy, I had to run the gauntlet of mothers and children as I hobbled through the hall in my tight boots. I was aware that a few of them tittered as I tiptoed past. Finally, in the blessed haven of the staff toilet, I changed back into my sports jacket and flares.

*   *   *

Back in the hall, Beth was busy talking to a group of mothers. Alongside her stood Simon, her handsome, flaxen-haired, deputy headteacher, who bore a passing resemblance to Robert Redford. He seemed very attentive to Beth's every word. Then Beth's cook ushered me into the staff-room, where I was served with a large mug of black tea plus a slice of Christmas cake and a slab of Wensleydale cheese. It was a feast after my ordeal and I gradually relaxed.

Darkness descended quickly and out of the high Victorian windows, in the distance, the bright moonlight illuminated the crumbling remains of a twelfth-century abbey on the banks of the River Hart. It had been built by Cistercian monks and was etched against the winter skyline. History lay heavy on this land.

Gradually the school emptied and I was standing in the entrance hall as the last two mothers walked out, each pushing a pushchair and engrossed in loud conversation.

'Ah'll tell y'summat f'nowt, Sandra.'

'What's that, Donna?'

'That Miss 'Enderson's lovely an' my Tracy's coming on a treat, but ah didn't reckon much to 'er choice o' this year's Father Christmas.'

'Ah know what y'mean, Donna. Mebbe 'e were jus' a beginner.'

'Well, somebody definitely needs t'fatten 'im up.'

''E were proper skinny.'

'Skinny? 'E mus' be t'thinnest Father Christmas in the world.'

I smiled and walked into the empty school hall. Beth was turning out the lights and carrying a large bunch of keys. She looked tired.

'Goodbye, Beth,' I said. 'Thanks for the invitation.'

'Thanks, Jack – you've been wonderful.'

The school was quiet now; only the ticking of the hall clock echoed round the Victorian building. I squeezed her hand and walked away into the darkness.

Chapter Eight

An Angel Called Harold

A large audience supported the school Christmas concert,
2.00 p.m.–3.30 p.m. Every child took part and members of
the PTA served refreshments afterwards.
        Extract from the Ragley School Logbook:
                Thursday, 20 December 1979

The turkey was definitely limping.

It hopped forward on its left leg and then dragged its right leg behind it. I peered out through the frozen windscreen of my car and stared at the strange scene.

Jimmy Poole, his ginger curls hidden under a huge hand-knitted balaclava, had made a lead out of a length of orange baling twine and was guiding a limping turkey across the village green towards school. I decided to ask him about it later. It was Wednesday, 19 December, the day before our Christmas concert and a busy day was in store.

In the entrance hall, Jo Hunter was in conversation with Mrs Audrey Bustard, mother of seven-year-old Harold.

''E's a proper little angel is my 'Arold,' announced Mrs Bustard proudly. 'Ah've made 'im this pair o' wings,' and she handed over a pair of wings that would have looked more at home on Batman.

'Thank you,' said Jo uncertainly.

I glanced at little Harold Bustard as I walked into the office. With his skinhead haircut, jug-handle ears and toothless grin, he didn't look particularly angelic. The two green candles of snot that were fast approaching his upper lip appeared to go unnoticed by his mother.

'Burra wanna be a sheep,' grumbled Harold.

'Shurrup, 'Arold,' said Mrs Bustard. 'You'll do as y'told.'

'Well, actually, Mrs Bus-taaahd,' said Jo, remembering to put an extended and heavy emphasis on the second syllable of 'Bustard' so that it didn't rhyme with custard or mustard, 'we do need a few more sheep.'

'Ah don't want 'is dad t'be disappointed, Mrs 'Unter. 'E's set 'is 'eart on it. It runs in t'family. 'E comes from a long line of angelic Bus-taaahds.'

'Well, I'll talk to Harold and we'll decide what's best,' said Jo, ever the peacemaker. She crouched down in the staff-room doorway and wiped little Harold's nose with a tissue. 'I'm sure Harold will do well,' she said cheerfully but not entirely convincingly.

Harold looked up at his mother with a fierce expression. 'Burra wanna be a sheep.'

'You'll do as y'told an' be a ruddy angel,' said Mrs Bustard with a finality that brooked no argument.

Jo took a step backwards. 'We really don't mind,' said Jo hopefully. 'In fact, another sheep would be really useful.'

Mrs Bustard glared at Jo. 'T'angelic 'ost jus' wouldn't be t'same wi'out our 'Arold,' she said. ''Is uncle 'Enry were an angel, 'is dad were an angel an' ah were an angel . . . an' a bloody good'un an' all.'

'I'm sure you were, Mrs Bus-taaahd,' said Jo with a sigh. 'In that case . . . we'll let Harold be an angel.'

Mrs Bustard nodded. She'd got what she came for. 'C'mon, 'Arold,' she said. Then she dragged little Harold across the entrance hall towards the front door, where she paused and shouted, 'An' ah'll mek 'is 'alo tonight.'

Jo breathed a sigh of relief and walked into the office.

'Well done,' I said. 'I imagine it's a bit wearing having to deal with Mrs Bustard.'

'Actually, it's Mrs Bus-taaahd, Jack,' said Jo with a grin and she skipped out into the corridor to the stock cupboard to collect some white card, red crêpe paper and a new brand of rubber glue with a distinctive but strangely compulsive smell.

Our annual Christmas concert was almost upon us and, traditionally, each class was to present a short play. However, this year, Anne and Jo had decided to combine their classes in a joint Cecil B DeMille production of the nativity. Sally's class had prepared a tear-jerking adaptation of Charles Dickens's *A Christmas Carol* and my class had rehearsed the world première of Jodie Cuthbertson's original play *Christmas in the Eighties*, which relied heavily on miming to Abba records while wearing lots of make-up.

By morning break the staff-room was so full of costumes, shepherds' crooks and kitchen-foil crowns that, in spite of the temperature dropping like a stone and the forecast of snow, it was a relief to do playground duty. I was warming my hands on my mug of coffee when I noticed Jimmy Poole standing by the cycle shed. He looked dejected, so I walked over to him.

'What's the matter, Jimmy?' I asked.

'Thpartacuth hath gone, Mr Theffield,' said Jimmy mournfully.

'Spartacus?'

'Yeth. Ah tied 'im up 'ere an' he'th gone.'

I remembered the turkey. 'Is Spartacus a turkey?' I asked.

'Yeth, Mr Theffield,' said Jimmy, totally unimpressed by my powers of deduction.

'You've got a turkey called Spartacus?'

'Yeth. Cauth of that thtory you told uth in athembly.'

I recalled I had just related the epic story of Spartacus the slave. 'And why did you bring him to school, Jimmy?'

'Ah'm trying to thtop Thpartacus getting killed for Chrithmath, Mr Theffield, cauth he'th my friend 'an' ah feel thorry for 'im.'

'I'm sure we'll find him,' I said unconvincingly and Jimmy walked back into class. I took a quick look round the cycle shed, but the limping turkey and the length of baling twine had disappeared. Spartacus was a free turkey.

Back in my classroom two of the mothers, Staff Nurse Sue Phillips and Margery Ackroyd, had called in to make glittery Abba outfits, while I helped ten-year-old Katy Ollerenshaw prepare a compilation of Christmas carols on our Grundig reel-to-reel tape recorder. It was noticeable that, compared with me, Katy was much more competent.

At twelve o'clock, Jungle Telegraph Jodie made an announcement. 'Vicar's coming up t'drive, Mr Sheffield, an' 'e's walkin' funny.' It was true. The Revd Joseph Evans was walking like a man wearing sandpaper underpants. I went to meet him in the entrance hall.

'Come into the staff-room, Joseph, and sit down,' I said, clearing colourful parcels of gold, frankincense and myrrh from the nearest chair.

Joseph gave me a strained look. 'I'd rather not, Jack. My, er, little problem's back again.'

It was obvious that Joseph's haemorrhoids had made an unwelcome return. No one ever used the 'h' word; we always referred to Joseph's 'little problem'.

'Oh, I'm sorry to hear that, Joseph. Would you like a cushion?'

'Thanks, Jack, that's very kind.' He lowered himself very gingerly on to one of the cross-stitched cushions that Vera had made for the staff-room. 'I wondered if we could have a word about the Bible readings for the church services over Christmas,' he said.

'Why not call round to Bilbo Cottage after school?' I asked. 'I should be home by six.'

Joseph stood up with some relief. 'Good idea, Jack.' He paused in the doorway, looked back and smiled. 'And I'll bring a bottle.'

It was six fifteen when I arrived home in Kirkby Steepleton. A sharp wind had sprung up and, over the distant Hambleton hills, heavy grey clouds promised snow. A little white Austin A40 was parked on my driveway, which meant Joseph had arrived. I hurried into the warm house, where loud Scottish voices could be heard in the kitchen.

My little Glaswegian mother, Margaret, and her sister, May, had arrived for their annual Christmas visit and it hadn't taken them long to work out what was wrong with Joseph. He was standing by the kitchen door, looking utterly bemused and clutching a wine bottle with a home-made label.

'Hello, Jack,' said Joseph. He gave me the bottle of murky yellow-green liquid. Joseph was very proud of his home-made wine. 'It's my peapod and nettle,' he said.

Meanwhile, a strong unpleasant smell drifted out of the kitchen and Joseph and I twitched uncomfortably. Cooking was not Aunt May's forte.

'Och aye, Vicar, this'll cure y'asteroids,' said Aunt May, who possessed a very individual but perfectly understandable use of the English language.

'After a wee portion of May's dock pudding,' said Margaret, 'ye will nae have haemorrhoids.'

May had cooked the spinach-like leaves of *Polygonum bistorta*, known locally as 'snakeweed', in a large, blackened pan. Then she had stirred in oatmeal, a knob of butter, spring onions and bacon fat. Finally, she had slapped a large spoonful of it into a bowl with a few rashers of bacon and served it to Joseph.

'You're a paragon of virtue,' said Joseph, accepting the bowl with a forced smile and inner dread. He carried it into the lounge.

'Och aye, thank you, Vicar,' shouted Aunt May, who, like my mother, was partially deaf.

'What did the wee man say?' asked Margaret when May returned the kitchen.

'He said you're a polygon of virtue,' replied May.

'He's nae bad for a Sassenach,' said Margaret.

'Shame aboot the asteroids,' said May.

Meanwhile, Joseph stared out of the lounge window at the starry sky but at that moment his body felt far from heavenly.

Three miles away, in the Bustard household, Mrs Bustard was putting the finishing touches to Harold's halo and Mr Bustard had arrived home from work. The family had returned recently to the council estate on School View after four years in the Midlands. Harold Bustard senior had worked at Calverston Colliery in Nottingham but, after receiving his redundancy package, he had come back to his native Yorkshire and started work as a traffic warden in York.

By the end of his first day, the portly, bespectacled

Harold 'Bertie' Bustard reflected that he had not been blessed with the best of names. His first seventeen customers had called him a 'four-eyed bustard' – at least, that's what it sounded like. His mother had once told him that a bustard is a tall elegant bird with long legs, a rotund body and a long neck that lives in open grassland in Africa and Australia. However, there was little opportunity to share this ornithological gem with the irate drivers who ripped up their parking tickets and scattered the pieces at his feet.

At the kitchen table, ten-year-old Carol Bustard was immersed in her *1978 Jackie Annual* and little Harold was tucking into his fish fingers, chips and mushy peas. Suddenly a thought struck him and he screwed up his face with the inner torment of the misunderstood thespian. 'Ah won't know what t'say,' he pleaded – 'ah don't know 'ow angels talk.'

Harold senior sat down and studied the back of the HP Sauce bottle for inspiration. 'They talk like someone himportant,' he said.

'Like yer uncle 'Enry,' added Mrs Bustard triumphantly as she applied some gold tinsel to a bent coathanger.

Harold senior glared at her. His brother Henry earned twice as much as he did and wore a suit to work. It was a popular topic of conversation in Bustard family circles that in 1975 he had sold more vacuum cleaners than any other salesman in Halifax. 'No,' he retorted in a determined manner, 'more himportant than 'im.'

'Mebbe as famous as Bob Geldof,' said Carol, looking up from her annual.

'Bob Geldof?' said Mrs Bustard with a hollow laugh. 'In a few years' time no one'll know 'is name.'

Carol glowered at her mother, bit savagely into her chip buttie and returned to the step-by-step guide of how to apply blusher like a professional.

'Or like Darth Vader?' said Harold junior, through a mouthful of mushy peas.

'Or Cliff Richard?' added Mrs Bustard.

Harold senior pondered this for a moment. 'Mmm,' he said, 'prob'ly more like Cliff Richard.'

On Thursday morning the world outside my bedroom window had changed. The first snow of winter had fallen. Kirkby Steepleton was cloaked in a mantle of silence, all sound muffled and frozen in time. In the distance the boughs of elm, sycamore and oak stooped under the weight of snow and, on my driveway, tiny prints of sparrow, cat and fox made patterns on the smooth frosty crust. It was a strange, eerie journey to Ragley village through countryside empty of wildlife and still as stone.

By the time I arrived in the school car park the first excited children were in the playground, rolling snowballs and making the first snowmen. Ruby, in a headscarf and old coat, had swept the steps leading to the entrance and was sprinkling them with salt.

'Morning, Mr Sheffield,' she shouted. 'Ah've turned 'eating up.'

'Thanks, Ruby – you're a gem,' I said.

As I walked across the car park, I saw Jimmy Poole leaning against the school wall and looking thoughtful.

He was holding a carrier bag in which his mother had packed a bright-green rolled-up curtain destined to be a Wise Man's cloak. I stopped to talk to him.

'Good morning, Jimmy,' I said.

'Good morning, Mr Theffield. Would you like a thweet?' he said.

'Not just now, thank you, Jimmy,' I said.

'They're athid dropth,' said Jimmy, opening the sticky brown paper bag.

'OK, then.' I took a sweet and suddenly remembered I should have done something about Spartacus but I had been so busy I had forgotten all about it. 'Are your parents coming to the concert, Jimmy?'

'Yeth, Mithter Theffield.'

It was quicker to wait for them to arrive to discuss the missing turkey. 'So have you been back to the cycle shed, Jimmy?' I asked.

'No, Mithter Theffield. Ah don't want to arouthe thuthpithion,' said Jimmy conspiratorially, looking furtively over his shoulder. I was quietly impressed. Jimmy's vocabulary was improving dramatically. 'Ah think it wath like that thtory of Captain Oath when 'e walked out into the thnow,' said Jimmy.

I recalled the sad tale of Captain Scott's fateful journey to the South Pole and there was barely a dry eye in the assembly hall when I described Captain Oates's heroic gesture to leave the frozen tent to give his comrades a better chance of survival.

I smiled down at the intense little boy. 'And is that what Spartacus did, Jimmy, walk out into the snow?'

Jimmy looked up at me forlornly with his black-button eyes under his curly mop of ginger hair. 'Yeth, Mr Theffield: it wath thuithide.'

It was a hectic morning and at twelve o'clock I returned home on the snowy back lane to Kirkby Steepleton to collect Margaret and May. They were very excited about the Christmas concert and, when we returned to school, Anne enlisted their help sewing strands of glitter on the kings' cloaks.

After lunch, Ruby swept the hall and the children in my class put out all the dining chairs in neat rows. I wheeled out our Contiboard music trolley with its built-in record deck and two huge speakers. Anne carefully wiped the vinyl surface of her precious Harry Belafonte LP record, clicked the dial to 33 rpm and placed it on the circular rubber mat on the turntable.

There was an air of expectancy as the first parents walked into the hall and selected the best vantage points. Many had brought cameras to record their angelic offspring. Mrs Petula Dudley-Palmer was one of the early arrivals and sat down next to Sue Phillips.

'Had a good day, Petula?' asked Sue politely.

'Simply wonderful!' exclaimed Petula. 'I've been to Leeds and bought some quite delightful presents.' She then spent five minutes describing her state-of-the-art, revolutionary new A530 Food Processor-De-Luxe. Sue responded with a glassy-eyed smile, knowing full well that Petula Dudley-Palmer would never be able to cook in a month of Sundays and couldn't tell a parsnip from a tent peg.

'You really must see this present I've bought for my Geoffrey,' said Petula as she pulled out of her leather shopping bag a small shiny box.

'What is it?' whispered Sue.

'It's an executive toy for the businessman of the eighties,' said Petula – 'at least, that's what the nice young man said.'

'Yes, but what is it?' repeated Sue.

'He said it was a desktop status symbol for the modern man,' recited the brainwashed Petula.

Sue stared at the picture on the side of the box showing a row of five large chromium ball bearings hanging from wires on a steel frame. 'Yes, but what exactly is it?'

'It's Newton's balls,' said Petula simply.

'Oh,' said Sue and settled back in her chair. 'No wonder the poor man discovered gravity,' she muttered to herself.

The hall filled up with parents and grandparents and last to arrive was Mrs Earnshaw, who walked into the hall and parked her pram next to our makeshift stable. This relied heavily on the audience having a good imagination as it comprised two PE mats, a bale of straw and a cardboard donkey.

Mrs Earnshaw lifted her six-week-old baby from the pram and, immediately, a group of cooing mothers gathered round. The imminent birth of baby Jesus could not compete with this real-life alternative. I found a spare chair and put it near the doorway.

'You should be fine here, Mrs Earnshaw,' I said.

'That's reight kind, Mr Sheffield,' she said.

'So you got your little girl after all?' I said. 'What did you decide to call her?'

'This is Dallas Sue-Ellen Earnshaw,' said Mrs Earnshaw proudly.

'Lovely, er . . . names,' I said.

'Ah like Dallas, it suits 'er,' said Mrs Ackroyd, while she counted the baby's fingers and toes.

'It's our fav'rite programme,' explained Mrs Earnshaw. 'Would y'like to 'old 'er, Mr Sheffield?' she asked.

'Yes, go on,' urged Ruby, who had joined the throng.

Reluctantly, and terrified I would drop this little bundle, I took the baby gingerly from Mrs Earnshaw's outstretched arms. 'Yurra natural, Mr Sheffield,' she said. 'My Eric dunt know which end's which.'

'Good job 'e doesn't feed 'er, then,' added Mrs Ackroyd with a chuckle.

Suddenly, Dallas began to make strange noises and I handed her back.

''As little Dallas done a big poo-poo, then?' said Mrs Earnshaw. The resulting smell that lingered round our stable had nothing to do with our cardboard donkey.

At two o'clock we were almost ready. In the reception class, Anne was telling the sheep to stop baaa-ing until it was their turn to appear and Jo was breaking up a fight between two of the three kings. Sally's recorder group had assembled round the donkey and, after she had sprayed it with air freshener, they played 'Away in a Manger' in a toxic-free zone. Meanwhile, in my classroom, Jodie Cuthbertson was telling Adam and the

Ants to stop trying on her Abba blonde wig, recently 'borrowed' from her big sister's wardrobe.

Joseph had arrived and Vera looked irritated that he wouldn't sit down.

'Margaret,' whispered May, 'the poor wee vicar still canna sit doon.'

'Och aye,' said Margaret, 'he nae looks comfortable.'

'Asteroids,' mouthed May.

'Piles,' whispered Margaret.

'Och aye,' said May.

'D'ye ken what Miss McKenzie told us in school?' said Margaret.

May nodded in acknowledgement. 'Dinna sit doon on cold floors,' she said.

'. . . Or hot radiators,' added Margaret. She folded her arms in a self-satisfied way and sat back in her chair. Like a perfect mirror image, May did the same and they returned their attention to the arrival of a flock of lively sheep wearing outsize Arran sweaters and painted masks. The nativity had begun.

Little Benjamin Roberts walked round his flock and used his shepherd's crook to administer a sharp thwack to the backside of anyone he disliked. Meanwhile Sally had removed her multicoloured random-striped poncho, her favourite Bernat Klein design, in order to conduct her recorder group while the choir sang 'Hark the Herald Angels Sing'. That is, all except for young Harold Bustard, who replaced the word 'Herald' with 'Harold' as he always had done, totally oblivious of his error and secretly pleased that his name was special enough to feature in a Christmas carol. He looked down at his flock of friends and wished he could be part of them as his moment of fame approached.

'And an angel of the Lord came down and glory shone around,' said little Benjamin Roberts. Harold was ushered on from the side of the hall by Jo. He certainly looked the part in his white sheet and batman wings. Fortunately his sticking-out ears provided the perfect support for his coathanger halo.

Harold climbed on to a wooden stage block behind the nativity scene and looked down at the audience. Mr and Mrs Bustard held hands tightly and stared in admiration at the next generation of angelic Bustards.

Elisabeth Amelia Dudley-Palmer as Mary, in a professionally refitted bridesmaid dress and a flowing royal-blue headscarf, looked up in anticipation.

Harold stood there, his halo twinkling under the fluorescent lights.

Elisabeth Amelia decided to help him out. 'Have you any news?' she asked.

Harold stared longingly at the flock of sheep. All his friends were there.

'So, you've got a message for us, haven't you?' insisted Elisabeth Amelia. 'It's about the birth of Jesus, isn't it?'

Harold took a deep breath and then in a big voice he shouted, 'Baaah-baaah.'

The sheep looked up in surprise and then, led by Heathcliffe and Terry Earnshaw, they responded as one united flock. 'Baaah-baaah,' they all cried.

Mrs Bustard immediately began to clap, little Harold

waved in acknowledgement and all the sheep, led by Heathcliffe, stood up and bowed.

'There's a lot o' wee sheep,' said Margaret.

'Och aye,' said May. 'I almost fell asleep counting 'em.'

They both burst into fits of laughter and joined in the applause.

Meanwhile, in the entrance hall, I was standing quietly next to the Three Kings, mainly to ensure Caspar and Melchior did not resume their dispute over who was going to be the first king to present a gift to baby Jesus. Jimmy Poole, as Balthazar, looked regal in his green curtain-cloak and cardboard crown, although his York City football socks did slightly reduce the overall effect. The three boys picked up their parcels of gold, frankincense and myrrh: or, to be more precise, a box of Pagan Man aftershave, an empty foil-wrapped packet of Klondike Pete Golden Nuggets and a tissue-covered empty can of Watney's Party Seven Draught Bitter and waited for their moment to walk on.

Suddenly the outside door opened and in walked Old Tommy Piercy, leading a turkey by a strand of baling twine. 'Jus' found this in t'yard, Mr Sheffield,' said Old Tommy. 'Shall ah tie it up outside f'now? Ah can see y'busy.'

'Oh, er . . . thanks, Mr Piercy,' I said.

Jimmy stared in amazement and dropped his parcel. 'Thpartacuth!' he yelled and grabbed the length of twine.

Suddenly, Jo opened the hall door and whispered

urgently, 'Come on, you kings, you're on!' The Three Kings knew when their teacher meant business and rushed on together. Jo stared in horror as, in a surprising diversion from the traditional script, her three little kings presented baby Jesus with gold, frankincense and a turkey with a limp.

Another ripple of applause echoed round the hall at this unexpected development, followed by a communal 'Aaaaah!' as Spartacus limped his way bravely towards baby Jesus. Then Jo, with consummate professionalism, led Jimmy and Spartacus back into the entrance hall and they received another ovation.

Mrs Poole left her seat in the front row and hurried after her son. His explanation was received with a big hug. 'Ah wondered where that turkey 'ad gone,' she said with a smile. 'That were a wonderful play, Mrs 'Unter. That turkey brought tears t'me eyes.' All seemed forgiven and it was clear from Mrs Poole that Spartacus had been reprieved.

The concert continued without mishap. Sally's class were superb with their version of *A Christmas Carol* and my class finished up with a rousing rendition of Slade's 1973 Christmas hit 'Merry Xmas, Everybody'. While Joseph frowned slightly at Noddy Holder's line about Father Christmas's fairies keeping him sober for a day, it was a fitting end to the entertainment.

Finally, cameras flashed, the children bowed and I thanked everyone. The hall was cleared and members of the PTA served coffee from Shirley's Baby Burco boiler along with turkey sandwiches and mince pies.

Soon parents and grandparents made their way home accompanied by their children, many still in costume.

Mr and Mrs Bustard paused in the entrance hall and looked down proudly at little Harold.

'Well done, Harold,' I said a little hesitantly.

'Oh, ye of little faith,' said Mrs Bustard, wagging her finger in my face. 'Ah told yer my 'Arold would mek a proper little angel.' She walked to the door and then, as an afterthought, stopped and called back: 'An' talking t'them sheep in their own lang-widge were reight clever.' Then, hand in hand with an angel called Harold, she walked out in triumph.

It had begun to snow again and the lights of the school reflected on the frosty school drive. Anne, Jo, Sally and Vera came to stand beside me as we watched the last families leave. Making their way very slowly across the playground was Jimmy Poole and his mother. Jimmy was holding the baling twine as if his life depended upon it and Spartacus followed behind.

'Are you sure it's the same turkey, Jack?' asked Jo. 'They all look alike to me.'

I peered into the darkness. There was no doubt about it. The turkey was definitely limping. 'Yes, it's the same one,' I said: 'that's definitely Spartacus.'

'Spartacus?' said Anne in surprise.

'It's a long story,' I said.

'Come on, let's shut the door,' said Sally. 'I'm hungry.'

'Refreshments in the hall, everybody,' announced Vera.

Back in the hall, I picked up a mince pie and a coffee, walked to the window and stared out on to the empty playground. It had been a day of unexpected surprises. Little Harold, unwittingly, had succeeded as a bilingual angel and, while Spartacus had lost his freedom, at least he could look forward to Christmas.

As the snow fell on Ragley School, it was a happy group who drank hot coffee and shared the experiences of yet another Christmas concert. No one noticed that I was the only one who didn't have a turkey sandwich.

Chapter Nine

Goodbye, 1979

The seventies were nearly over and the eighties beckoned, but some things didn't change.

'Ah dinna think he was in *South Specific*, Margaret,' shouted Aunt May across the kitchen.

'I think Aunt May means *South Pacific*,' I said, looking up from my mug of tea.

My little Scottish mother didn't hear. She was studying an advertisement most intently in her *Daily Mirror*. It read: 'Constipation? It needn't be a problem. Feel great again with Beecham's Pills, the natural laxative.' I refrained from asking her why she was so interested.

It was Boxing Day morning and my mother and her

sister were coming towards the end of their holiday with
me before travelling to Glasgow to share Hogmanay with
their Scottish clan. I looked around and smiled. On the
old dark-oak Welsh dresser, incongruously side by side,
were two of my presents from my mother. A copy of the
poems of T. S. Eliot was propped against a large Fabergé
box containing "Enry's 'ammer'. This was a large bright-
red bar of soap in the shape of a boxing glove and attached
to a thick coil of rope. My mother had been a big fan of
Henry Cooper, the heavyweight boxer, ever since he had
put Cassius Clay on the seat of his fancy silk pants.

After yesterday's Christmas dinner I never thought
I would need to eat again but Aunt May was making
a traditional Scottish breakfast – at least, her distinct
version. The smell of burnt porridge was overpowering
and the glutinous mixture had the consistency of heavy-
duty Polyfilla. As I opened the kitchen window to breathe
in the sharp cold air, a startled woodcock took off and
zigzagged through the sleeping trees.

'Och aye, an' 'e sings like that Barry Manifold,' continued Aunt May, stirring the contents of the pan
vigorously – 'that wee boy wi' a nose like Concorde.'

Margaret flicked through her *Daily Express*. 'Dinna
worry, May, ah've foond it an' it's on at two o'clock.' The
Boxing Day film on ITV was the 1956 classic *The King and
I* with Yul Brynner and Deborah Kerr. It was one of their
favourite films. 'An' he sings more like that lovely wee
man from America, Louis Armstrong,' said Margaret.

'Nae, it canna be Louis Armstrong,' replied Aunt May,
serving up the blackened porridge. 'He's the wee boy

that landed on the moon.' A large tablespoon of golden syrup made the porridge edible and I left them to settle for another day in front of the television.

On Christmas Day, Margaret and Aunt May had been among the twenty-eight million viewers of the Queen's Christmas message and later that evening they had settled down to watch the first in a new series of *All Creatures Great and Small*, followed by the *Mike Yarwood Christmas Show* and the wonderful Penelope Keith in *To the Manor Born*. After a break to prepare turkey sandwiches and Christmas cake with a crumbly slice of Wensleydale cheese, they had switched over to ITV for the highlight of their Christmas viewing, *The Morecambe and Wise Christmas Show* with special guest Glenda Jackson.

'It's nae Christmas withoot Morecambe and Wise,' said my mother.

Aunt May had kicked off her tartan slippers, put her feet up on the battered pouffe and nodded in content- ment. By the time I had switched back to BBC1 to watch Michael Parkinson interviewing Dame Edna Everage they both looked tired and ready for their beds.

'An' we're nae watching that scary Alfred Hitchcock film *Sago*,' Aunt May had announced.

'It's nae *Sago*,' said Margaret, 'it's *Psycho*.'

'Och aye, Margaret,' said Aunt May, 'ah canna stand t'see that bonny wee lassie stabbed in the shower by that terrible American cyclepath.'

I had stayed up to wash the dishes and clear the kitchen ready for a prompt start the next day. Laura had telephoned to ask if I wanted to meet her on Boxing Day

morning in Ragley on the village green to see the annual
hunt. I had heard it was a spectacular affair and one of
the features of country life. Also, it was difficult to say no
to Laura.

The next morning was bright, clear and cold as I drove
the three miles to Ragley village. The sun had broken
through the mist and in the distance the frozen fields
were lit up with a diamond light in among the long
grey-blue shadows of the bare trees. On the outskirts of
Ragley the hedgerows were rimed with white frost and
the Christmas berries on the holly bushes shone through
the dark ivy.

When I pulled up on Ragley High Street outside
Nora's Coffee Shop the scene in front of me was full of
movement and colour. Albert Jenkins had explained to
me over a glass of home-made wine in the vicarage that
each Boxing Day it was traditional for the hunt to meet
at midday outside The Royal Oak. On the village green,
riders in their 'pinks', as they called their bright red coats,
sat proudly on their horses. In among their stamping
hoofs, a pack of about thirty very noisy beagles, mostly
tan and black and white, with long tails and floppy ears,
were milling round. Don the barman was topping up hip
flasks from a shiny stirrup cup while Sheila handed out
plates of beef sandwiches.

Perched on the arm of the wooden bench by the duck
pond was Beth. In a pink bobble hat and matching scarf,
she stood out from the crowd and appeared to be in
animated conversation with a tall flaxen-haired man. I

recognized him as Simon, her deputy headteacher at Hartingdale Primary School. They looked relaxed together and his bright-red Morgan, its soft-top patterned with frost, was parked outside The Royal Oak. I waved to her and caught her eye. She waved back and got up and started to walk towards me. Then, for some reason which I couldn't understand, she stopped suddenly and turned round.

Seconds later, to my surprise, Laura slipped her arm in mine.

'Hi, Jack. Isn't this fantastic? I just love the horses.'

Her dress sense always seemed perfect for every occasion. She was wearing a Daks country classic suit in herringbone tweed with patch pockets and leather buttons. The suede-edged buttonholes matched the pockets of the skirt and the ensemble was completed to perfection with a checked brown and black scarf. Her matching flat cap was set at a jaunty angle. She looked as if she had stepped from the front cover of a *Country Life* magazine.

'Mmmm . . .'

'Penny for them, Jack,' said Laura, tugging my sleeve.

I looked back, hoping to catch a glimpse of Beth, but she had gone and I guessed that the handsome Simon had lured her away with a glass of mulled wine.

'Sorry. I was miles away,' I said.

'Jack, I was wondering what you are doing on New Year's Eve, because I've been invited to Jo and Dan's party.'

'Oh, so have I.'

'Have you seen their house yet?'

'No. Have you?'

'Yes. It's super. Beth and I went round there the other evening. They're renting a lovely old terraced cottage in Easington and they're combining a New Year's Eve party with a house-warming.'

My mind flickered back to a memory of two years ago when Beth and I had danced in the village hall on New Year's Eve. It was still vivid in my mind.

From the far side of the village green, Vera and her friend Joyce Davenport walked over to us. Both were wrapped in warm hand-knitted scarves and matching gloves.

'Good morning, Mr Sheffield,' said Vera with a smile, 'and good morning to you, Miss Henderson,' she added quickly.

'Good morning, Vera. Hello, Mrs Davenport,' I said. 'Isn't this an exciting occasion?'

'I don't altogether approve of fox-hunting,' said Vera guardedly, 'but the horses and the colour make such a wonderful spectacle.'

'And the major is quite splendid,' added Joyce with a knowing look at Vera, whose cheeks flushed momentarily.

The departure of the fox-hunt appeared imminent and, as Master of Foxhounds, Major Rupert Forbes-Kitchener was at the centre of everything. His favourite steeplechaser was pawing the ground in expectation and he leaned forward in his saddle to pat its proud head. He looked magnificent in his bright-red coat with leather patches on the elbows, cream jodhpurs, high leather boots and a riding hat with a black ribbon on the back. The finishing touch was a long crop of white silk round his neck, pinned neatly with a family heirloom, a cameo with a silhouette of his mother. Inside a flap on his coat, hanging from a braided rope, was a brass hunting horn. He caught sight of us and waved but his eyes were on Vera, who smiled back at him.

Everything was ready. With a blast from his hunting horn, the major led the way and the hunt trotted up the Morton Road towards the vast acres of farmland that formed part of the estates of Old Morton Manor House. Soon the big horses, the powerful steeplechasers, would gallop a familiar route from one steeple to another over heather, hills, rivers and tall hedges. In the crowd round us, anxious but proud mothers, who frequented the local gymkhana circuit, cast admiring glances towards their daughters, destined, they hoped, to be the show-jumping prize-winners of the future.

Finally, the hunt had disappeared from view and Laura and I followed the crowd into the warmth of The Royal Oak. As we walked in, Pink Floyd's 'Another Brick in the Wall', the Christmas number 1 record, was playing on the jukebox in the taproom. Laura walked through to the lounge bar and I set off to buy some drinks. I looked around but there was no sign of Beth.

'What's it t'be, Mr Sheffield?' said the voluptuous Sheila. She was wearing a fluorescent strip of material that exposed her midriff and left her shoulders bare. My eyes widened at the vision before me. 'It's t'latest fashion,

Mr Sheffield,' said Sheila proudly, as she hitched up the straining sequinned fabric: 'it's called a boob-tube.'

'At least she's got summat t'keep it up, Jack,' shouted the appreciative Don from the other end of the bar.

I hesitated to answer. To agree was to suggest I had made an assessment of Sheila's main attribute. To disagree could be taken as an insult. So I just smiled and put a pound note on the bar. 'Er, a white wine and a glass of Chestnut Mild, please, Sheila,' I said, trying hard to avert my gaze.

"E's reight, Mr Sheffield. Without these it'd migrate south, if y'tek me meaning,' said Sheila, putting her hands on her hips and straightening her shoulders. The result was extraordinary and all the men leaning on the bar immediately stopped talking about Sebastian Coe, who had just been voted the 1979 BBC Sports Personality of the Year. For a brief moment they were united in thinking about something other than sport.

Next to me, Old Tommy Piercy was sitting on his familiar stool under the signed photograph of Geoffrey Boycott. 'Sir' Geoffrey, as he was known to the regulars, had been captured by the photographer with arms aloft after scoring his one hundredth century in the 1977 Test Match at Headingley against the old enemy, Australia. Old Tommy was the salt of the earth and he sat there smoking his briar pipe. At sixty-seven years old and a Yorkshireman through and through, he was independent, stubborn and warm-hearted. He was rarely one for excessive expression. Tommy was not one to waste his words.

'Hello, Mr Piercy,' I said cheerily.

'Hmmf,' grunted Old Tommy through a haze of Old Holborn tobacco.

'Business looks to be booming at your butcher's shop,' I said encouragingly.

'Hmmf,' muttered Old Tommy.

'I see Young Tommy is learning his trade,' I added thoughtfully.

'Hmmf,' murmured Old Tommy.

I looked through the leaded bay window at the vast cloudless primrose-blue sky. 'Lovely day, Mr Piercy,' I said.

Old Tommy took his pipe out of his mouth and looked up at me warily. 'Now, don't let's get carried away, young Mr Sheffield,' said Old Tommy.

It appeared I'd reached an impasse.

'Well, I can't stop to talk, Mr Piercy.'

Old Tommy continued to puff on his pipe for a while and then he nodded. 'Nay, lad, ah've said too much already.'

I picked up the drinks and headed back to the table. 'Laura, don't you just love Yorkshire on days like this?' I said appreciatively.

Laura sipped her white wine. 'It's lovely, Jack, but, as I've said before, London's the place to be. Beth and I are always arguing about this. She thinks Yorkshire is God's Own Country.'

'So do I,' I said.

We were both wrapped up in our own thoughts until Laura suddenly picked up her handbag. 'I'm going to the Ladies, Jack,' she said and hurried away.

I leaned back in my chair and surveyed the crowd enjoying their holiday drinks. Deke Ramsbottom and a group of farmers had gathered round the roaring log fire to listen to the latest tales from Royston Tupp. In between leisurely puffs of his old pipe, Royston was regaling his audience, who kept him well lubricated with Tetley's bitter and the occasional whisky chaser. 'It's to warm t'cockles of 'is 'eart,' explained Deke to Sheila.

Royston, or 'Rabbit Roy' as he was known in the village, was every inch a rugged old North Yorkshire moors countryman. He lived in the deserted hillside hamlet of Capton and the sign over his door read: 'Licensed Game Dealer'. There, in his cold-rooms, he eked out a living plucking and storing game for the Easington market.

Thirty years ago, as a young man, he had been a trawlerman in Hull. He remembered fondly the time when cod was king and a third of all the cod eaten in England had been gathered in by the fleet of tiny boats that braved the North Sea each day, but now those days were gone. 'An' nowt'll come o' that peace treaty,' announced Royston. The so-called Cod War between Britain and Iceland had ended just three years before in an uneasy peace.

'Go on, then, Rabbit,' said Deke enthusiastically. 'What 'appened las' winter?'

'Well, 1979 were a reight disaster f'me,' said Rabbit Roy mournfully, 'wi' a long winter an' a short spring. Usually, ah'm busy from Twelfth Night reight through t'January. 'Eather's been poor, not much grouse abart, an' birds 'ave got t'worm, tha knaws.'

The farmers all nodded and shook their heads in equal measure. They all respected Rabbit Roy, not least because he was North Yorkshire's clay pigeon single-barrel champion. I looked at him and wondered about his life. He had found peace and clearly enjoyed the outdoors. With his dog and his gun, he walked the wild and desolate moors living the life of a free man.

In complete contrast, in the lounge bar, Geoffrey and Petula Dudley-Palmer were discussing their forthcoming holiday. Geoffrey stretched back contentedly and smoked his 'Old Port Straight', a Canadian cigar, rum-flavoured and dipped in wine. He flicked idly through the brochure showing the nightlife of New York. It had been a late decision but he had snapped up two standby tickets on a Freddie Laker flight to JFK Airport for £99 each. Meanwhile, Petula was staring at the young jodhpur-clad women from the local country set. 'It's all down to good breeding, Geoffrey,' she said, but Geoffrey didn't hear. He was thinking about buying an American lime-green Cadillac.

In the corner of the lounge bar sat Margery Ackroyd with her husband, Wendell. Margery always liked to be at the cutting edge of fashion and was proud to be the first in the village to wear Linda Gray shoulderpads under her blouse. Linda Gray was becoming a popular television star as the downtrodden Sue Ellen, wife of the villainous JR Ewing in *Dallas*. Margery had chopped-off white shoulder pads for her large blouses, curved Velcro ones for her jumpers and double-flapped ones to slip under her bra straps. At the travel agent's in York where she worked as an assistant manager, she said she wanted 'to be the boss but stay sexy'. Meanwhile, Wendell secretly believed he now had a wife who resembled a vertically challenged American footballer

Back in the taproom, Big Dave Robinson was talking loudly about ferret-racing, while Little Malcolm was looking adoringly across the table at the strikingly dressed Dorothy Humpleby. Dorothy didn't do things by halves and tended to stand out from the country set in their tweed jackets. Today she was wearing her skin-tight Abba outfit, complete with hipster trousers in blue and lavender Lycra with flared bottoms. To Little Malcolm she was the girl of his dreams.

I sat back and sipped my drink and reflected how much I enjoyed living in this wonderful village with such a diverse collection of characters, most of whom were now my friends. Half an hour later Laura and I walked out to our cars. She hugged me tightly before we said goodbye and smiled when I said, 'See you on New Year's Eve.'

Back in Kirkby Steepleton, snow began to fall again as darkness descended. I chopped a supply of logs for the fire and settled down for another amusing evening with my mother and Aunt May.

'Have y'been tae see y'wee lassie, Jack?' asked my mother.

I picked up the *Radio Times* and pretended to look engrossed. 'It depends which one you mean, Mother,' I said. She looked at me curiously but said no more.

*　　　*　　　*

New Year's Eve arrived and Bilbo Cottage was quiet at last. My mother and May had gone to Scotland and I sat in the kitchen, drinking black tea and looking forward to whatever the evening might bring.

Jo had telephoned to say that everyone was expected around eight o'clock and she and Dan had planned a few party games. She also mentioned that both Beth and Laura would be there.

Dan and Jo's new home was a tiny, middle-of-terrace cottage built of old reddish-brown bricks with a rustic pantile roof and a tall chimney stack from which wood smoke billowed into the night.

'Hello, Jack. Glad you could make it,' said Jo.

'Thanks for the invitation,' I said, stepping into the hallway. 'You've worked wonders in the house.'

'It looks better in the dark, Jack,' said Dan with a big grin. 'Come on, I'll get you a beer.'

I enjoyed Dan's company. It was simple and uncomplicated and we chatted happily as he described their attempts to furnish their new home on a shoestring. They had gathered together an uncoordinated collection of second-hand chairs, two old-fashioned sofas and off-cuts of vividly patterned carpet that covered most of the bare floorboards. However, with the flickering log fire, the soft candlelight and the coloured lights on the Christmas tree, it was warm and cosy and I relaxed as I sipped on my glass of beer from Dan's huge can of Watney's Party Seven Draught Bitter.

In the lounge, Beth and Laura were sitting on a sofa

together, chatting and drinking white wine. Beth was
casually dressed in a white polo-neck sweater and tight
black cord trousers. In contrast, Laura was wearing a
smart, fitted scarlet dress and they both looked up and
smiled when I walked in. I kissed Beth on the cheek and
then Laura.

'Hello, Beth,' I said and then looked round the room.
'Is your deputy, Simon, here?' I asked.

Beth looked puzzled. 'No, Jack. He's up in Northallerton at a family party.'

'Oh, I see,' I said. 'I just thought . . . oh, nothing.'

There was a moment of silence. Her green eyes studied
me for a while and then Laura leapt up. 'Jack, let me get
you something to eat. Vera's just put the most wonderful
home-made sausage rolls in the oven.' She took my hand
and led me quickly towards the kitchen.

I looked over my shoulder and waved at Beth. She
waved back and then stood up to chat with Jo, who was
busy serving a 'hedgehog' of cocktail sticks to John and
Anne Grainger. On each stick Jo had carefully speared a
piece of pineapple, a cube of cheese and a silver onion. A
chilled bottle of Blue Nun wine stood alongside. In the
far corner, Sally and her husband Colin were leaning
against the window ledge, deep in conversation. Sally, in
a loud, bright-tangerine party dress, was pouring a fresh
glass of Blue Nun, and Colin, a slim, balding man in a
crumpled suit, relaxed with a hand-rolled cigarette. A few
local policemen I vaguely recognized and their partners
were gathered round the record player, flicking through
a selection of Elton John LPs. It was a lively party and,

while the music was not to Joseph's taste, the contents of his bottle of home-made wine soon made him relax.

At midnight Dan turned on the television for the chimes of Big Ben and we gathered in a circle to sing 'Auld Lang Syne'.

'Welcome to the eighties,' yelled Dan and raised his glass.

Laura was the first to put her arms round me and kiss me. 'Happy New Year, Jack,' she shouted above the din.

'Happy New Year, Laura,' I replied.

Then the room seemed to erupt with cheers and the sound of a popping champagne cork. In the huddle of people, Anne pecked me on the cheek, Joseph shook my hand, Vera gave me a slightly tired smile, Sally hugged me and Jo refilled my glass. It felt like being in a pinball machine as I bumped from one couple to the next. Finally, I came face to face with Beth.

Our glasses clinked together. Her hair was filled with the scent of wild flowers. 'Happy New Year, Jack,' she said. 'I hope it's a good one for you.'

'Happy New Year, Beth,' I said. 'May all your dreams come true.'

I kissed her on the cheek and she looked up at me. 'A year ago we built a snowman,' she said, almost in a whisper.

'I remember . . . and two years ago we danced in the village hall.'

There was an instant when her look softened. Then Laura reappeared and grabbed my hand. As Beth walked away, it occurred to me that while time might be a great healer, love was better.

The party went on into the early hours and everyone relaxed and talked about their plans for 1980. Vera, once again, tried to persuade Beth to join the church choir and I finally had my first conversation with Colin Pringle, who appeared to be worse the wear for drink. He and Sally were the first to leave, with Sally holding the car keys. Everyone gradually followed on and I walked out with Anne and John Grainger, Beth and Laura.

'Goodnight, Jack,' said Anne. 'See you on Thursday morning,' and I realized how close we were to the start of the spring term.

Beth and Laura both waved goodbye and I watched them walk across the icy cobbles of Easington market square towards their cars. As the snow settled on my shoulders I watched Beth drive off in her Volkswagen Beetle towards the Morton Road and Laura speed away in a spurt of frozen snow towards York. Gradually the darkness enveloped me and I looked around. Wood smoke billowed from the chimneypots and the pantile roofs were patterned in snow. I climbed into my car and drove back to Kirkby Steepleton. Above my head there were only dead branches in a frozen sky.

Back in the silence of Bilbo Cottage, I sat with a mug of coffee and reflected on the end of 1979, a time of closed doors and the ache of distance.

Finally, I made a decision. Before I turned out the light

Goodbye, 1979

I took down my 1979 calendar from the kitchen wall and dropped it in the bin. Then I hung up my 1980 Yorkshire Landmarks calendar and smiled.

It was a new year, a new decade.

I smiled and decided . . . this year was going to be a good one.

Chapter Ten

Reluctant Resolutions

School reopened today for the spring term with 89 children registered on roll.

Extract from the Ragley School Logbook:
Thursday, 3 January 1980

It was Thursday, 3 January, the first school day of 1980 and the driveway of Bilbo Cottage was coated with a blue film of crystal on this freezing morning. With my lesson plans in my battered leather briefcase and my college scarf flying behind me, I strode confidently towards my Morris Minor Traveller, which was encased in ice.

A new decade stretched out before me, the spring term beckoned and, reluctantly, I had made my New Year resolutions. There were three of them. First of all, I intended to get fit. My body was now my temple. Second, I intended to cut down on coffee and biscuits. I had put on weight over the Christmas holiday but soon

I would be a lean machine. Third, I intended to make a bigger effort to understand women. I would listen to them sympathetically, display a new empathy for their feelings and become a 'new-age-eighties-man'. At least that's what was advised in an article in the New Year *Radio Times* that I had read while I was finishing the last three slices of my mother's Christmas cake.

As I scraped the ice from my windscreen and blew hot air on the boot handle to defrost the lock, I had the confidence of a man who was about to become a better human being, with a generous smattering of martyrdom thrown in for good measure.

The previous day I had braved the cold to prune the hard, woody stems of the blackberry canes that were rampant against the south-facing fence that separated my garden from the back road into Kirkby Steepleton. Beneath my feet the silent roots lay still beneath the frozen soil, waiting for the trigger of warm sunshine and the onset of a distant spring. As I removed the spent and skeletal canes, now bleached of colour and life, I wondered what 1980 would bring. Laura had proved an exciting companion in recent months. This new friendship was a cathartic experience but I knew that I was cutting out the old to make way for the new.

The drive from Bilbo Cottage to Ragley village was hazardous and my car struggled in the sub-zero temperature. On either side of the narrow road the frozen trees looked unreal, as if sketched with a silver pencil against the vast grey sky. With some relief I skidded to a halt in the High Street, outside Prudence Golightly's

General Stores & Newsagent. As usual, Prudence had my copy of *The Times* ready for me and I frowned at the headline announcing that Mark Carlisle, the Education Secretary, was planning to make further cuts in school expenditure.

'Happy New Year, Mr Sheffield,' said Prudence with a smile.

Jeremy, her ancient, much-loved teddy bear and life-long friend, was sitting on the shelf behind her in his usual spot alongside a tin of loose-leaf Lyons Tea and an old advertisement for Hudson's Soap and Carter's Little Liver Pills. Miss Golightly made all his clothes and on this frosty morning he sported a bright-red bobble hat, an Arran sweater, brown cord trousers and mint-green wellington boots.

'Happy New Year, Miss Golightly, and a Happy New Year to you, Jeremy,' I said.

Miss Golightly smiled appreciatively and then pointed to the display of biscuits and chocolates behind the jars of Seven Seas Castor Oil. 'Would you like something for the staff-room, Mr Sheffield? They're all reduced after Christmas,' said Prudence, pointing to the packets of Brontë Biscuits, sumptuous boxes of Sarah Bernhardt Butter Cream & Fondant Fancies and a magnificent Rich Yorkshire Tea Loaf.

I couldn't resist. 'I'll have one of each, please,' I said quickly.

After she had packed them in a carrier bag, Miss Golightly stepped on to the higher wooden step behind the counter so that we were almost eye to eye. 'And have you made a New Year resolution, Mr Sheffield?'

I glanced down at the rich assortment of biscuits and chocolates. 'I'm going to get fitter,' I said. I hurried out and the jangling bell on the door seemed to echo, 'Oh, yes? Oh, yes?'

After parking in the school car park I tiptoed across the frozen cobbles, carrying my briefcase and carrier bag.

'G'morning, Mr Sheffield,' shouted Ruby, as she showered the frosty school steps with salt. She sounded in good spirits. ''Ave y'made a New Year resolution?'

'Happy New Year, Ruby,' I said. 'Yes, I have. I'm going to try to understand women.'

'Huh! Well, ah suggest y'don't talk t'my Ronnie, cos y'won't learn much from 'im,' muttered Ruby.

As I walked into the staff-room, Jo sneezed loudly and I handed her the box of tissues.

'Thanks,' she said and blew her nose loudly.

'Oh dear,' I said, 'have you got a cold?'

'Yes,' said Jo with a sniff.

Anne walked in and quickly summed up the situation. 'I'll do your playground duty today, Jo,' she said helpfully.

'I don't really mind,' replied Jo and then sneezed again. 'Oh no, I'm off to my classroom.'

Anne sat down and picked up her mug of coffee. 'Jack, Shirley looked concerned this morning. Perhaps you should call in the kitchen.'

I remembered my New Year's resolution. I would

listen to her problem, show understanding and provide a solution. When I arrived in the kitchen, Shirley was writing out a menu and her assistant, the fiercesome Mrs Critchley, was emptying a huge sack of potatoes into a large aluminium bowl with effortless ease. Her muscles bulged and she stared at me as if I was an intruder.

'Ah'm worried about t'school meals, Mr Sheffield,' said Shirley. 'Ah've brought the *Easington 'Erald & Pioneer* t'show you.' The article said that the cost of school meals would be raised to fifty pence, so I could see why Shirley was concerned. Many parents in the village would soon be faced with a difficult choice.

'Your meals are excellent, Shirley,' I said, 'and I'm sure the majority of parents will think they're still real value for money.'

Shirley gave me a wan smile and shook her head sadly. It was when I looked at Mrs Critchley that I realized my resolution of understanding women might take longer than I thought. She flashed me a scathing glance and began peeling potatoes with the fervour of Sweeney Todd. I made a mental note to stay out of the kitchen for the rest of the day.

Back in the staff-room, Vera and Sally were looking at the front page of Vera's *Daily Telegraph*. 'It says here the government is determined to spend £500 million on an M25 motorway around London,' announced Vera, 'but there's not enough traffic to justify it.'

'I agree, Vera,' said Sally. 'Instead of a vast empty roundabout we need more investment in schools rather than closing them down.' Anne and I looked up in surprise. It was unusual for Vera and Sally to agree. Then Sally pointed again to the front page. 'Look at it,' she said. 'Russia has invaded Afghanistan, energy costs are rising, the standard of living is falling and every day there are new cuts in public services. We need Maggie to pull her finger out.'

Cordial relations dashed, Vera buried her head once again in her newspaper and Sally ripped open my packet of Brontë Biscuits with a vengeance. I stared hard at the Butter Cream & Fondant Fancies and wondered if I could resist. Anne, ever the peacemaker, answered the question for me by opening the packet on to a plate and handing them round. I told myself it would have been ungracious to resist.

There was a knock on the staff-room door. It was Mrs Daphne Cathcart, who was without doubt our strangest parent. With candy-floss pink hair, huge purple earrings that resembled mini hula-hoops, teeth like broken tombstones and a Darth Vader wheeze, she stood out from the crowd. Alongside her was a smaller version of her mother, ten-year-old Cathy, who was now in my class.

We had just purchased a new graded reading scheme called Ginn Reading 360 and Cathy was clutching one of the attractive and brightly coloured readers.

She held it up proudly. 'Ah like reading, Mr Sheffield,' she said with her usual boundless enthusiasm, 'an' my New Year resolution is t'get good at it.'

Mrs Cathcart looked proudly at her chip off the old block. 'It's all about positive thinkin', Mr Sheffield,' said

Mrs Cathcart with a determined nodding of her head. 'Ah read in my *Reveille* that this positive thinkin' is the answer. It's gonna change me life.'

'I'm pleased to hear that, Mrs Cathcart,' I said, staring fixedly at her nose to avoid the startling vision of her lurid pink hair and improbable teeth.

'An' ah've made me resolution, Mr Sheffield. Ah'm going t'stop blushing,' she said.

'Oh, I didn't know you blushed,' I said.

Mrs Cathcart immediately went puce, then leaned forward and whispered: 'Ah'm goin' to a 'ypnotist in York, Mr Sheffield. Ah've got an appointment. 'E'll put me reight.'

'Oh, er, well, good luck, Mrs Cathcart.'

'Well, when you've made a resolution y'ave t'keep it,' she shouted over her shoulder. 'An' our Cathy will keep 'ers with 'er reading, won't you, luv?'

Cathy had her nose buried in her new reading book as they walked away.

It was a busy first day back at school but during the afternoon I called into Jo's classroom to see how she was coping with her dreadful cold. She was checking each child's writing about their New Year resolutions.

'Thanks, Jack – not to worry, it's nearly hometime,' she said, while wiping her shiny red nose.

I looked down at Heathcliffe Earnshaw's exercise book. He had simply written one word: 'Peas'. It was to the point if nothing else. 'So what's your resolution, Heathcliffe?' I asked.

'Peas, Mr Sheffield,' said Heathcliffe bluntly. 'If ah crush 'em in potato they won't taste as bad.'

It struck me that there was a lot to be said for having achievable resolutions.

Jimmy Poole was waving his hand in the air so I stepped in to help out. 'Yes, Jimmy, what is it?' I asked.

'Ah want t'try my betht, Mr Theffield.'

'That's a good resolution, Jimmy,' I said.

'Ith jutht that I can't alwayth be my betht.'

'But as long as you try, Jimmy, that's the main thing,' I said.

Jimmy smiled, picked up his well-chewed HB pencil and proceeded to write.

Next to him, Elisabeth Amelia Dudley-Palmer was looking up the word 'mistakes' in her *Oxford First Dictionary*. She gave me a big smile and showed me her book. She had written, 'I know I make a lot of mistakes but the more I make the cleverer I get.'

I was beginning to wish I had talked to Jo's children before making my own resolutions. As I walked out I noticed Joey Wilkinson staring intently up at the map of England on the classroom wall. Puzzled, I glanced down at his exercise book. Joey had written, 'I am going to be good to my great grandma cos my great granddad died. I asked her where he had gone. She said he'd gone to Devon.'

It occurred to me that the afterlife could be spent in worse places.

*   *   *

Meanwhile, at the far end of the village, Petula Dudley-Palmer was in heaven. Thanks to her monthly issue of *Cosmopolitan* magazine, her prayers had been answered and her New Year resolution was about to be achieved: 1980 would definitely be the year she would become a slim, athletic, bronzed beauty.

For the tiny sum of £7.95 + 75p post & packing from a far-away address in Surrey her Sensational Sauna Suit had arrived in the post. The suit had been designed by a famous 'figure-culture expert' (although it didn't say who) and was made of soft, pliable waterproof fabric with airtight cuffs and wristbands. She had been assured that the suit would 'create its own atmosphere' when she did her exercises. All she had to do was wear it just like the slim goddess in the photograph while she did her dusting and hoovering. Although she had Ruby's daughter, Natasha, doing a bit of cleaning for her twice a week, she was still left with a few household chores. So, after donning the suit in the privacy of her bedroom, she decided to polish a set of crystal glasses from the cabinet in the lounge.

In contrast, Clint Ramsbottom's New Year resolution involved a life-style change. The eighties had opened up a whole new world of culinary delights. Supplementing his range of Monster Munch snacks was a choice between a new, revolutionary Golden Wonder Pot Noodle or a Batchelor's Snackpot (curry and rice with chicken). His *Smash Hits* magazine told him the eighties would be a decade of sex, drugs and rock and roll. He was encouraged. There were only two left for him to experience. So starting off with a trendy carton of pot noodle certainly seemed a step in the right direction to achieve the status of the new-age man.

By Friday morning, the Revd Joseph Evans had accepted that his New Year's resolution was in tatters. Joseph had decided he would make an effort to understand the world of children that up to now had proved to be a secret garden. In the middle of his Bible story with Anne's class he paused and, with great gravitas, delivered the immortal line 'And Jonah was swallowed by a whale'.

Terry Earnshaw's hand shot in the air. 'Ah've been t'Wales,' he shouted.

'So 'ave I,' yelled Molly Paxton, not to be outdone. 'We stayed in a caravan.'

And for the next ten minutes Joseph found himself involved in a discussion about caravan holidays.

During morning break we finished off the last of the Brontë Biscuits. By lunchtime, the boxes of Sarah Bernhardt Butter Cream & Fondant Fancies had been emptied and, during afternoon playtime, Sally shared out the Rich Yorkshire Tea Loaf. By the time Jodie Cuthbertson rang the end-of-school bell my trouser belt was straining and I vowed to begin my strict fitness and diet regime over the weekend.

Back at Bilbo Cottage, I was looking in my empty fridge when the telephone rang. It was Dan Hunter.

'Hi, Jack. Fancy a pint?' he said.

'I thought you would be looking after Jo,' I said.

'No. Her mother's just arrived and Jo wants me out from under her feet.'

'Fine,' I said. 'Have you eaten?'

He read my mind. 'How about a pie and a pint in the Oak about seven?'

'Sounds good. See you there,' I said. The diet could start tomorrow.

When I arrived in The Royal Oak, the football team had gathered as usual and Little Malcolm was facing a crisis.

'Ah'm off t'York tomorrow wi' Dorothy,' he said.

'What for?' asked Big Dave abruptly.

'It's me resolution,' said Little Malcolm meekly. He looked nervously left and right and then leaned over the table. 'Shoppin',' he whispered.

'Shoppin' . . . wi' a woman?' exploded Big Dave.

The whole team stopped supping momentarily and stared at Little Malcolm.

'It's jus' that ah promised 'er ah'd go.'

Then Big Dave gave Little Malcolm the worst insult any Yorkshireman could bestow on a friend – apart, of course, from calling him a southerner. He gave him his 'big girl's blouse' look.

Little Malcolm recoiled but then tried to salvage some pride. 'It can't be that bad, Dave,' he pleaded. 'She says it's t'January sales. Y'get stuff cheap.'

There was silence as the rest of the football team tried

to accommodate the sheer horror of shopping with a woman. Clint Ramsbottom eventually spoke up.

'Ah went shoppin' once wi' 'er from t'fish 'n' chip shop in Easington,' he announced.

''Er wi' t'big chest?' asked his big brother, Shane.

'Y'reight there, Shane. It's big all reight,' said Little Malcolm, relieved at the diversion.

'Took two hours t'buy three pair o' shoes,' said Clint.

'Two hours?' chorused the rest of the team.

'An' nex' day she took two pairs back.'

'That's reight, lads,' agreed Don from behind the bar. 'My Sheila does that wi' 'er underwear.'

Everyone stared once again at the curvaceous Sheila but wisely kept their thoughts to themselves. After all, Don had once wrestled on the professional circuit under the name 'The Silent Strangler'.

Dan and I found a corner table and made short work of pie, chips and mushy peas, two bags of crisps and a few pints of Chestnut Mild.

'So have you made a New Year resolution, Dan?' I asked as we began our third pint.

'Yes,' he said mournfully. 'I had such a bad head after our party I promised to give up beer.'

'Oh, I see,' I said.

'What about you?' he asked.

'Usual,' I said defensively: 'getting fit and suchlike.'

'And how's it going?' said Dan, sinking the rest of his pint.

I emptied my glass slowly and put it down on the table top. 'I'm starting tomorrow.'

*   *   *

The next morning bright light pierced my eyelids and I recoiled at the pain. My head was thumping and I decided to drive into Ragley for a black coffee in Nora's Coffee Shop.

Three miles away, Anita Cuthbertson, Jodie's big sister, had the same idea. She was sitting behind the sofa reading her *Jackie* magazine. For ten pence this was teenage heaven. While the article 'How not to get talked about' had been mildly interesting, it was the 'Problem Page' that had captivated her attention. The question 'Should you keep your eyes open or closed when kissing a boy?' had reverberated round her teenage brain all morning. Suddenly, Anita realized what her New Year resolution must be. But first she had to do some research. She needed to talk and that meant only one place.

In the days before mobile phones, opportunities for discussion on the important things in life – namely, boys, music and clothes – were limited. However, in Ragley village the obvious answer was to meet a fellow soulmate in the ultimate forum for village gossip – namely, Nora's Coffee Shop. So, after watching Noel Edmonds present *Multicoloured Swap Shop* on BBC1 while she ate a bag of Monster Munch, Anita decided to hurry down the High Street, sit in her usual table next to the jukebox and wait for her best friend, Claire Bradshaw, the cheerful daughter of Don and Sheila Bradshaw.

I got there at the same time as Anita. 'Hello, Mr Sheffield,' she said. Anita had been in my class when I first arrived in Ragley.

'Good morning, Anita,' I said, 'and a happy New Year.'

'Thanks, Mr Sheffield,' said Anita. 'Ah'm gonna work 'ard at school this year – it's me resolution.'

'Well done, Anita,' I said as I ordered a jam doughnut and a black coffee from Dorothy behind the counter.

'Do teachers mek resolutions, Mr Sheffield?' asked Dorothy.

I looked down at the large, sticky doughnut. 'Er, sometimes, Dorothy,' I replied and hurried away.

Anita put her current favourite record, 'I Don't Like Mondays' by the Boomtown Rats, on the jukebox for the umpteenth time, accompanied by a despairing groan from Nora Pratt. 'Ah'm sick o' them Boomtown Wats,' she shouted from behind the counter. ''Ow about a pwoper song like "Day Twip t'Bangor" by Fiddler's Dwam?'

Anita's expression made it clear what she thought of a day out in a Welsh seaside resort and she hung her sparkly Blondie shoulder bag over a plastic chair. She glanced at the clock above the peeling posters of the Ragley Amateur Dramatic Society's recent pantomime. The photograph of Nora in her Alpine corset staring appreciatively at Aladdin's magic lamp, which was actually a gravy boat covered in tinfoil, stared down over the coffee machine. Anita knew with absolute certainty that, once Claire Bradshaw had read the same article, she would make a beeline for Nora's Coffee Shop to seek mutual solace for her equally troubled teenage mind.

Behind the counter, Nora Pratt was filling the plastic display case with slightly stale currant teacakes, while her assistant, Dorothy Humpleby, was reading her brand-new *1980 Top of the Pops Annual*. For Dorothy it was sixty-four pages of heaven. A photograph of a youthful Paul McCartney was on the front cover and the full-page colour pin-ups of the Bee Gees and Legs & Co would soon decorate her bedroom walls. She was flicking through the features on Blondie, David Essex, The Who, Status Quo, Barry Manilow and Thin Lizzie when Anita placed her order.

'A Milky Way an' a frothy coffee, please, Dorothy,' said Anita.

''E's dreamy,' mumbled Dorothy, pointing to the photograph of David Essex.

''E's a bit old f'me,' said Anita. As Dorothy transformed the splash of lukewarm milk into a bubbling inferno, Anita had a thought: 'If y'kissed 'im would y'keep y'eyes open, Dorothy?'

Dorothy looked across to the table where Big Dave and Little Malcolm were enjoying their mugs of sweet tea. Before Dorothy could answer, Nora leaned over the counter. 'D'you weally want t'know?' asked Nora.

Anita nodded vigorously.

'Allus keep 'em open, luv, else you'll wegwet it. Y'can't twust men.'

When Nora returned to the till, Dorothy whispered, 'Some aren't that bad, Anita, but mebbe y'ought t'keep 'em open till y'sure.' Then Dorothy cast a wistful glance at Little Malcolm, who was listening to Big Dave's complaints about New Year resolutions concerning shopping with women.

*   *   *

On Saturday evening my fridge was still empty so I drove to the fish-and-chip shop in Easington. By six forty-five I was settled in front of the television, eating a large battered haddock, double chips, mushy peas and four thick slices of white bread. Meanwhile, Jimmy Savile on *Jim'll Fix It* was showing me how to eat spaghetti correctly, go tracking with bloodhounds and how to make model trains. This was followed by *All Creatures Great and Small* and *The Dick Emery Show*, during which time I enjoyed a Mars bar and a cup of coffee. In *Dallas*, Sue Ellen was romantically attracted to a lean, fit, rodeo cowboy whose diet appeared to be different from mine.

It was about that time I realized my resolutions were reluctant ones and I wasn't destined to become a 'new-age-eighties-man'. In fact, I was two pounds heavier, felt completely unfit and understanding women was as likely as a knighthood for Bob Geldof.

Chapter Eleven

Sex and the Single Teacher

The Ragley and Morton Weight Watchers Club have hired the school hall from the County Council for their weekly meetings.

Extract from the Ragley School Logbook:
Thursday, 31 January 1980

'He wants to take me to a nudist beach!' exclaimed Sally.

'Pardon?' said Vera, presuming she had misheard and almost spilling her Earl Grey tea. She took off her spectacles, polished them vigorously and stared at Sally.

'Colin says he wants to spice up our life,' said Sally, shaking her head in dismay.

'Did you say a nudist beach?' asked Anne, almost choking on her garibaldi.

'Where is it?' asked Jo, suddenly interested and closing her *Ladybird Book of the Weather*.

'It's in Yorkshire,' said Sally.

'A nudist beach in Yorkshire!' exclaimed Anne.

'Yes. It's near Bridlington,' said Sally, staring forlornly at the colourful brochure.

Anne and I put our coffee mugs down with a nervous clunk on the staff-room table.

'Don't tell my Dan about it,' said Jo nervously.

It was the last day of January and the travel agents in York had begun their annual onslaught on the local population. Scores of assorted holiday brochures had been pushed through the letterboxes of everyone within a ten-mile radius of the city centre.

However, Sally's brochure was very different. 'It's in here,' she said and pointed to the cover. Two shapely young women were holding huge, brightly coloured beachballs at a strategic height in front of their supposedly naked bodies. Nearby, two broad-shouldered men with Charles Atlas biceps were setting up a badminton net while standing behind a row of dwarf conifers. Fortunately the conifers were not so dwarf as to expose the parts that would otherwise not see the light of day.

'You don't look too happy about it, Sally,' I said cautiously.

'I'm not,' replied Sally. Her response left everyone in no doubt that this was not the time to pursue Colin's unusual idea of a romantic holiday for two.

Vera felt concerned about Sally, who had seemed low in spirits for some time. It was obvious to the women on the staff, if not to me, that everything was not as it should be between Sally and her husband Colin. For several years now, the love of his life had been woodwork and Sally was seeking consolation in the biscuit jar. As the bell rang for afternoon school Sally lifted herself from the chair. 'And there's something wrong with my washing machine,' she said. 'It shrinks every pair of jeans I put in it.'

Vera replaced her spectacles and stared hard at Sally. 'Are you all right?' she asked.

'No, I'm not, Vera,' said Sally. 'I really don't want to be one of the first customers at a nude bathing beach in Bridlington. It's not my idea of romance.' Then, suddenly, she burst into tears.

'I'll keep an eye on your class,' I said and sidestepped quickly into the entrance hall. I knew from past experience that Sally was best left in the capable hands of my ever-dependable secretary. Vera ushered Sally into the school office and the floodgates opened as she told her how fed up she was with life.

'Oh, Vera,' she said, 'I'm only a couple of birthdays away from forty and look what's happened to me.'

'Tell me about it,' said Vera, offering Sally her handkerchief.

Sally dried her eyes and then fingered the lacy edge of the handkerchief. 'When I first met Colin we had such fun,' she said, staring out of the window. 'He had long hair then, you know,' she added with a strained smile. Vera looked suitably surprised. 'Yes, he did!' continued Sally, suddenly animated. 'He was so adventurous and we did lots together. We went dancing . . . I suppose that helped to keep me slim and active. But then . . . slowly things seemed to change. He wasn't as interested in doing anything any more.' She dabbed her eyes once again. 'Well, that's not quite right. He enjoys his woodwork class . . . but he's got no time for me.'

Vera realized this was a time to stay quiet. She smiled gently at Sally, who seemed to gain momentum with the story.

'You see, Vera, I've just had enough! I told him to buck up his ideas and get some romance back into our lives or else. And then he comes up with this ridiculous idea. Well, that's it!'

Vera's startled look must have registered with Sally, who shut up immediately and the tears began again.

'Sally, why don't you come to the vicarage for a couple of days?' said Vera. 'It would give you time to think things through.' Vera had recently read that the number of divorces had reached a peak of 143,000 and she did not want Sally to add to that statistic.

'Thanks, Vera,' said Sally. She took a deep breath, 'I think I will.' Then she dried her eyes, readjusted her tightly fitting skirt, and they both walked back to her classroom.

Vera nodded at me to indicate all was in hand and Sally gave me a brave smile as she passed me in the doorway. 'Thanks, Jack,' she said. When she walked in and stood in front of the blackboard, Sally moved smoothly into teacher mode. 'Now, girls and boys, please put on your painting shirts.'

'Mr Sheffield,' said Vera, 'I need your help.' Vera was at her best in a crisis and her organization was second to none. 'I need you to contact Colin and ask him to meet you this evening after work.' I looked nonplussed. 'You need to talk to him about getting some romance back into his life.'

'I don't think I'm the best person to be doing that, Vera!' I said ruefully, given the lack of success I was having with my own love life.

'With respect, Mr Sheffield, if you say what I tell you to say,' she replied, 'you will be fine.' Vera had that look of absolute confidence about her that I had come to admire.

Colin was puzzled when he took my call but agreed to meet me in The Royal Oak that evening. 'I'm free this evening,' he said. 'Intermediate woodwork is on Tuesdays and the advanced class is on Fridays.'

After school, Sally drove home and packed her overnight bag with a heavy heart. As she rummaged round her cluttered wardrobe she smiled grimly as she discovered their copy of the classic seventies sex title *The Joy of Sex*. It featured the iconic bearded man in a variety of athletic positions. Then she sighed deeply as she recalled it was shortly after buying the book that Colin had become clean-shaven and boring.

At seven o'clock, as I drove back from Kirkby Steepleton towards Ragley, I reflected on the story that Sally had shared with us all in the staff-room at the end of school. She had met Colin in 1965 at the Ragtime Ball at Wembley and for her it was love at first sight. She was twenty-three years old and, with her geometric haircut, hoop earrings and black and white 'op art' PVC coat, Sally felt like a Carnaby Street model. Colin, in his navy-blue duffel coat, shoulder-length hair and faded, skin-tight jeans, told her he was a 'beatnik' and she was definitely 'with it'. While Sally wasn't entirely sure what 'it' was, after sharing a few of Colin's mind-blowing, roll-up cigarettes she had ceased to care.

They had agreed to meet up again in Colin's home city of Leeds and so it was that, on a summer night in the swinging sixties, Colin arrived under Dyson's Clock in the city centre, clutching a bunch of flowers. This was a popular meeting place for young lovers and he stared at the ornate clock with the roman numerals and watched the minutes tick by. Above the clock, Old Father Time, with his hourglass and scythe, stared down silently as each new generation of lovers smiled nervously and young men handed over bunches of roses with the awkwardness of youth.

Sally loved the fashionable Colin who changed his image with the times. His 1966 Native American look, adopted after watching Sonny and Cher singing 'You Got Me, Babe', had been quickly dispensed with in 1967 when he began to wear a beret after seeing the film *Bonnie and Clyde*. In 1969, after Joe Cocker's performance at Woodstock, he adopted psychedelic tied-and-dyed shirts. Then in the seventies, with his Elton John platform boots, he had increased his height by four inches. Finally, he had found his true identity and settled for an Afghan sheepskin coat, John Lennon circular spectacles and rapidly receding hair with an ever-widening centre parting.

But the dreams of youth had long since gone. When Sally had started her teaching career at Ragley School, Colin began work as a filing clerk at the local architects' department in York. He became just another man in a suit and it was about this time they had begun to drift apart. Sally spent her evenings marking children's work and preparing music lessons while listening to the Carpenters, her favourite group. She loved their songs and in 1973 she sang along to 'Rainy Days and Mondays' and 'Goodbye to Love'. However, by the time 'Please, Mr Postman' was released in 1975, Colin was spending more time in the shed at the bottom of the garden.

One Saturday afternoon in 1976, Sally bought 'There's a Kind of Hush' and, as an afterthought, a large packet of chocolate-coated digestive biscuits. Slowly, she began to put on weight, unlike the waif-like Karen Carpenter, who was now dreadfully thin. Although, much to Sally's relief, there was a rumour reported in the *Daily Express* that she was thinking of getting married.

When I walked into the lounge bar of The Royal Oak, Colin was already halfway down his first pint. In a haze of aromatic cigarette smoke, he waved a greeting and got up to buy me a drink. After a few moments of awkward silence, unexpectedly he launched in at the deep end. 'It all began with that bloody canoe,' he said. 'I've been depressed ever since.'

'Canoe?'

'Yes, Jack. I made a canoe in woodwork evening class in York.'

'But that's brilliant, Colin,' I said with slightly false enthusiasm. 'Building a canoe is a wonderful achievement.'

'Yes, but I couldn't get it down the staircase,' explained Colin. 'It was too long to get round the corners.'

'I see,' I said, trying not to smile. 'That's unfortunate.'

'It's still there, hanging up in the rafters,' he said, lighting another roll-up.

'So how are things?' I asked tentatively.

He put down his drink and looked at me with red-rimmed eyes. 'I guess you know Sally's gone to stay at the vicarage. We've been going through a sticky patch. She said she needs to "find herself" . . . whatever that means.'

'Maybe she just needs some space. She's looked a bit down at school.'

'I'm lost without her, Jack. Is there anything you can say to her?'

I supped deeply on my Chestnut Mild. 'Tell me about this nudist camp idea,' I said.

A mile away, the sad sound of an owl echoed with a hollow grief round the silent towers of the churchyard. Jo Hunter's car crunched over the pebbled courtyard of the vicarage and parked by the front door. She had driven from Easington and picked up Anne en route in her new 'F'-registered two-tone-green Wolseley Hornet with a dark-green roof. Dan and Jo had bought it for the princely sum of £300 and they were proud of their first car.

Soon they were in the warmth of the beautifully furnished lounge and Vera was pouring tea through a silver tea-strainer for Sally. 'We've had a thought,' said Vera and she looked expectantly at Anne, who launched into the opening gambit.

'Sally, we wondered if you might be interested in the new club that's starting at school,' said Anne, pointing to the advertisement she had removed from the staff-room noticeboard.

'Weight Watchers!' exclaimed Sally.

'You've been saying for a while you've been eating too many biscuits,' said Vera.

'Yes, but Weight Watchers!'

'It says here, "It's time to rekindle your lost youth",' said Vera, reading from the advertisement.

'And it might be fun,' said Anne.

Sally put down her china cup and saucer and looked at Jo. 'You're quiet,' she said.

Jo took a deep breath. 'I'll come with you,' she said in a determined manner.

Sally was surprised. 'But you're thin as a rake,' she said.

'Not really,' said Jo. 'Dan seems to think we can live on fish and chips.'

'I don't know,' said Sally, looking down at her tea.

'Anne's right, Sally,' said Jo. 'It could be fun. So come on, let's at least give it a try.'

Everyone held their breath. It was their first step towards getting Sally to feel good about herself.

Sally grinned. 'OK,' she said. 'Weight Watchers it is, then.'

Back in The Royal Oak, Colin was pouring out his heart. 'I was just trying to get some spark back, if you see what I mean . . . like when we were both single.'

'Maybe she's moved on in her life and wants something different. Perhaps you should ask her.' I was keeping faithfully to Vera's script.

'I need to talk to her,' he said.

I remembered what Vera had told me to say. 'Colin, what are you doing tomorrow night?'

'It's advanced woodwork class,' he said with sudden enthusiasm. 'I'm making those kitchen cupboards in *The Reader's Digest Complete Do-It-Yourself Manual*.'

'How about coming here afterwards and we can continue this chat?'

'Don't you think I should drive round to see her at the vicarage?'

'Not just yet, Colin. Sally needs a bit of space right now.'

He sat back and stared at the ceiling.

'Are you hungry?' I asked.

He nodded and fifteen minutes later Sheila arrived with chicken and chips in a basket followed by her famous bread-and-butter pudding. Colin looked at the food with little interest, but for me it was heaven.

* * *

The first morning of February was grey and still as Vera and Sally walked out to Vera's car parked under the giant elm trees of the vicarage. Against the old red-brick wall, beyond the damp grass and decaying leaves, tiny yellow flowers of winter jasmine brightened the gloom and, at their feet, the grey-green florets of saxifrage jostled for space in the frozen earth. Alongside, a tall, solitary teasel stood incongruously like a giant sentinel, its brown, spiky honeycombed crowns swaying in the breeze.

'Thanks, Vera,' said Sally. 'I appreciate the lift.'

'You look more rested today,' said Vera.

'Thanks, Vera . . . Lovely suit, by the way.'

Vera smiled. 'Thank you, Sally.'

Vera had bought a smart dark-blue, tailored suit with a cream, kitten-bow blouse, high buttoned to the neck. One day she knew she would visit the Aquascutum store in London's Regent Street where Margaret Thatcher did her shopping but, for now, Marks & Spencer's was fine.

Morning school went smoothly and Vera reappeared in the staff-room at lunchtime after completing her register of late dinner money. Sally was on playground duty during afternoon break, so Vera gathered Anne, Jo and me in a huddle that felt like a secret society. A few minutes later we all knew what to do next.

That evening at seven o'clock Sally and Jo, giggling like schoolgirls, returned to Ragley School to register for Weight Watchers.

A slim, strikingly dressed lady was sitting behind the old pine table in the entrance hall, collecting money and giving out registration cards. She was wearing a hip-hugging jumpsuit with a zip from neck to navel and fashionable Adidas Pacesetters trainers, bright blue with three loud yellow diagonal stripes down the side. However, the outstanding feature was a pair of the most vivid multicoloured leg warmers Sally and Jo had ever seen.

'Hello, ladies,' said Miss Leg Warmers. 'I'm Mandy. Just fill in these forms and then I can give you your membership registration card and your personal weight record.'

'So, how does it all work?' asked Jo. 'We've not been before.'

'Well,' said Mandy, going into automatic pilot, 'Weight Watchers is based on measured portions of food and is a wonderful way to lose weight and feel good.'

'I see,' said Sally uncertainly.

'Just pay now to register, plus your weekly fee, and then we'll get you weighed,' said Mandy, adding two more names to her alphabetical index. She gave Sally and Jo a small weight-loss record card and a white sticker.

After weighing themselves, Sally and Jo returned to the ever-smiling Mandy.

'So what would you like to weigh?' asked Mandy. 'This is your goal weight.'

'Er, not sure,' said Sally. She turned to Jo. 'I just want to feel good about myself again,' she whispered.

They both walked into the hall. There were four rows of chairs and Sally and Jo sat on the back row, feeling nervous. One or two parents of children at Ragley School were in the audience and waved in acknowledgement, including Petula Dudley-Palmer and Margery Ackroyd. Margery was reflecting on her day. She had starved herself after taking a laxative tablet the previous night and then, before getting weighed, she had taken off her shoes and removed all her jewellery, including her earrings and the toggle for her pony-tail. Margery was determined to succeed.

Suddenly, the leader, Valerie Ormskirk, struggled into the hall, dragging a life-size cardboard cut-out of the fattest lady Sally had ever seen. Valerie propped it up against the folding trestle table at the front of the hall and stared at her assembled flock. 'Good evening, ladies,' she said, with the inner confidence of the successful Weight Watcher.

'Good evening, Valerie,' answered the assorted group of ladies.

Sally looked around her in trepidation and began to regret eating that second slice of Black Forest gateau for her supper the previous evening.

'This was the old me,' announced Valerie, coyly pointing towards the giant photograph. 'And this is the new me,' she added, smoothing her skin-tight Olivia Newton John leather trousers.

To Sally's surprise, all of Valerie's disciples burst into spontaneous applause.

Valerie bowed in acknowledgement and then held up one finger. Silence fell and the room suddenly crackled with tension. 'Now, ladies, let's see how you've got on,' she said. Nervous glances were exchanged. 'Put up your hand if you've lost a pound.' A few hesitant Weight

Watchers responded. 'And now two pounds,' continued Valerie. The ladies on either side of Sally and Jo raised their hands. 'And who has lost three pounds?' A few slightly more enthusiastic ladies responded. 'Now, has anyone lost more than three pounds? And remember, there's a special badge for anyone who has lost seven pounds.'

No one moved.

'And who's been naughty this week?'

A contrite lady in the front row coughed nervously.

'Never mind, Jenny,' said Valerie. 'Tell us all, what went wrong?'

'I had lots of toast and sandwiches,' said Jenny.

Sally thought she was very brave.

'Get your neighbour to post you *one slice* of bread through your letterbox, my dear,' said Valerie. 'We must all help one another to achieve our goals and don't forget to put your *fat* photos on the fridge door. That always provides motivation.'

A severe-looking lady in the second row put up her hand. 'I'm a vegetarian,' she said apologetically.

'Oh dear,' said Valerie. 'Well, you'll have to be careful you get enough vitamins, particularly Group B and especially B6 and B12.'

And so it went on and Sally and Jo gradually relaxed into the pattern of the evening. As they put on their coats at the end of the session, Sally whispered in Jo's ear. 'I'm glad I came,' she said. 'I feel, well . . . part of something again. Recently it's just been school work, books and biscuits and not much else.'

Jo gave her a hug. 'We'll be fine,' she said. 'Come on, let's have a drink before we go home.' Then she put her weight record card in her handbag, took Sally by the arm and walked out into the night.

Meanwhile, at the far end of the village Petula Dudley-Palmer slipped off her designer Chris Evert tennis shoes, with the distinctive blue star and stripe down the side, and walked barefooted across the deep-pile Axminster carpet.

Geoffrey was enjoying a whisky and soda. 'Hello, darling. How did it go?' he said with absolutely no recollection of where she had been.

'Excellent,' said Petula, pouring herself a gin and tonic. 'I've lost another two pounds.' She stared thoughtfully at her husband and wished he could be more like Val Doonican sitting in a comfortable rocking chair in a beautiful hand-knitted jumper while singing 'Scarlet Ribbons' or 'Walk Tall'.

Meanwhile, Geoffrey looked at his wife and wished she could be more like Babs, Dee Dee or Cherry in Pan's People, the *Top of the Pops* dancers, or even his ultimate fantasy, Agnetha Fältskog of Abba in her satin-blue knickerbockers. As he closed his eyes a broad smile crossed his face.

'What are you thinking about, Geoffrey?' asked Petula.

'You, my beloved,' said Geoffrey smoothly. He hadn't achieved the dizzy heights of chief executive at the Rowntree's chocolate factory without some important management skills.

*   *   *

Sex clearly meant different things to the people of Ragley village. To Timothy Pratt, who had never had a girlfriend, sex was something visually beautiful and ethereal, yet precise and well organized.

After switching on his television to watch *Come Dancing* for the first time many years before, Timothy realized that sex was for other people and, when the Frank and Peggy Spencer formation dancing team from Penge walked on to the dance floor, Timothy's life was complete. The sequins, sewn with the same precision as their perfect dance steps, glittered under the lights and the couples moved in exact symmetry. Then, in 1979, Alan Yentob, the BBC director general, banished the programme from our screens and Tidy Tim had mourned for a week.

It was clear that something was missing in his life but he didn't think it was sex. With a measured tread he walked to the store cupboard and took out his Meccano set. He stroked the lid of the box with deep affection. Now, this is better than sex, he thought.

Back in her kitchen, Anne Grainger wondered how Sally and Jo's night was progressing. As she combed a pattern with a fork on top of her fish pie, she knew she was content with her life. Her husband John was a caring man and, while the enthusiastic days of their youth were behind them, she was happy. Even so, after adding sliced tomatoes and putting the casserole dish under the grill, she glanced wistfully at the photograph of David Soul on the front cover of her *Radio Times*.

*   *   *

At nine o'clock, in the taproom of The Royal Oak, the members of the Ragley football team were all thinking about sex. For this trusty band of brothers, these thoughts occurred as regularly as breathing. However, for them sex was something that, if you were lucky, happened on a Saturday night after *Match of the Day*. When I walked in, they were all staring at the sheer magnificence of Sheila's straining boob tube as she pulled another foaming pint of Tetley's bitter.

'That's a funny tank top, Stevie,' said Sheila, looking up from behind the hand pumps at Stevie's multicoloured creation. The word STRIPPER appeared to be emblazoned across the front.

'My Aunty Maureen knitted it,' explained Stevie. 'She's colour-blind,' he added apologetically.

'That explains it, then,' said Sheila.

'She says she wants t'teach me t'knit,' said Stevie mournfully.

There was an intake of breath. All the members of the football team looked at Stevie as if he had just told them Geoff Hurst's third goal in the World Cup Final of 1966 should have been disallowed.

Finally, Big Dave broke the silence. 'Only poofters knit,' he said.

Everyone nodded at this well-known fact, except Sheila.

'Ah've 'eard Norwegian seamen knit their own socks,' said Sheila, folding her arms in a determined fashion, although this was achieved with difficulty.

Again, it was left to Big Dave to respond. 'Mebbe so,' he conceded graciously, 'but ah'll tell y'summat: me an' Malcolm won't be going t'Norway for us 'olidays.'

'Y'reight there, Dave,' agreed Little Malcolm, looking relieved.

Colin saw me sitting at the same table, walked in and slumped down.

'I've been thinking,' he said.

'Yes?'

'Maybe I should give up woodwork classes.'

'Why not just go on Friday nights and meet Sally for a drink after her Weight Watchers class?' I was word perfect with my script.

Suddenly Sally and Jo walked in. Colin looked up in expectation and Sally stared hard at Jo and then me. 'What's going on?' she said.

'We hoped you might like to talk things through,' said Jo.

Colin walked up to the bar. 'I've missed you,' he said, with the eyes of a homeless puppy.

'Have you?' said Sally.

'Did you enjoy Weight Watchers?' asked Colin.

'It was really good,' said Sally. 'I'm going to stick at it.'

'That's good,' said Colin.

'So what have you been making?' asked Sally.

'Kitchen cupboards.'

'Are you sure you'll get them down that staircase?' asked Sally.

Colin's eyes widened. 'Bloody hell, I hope so!'

Then they burst into fits of laughter.

'I'm sorry, Sally,' said Colin. 'I want to make it right. The nudist camp idea was stupid.'

'Oh, maybe not,' said Sally, with a mixture of relief and mischief in her eyes.

Jo and I smiled at each other and walked away, while Colin and Sally talked as if they had a lot to catch up on. By ten o'clock they left together, hand in hand. Colin had parked his car on the other side of the village green, near the school gates. On one of the pillars was a large hand-written notice which read: *Weight Watchers – please use the double doors at the side of the hall.*

Sally and Colin burst into laughter, climbed into their car and roared home.

Back in their tiny kitchen, Colin prepared two mugs of Horlicks. 'I'm going to give up woodwork,' he said, taking two biscuits out of the biscuit barrel and then, as an afterthought, replacing them.

Sally gave him a hug. 'Being single didn't suit me,' she said with a grin.

'Nor me,' said Colin.

They went upstairs and Sally placed the nudist camp brochure on the shelf in her wardrobe where she could find it again. It was then she noticed a certain book she hadn't read for a long time. She picked it up, flicked through the pages and smiled.

Chapter Twelve

Look Before You Leap

School closed today for the spring half-term holiday and will reopen on Monday, 3 March.

Extract from the Ragley School Logbook:
Friday, 22 February 1980

As I drove towards Ragley village on the winding back road from Kirkby Steepleton, the plain of York was still in the grip of winter. Snowflakes drifted like north wind confetti, weightless in the pale beam of the headlights, while a vast darkness lifted reluctantly from the frozen earth. It was Friday morning, 22 February, and the half-term holiday was almost upon us.

'G'mornin', Mr Sheffield,' shouted Ruby as she swept the snow from the steps in front of the entrance porch. Ruby's headscarf was tightly knotted under her chin and her breath steamed in the cold morning air.

'Good morning, Ruby,' I shouted across the car park. 'And how's Ronnie?'

''Ibernatin',' said Ruby in disgust, as she clattered her yard broom against the school wall to shake the snow from the bristles. ''E allus does in winter.'

Suddenly Sally drove through the school entrance. Sally and Colin had bought a new second car and her 'S' registration, dark-blue Ford Fiesta bumped over the frozen cobbles and parked next to mine. Her old zest for life had returned.

'Morning, Jack. Morning, Ruby,' she said, as she grabbed her shoulder bag, filled with exercise books, and scurried up the steps into the entrance hall.

In the staff-room, Vera picked up a third of a pint milk bottle, shook it to mix in the cream and removed the foil top. Then she poured the milk into a small saucepan and began to heat it over our single electric ring. 'Coffee, everybody?'

'Yes, please, Vera,' chorused Anne and Jo, who were sitting by the gas fire and checking the half-yearly reading-age figures for each child of seven and under.

'Did you notice the holiday includes a leap-year day?' said Vera, pointing with a wooden spoon at the calendar on the staff-room noticeboard.

Jo looked up. 'Dan said something about it being a day when women could propose to men.'

'Sally will know,' said Anne, putting down her Berol pen.

As usual, Sally, our resident historian, was a fund of

information. 'Dan's right, Jo,' she said. 'It all began with St Patrick. He started the tradition when St Bridget complained that women were fed-up having to wait for men to pluck up courage to propose.'

'Not like my Dan, then,' said Jo confidently.

Little did she know it but, at that moment, Dan was cursing her down at the local police station. Jo had misguidedly bought her six-feet-four-inch policeman-husband a bottle of Macho by Fabergé, a powerful new scent for men, much to the amusement of his less-liberated colleagues.

Undeterred, Sally pressed on. 'Eventually, a law was passed in Scotland in 1288,' she explained. 'It allowed women to propose to men. If they refused, they had to pay a fine.'

'Sounds a good idea,' said Anne.

'Quite right,' agreed Sally. 'Refuse and you pay a fine. Accept and you pay for an engagement ring.'

'It might be the night for me then,' said Vera. Sally, Anne and Jo looked at one another in surprise. 'Only joking,' added Vera with a smile.

The morning progressed quietly except in Jo Hunter's classroom, where the Revd Joseph Evans was leading a Religious Education lesson on the theme of Lent. He explained that Lent lasts for forty days and forty nights, from Ash Wednesday to Easter, the time spent by Jesus in the wilderness. He then explained the concept of self-denial, a tough task with seven-year-olds.

'Does this mean we can't 'ave Easter eggs?' asked Heathcliffe, who was rapidly emerging as Class 2's equivalent of Arthur Scargill.

'Yes, you can have Easter eggs,' said Joseph.

Elisabeth Amelia Dudley-Palmer, one of the few who had been paying attention, raised her hand. 'It's because Jesus rose again on Easter Sunday,' she said.

''E prob'ly didn't want t'miss out on 'is Easter egg,' said Heathcliffe.

The bell for morning break was always a relief for Joseph.

By lunchtime Vera had completed all her paperwork, tidied her desk and put the tin of late dinner money in her shopping bag to deposit at the bank. 'Enjoy your holiday, everybody,' she said and drove away with Joseph to Easington.

On this freezing day, Shirley had made one of my favourite school dinners – mince and dumplings followed by gooseberry crumble and custard – and I felt content when I walked into the staff-room for a cup of tea.

The telephone rang and Anne picked it up. 'Yes, Laura, he's here now,' she said and passed over the telephone, while my colleagues began to drink their tea in complete silence.

'Jack, I just need to check if you're free next Friday,' said Laura. She sounded in a hurry.

'Er, yes, I should be: it's half-term.'

'Perfect,' said Laura. 'Just leave the whole day free.'

'Why? What's happening?'

'You'll see,' she said. 'Let's just say it's a nice surprise,' and she rang off.

The conversation round me recommenced and I was left to wonder what Laura was planning. She had certainly captured my interest.

It had been a busy half-term and at the end of the school day we all gathered in the staff-room to say goodbye.

Sally had spent 35p on this month's *Do It Yourself* magazine and was flicking through the pages. 'It's for Colin,' she said, looking in bewilderment at the article on how to build an antique pine bookcase. 'I thought he would enjoy it. There's a free filler knife, so it looked like a bargain.' She stuffed it in her bag. 'Don't worry, I still prefer *Cosmopolitan*,' she added with a grin.

Jo gave Anne a lift home and Sally, who was meeting Colin outside the Odeon cinema to see *Bedknobs and Broomsticks*, sped off towards York. I decided to make the most of the peace and quiet of the school office and catch up with a few hours of paperwork. With Ruby singing 'Edelweiss' while she mopped the hall floor, I completed a report for the school governors and, finally, added another entry into the school logbook. I had just written *'School closed today for the spring half-term holiday and will reopen on Monday, 3 March,'* when the telephone rang. It was Laura again.

'Hi, Jack. It's all fixed,' she said excitedly. 'I'll pick you up at Bilbo Cottage at ten o'clock next Friday and have you home again by early afternoon.'

'So, what is it?'

'Let's just say you'll find it an uplifting experience . . . and I guarantee it will be fun!'

'Well . . . er, thanks, Laura, whatever it is,' I mumbled.

'So just wear casual clothing – jeans and a sweater will be fine – and I'll see you then.'

'Laura?'

'Yes?'

'I'd like to reciprocate, so maybe we could go for a meal in the evening as a thank-you from me?'

'Perfect, Jack. Let's do that.'

'So where would you like to go?'

'How about the Dean Court?'

'Oh, well . . . er, OK. I'll book a table for seven o'clock.'

'That's lovely. See you on Friday.'

'OK. 'Bye.'

'Bye.'

I stared at the receiver and smiled. Laura was definitely different.

I looked at my watch. I was tired and hungry and The Royal Oak beckoned. I locked the door behind me, breathed in the cold night air, wrapped my old college scarf a little tighter round my neck and fastened the top toggle of my duffel coat. Then I climbed into my car and drove out of school with a week's holiday stretching out before me. I wondered what Laura had planned for the following Friday and smiled in expectation.

The Royal Oak was welcoming and warm with a roaring log fire and I ordered a pint of Chestnut Mild and a hot meat pie. Don the barman had switched on the television in the taproom and assorted members of the

Ragley Rovers football team were staring blankly at a strange man who was standing next to one of the new television-detector vans.

'The anti-television-licence-evasion scheme begins on 25 February,' said the grey-suited, bespectacled man with the appearance of a mad scientist. 'Our television-detector vans incorporate the latest technological innovations,' he continued smugly. 'The detector consists of a highly sensitive receiver and a directional aerial array mounted on the roof of the minibus body.'

'Who's 'e?' mumbled Deke Ramsbottom. Deke was wearing a black armband, upset at the news that John Wayne had died at the age of seventy-two.

'Yeah, what's 'e on abart?' asked Big Dave.

'Dunno,' said Little Malcolm.

The mad scientist was building up to the big finish. 'Television receivers work on the supersonic heterodyne principle. Energy from this signal escapes from this receiver in the form of radio waves. By examining the radiations generated in the frequency-changing process, they can discover the programme that is tuned to and the television's location.'

There was a stunned silence.

'So what's all that about?' asked Clint Ramsbottom.

Don cleaned a pint glass thoughtfully with a York City tea towel. Then he placed the glass on the counter, put down the tea towel and leaned over the bar. 'Tell me this, Dave,' said Don: ''ave you an' Malcolm got a TV licence?'

'Y'mus' be joking,' said Big Dave.

'Y'joking all reight,' echoed Little Malcolm.

Don shook his head sadly. 'Lads, ah'm not joking.'

'So what's it all about, then?' asked Deadly Duggie Smith.

'Yeah, what did Brainbox 'ave t'say, then?' asked Shane Ramsbottom.

'D'you want me t'tell y'gently?' asked Don.

Big Dave and Little Malcolm nodded.

''E says you an' Malcolm are stuffed.'

Big Dave stared at Don uncomprehendingly. ''Ow d'yer mean, Don?' he asked.

'You lads need t'buy a TV licence, 'cause they'll find you if you 'aven't.'

'Bloody Nora!' exclaimed Big Dave.

Little Malcolm just shook his head, which at least made a difference from nodding.

'Remember this day, lads,' continued Don. 'It's t'beginning o' t'end. Big Brother's come t'Ragley.'

The holiday flew by and, on Thursday morning, I decided to drive into school to complete an audit of the contents of the stock cupboard and send off a new order to the educational suppliers in Wakefield. We were running short of powder paint and sheets of A3 paper. Anne had been tearing up old wallpaper sample books to provide paper on which her children could paint their wonderful creations. We also needed a few more rolls of sticky-backed plastic to cover our precious but increasingly well-thumbed *Ginn Reading 360* reading-scheme books.

The road into Ragley village was lonely and quiet but

Mother Nature was trying to lift the spirit and give hope for better days ahead. Hazel catkins shivered defiantly in the bleak hedgerows and the tiny yellow stars of winter aconites brightened the dark woodland. As I drove into the school car park, icy blasts rattled the grey slate roof tiles and flurries of snow settled in curve-stitching patterns on the Victorian windowpanes.

After an hour of silent endeavour I switched off the staff-room radio, even though the Nolan Sisters were telling me they were in the mood for dancing. I definitely wasn't. On this cold morning what I really needed was a coffee. I pulled on my duffel coat and scarf and walked out of school.

I hurried across the High Street and, as I opened the door of Nora's Coffee Shop, Stan Coe was on his way out and barged past, nearly knocking me over. 'Mind where y'goin', Sheffield!' he shouted gruffly.

The place was almost empty and Dorothy had come round the counter to sit with Big Dave and Little Malcolm. 'Tek no notice of 'im, Mr Sheffield,' said Dorothy. ''E's the sort that doesn't put t'top back on t'sauce bottle.' In the catalogue of rebukes, this was obviously a serious one and I nodded in agreement.

Meanwhile, Big Dave and Little Malcolm had a problem to solve. On Friday night it was the refuse collectors' annual ball at the Working Men's Club in York and this year the organizers had stipulated that fancy dress should be worn. Dave had suggested that he and Malcolm should put on their best suits and go as the Kray twins, but, much to his disgust, Little Malcolm had invited Dorothy to be his partner and she had jumped at the chance.

'What we gonna do, Dave?' asked Little Malcolm.

'Shurrup. Ah'm thinkin',' said Big Dave.

''Ow about still goin' as t'Kray brothers,' suggested Little Malcolm, 'wi' Dorothy as a gangster's moll?'

'Ah don't remember no molls,' said Big Dave gruffly.

'Oooh, Malcolm, 'ow about we go as super'eroes?' said Dorothy excitedly. 'Ah can wear m'Wonder Woman outfit an' you can go as another super'ero.'

Little Malcolm had never thought of himself as a superhero. He was just a vertically challenged bin man with a big heart. His only claim to fame was that he could always finish on a double three at darts and play 'Mull of Kintyre' on his harmonica. He didn't think this would frighten many inter-galactic psychopaths.

''Ow about Superman? Ah've got a lovely pair o' blue tights,' said Dorothy. Big Dave shook his head in anguish, Malcolm went a shade of puce and Dorothy considered Little Malcolm's legs. 'An' ah could tek 'em up a bit,' she added helpfully.

Little Malcolm stared at the ground and gradually came to realize that true love can have a strange effect on bin men, even ones that were only five-feet-four-inches tall and born and bred in Yorkshire. He craned his neck and stared up at Dorothy's false eyelashes. They fluttered just once and, even though he knew he was destined to look a complete prat, all resistance left him. 'All reight,' he mumbled.

Big Dave gave Little Malcolm his 'southern softie' look.

'Ah'll jus' go as *one* o' t'Kray twins, then,' he said with exaggerated pathos.

'OK, Dave,' said Malcolm. Dorothy gave him a hug and for a delicious moment, Little Malcolm was completely but pleasantly deaf.

''Ave y'got any red underpants?' asked Dorothy.

'Y'what?' asked Little Malcolm in a muffled voice.

I smiled as I watched the effect true love could have on the most unlikely of men. However, by the time Dorothy had walked back behind the counter, Little Malcolm had considered his future role as Clark Kent, Man of Steel. The only consolation he could think of was that on the night of the party it would be dark by six o'clock.

It was leap-year day and the weather was bright and clear. At precisely ten o'clock my doorbell rang and there stood Laura. Her high cheekbones were flushed with the biting cold and she looked simply wonderful in her tight Burberry jeans, blue denim shirt, green denim jacket and a red neckscarf tied in a knot.

'You look amazing,' I said.

She grinned. 'It's nothing really, Jack – we're just promoting the Ralph Lauren Western Collection. It's the latest casual gear.'

I grabbed my anorak and college scarf and we walked out to her Mini Clubman. Laura drove at her usual break-neck speed towards York but then I was intrigued as we headed south through Stillingfleet and Cawood towards the aerodrome on the outskirts of the tiny village of Kirk Fenton.

When we reached the red-and-white-striped security barrier we stopped and waited. Almost immediately, from a nearby hut stepped a tall, rangy pilot officer with a severe military haircut and a neat salt and pepper moustache. He looked about forty years old with clear blue eyes and his baggy flying suit flapped in the cold breeze as he walked towards me. The Perspex pockets above each knee flashed in the morning sunlight. Two thick white stripes separated by a single thin stripe against the pale-blue background of each epaulette marked him out as a squadron leader. The guard on duty saluted with elaborate formality, while he responded with curt acknowledgement.

'Hello again, Laura,' he said and gave her a kiss on the cheek. 'And this must be Jack.' He shook my hand with a firm handshake. 'I'm Tom Bannister. Laura and I go way back. Welcome to Kirk Fenton.'

'Er . . . thanks,' I replied, looking round me in wonderment. 'This is all new to me, I'm afraid.'

The guard stepped forward. 'I've checked in Miss Henderson's car, sir,' he said, tapping his clipboard with a chinograph pencil.

'Roger,' replied Tom, with a friendly nod, and we set off towards the hangar.

'I'll see you later, Jack,' said Laura, her eyes twinkling.

'You grab a coffee and I promise I'll bring him back in one piece,' said Tom.

Laura walked away with the guard and, even more puzzled, I followed Tom.

'We're only on security level C, Jack, so things are fairly

relaxed,' he explained. 'It's not as if we're at war with anyone at the moment,' he added with a grin.

Around thirty planes were lined up in a perfect row outside the hangar. 'These are our Jet Provosts, Jack,' said Tom. 'They used to be piston-driven but now we're in the jet age. They're two-seater with duplicate controls, so they're ideal for training.'

'I've seen them flying over the moors,' I said in awe, 'but I've never been so close to one before.'

'Well, I've a surprise for you, Jack. Thanks to Laura, you're going up in one.'

'What!'

'Don't worry, Jack, it will be fun.'

'I'm speechless!'

I couldn't believe my luck and I stared at the planes. Their colour matched the leaden sky, pale grey, except for the vivid red wing tips and fuel tanks. Gathered round the first of the aircraft, members of the civilian ground crew were busy making final checks. One of them glanced up and in a confident, clipped tone said, 'Alpha-One, ready for take-off, sir.'

'Roger, Dave,' replied Tom casually. Briefly, I wondered if any of the ground crew might actually be called Roger.

'Alpha-One is the weather ship, Jack,' explained Tom. 'It goes up an hour before the students to check on weather conditions.' He paused and stared at the sky. 'But we should be fine this morning, clear and cold.'

An hour later, dressed in a flying suit and helmet, and after a crash course in what not to touch in the cockpit,

I sat petrified in my seat listening to Tom's voice in my earphones.

'Ready for take-off,' said Tom. His voice seemed strangely tinny.

'Clear for take-off, Alpha-One,' was the instant reply from the tower.

We bumped along the runway until our air speed reached eighty-five knots, and I stared in horror as the end of the runway appeared all too quickly. Tom gripped the control column a little tighter and, as our speed flickered up to ninety-five knots, he gently eased it back and we left the ground. I said goodbye to my stomach as rooftops and green fields sped below us and we headed off towards the distant hills.

Gradually we levelled out and turned north on a course towards Leeming and then east, past Thirkby, over the Hambleton hills and on to the vast flatlands of the Vale of York. Below us, in a beautiful and secluded valley, stood the ruins of the Cistercian monastery of Rievaulx Abbey and the spectacular Ampleforth College, a Roman Catholic school run by a community of Benedictine monks. Then, as we gained height, we approached the Bilsdale television mast near Hartingdale. I knew it was over one thousand feet high but we soared above it.

Suddenly, there was a message in my headset that I didn't expect to hear. 'Do you want to loop the loop, Jack?'

Through a gap in the thinning layer of strato-cumulus clouds at around two thousand feet we flew into a bright new world of empty blue sky. Below us a hazy carpet of soft grey clouds stretched out in all directions and suddenly the world seemed a distant place.

We climbed to over five thousand feet and Tom glanced across. 'Settle back, Jack. Try to relax with your hands on your knees.'

I did as I was told and glanced furtively in the direction of the sick bag. 'OK, Tom. I'm ready.'

The horizon disappeared beneath me and clear sky filled my range of vision. I was completely disorientated when the layer of clouds reappeared upside down and tumbled across the cockpit and I recalled falling backwards from a swimming-pool diving board as a child and tumbling helplessly into the water.

'Geronimo!' I yelled.

'Roger, Jack,' replied a calm voice in my headphones.

Then a giant fist appeared to be pushing me through the seat. The weight of my helmet crushed into my skull and, at four times gravity, I couldn't raise my hands from my knees. I was utterly helpless.

With a life-jacket on top of my flying suit the cockpit had gradually become uncomfortably hot, but at that moment cold, naked fear froze my bones.

A minute or two later, when terror had given way to exhilaration, it was all over and, after a smooth landing, my stomach returned to normal. Tom helped me out of the cockpit and we walked back towards the barrier, where Laura was waiting. She rushed towards me, her green eyes full of excitement, and hugged me.

'Oh, Jack, how was it? I couldn't believe the loop the loop!'

I held her, feeling elated. 'It was fantastic. Thank you so much.'

Tom stood quietly alongside. 'Thanks, Tom,' I said, shaking his hand. 'It really was an amazing experience.'

'My pleasure, Jack. I hope we meet up again sometime.' He turned to Laura, who was still gazing up at me. ''Bye, Laura, and best wishes to your father.'

Laura stretched up and pecked him on the cheek. 'Thanks, Tom. I'll tell Dad when I see him.'

Then she took my arm, led me back to her car and we raced off down the country lanes and back towards York.

Outside Bilbo Cottage Laura leaned over, looked at me intently and kissed me on the cheek. 'I'm dashing now but I'll see you at the Dean Court,' she said, 'seven o'clock sharp.'

'See you soon,' I shouted as she drove away.

In the Dean Court's luxurious entrance Laura gave her charcoal-grey maxi-length coat and her cyclamen-pink scarf to the receptionist and the maître d'hôtel showed us to our table. I looked across at Laura in the flickering candlelight. She looked stunning in a sheer black dress, straight from *Breakfast at Tiffany's*.

'You look sensational,' I said, 'and I love the perfume.'

'Opium by Yves Saint Laurent,' she said, 'and you don't look bad yourself, Jack.' Then she leaned over and removed my large, black-framed Buddy Holly spectacles and put them on the white linen tablecloth. 'There, now you look almost handsome,' she said, her green eyes full of mischief.

The meal was excellent and the Bordeaux wine complemented the tasty Yorkshire beef. The conversation ebbed and flowed with easy banter until we were nibbling at cheese and biscuits and then Laura went quiet as if deep in thought. Finally she said, 'Did you know it's a special day today, Jack, leap-year day . . . the day women can propose to men.'

'So I heard,' I said. 'Sally told us all about it at school.'

Then Laura gave me that special look I had come to know so well and, once again, her green eyes reminded me of Beth. 'How would you feel if someone proposed to you on 29 February?' She stretched her right hand across the table and laid it gently on top of mine.

I laughed. 'That would never happen to me.'

'It might,' said Laura softly and she stared at me intently.

'No, it wouldn't.' I laughed. 'I'm not the marrying kind, Laura.' I picked up my glasses and put them back on.

For a few brief moments the colour drained from her face and she turned away, her green eyes moist. Then it hit me like a thunderbolt. I realized that our months of friendship had meant more to Laura than they had to me . . . much more.

'Yes, of course,' she said and, unexpectedly, she laughed loudly. 'I know you aren't the marrying kind.' She looked down and began to fiddle with the clasp of her handbag. 'Oh, you didn't think I was proposing to you, did you?'

'Of course not,' I replied, though in reality I wasn't quite so sure.

The next few seconds seemed like hours. Laura looked

at her wristwatch. 'I'm tired now, Jack. I think I'd like to go home.'

The evening had come to an abrupt end.

'Yes – it has been a long day. I'll pay the bill.'

Laura got up quickly and walked towards the reception area where Abba's 'Knowing Me Knowing You' was playing softly in the background. The maître d'hôtel ordered our coats to be retrieved and looked concerned when he saw Laura's face. 'Everything to your satisfaction, sir?' he asked. I nodded and he accepted his tip, bowing politely, and we stepped out into the cold night.

We walked to the gate of Laura's flat near the Museum Gardens and said goodnight. Then she walked to her front door without looking back.

As I drove back to Kirkby Steepleton I felt too much had been left unsaid. It was a sad end to an exhilarating day. Laura's life appeared to have clearly defined borders; mine simply had frayed edges. Above me a sickle moon, alone in the vast ebony sky, looked down over the plain of York like a silent sentinel. There was peace on the land but no longer between Laura and myself.

Chapter Thirteen

Nicholas Parsons and the Rhubarb Triangle

County Hall requested a copy of our scheme of work for mathematics in support of their proposal for a 'common curriculum' for schools in North Yorkshire.
                              Extract from the Ragley School Logbook:
                                        Wednesday, 5 March 1980

'He can't possibly like rhubarb!' said Vera emphatically.

'But ah read it in our Ronnie's *News of the World*, Miss Evans,' insisted Ruby: ''e definitely likes rhubarb.'

'Are you quite sure?' asked Vera, taking off her coat. She stared thoughtfully out of the staff-room window. 'It never occurred to me he would like such a thing. He's not really the type,' said Vera.

'Fifteen, sixteen . . . Who likes rhubarb? . . . seventeen, eighteen,' asked Jo as she turned the handle of the Roneo duplicator.

''Im on t'telly what gives away that posh furniture,'

said Ruby, as she absent-mindedly polished the handle of the staff-room door.

'You may be right, Ruby. I remember reading something like that in the *Radio Times*,' continued Jo, while sniffing the Roneo spirit appreciatively.

'Mind you, I've got a wonderful recipe,' mused Vera to herself.

'What's all this about rhubarb?' asked Sally, rummaging through the *Art and Craft* magazines on the coffee table until she found a pull-out poster on 'How to make clay coil-pots'.

Anne and I were huddled next to the gas fire and we were making a final check of the summary of our scheme of work for mathematics. Intrigued, we looked up from the section on 'special needs provision'.

'I wonder if Prudence at the General Stores has some rhubarb in stock,' said Vera, thinking out loud. 'I'd need to make it today and take it with me tomorrow morning.'

'Make what?' asked Anne.

'Take it where?' asked Sally.

Vera, clearly preoccupied, walked from the staff-room, down the little corridor past the staff toilets and opened the door to the school office. Then she paused and called over her shoulder, 'Rhubarb crumble, of course.'

It was Wednesday lunchtime, 5 March, and Vera was obviously in a world of her own. The snow and ice had gone but now heavy rain lashed against the window and dark grey clouds scudded across the bleak sky towards the distant line of the Hambleton hills. Anne turned up the gas fire again and shivered as the windows shook in their Victorian casements. 'That so-called "common curriculum" will be here one day,' she muttered as she scribbled notes next to the section on 'Early Numbers'.

I picked up my copy of *The Times* from the staff-room coffee table and scanned the front page. There was a large photograph of Peter Walker, the Minister for Agriculture, being presented with a fluffy white lamb by an irate French farmer following talk of a 'lamb war' between England and France. It was clear from their expressions that the *entente* was not so *cordiale*. Alongside was a photograph of Prince Charles, nattily attired in riding breeches, in preparation for an amateur race at Cheltenham on Saturday. He was going to ride a horse called Sea Swell and the odds were ten to one. I was surprised that Vera, as a fervent royalist, hadn't commented on it but it was clear her mind was elsewhere.

Meanwhile, Anne was flicking through the local paper, the *Easington Herald & Pioneer*. 'Look at this, everybody,' said Anne, pointing to an advertisement that had been circled in red ink. It read: 'Meet Nicholas Parsons in the Cavendish Furniture Store in York on Thursday, 6 March, at 11.00 a.m.'

'Now we know why Vera is so agitated,' said Sally.

'It's Nicholas Parsons,' I said, 'the handsome and debonair *Sale of the Century* man.'

'Vera's perfect English gentleman,' said Jo with a grin, looking up from her duplicating.

'And she's going to make him a rhubarb crumble,' added Anne with a chuckle.

We all laughed and I wondered what the television star would have made of the impact he had created in Ragley School.

I walked through to the office, where Vera was pacing up and down the carpet and casting anxious looks out of the window. 'Of all the days for Joseph to use the car!' she exclaimed. Her brother had dropped her off at school that morning and then set off to attend an ecclesiastical meeting in York. He had looked so preoccupied that it wouldn't have surprised me if he had forgotten all about his sister. Suddenly the telephone on my desk rang out with shrill urgency.

'Vera, it's Joyce Davenport for you,' I said, handing over the receiver. Joyce was the local doctor's wife and the vice-president of the Women's Institute. She was also one of Vera's most loyal and trusted friends.

'Vera, is that you?' she said.

'Yes, Joyce,' said Vera. 'It's unusual for you to ring me at school.'

'I simply had to tell you straight away, Vera,' said Joyce, sounding very agitated. 'It's that dreadful woman Deirdre Coe. You know how she always tries to grab the limelight.'

'What's she up to now?' asked Vera.

'Well, she's only invited that irritating little entertainer-chappie from Easington, Troy Phoenix, to run her stall at tomorrow night's bring-and-buy sale. She's determined to make more on her stall than anybody else . . . and especially you, Vera.'

'Oh dear,' said Vera. 'Well, I appreciate you letting

me know. I must go now, Joyce. Goodbye and thank you.' She knew that, as president of the Ragley and Morton Women's Institute, it was very important to set an example. Ever since Vera had demoted Deirdre Coe to the role of cupboard secretary she had been a thorn in her side.

I glanced at my watch. It was twenty past twelve, almost an hour before afternoon school restarted. 'Come on, Vera, I'll take you home and we can call into the General Stores on the way.'

'Oh, thank you, Mr Sheffield – that's very kind.' Vera collected her coat, scarf and handbag and we drove out of school into the High Street.

Half a mile away, in Stan Coe's kitchen, his sister Deirdre was on the telephone and putting the final touches to her plans.

'Troy, make sure y'wear y'posh clothes like y'did when y'introduced t'Ragley talent contest. Y'looked a proper star in them sparkly flares,' said Deirdre, while chewing greedily on a gammon, chutney and pickle sandwich.

'Leave it t'me, Deirdre. Ah'll knock 'em dead,' replied the confident Troy.

Deirdre replaced the receiver and wiped the dribbles of chutney from her chin with the frayed sleeve of her cardigan. 'OK, Miss la-de-dah Evans,' she said out loud, 'let's see who's top dog now.'

Deirdre was absolutely confident that by inviting Troy Phoenix, the Easington entertainer, to come along to the annual bring-and-buy sale, she would show the rest of the ladies just who was the real influential force in the Ragley and Morton Women's Institute.

Troy, known locally as Norman Barraclough, made a living selling fresh fish from his little white van. It had to be said that, although Troy was an entertaining local celebrity, it was wise not to stand too close as the strong smell of Whitby cod permeated every pore of his diminutive, fishmonger's frame.

In the General Stores & Newsagent, Prudence Golightly was always pleased to see Vera. 'Good afternoon, Mr Sheffield, and my dear friend, Vera. How are you today?'

'Hello, Prudence. Fine, thank you,' said Vera and then, as an afterthought, she glanced up at the teddy bear on the shelf behind Prudence, 'and, er . . . good afternoon, Jeremy.'

Prudence beamed. 'And what can I do for you today, Vera? You seem a little rushed.'

'I need some rhubarb, Prudence, for a special crumble. It would need to be your best-quality rhubarb.'

Prudence looked thoughtful. 'I'm sorry, Vera,' she said, 'I've only got rhubarb in tins – that is, until Maurice delivers some more. He gets it delivered every week from his brother in Leeds, you know.'

'Maurice?' said Vera.

'Yes, Maurice Tupham just across the street,' said Prudence, pointing. 'It's the blue door.'

'Shall I go across to ask him?' I said.

'Say I sent you, Mr Sheffield,' said Prudence.

'I'd better come with you,' said Vera, 'and thank you, Prudence. Perhaps you could put a tin on one side for me just in case.'

Maurice Tupham was a quiet, retired man in his sixties who kept himself to himself. He had few visitors and, though he doffed his flat cap to Vera when he left church each Sunday morning, he had never spoken to her. However, his passion in life was rhubarb and, when Vera asked him if he had any, it was as if we had said, 'Open sesame!' Seconds later we had been ushered into his Aladdin's cave – except, on this occasion, the treasure was rhubarb. He had a fresh batch in his kitchen and held up a handful of the tall slim bright-red stalks. He sniffed the air appreciatively like a connoisseur and smiled.

'Beautiful, aren't they?' he said lovingly. 'Me an' m'brother were rhubarb-growing champions in t'rhubarb triangle,' he added without a hint of modesty.

I had heard of the Bermuda Triangle but not this one. 'The rhubarb triangle?'

'That's reight, Mr Sheffield. All that land bordered by Wakefield, Leeds and Bradford is jus' perfect f'growing rhubarb. Up to abart fifteen year back, there were two 'undred rhubarb-growers like me an' our kid. We used t'load it every day on t'Rhubarb Express to Covent Garden. Then after 1962 it went by road.'

It was clear that Maurice was an encyclopaedia of rhubarb facts and we weren't going to be allowed to leave until he had shared some of his knowledge. He knew he had a captive audience.

'We grew t'plants for two years, Miss Evans, an' then

put 'em in forcing sheds,' said Maurice, pointing to a faded black-and-white photograph on the wall. The youthful Maurice was standing with a similar burly, short man, who was clearly his brother, in front of a long, low windowless shed, about two hundred feet long and ten feet high. 'It were reight dark an' warm in there. We even picked by t'light of a shaded lantern an' t'rhubarb grew about an inch every day.' He nodded in satisfaction. 'Same routine f'generations . . . ever since t'Industrial Revolution.'

Maurice handed over a large bag of rhubarb stalks. 'No charge, Miss Evans,' he said, 'an' if y'ever fancy a trip t'annual Festival of Rhubarb y'can be my guest.'

'Thank you so much,' said Vera. 'You've been very kind and I'll keep it in mind.'

As we drove towards Morton village I glanced across at Vera and there was a gleam in her eyes. 'I think you made a hit with Maurice,' I said playfully, but she did not seem to hear. The rhubarb triangle seemed far away now and her mind was filled with thoughts of meeting her television heart-throb.

On Thursday morning the harsh cawing of the rooks from the high branches of the distant elm trees woke me from a pleasant dream. I was on a tropical beach, paddling in the warm sea and walking hand in hand with someone who appeared to be Beth . . . except, every time I glanced across at her, she became Laura. I rubbed the sleep from my eyes, turned on the Bush radio perched on my bedside table and padded across the worn wooden floor of my bedroom. When I drew the curtains, cold, grey light flooded in through the leaded panes.

'Hello again. Rise and shine, all you lazybones. You're listening to Ray Moore on wonderful BBC Radio 2. It's seven thirty-five on Thursday, 6 March, with another two and a half hours of popular music before our national treasure, Jimmy Young, sorts out our great nation and asks the questions "Will daytime television be a dream or a nightmare?" and "Can Robin Cousins become the next world figure-skating champion?" In the meantime Marti Webb tells us to "Take That Look Off Your Face" . . .'

Four miles away on the Morton Road, the sound of rooks was lost amid the clatter of milk bottles. Ernie Morgetroyd's milk float had pulled up outside the vicarage. His nineteen-year-old son, Handsome Rodney, his golden locks hidden under a red-and-white York City bobble hat, crunched up the driveway and delivered two pints of gold-top full-cream milk along with a half-pint carton of single cream and a half-dozen fresh farm eggs.

Rodney extended a finger and thumb and deftly picked up the two spotlessly clean and recently washed empty milk bottles from the vicarage steps. Then he set off back down the driveway, whistling Rod Stewart's 'Do You Think I'm Sexy?'. Meanwhile Ernie Morgetroyd hoped the battery on his little electric milk float would last until he had completed his round. Apart from that and Handsome Rodney's never-ending girlfriend problems, life was uncomplicated for the milkmen of Morton.

Vera looked through the open casement window of the

vicarage window and smiled. She turned up her radio a fraction and walked to the front door.

'Good morning. It's seven thirty-five on Thursday, 6 March, and this is BBC Radio 4 wishing you a pleasant morning. From Handel and Dussek we now continue with the Schumann Cello Concerto . . .'

At number 7, School View, life was not quite so serene. Ruby's daughter, Sharon Smith, turned up the radio and rummaged in the wash basket for her overalls.

'Hello, everybody. It's the Hairy Monster, Dave Lee Travis, on your very own BBC Radio 1 saying get into gear and pin y'ears back 'cause its twenty-five to eight on Thursday, 6 March, and 'ere we go with the gorgeous Blondie at number 3 with, wait for it . . . "Atomic".'

When I walked into the staff-room before the start of the school day, Anne and Jo were checking the new delivery of sugar paper, while Sally was deep in thought. She opened her teacher's copy of *Apusskidu*, her new song-book for her 'school orchestra', turned to number 27, 'The Wombling Song', and began to convert Mike Batt's music into a few simple guitar chords for her beginners' group.

Suddenly Ruby was standing in the open doorway, leaning on her mop. 'I 'eard from Margery Ackroyd that Miss Evans was given some rhubarb by Maurice Tupham in the 'Igh Street,' she said.

Sally looked up from her songbook. 'So Vera got her high-quality rhubarb after all,' she said.

'Yes, and she went home to make the crumble,' I said,

while picking at the loose threads on the leather patches on the sleeves of my sports jacket.

'For Nicholas Parsons,' said Anne.

'The man of her dreams,' giggled Jo.

''E's a bit on t'skinny side f'me,' said Ruby. 'Mind you, ah'll be s'pportin' Miss Evans tonight an' ah gave 'er a bag o' my chocolate t'sell.'

Ruby would have done anything for Vera and this was a generous gesture. With great ceremony, she had presented to Vera a large bag of chocolate bars known as Rowntree's 'waste' and Vera had accepted it with great dignity.

Ruby's daughter Sharon was currently working in the 'waste' department at Rowntree's factory in York, a sort of orphanage for misshapen bars of chocolate Lion Bars and broken Kit Kats. The pristine packaging afforded to their perfectly shaped companions was replaced by a large crumpled paper bag into which a dozen un-wrapped chocolate bars were thrown unceremoniously. Every Friday night Sharon delivered two or three bags to her mother and each week Ruby's weight increased and it was a trade-off she accepted without a shred of guilt. 'Ah work 'ard,' said Ruby as she sat down at the end of each working day. 'Ah deserve me little treat.'

Vera was full of anticipation as she drove her car into York. It was the Year of the Viking and the Jorvik excavation had entered its final year in Coppergate, so Vera negotiated the traffic surrounding the building works and parked in Micklegate. She had completed her rhubarb crumble and it was packed safely in her shopping basket as she strode purposefully into the Cavendish Furniture Store.

Nicholas Parsons was sitting behind an ornate, hand-carved desk and Vera stopped in her tracks with an admiring gaze. He was even more handsome in real life than he was on the television. The floppy silk handkerchief that hung casually from the top pocket of his navy-blue jacket exactly matched the yellow and blue-checked cravat round his neck. Sitting alongside was a busy, slightly agitated, bald-headed little man in an ill-fitting pin-striped suit. The badge on his lapel read 'Cyril Backhouse, General Manager'.

'Good morning, madam,' said Cyril. 'How can we be of assistance?'

Vera had studied the catalogue very carefully. 'I'd like to purchase the Grosvenor wall unit with brass handles at £69.95,' said Vera, pointing to the photograph in the catalogue.

'My pleasure, madam,' said Cyril, 'and if you would like a signed photograph of Mr Parsons I'm sure he will oblige.'

'Well, actually, Mr, er . . . Backhouse,' said Vera, putting on her steel-framed spectacles and staring at the little man's badge, 'I've got something for Mr Parsons.'

Nicholas Parsons stood up, took Vera's hand and bowed slightly. 'Good morning,' he said with a disarming smile. 'I'm Nicholas.'

Vera's cheeks reddened but she remained composed. 'And I'm Miss Evans, er . . . well, actually, Miss Vera Evans.'

'It's a pleasure to meet you, Vera,' said Nicholas. 'But I'm intrigued. What have you brought for me?'

Vera put the basket on the table and lifted the edge of the embroidered tea towel. 'If I may, Mr Parsons, I should like to present you with this rhubarb crumble on behalf of the Ragley and Morton Women's Institute.'

Nicholas Parsons looked up in surprise. 'My very dear lady, it is the most wonderful gift. I'm a great fan of rhubarb.'

'Actually, I heard you were a connoisseur,' said Vera.

Nicholas's eyes creased as he gave her a warm smile. 'It's a pleasure to meet such a discerning and, may I say, elegant lady.'

In that moment, Vera felt her life was complete. 'You may keep the basket,' said Vera. 'I have many of them at the vicarage.'

'The vicarage?' said Nicholas.

'Yes. I live there with my brother. He's the vicar of Ragley and Morton,' explained Vera.

'I will make sure it is returned forthwith,' said Nicholas, 'and I shall enjoy this for my lunch.'

Back at Ragley School my class were completing a punctuation exercise in their English books. I watched, intrigued, as Tony Ackroyd carefully prised open the metal staples that held together his English exercise book and then removed the centre pages. He had worked out that if he did this once each week for the next four weeks he would fill his book rapidly and it would appear he was working quicker than anyone else. Even though I made him replace the pages and told him it was a silly thing to do, I had to admire his lateral thinking.

At lunchtime Vera returned, full of excitement, and a captivated audience listened to every word of her meeting with the handsome television personality. It was only when Vera received another call from Joyce Davenport, telling her about the grandiose scale of Deirdre Coe's stall that her spirits were dampened. It was clear Vera would have her work cut out and we all agreed to turn up and support her.

By seven o'clock the village hall was full for one of the most popular events of the year. However, Troy Phoenix was standing on a chair next to Deirdre's stall and a small crowd was gathering.

'C'mon, ladies, we've got a job lot o' fancy tin openers an' some 'igh-quality tea towels 'ere. First come, first served,' he shouted.

Ruby's daughters Sharon and Natasha were first in the queue in spite of Ruby's protests, while only a trickle of customers seemed interested in the items on Vera's stall. Deirdre Coe leered at Vera in delight. 'Judgement Day, as my Stanley says,' she said and began to count her takings.

Suddenly, in walked the Revd Joseph Evans with a huge smile on his face. Behind him was Nicholas Parsons, the perfect English gentleman and the picture of sartorial elegance. His cuff-links sparkled, his shoes shone and there were knife-edge creases in his three-piece navy-blue suit, fashioned at a leading gentleman's outfitter in

London. A stunned silence descended as, with debonair grace, he walked up to Vera's stall, bowed slightly and kissed her hand.

'Mr Parsons!' exclaimed Vera.

'Please, it's Nicholas,' he said as he went round the stall and stood beside her.

'But . . . how . . . ?'

'Your brother told me of the event when I returned your dish and basket to the vicarage,' said Nicholas, 'and I asked him to bring me here so I could thank you in person.'

Vera had just about gathered her senses. 'There was no need, Mr . . . , er, Nicholas . . . but it really is most kind of you.'

Nicholas Parsons suddenly became aware of the huge number of ladies surrounding Vera's stall. 'Now, perhaps you will allow me to assist you in the sale of these items?'

'But of course, Nicholas, I should be most grateful,' said Vera.

He surveyed the collection of artefacts and transformed instantly into his *Sale of the Century* persona.

'May I?' he asked, picking up one of the vases on the stall and peeling off the fifty-pence sticker. 'Now, who will give me five pounds for this elegant vase?'

'I will,' said Petula Dudley-Palmer, almost swooning at his feet.

'And how much for this pair of candlesticks?' continued Nicholas. 'How about six pounds the pair?

'Done,' shouted an enthusiastic Joyce Davenport.

Deirdre Coe's face went red, then purple, and finally settled on a shade of green to match Vera's presidential sash. Troy Phoenix had left Deirdre's side, deserted his post and was queuing up for an autograph.

Minutes later, every item had been sold and Vera had raised the highest total ever recorded by a single stall in the whole distinguished history of the Ragley and Morton Women's Institute.

'I'm afraid time is pressing, Vera,' said Nicholas, looking at his wristwatch.

'You've been wonderful, Nicholas. Thank you so much,' said Vera.

On his way out, Nicholas stopped to talk to Old Tommy Piercy, who was sitting down next to Mrs Patterson-Smythe's stall after purchasing a large jar of orange, apple and rhubarb chutney.

'So where were you born?' asked Tommy.

'I was born in Grantham in Lincolnshire,' said Nicholas.

'The same as Margaret Thatcher,' said Vera proudly.

'So yurra southerner, then,' said Old Tommy disdainfully.

'Well, I'm not a Yorkshireman if that's what you mean,' said Nicholas.

'Pity,' said Old Tommy gruffly.

'You're obviously proud of Yorkshire,' said Nicholas engagingly.

'Yorkshire's a proper kingdom,' said Old Tommy defiantly. 'We've got fishing on t'east coast, plenty o' coal, millstone grit f'building an' acres o' arable 'n' pasture land f'vegetables 'n' corn. We've got sheep 'n' cattle so we'll not go 'ungry. Y'can keep y'southerners f'me. We're 'appy enough up 'ere.'

'I couldn't agree more,' said Nicholas, 'and it's been a pleasure talking to you.'

'Mebbe y'not so bad after all,' said Old Tommy.

'And believe me, Nicholas, that's a real compliment from Mr Piercy,' said Vera as they walked towards the door.

'I've so enjoyed my visit, Vera, and I hope we meet again.'

Vera's cheeks flushed and she smiled as they walked out together towards the High Street.

Joseph and quick thinking were not natural allies. However, on this occasion, before leaving the vicarage, he had picked up Vera's camera. As he had no idea how to use it, he thrust it into Joyce Davenport's hands. 'Excuse me, Joyce . . . but could you take a photograph for me?'

Joyce snapped the happy couple standing by the old wooden gate that led to the front door of the village hall. Nicholas had his arm round Vera's slim waist while Vera looked up at a profile she knew so well. It was a photograph she was destined to keep in the years to come in a small wooden frame and placed discreetly at the bottom of her handkerchief drawer.

That evening, Vera sat down in the vicarage and reflected on her perfect day. Then she opened the sloping lid of the old writing bureau, selected a sheet of vicarage-headed notepaper and wrote a letter of thanks to be hand-delivered. As an afterthought, she smiled and wrote on the crisp white envelope in her beautiful cursive script, *Mr Maurice Tupham, The Rhubarb Triangle.*

Chapter Fourteen

The Pontefract Strippers

Two visitors from West Yorkshire came to school today and gave the staff an impromptu talk on 'The Production of Liquorice'.

Extract from the Ragley School Logbook:
Friday, 28 March 1980

As I drove to school on the last Friday in March the rooks cawed in the elm-tops, announcing the end of winter. An imperceptible change had come at last with the morning sunshine. The cuckoo, the messenger of spring, had arrived along with new grass and primroses. The days of log fires and mulled wine were finally over.

When I walked into school, to my surprise Shirley the cook was standing in the entrance hall alongside two ladies who looked to be in their sixties. One was a very tall, big-boned lady and the other was short and plump. They both wore tightly knotted headscarves and thick overcoats buttoned up to the neck. It was a day I would come to remember with great affection – the day I met the two sisters Edie and Florence Ramsden.

'Good morning, Mr Sheffield,' said Shirley. 'This is my aunty Edie and my aunty Flo. They've come up from West Yorkshire to stay with me for the weekend and I hoped you wouldn't mind them looking round my kitchen.'

The short cheerful Florence gave me a hesitant smile, while the tall uncompromising Edie shot me a look that would have crushed many a man.

'Good morning, Shirley. Good morning, ladies,' I said.

'That is, if it's no trouble . . .' began Florence hesitantly.

Edie gave her sister a withering look, stepped forward and took my hand with a grip like a wrestler's. Her eyes stared defiantly into mine. It was clear Edie was no lover of authority. 'We're from Pontefract,' she said. Edie obviously did not waste words and it appeared the subtle nuances of the English language had passed her by. The handshake crushed my fingers and I winced and flexed them when she let go.

Shirley saw my discomfort. 'Sorry, Mr Sheffield,' said Shirley. 'My aunty Edie used to be a thumper.'

'She doesn't know 'er own strength,' added Florence, looking up in awe at her big sister.

'A thumper?' I asked, while I readjusted my knuckles. 'What's a thumper?'

'It were t'name of 'er job, Mr Sheffield,' explained Florence. 'That is, until she were replaced by a machine.

Our Edie used t'stamp thirty thousand liquorice Pontefract cakes a day by 'and. She were t'best thumper i' Pontefract.'

Looking at Edie's massive fists, I could well believe it.

'Oh, well, I'm very pleased to meet you,' I said. 'We should be lost without Shirley. She works wonders in her kitchen.'

Shirley's cheeks went pink, Florence smiled warmly and Edie's glare softened from sub-zero to marginally above freezing point.

'You're very kind, Mr Sheffield,' said Shirley. 'So, is it all right for my aunties to spend a bit of time with me today?'

'Of course, Shirley, and perhaps you would all like a cup of coffee in the staff-room? It's more comfortable there.'

'Thank you, Mr Sheffield,' said Shirley.

Edie marched off with Shirley to the staff-room but Florence hung back and began to undo her headscarf.

'Don't mind our Edie, Mr Sheffield,' said Florence quietly. 'She's never tekken t'men, 'specially bosses.' And with a sly wink she scurried off to follow her sister and her favourite niece.

In the entrance hall Ruby was putting away a box of paper towels. Hazel was standing next to her. 'Mummy,' she said, looking thoughtfully up at her mother, 'why 'ave y'got grey 'airs?'

Quick as a flash Ruby said, 'Cos every time y'do summat wrong ah get a grey 'air.' Then she smiled at me in a self-congratulatory way.

Hazel turned to walk away and then looked over her shoulder. 'So 'ow come Grandma's 'air is *all* grey?'

It was morning playtime before I recalled Shirley's aunties. 'Two old women in t'playground, Mr Sheffield,' announced Jodie Cuthbertson.

Through my classroom window I saw them walking out to join the children in the playground. They were carrying a long length of rope. On entering the staff-room I passed Sally in the doorway. She had grabbed her coffee quickly and was going out to do her playground duty.

Meanwhile, Vera's face was wreathed in smiles. With the exception of Margaret Thatcher, Vera's favourite woman was the Queen and, in her eyes, the royal family could do no wrong. To emphasize the point she picked up her *Daily Telegraph* and studied the photograph of Prince Andrew on the front page. 'He ran nine miles in ninety minutes across Dartmoor and waded through freezing water,' announced Vera triumphantly.

'Who did?' asked Jo, looking up from checking her box of coloured netball bibs. The school team were playing Morton School during our afternoon games session on the netball court painted on our tarmac playground.

The door opened and Joseph walked in from his weekly Religious Education lesson and sat down disconsolately. Nobody dared ask how he had got on with Heathcliffe Earnshaw and the rest of Jo's class. He picked up his mug of coffee and settled down to listen to Vera, who was now in full flow.

'He is strong and fit and will make an exceptional naval

officer,' recited Vera. She peered through her steel-framed spectacles at the tiny text below the photograph of the twenty-year-old Prince Andrew being presented with the award of the Green Beret from the Royal Marines.

'Who is?' asked Joseph, reaching for the biscuit tin and selecting a custard cream.

'All he needs now is a nice young woman, someone quiet and genteel, to keep him on the straight and narrow,' said Vera wistfully.

'Who does?' mumbled Joseph through a mouthful of biscuit crumbs.

'Don't speak with your mouth full, Joseph,' said Vera, looking irritated at the interruption.

Joseph swallowed quickly. 'I just wondered if it was one of my parishioners.'

'No, Joseph. Pay attention,' said Vera, rather sharply. 'I'm talking about our Queen's second son.'

'Oh, that one,' said Joseph without enthusiasm.

Suddenly we heard cheering in the playground and we all looked out of the window to see an unlikely sight. Shirley's aunties, Edie and Florence, were furiously winding the long rope and a line of red-faced children were skipping in and out and obviously loving the game.

'Who are they?' asked Joseph.

'They're relations of Shirley,' I explained. 'Just visiting for today.'

'Yes, nice people,' said Vera. 'The tall one's a bit brusque but they're both very pleasant. I wonder if they would like a cup of coffee?'

'I'll take it out to them,' I said.

When I walked out Sally gave me a wave and pointed to the skipping group.

'You go in to get warm,' I said to her. 'I'll finish your duty.'

As I walked closer to Edie and Florence I could hear their voices joined in a skipping chant.

> *'Little fat doctor*
> *How's your wife?*
> *Very well thank you*
> *That's all right*
> *Eat a bit o' fish*
> *An' a stick o' liquorice*
> *O-U-T spells OUT!'*

They paused, passed the ends of the skipping rope to Jodie Cuthbertson and Katy Ollerenshaw and took the welcome hot drinks from me.

'Teks us back,' said Florence with a smile.

'It does that,' added Edie, sipping her coffee.

A group of children had gathered round. 'Ah love sticks o' lick-rish,' said Heathcliffe both politely and hopefully.

'It's fascinating stuff,' said Florence, ruffling his hair.

When Heathcliffe realized no free samples were forthcoming he ran off.

'If you would like to call into the staff-room at lunchtime you could tell us about it,' I said.

Edie looked at me suspiciously. Florence tugged at her sleeve. 'That's reight kind, Mr Sheffield. We'd luv to, wouldn't we, Edie?'

*   *   *

At half past twelve a blue minibus, purchased by the Morton Church of England Primary School PTA, pulled up outside school and a group of girls and parents tumbled out. From the front passenger seat stepped the headmistress, Miss Tripps. Edith Tripps was now in her sixty-fifth year and was about to retire after over thirty years' service. Twice a year she visited Ragley School with her netball team and her rounders team. It was always a happy event and her good friend Vera had stayed on after her morning's work to meet her. Both were members of the Ragley and Morton Women's Institute.

'Hello, Vera,' said Miss Tripps with a warm smile.

'Good to see you, Edith,' said Vera. 'Come on into the staff-room. We've got some interesting visitors today.'

When they walked in, Edie and Florence were chatting happily with Anne, Jo and Sally.

'Edith,' said Vera, 'these are Shirley's relations from West Yorkshire and they used to work in a liquorice factory there.'

'Oh, I absolutely love liquorice,' said Miss Tripps enthusiastically, 'but it's ages since I've had any.'

'Prudence sells it at the General Stores in the High Street,' said Vera.

'I must call in and buy some,' said Miss Tripps.

Edie looked in appreciation at a fellow lover of liquorice and Florence beamed from ear to ear. Vera poured Miss Tripps a cup of tea and I stood up to give her my seat and perched on the arm of Anne's chair.

'By the way, Vera,' said Miss Tripps, 'thank you for

sending me the information about coal and coke stocks for the school boiler. Sadly, we seem to be using more than any other school in the area and I don't know why,' she said.

'Yes, it is strange, Edith,' said Vera, passing her a cup of tea.

'It's just that our supply seems to go down so quickly but, even so, the school is still cold,' explained Miss Tripps. 'I've asked Mr Sharp the caretaker to look into it.' She sipped her tea and then looked at Edie and Florence. 'So what exactly did you do in the liquorice factory?'

There was a twinkle in Florence's eyes as she recalled happy memories of times gone by. 'Well, when ah started ah were a jolloper.'

'A jolloper?' said Miss Tripps in surprise.

'Aye, that's reight. Ah brushed gum on to cream an' liquorice t'make 'em stick together. It were called jolloping.'

'Oh, yes,' said Miss Tripps.

'An' then ah were a stalker.'

'A stalker?' I asked.

'That's reight,' said Florence. 'Ah used t'stick stalks into coconut mushrooms.'

'Oooh, they're my favourite,' said Jo.

'Mebbe so, but it were boring,' added Edie with a frown.

'"Cept we 'ad some fun, 'specially when it were y'birthday, didn't we, Edie?'

'What happened then?' asked Sally.

'Y'got thrown in t'starch bin an' y'came out looking

like a snowman,' said Edie. 'Mind you, nobody ever threw me in,' she added darkly.

'An' when we were making jelly babies, t'starch even got inside y'knickers,' said Florence with a laugh. Even Edie's steely gaze softened with reminiscences and we all laughed at the thought. 'Friday night were wages night,' continued Florence, 'an' then we'd rush t'Woolworth's t'buy silk stockings for a shilling.'

'We earned thirty-two shillings a week in 1950, an' a man earned twice as much . . . jus' 'cause 'e were a man,' muttered Edie.

'But it were a tough place t'work, weren't it, Edie?'

'That's reight,' agreed Edie. 'Young Betty Arkwright 'ad three fingers chopped off on t'machine that cut all-sorts into squares.'

Everyone stared in horror.

'But there were some good times,' said Edie, breaking the spell.

''Specially one Christmas,' continued Florence. 'We 'ad a Christmas fancy-dress party an' our Edie made me a South Sea Island costume out o' liquorice. Ah won first prize.'

We all laughed.

'And what happened then?' asked Sally, eager to know more.

'Well, ah s'ppose best time of all was when me an' Edie worked together,' said Florence wistfully. She looked up at Edie, who nodded slowly.

'And what job was that?' asked Anne.

'Well . . . we were both strippers,' announced Florence.

'Strippers?' exclaimed everyone in unison.

'That's reight, we were strippers,' Edie joined in. 'We 'ad a big scraper an' we used t'strip all t'liquorice off every board that were in t'stores. It were 'ard graft . . . but me an' Flo were t'best strippers in Pontefract.'

Everyone stared in wonderment at these two York-shirewomen, one happy with the lot she had been given in life and the other apparently full of resentment for the injustices she had been forced to endure.

'It's allus been jus' two of us,' said Edie.

'Neither of us ever married but ah 'ad a boyfriend once,' said Florence. "E were a sort of a cross between Sacha Distel an' Val Doonican.'

'Was he French, then?' asked Miss Tripps.

'No, 'e were from Cleethorpes, but 'e 'ad sinus trouble an' 'e talked funny,' said Florence, 'and 'e used t'wear these lovely 'and-knitted cardigans.'

Edie's gaze softened slightly and she looked fondly at her little sister. 'Y'better off without 'im,' she said firmly.

'Y'probably right,' said Florence.

At one o'clock it was time to get ready for afternoon school and the netball match. Parents were gathering in the playground and Ruby had set up the netball posts.

'We're jus' going t'walk down the 'Igh Street an' 'ave a look at y'local shops before t'netball match,' said Edie. 'C'mon, Flo, get y'coat on.' They buttoned up their heavy coats to the neck, checked the knots on their headscarves and walked out of school.

Joe Sharp, the Morton caretaker, had parked the

minibus under the row of horse-chestnut trees at the front of the school. He threw his cigarette on the ground and crushed it with the heel of his boot. Next to him, Deirdre Coe was looking distinctly furtive. 'So what's it t'be, Deirdre?' muttered Joe.

'Same as usual,' said Deirdre. 'A couple o' bags'll do, but none o' them big lumps like las' time.'

'OK, Deirdre,' said Joe. 'Cash in advance?'

'On delivery, Joe, same as usual,' said Deirdre. 'Jus' slip 'em round tonight.' Then she scuttled away towards her Land-Rover parked outside The Royal Oak.

Edie had stopped on the other side of the minibus, pretending to look in her bag, while Florence walked on. Her hearing was uncanny and she recognized wrongdoing when she stumbled across it. Both Deirdre and Joe had ignored the two strangers.

Edie zipped up her bag and strode on, a glint in her steely eyes.

At half past one Sally took her class and Jo's class into the hall for singing practice, while, out on the playground, Jo blew her whistle for the start of the netball match. I stood with the children in my class cheering them on. Edie and Florence had returned from the village and went to stand alongside Miss Tripps.

'Excuse me, Miss Tripps,' said Edie, pointing towards the minibus, 'but is that man your caretaker?'

'Yes. That's Mr Sharp,' said Miss Tripps.

'An' if y'don't mind me asking, 'ow long 'as 'e worked for you?'

'Since January,' said Miss Tripps. 'Why do you ask?'

'Nothing special,' said Edie, returning her gaze to the netball match. Then she walked over to Vera. 'Excuse me, Miss Evans, but 'ow long as coal been disappearing from Miss Tripps's school?'

'She first mentioned it at the start of this term, I think,' said Vera.

'That's int'resting,' said Edie. 'Ah'll be back in a minute,' and she set off down the school drive.

Joe Sharp was enjoying a quiet cigarette and looking forward to a good meal and a few pints of Tetley's bitter as a result of his ill-gotten gains. Suddenly a long shadow was cast on the grassy bank in front of him and he looked up. The fiercesome bulk of Edie came as a surprise.

'Mr Sharp?' said Edie, stepping forward with an outstretched right hand.

It was an automatic reaction. He shook hands and immediately regretted it. With the strength of a woman who had stamped a million Pontefract cakes, Edie began to crush his hand. Joe looked up, alarmed and in pain.

'What y'doing?' he yelled.

Edie gradually increased her grip and Joe's knuckles crunched.

'It's about the coal, Mr Sharp,' said Edie coldly.

'Aaaagh . . . What about it?' screamed Joe.

'Promise me y'll not be stealing any,' said Edie.

'What? . . . Aaagh.'

'Ah sed promise,' said Edie, squeezing harder.

Joe fell to his knees. 'Ah promise, ah promise.'

Edie let go and tears sprang from Joe's eyes as he

massaged life back into his hand. 'If ah 'ear any coal's gone missin' from school . . . ah'll be back,' said Edie. Then she turned on her heel and walked away.

At the end of the school day Edie and Florence came into the office to say farewell.

'It's been a smashing day,' said Florence. 'Our Shirley says you're a nice man t'work for.'

Edie stood quietly, an ominous presence. She was clearly still weighing me up. 'Y'not bad,' she said bluntly. I took it as a compliment and she stretched out her hand. I took a deep breath and shook it. Thankfully, this time, it was firm but no more.

Anne and I watched them drive off in Shirley's car. 'Lovely ladies,' said Anne.

'Not bad for a pair of strippers,' I said.

Anne gave me a dig in the ribs. 'So what are you doing tonight, Jack?' she asked.

I sat down at my desk and pulled out my notes about our mathematics scheme of work for the local authority. 'I'm going to finish this if it kills me,' I said, unscrewing the top from my fountain pen.

'Oh dear,' said Anne. 'Well, don't stay too late.'

Darkness fell and I worked on. Suddenly, the telephone rang and to my surprise it was Beth. She sounded tired.

'Hello, Jack. I guessed you might still be at school,' she said.

'Beth, good to hear from you. How's it going?'

'Well, like you, I have to complete this scheme for

mathematics and I'm finding it difficult. I wondered if you could have a look at it before I send it off.'

'Of course I will. I'm working on it myself as a matter of fact. When I've finished I'll send you a copy.'

'That's kind, Jack. This so-called "common curriculum" could become a reality the way things are going.'

'Perhaps, but I can't imagine how the government would organize it.'

There was a pause and I could hear the church bells of St Mary's striking seven o'clock.

'OK, Jack . . . Well, thanks.'

'Beth . . . there's something I'd like to ask you.'

'Yes?'

'Are you alone in the office?'

'Yes. The school's been empty for half an hour.'

'I have to ask . . . is Laura OK?'

'Well, Jack . . . you must know she was very upset.'

'I'm so sorry, Beth. I enjoyed her company but it had never occurred to me that she might have thought I felt more than that.'

'But, Jack, by going out with her you did give her that impression.'

'I just didn't realize . . . I'm sorry, Beth.'

There was a pause and I waited for Beth to respond.

'She seems OK now. She's been approached by Desmond, her manager in London, to do some more training down south. She told me she was going to take him up on it.'

'I see . . . Well, I wish her luck.'

'Jack . . . I have to ask . . . did you care for her?'

258

'She was a good friend, Beth.'

'Laura told me she wondered if you might care for somebody else.'

I couldn't answer. As I sat there I heard the clock ticking in the school bell tower but words failed to come. 'Oh, Beth . . .'

There was a long silence before she finally spoke. 'I'll ring you, Jack.'

And the line went dead.

Further work was impossible so I packed my old leather briefcase and collected my duffel coat and scarf. The ringing of the telephone again made me jump. I thought it might be Beth.

'What on earth are you doing still there?' It was Anne Grainger. 'I rang your home but there was no answer and I guessed you might be still working on that dratted maths scheme.'

'Hi, Anne. I'm just going home now.'

'No, you're not, you're coming to join John and me at the Oak for a bar meal.'

'Oh, thanks. Well . . . er, I'll see you there.'

'Everything all right, Jack? You seem preoccupied.'

'I'm fine. I'll be there in five minutes.'

I put down the telephone and smiled grimly. It had been a long day.

In The Royal Oak Anne and John Grainger were at the bar, ordering food, when I walked in. John Grainger stood there thoughtfully stroking his curly beard with his woodcarver's hands. As usual, tiny flecks of sawdust coated his bushy eyebrows like fresh snow on a window ledge.

'Hello, Jack. You OK?'

'It's been a busy day, John. How about you?'

'I've been adzing a huge table top.' I recalled seeing John using one of these heavy axe-like tools. It had appeared light in his large hands as he chipped out the special rough-hewn effect on the surface of an oak panel. 'The woodcarvers of two hundred years ago used them to shape a ship's timbers,' he said.

'Sounds like a satisfying day, John.'

'Doing *my* job, Jack, every day's a good day. I wouldn't change it for all the tea in China.'

Anne looked at him and smiled and I could see where she found her sense of peace beyond the hectic world of Ragley School.

I sat back and relaxed. As usual, The Royal Oak was filled with characters. At the dominoes table, the local champion fisherman, seventy-four-year-old George Postlethwaite, was deep in conversation with Deke Ramsbottom. The trout-fishing season had begun on 25 March. George was excited because the new legislation allowed fishermen to keep their catches if the trout measured over eleven inches long. He regularly stuck out his left hand to demonstrate the length of his catches, but, as he had lost his right arm fighting for the Desert Rats in the war, it was difficult for him to be precise.

At the piano in the taproom sat Freddie the Finger, the nine-fingered piano player from Thirkby, who was on tour. He had modelled his honky-tonk style on Russ

Conway and his version of the 1959 number 1 hit 'Side Saddle' was always the feature of his grand finale. It was a relaxing evening with John and Anne and when we stepped out into the cold night air they waved goodnight and walked home up the Easington Road.

I drove back to Bilbo Cottage and thought of Beth.

The following Monday morning, when I walked into the school office I was surprised to see a large box of liquorice all-sorts on my desk. Vera looked up at me and smiled, while Sally and Jo just grinned like Cheshire cats.

Anne broke the silence. 'Shirley delivered them for you this morning,' she said. 'I think you ought to read the label.'

I walked over to the desk and looked closely at the card attached to the box with red ribbon. In old-fashioned cursive script it simply read: *To Mr Sheffield with love from a pair of strippers. XX*

I smiled and looked at the two kisses. I guessed they were both from Florence.

Chapter Fifteen

The Day of the Daffodils

The Education welfare officer Roy Davidson and the school social worker Mary O'Neill visited school today to complete the report on Dean Pickles, following his extreme antisocial behaviour. The decision to transfer Dean to Netherbank Special School in the Yorkshire Dales was supported by the County Education Authority, the school governors and his mother, Mrs Pickles.

Extract from the Ragley School Logbook:
Wednesday, 16 April 1980

Pale spring had given way to warm breezes and the chill of winter was forgotten. The earth was new, reborn. It was a day of green shoots and bright-yellow forsythia and, when I arrived at school on this April morning, all seemed well.

From the office window I could see the children wandering up the drive, swapping stories and looking relaxed, their satchels and duffel bags swinging over their shoulders. Suddenly an irate woman in a miniskirt appeared at the school gates. When I saw the small boy alongside her, I knew immediately that this day would be different.

I had never witnessed such anger.

The boy's eyes were filled with torment and he bared his teeth in a ferocious snarl. The long stick he had torn from the hedgerow was a weapon of hate. I could see his mother shouting at him but I couldn't hear the words. She pointed towards the school and tried to grab him by the shoulder but he shook himself free and beat the stick on the ground.

Alongside the school driveway, clumps of daffodils bobbed in the morning sunshine, offering hope of warmer days after the long winter.

Then it happened. I could see it coming but I could do nothing about it. The boy raised his stick and systematically smashed through the stalk of every single flower. When he had finished, he threw the stick high in the air on to the school field. That was when his mother stubbed out her cigarette, grabbed his collar and dragged him into the school entrance hall.

It was destined to be a day I would never forget, a day when a little piece of my hope and optimism was destroyed.

It was the day I met a seven-year-old boy called Dean Pickles.

*   *   *

The first meeting with his mother did not go well.

'Ah can't do nowt wi' 'im,' shouted Stella Pickles. "E's jus' like 'is dad, a reight waste o' space.'

Dean looked round the school office like a hunted animal.

Vera took out a small Cadbury's chocolate egg from her shopping bag. 'Perhaps Dean would like to eat this while I get him a drink of orange juice from the kitchen,' she said in a quiet, calm voice.

Dean looked up in surprise and took the egg. He sat down and ripped off the silver foil eagerly and began to eat the egg.

Vera returned quickly with a plastic tumbler of orange juice and put it next to Dean. 'Don't forget to put the wrapper in the bin, please, Dean,' she said. Dean looked at Vera as if she was from another planet and carefully placed the ball of foil in the waste-paper basket.

'An' don't gobble it all at once!' shouted his mother.

Vera visibly winced at the sound, while Dean ignored her completely.

The previous evening I had received a telephone call from Roy Davidson, our Education welfare officer, to say he would call in to discuss a new pupil. He mentioned a history of significant behavioural disorder and a number of previous exclusions. It sounded serious. I could now see why.

"E's gone from pillar t'post,' said Mrs Pickles. "E can't settle in school. It's been like pass the bleedin' parcel.'

Vera recoiled at the bad language.

'Just calm down, please, Mrs Pickles, and we'll do our

best.' I glanced at Vera. 'And if you could just temper your language we can continue.'

Mrs Pickles flashed me a disdainful glance and began to chew on her fingernails. We learned that she had arrived in the village the previous weekend and had moved in with her mother on the outskirts of Ragley. Her husband, John Pickles, was a long-distance lorry driver and he had decided that a long distance from Stella was exactly what he wanted. A few weeks ago he'd telephoned from Inverness and told her he wasn't coming back. Since then Dean had run wild and his mother's attempts to curb his bad behaviour had failed.

So it was that on this April morning we knew we were about to enrol a boy with a problem.

By morning playtime, Vera had entered the name Dean Pickles in our register of new admissions but we were all unaware of the huge impact he was making in Jo Hunter's classroom as we relaxed in the staff-room at morning playtime.

I had spent twenty pence that morning on my copy of *The Times* and, as usual, after reading her *Daily Telegraph*, Vera had picked it up and scanned the headlines.

'Simply splendid,' Vera announced with enthusiasm. 'Doesn't he look smart?' She pointed to the front-cover photograph of Prince Charles in his white naval officer's uniform adorned with the striking sash of the Order of the Garter. Alongside him stood a smiling Robert Mugabe, Zimbabwe's prime minister-designate, at the independence ceremony in Salisbury. Both men appeared in a jocular mood. 'The last outpost of the British Empire in Africa and the last colony in the continent comes to an end at midnight on 18 April when Zimbabwe becomes independent,' Vera read aloud, 'and Mr Robert Mugabe has called for a new spirit of brotherhood.'

However, Jo had other things on her mind when she glanced down at the same front page. She looked at a photograph of the youthful Seve Ballesteros, who had just won the US Masters Golf Championship at Augusta. 'He is now the holder of both the US and British Open titles,' read Jo, and then held up the newspaper for Sally to see, 'and isn't he simply gorgeous?' Then she sipped her coffee and added, 'Oh, and by the way, Jack, the new boy's a real handful.'

I looked out of the window at a disturbance on the playground. Dean was pushing another child and I stood up to go to help Anne, who was on yard duty. As I was putting on my duffel coat, Sally was staring thoughtfully at Dean Pickles.

'Remember that sixteenth-century missionary, Jack?' she said. 'The one called Francis Xavier.'

I tried to recall the context. 'Ah, yes, I remember now. "Give me the child until he is seven and I will give you the man." . . . Yes, I see what you mean,' I said and hurried outside.

At lunchtime, Roy Davidson called in with Dean's educational records. They made unhappy reading. 'It's probably worse, Jack,' said Roy, 'now that his father has left home.'

*   *   *

So it went on, day by day, until one week later, after school on Wednesday, 16 April, Anne and I sat silently in the staff-room. It had been a long meeting and darkness had fallen. No one had got up to close the curtains. Our thoughts were elsewhere.

The Revd Joseph Evans sat with his head bowed and hands clasped tightly as if in prayer. Roy Davidson, his long, prematurely grey hair hanging over his lined forehead, was bent over his spiral notepad, making careful notes. Mary O'Neill, our visiting social worker, had completed her report and there was silence in the staff-room. I was now faced with the most difficult decision I had ever had to make as a headmaster.

'Well, Jack?' said Roy, looking up from his note-making.

I stared at the office clock. The second hand ticked round as I sought for solutions. Mary passed the neatly typed report to Anne, who scanned it and shook her head in anguish.

'I can't remember Ragley School expelling any child before, Jack,' said Anne. As usual, Anne had put into words what we were all thinking. 'Expulsion is so final,' she added quietly. 'If we send him away we're saying we've failed . . . Ragley School has failed.'

'You haven't failed,' said Mary firmly.

The Revd Joseph Evans had come to the same conclusion. 'We must consider the safety of the other children as well as the welfare of the boy,' he added.

'I really can't see what else we can do,' said Roy. Mary nodded in agreement.

I picked up the detailed report and studied it for one last time. It seemed more than a week since it had all begun. The list of violent acts of behaviour was lengthy – fighting in the playground, kicking a dinner lady, swearing at his teacher, damage to school property – and each day was worse than the one before. The procession of parents at my door complaining about the boy's behaviour had become too long to ignore. Dean Pickles was clearly a threat to the safety of the other pupils of Ragley School.

'If it's any help, Jack,' said Roy, 'I know the perfect place for Dean and my guess is we would get parental consent without any problem.'

'Where's that?' I asked.

'At a special school in the Yorkshire Dales that caters for children with behavioural and emotional difficulties. It's called Netherbank Hall and it's tucked away in the most beautiful countryside.'

'I know it well,' said Mary. 'Dean could have a chance to grow there in a stable community.'

I looked at Anne. 'I have to put the safety of the other pupils first, Anne.'

'I agree,' she said quietly.

I unscrewed the top of my fountain pen, signed on the line next to the word 'Headteacher' and passed it to Joseph. He signed, Mary added the date and Roy stood up and shook my hand.

'I'll ring you tomorrow from the office,' he said.

Mary paused in the doorway as she followed him out and turned back to leave a parting message. 'Don't worry, Jack. Sadly, I've seen this many times and what we're doing is for the best.'

Everyone left until there was just Anne and me checking windows and locking doors. I gave her a lift home and, as we pulled up in the Crescent and said good night, she leaned back in the car and said, 'Do you know what's really sad, Jack? This little boy doesn't even know what love is.'

There is something magnetic about puddles in the playground. Small children, like iron filings, are drawn irresistibly to their allure. Those with imagination were standing alone like castaways on their personal desert island. Others made lolly-stick boats and raced them. Then, of course, there were boys like Heathcliffe Earnshaw who simply took a running jump and landed in the centre, ensuring everyone in a ten-yard radius, particularly girls, was thoroughly soaked.

It was a damp Thursday morning and playtime had returned to normal. Dean Pickles was at home, packing a small rucksack, and his mother had made it clear she was glad to be rid of him. Mary O'Neill had arranged to take Dean and Mrs Pickles the following day to Netherbank Hall, where he would be admitted for full-time residential education at the school. Roy and I had agreed to drive out there on Sunday morning and check he had settled in. I leaned against the school railings and reflected on the difficult decision that had resulted in the little boy's departure.

At lunchtime, Vera made an announcement in the

staff-room. 'I trust you will all be coming to the church social in the vicarage on Saturday afternoon,' she said. It sounded like a command from on high and certainly not one to be refused.

'Of course, Vera. I shall look forward to it,' I said and everyone else nodded in agreement.

'Dan might be on duty, Vera, but I'll be there,' said Jo.

Vera looked at me knowingly and added, 'Miss Henderson is coming, Mr Sheffield, and I do hope you will help me persuade her to join the church choir.'

On Saturday afternoon the courtyard in front of the vicarage was filled with cars, notably a large, black classic Bentley. The chauffeur was leaning against the bonnet and Vera had come out to serve him tea.

'Hello, Vera,' I said. 'I see the major's here.'

'Good afternoon, Mr Sheffield. Thank you for coming,' said Vera, and she glanced through the trees towards the church. 'Rupert is with his daughter – it's a regular visit for them . . . His wife was a dear friend.'

Under a tall elm tree in a beautifully manicured grassy corner of the churchyard the major stood with his daughter, Virginia. The young woman replaced the flowers in the ornate cast-iron vase and put the spent ones in a small carrier bag. Then the major put his arm round her shoulders and together they stood quietly under a canopy of dappled sunlight and shadow. Many years had passed since the major's wife had died, but for both the major and his daughter it was important there were always fresh flowers on her grave.

'Let's leave them in peace,' said Vera, touching my arm. She was right. We were intruding.

Soon I was drinking tea from a delicate china cup and nibbling on a triangular cress sandwich, from which the crusts had been neatly removed, when I caught the familiar scent of Rive Gauche perfume and Beth was standing next to me.

'Hello, Jack. How are you?' She brushed her honey-blonde hair away from her high cheekbones and smiled up at me. Her green eyes looked tired.

'A bit weary, to be honest, Beth. It's been a busy week.'

'I heard about the expulsion. That must have been difficult.'

'Yes, but I'm going out to see him tomorrow at Netherbank Hall. I'm praying we've done the right thing . . . I certainly hope so.'

'I'm sure it will be fine, Jack.' Beth poured herself a fresh cup of tea from a large china teapot. 'And I appreciated the maths scheme. I was struggling with mine.'

'If I can ever help, Beth, you know I'm here.'

Around us everyone looked relaxed. Anne was deep in conversation with Sally, while Jo was asking Vera how to make vol-au-vents. Joseph, Albert Jenkins and John Grainger had crept out to the kitchen to sample Joseph's latest home-made, highly potent vintage.

'And . . . I'm glad we spoke about Laura,' I said.

Beth picked up a silver teaspoon and stirred her tea. 'Yes, Jack, so am I.'

Suddenly there was an explosion in the kitchen. 'I told Joseph *not* to open that dreadful wine!' said Vera in dismay. Everyone laughed as Joseph peered anxiously round the door and Vera rushed to the broom cupboard in the hall.

Beth smiled and, for the first time, she looked relaxed.

'There was something I wanted to ask you, Beth.' I looked round to check we couldn't be overheard. 'I wondered if I could ring you . . . to, er, go out possibly.'

Beth put down her cup and saucer and looked up at me. 'Yes, Jack. I'd like that.'

Vera suddenly reappeared, looking a little flushed. 'Now, Mr Sheffield, I do hope you have asked Miss Henderson to join our church choir.'

'I was just about to,' I said with a wink to Beth as the last of the April clouds scurried away and the room was filled with sunlight.

On Sunday morning, Roy Davidson and I set off in my car. The Vale of York is the heart of the vast county of Yorkshire, ninety miles from north to south. We sped through the rich agricultural flatland of wheat and barley, with occasional fields of sugar beet, potatoes, carrots, cabbages and brussels sprouts, and headed north-west towards Skipton, 'the gateway to the Dales'. Driving over the high ground of Blubberhouses I felt that familiar tingle of wonderment as I surveyed this great county. It was my kingdom of cathedrals, moorlands and mills, my home of beer and brass bands, Ridings and rugby, my land of coastlines and cricket. Beyond the market town of Skipton we drove on towards limestone hills and clear rivers. The purple bulk of the Pennines filled the far distance and memories of forgotten looms, cotton and cloth flickered across my mind.

Netherbank Hall was a solid Victorian building of local stone that reflected an amber light in the low April sun. It was set in a wooded area overlooking the River Wharfe and a huge grassy playing field had been created alongside. We stopped the car next to a group of young boys who were busy constructing a wigwam from stripped branches and stout rope. I could see Dean Pickles among them.

The tall, fair-haired, athletic man supervising them walked towards us. 'Good to see you again, Roy,' he shouted. He looked relaxed in his jeans and checked lumberjack shirt. They shook hands and he turned to me with a grin. 'And this must be Jack. Welcome to Netherbank. I'm the head, Rod Twelvetrees.' He saw my surprise and grinned. 'An old southern counties name,' he added by way of explanation.

We hit it off straight away and, after a tour of the school, we were drinking coffee in the staff-room with a dramatic view of the distant hills through the high arched window. The teachers were young, energetic and positive and spoke with enthusiasm about their work. They all shared the ethos of this special place based on strict discipline, self-esteem and mutual respect. I could see why Dean would have a chance to thrive in this well-organized and caring community.

'He'll be fine here, Jack,' said Rod, 'and I'll let you know how he progresses.'

As I left I walked over to Dean and ruffled his hair.

'Good luck, Dean,' I said. 'Make the most of your chance here. It's a great place and you'll make new friends.'

He looked confused but, strangely, not at all tearful. As I drove away I looked in my wing mirror and saw Dean being led into school by the tall figure of Rod Twelvetrees, his large hand resting on the little boy's shoulders.

The journey home was silent as we both reflected on the enormity of the impact we had made on the young life of Dean Pickles. The wild hillsides flew by and the grassy banks alongside the limestone walls were filled with brilliant-yellow daffodils.

Chapter Sixteen

The Prettiest Cow in Yorkshire

A selection of children's artwork was delivered to the City Art Gallery for the exhibition on Saturday, 26 April. A party of children, parents and staff will attend.
Extract from the Ragley School Logbook:
Friday, 25 April 1980

'This cow has just been insured for £10,000!' exclaimed Vera.

Sally and Anne put down their cups of coffee and stared at Vera in astonishment. It was Friday lunchtime, 25 April, and outside the staff-room window, through the mirage of mist, the mellow showers of April had arrived to refresh the countryside. However, at that moment, the beauty of nature was far from our minds.

'That's not like you, Vera,' said Sally tactfully.

'So . . . is it some Hollywood film star that you're not particularly keen on?' asked Anne cautiously.

Vera stared at the front page of the *Easington Herald &
Pioneer* and shook her head in dismay. 'How can a cow
like that be worth all that money?' she said.

'Who are you talking about, Vera?' I asked.

'Lulu,' said Vera.

'Lulu!' exclaimed Anne.

'Yes. She's a Canadian Holstein,' said Vera.

'I thought she was from Scotland,' said Sally.

'Scotland?' I said, puzzled.

'Well, she used to sing "Shout" in a Scottish accent,'
said Sally.

Vera held up the front page of the newspaper and
pointed to a photograph of a smiling farmer standing next
to a contented-looking cow in a muddy farmyard. 'No,'
she said, sounding exasperated. 'It's Mr Icklethwaite's
prize cow. His daughter, Betsy, is in Class 2. In fact, she's
just done a painting of this cow.'

'Ah, I'm with you now, Vera,' said Anne, looking relieved.

'I've seen the painting,' added Sally. 'It's excellent for a
six-year-old. It's in our collection for tomorrow's exhibition at the art gallery in York.'

Vera read out the bold text under the photograph.
'A Ragley farmer's prize cow has been selected for
the Milk Marketing Dairy event at Stoneleigh.' Then
she adjusted her spectacles as if she couldn't believe
what she was reading. 'Lulu, a Canadian Holstein,'
she continued, 'was chosen because she is particularly
good-looking and has been insured by the Board for
£10,000.'

I leaned over to stare at the photograph. 'How can a cow be good-looking?' I asked.

Joseph, sitting quietly in the corner, reached out for another custard cream. 'I suppose all of God's creatures have their own personal charm,' he said.

'Don't be greedy, Joseph,' Vera said.

'Well, most of them,' mumbled Joseph under his breath.

The awkward moment was interrupted by the shrill ringing of the telephone. Vera answered it, smiled and passed the receiver to me.

'It's Miss Henderson . . . Miss Beth Henderson,' she said.

'Hello, Jack,' said Beth. She sounded upbeat. 'My deputy, Simon, is taking some of our children's artwork down to the art gallery this evening and I wondered if you were going to the exhibition on Saturday. It starts at twelve.'

'Yes, I am,' I said, trying to hide my enthusiasm. 'Did you want to meet up?'

'How about ten thirty?' she said. 'We could go for a coffee first.'

'Fine,' I said. 'Where shall we meet?'

Around me the silence in the staff-room was deafening. Everyone sat like statues, listening in to the conversation – all with the exception of Joseph, who put his cup and saucer back on the coffee table with a clatter and the four women in perfect unison all shot him a disapproving stare.

'How about Minerva?' said Beth.

'Very appropriate,' I said. 'See you there.'

In the centre of York a popular meeting place was the corner of Petergate and Minster Gates, where the statue of Minerva, the Roman goddess of wisdom, kept her quiet vigil over the heads of the busy shoppers.

Predictably, I was in a good mood when I took morning assembly. Sally was leading the choir and playing her guitar. She was sitting down, which was strange for her, and looking a little more flushed and tired than usual. 'Daisies are our silver' sang the children. However, Benjamin Roberts, now just past his fifth birthday, remained silent and I gave him an inquisitive stare. Benjamin didn't actually mind daisies. They tended to brighten up his world. It was just that he didn't see much point in singing about them. With a crushing glance and the demeanour of martyrdom he sat up straight and began to mime the words like a professional.

Immediately after the end of school, Jo and Sally were using some of the dining tables in the hall to carefully mount the selection of children's artwork. Jo was trimming the pictures, using the deadly dangerous, long-handled guillotine that, for obvious reasons, we kept locked away in the stock cupboard while we waited for affordable new technology to replace it. Sally was double-mounting the paintings and drawings expertly on pastel-coloured sugar paper and then on to stiff white card. The results looked highly professional.

Sally held up Betsy Icklethwaite's painting. 'Isn't this good, Jack?'

'It's excellent,' I said. There were twenty paintings in all but the most colourful and vibrant was the one entitled 'Daddy's Best Friend' by Betsy.

'But are you sure it's a cow?' asked Jo, after carefully lowering the arm of the guillotine into a safe position.

We all studied the painting carefully. There was no doubt it was definitely an impressionist work. However, while the shape in the centre had the colouring of a zebra and the characteristics of a hippopotamus, it was the fact that the creature was watching television that tended to diminish the contextual clues.

Before going home, a group of children, seeing their work mounted, had gathered round, full of excitement.

'My mummy's going,' said ten-year-old Katy Ollerenshaw proudly. 'She says I'm the first in the family to have a painting in a proper gallery.'

Sadly, Katy's enthusiasm wasn't shared by everyone.

'Do we 'ave t'go?' asked Heathcliffe Earnshaw, who was not a natural patron of the arts.

'Well, your lovely drawing of your granddad is going on show, Heathcliffe,' said Jo encouragingly.

Heathcliffe looked at his masterpiece and frowned. He knew with certainty that his crayon picture was actually of God, but ever since his Plasticine ferret had been put in the nativity scene as a sheep he was getting used to the misinterpretation of his creative talents.

I helped Sally and Jo put the artwork in the back of Sally's car and then I called in to Nora's Coffee Shop before going home. Dorothy was sitting behind the counter and studying a catalogue, while Nora was fiddling with the coffee machine.

'A frothy coffee, please, Dorothy.'

Dorothy was engrossed in the colourful catalogue. 'Ah'm thinking o' buying one o' them sympathetic wigs, Mr Sheffield. Ah could 'ave a different look every day.'

'Oh, yes,' I said, staring curiously at the plate of rock cakes on the shelf of the plastic-fronted display case.

'Its synthetic, Dowothy,' corrected Nora as she added hot froth to my coffee. 'It says in the *Daily Expwess* that one in thwee women wear a wig.'

'So are you thinking of getting one, Nora?' I said, feigning interest.

'Yes, ah'm gonna get a Fawwer Fawcett,' said Nora, slapping down the mug of coffee on the counter.

I looked at the array of tired-looking pastries. 'So, what do you recommend, Dorothy?'

'Cream 'orns, Mr Sheffield,' said Dorothy returning to her catalogue. 'Fresh in day before yesterday.'

'OK, a frothy coffee and a cream horn it is, please.'

On my way out of the village I called in at Victor Pratt's garage and pulled up alongside the single petrol pump. Victor came out to serve me and, as usual, he had a problem. He walked painfully across the forecourt, like a cowboy who had lost his horse.

'Ah can't sit down,' he complained.

'Oh dear,' I said. 'What's the trouble?'

'Same as t'vicar, Mr Sheffield,' grumbled Victor. 'Las' Christmas your aunt May told me it were asteroids an' they're gettin' worse.'

'I see,' I said. 'I'm sorry to hear that, Victor.'

'It's embarrassin' walkin' like this, so ah only come out at night,' he said mournfully.

'That's probably about right for asteroids,' I said with the merest hint of irony.

'Y'spot-on there, Mr Sheffield. That's exactly what Dr Davenport said.'

As Victor hobbled away I guessed the doctor and I must share the same sense of humour.

That night I settled down with my new Toshiba 20-inch colour television set with the expensive rental of £7.67 per month. The spotty-faced salesman had told me that it had a state-of-the-art blackstripe tube for maximum picture clarity, but I was more concerned that my television licence had shot up to £34.00. The fact that the Home Secretary, Mr William Whitelaw, had encouraged me to use the savings-stamps scheme had fallen on deaf ears. So I switched on BBC1 and settled down to watch Terry Wogan interviewing Larry Hagman of JR Ewing fame and wondered why Americans needed such large hats.

On Saturday morning I drove into York and parked near the Minster, in Duncombe Place. While I was locking the driver's door, a couple who looked like tourists approached me in some confusion. They were staring at an upside-down street map of York.

'Tell me, mah friend, where is yur Minster of York?' asked the man in the Stars and Stripes baseball cap.

I pointed to the magnificent west tower of York Minster,

just fifty yards away and dominating the skyline. 'It's there,' I said.

Restoration work was in progress and his wife looked at the scaffolding. 'When they've finished building it ah'm sure it'll be real pretty,' she said with a voice of authority, peering over her Jodrell Bank sunglasses. Her heavy make-up and striking platinum blonde hair gave her the appearance of a Marilyn Monroe look-alike.

'They're just cleaning up the medieval stonework. It's a continuous process,' I explained.

'Well, ah do declare,' said Baseball Cap and then turned to his wife, who had taken a small mirror from her hand-bag and was checking her eye-liner.

'We sure lahke yur lil' bitty town of York, England,' she said, admiring the perfect jet-black crescents of her plucked eyebrows. 'It's the quaintest an' cutest lil' place ah ever did see.'

'I'm very pleased to hear it,' I said, trying to extricate myself from the conversation.

Baseball Cap took me by the arm and looked concerned. 'But can you kindly tell me, sir, why yur sidewalks are so narrow?'

I was beginning to lose the will to live. 'You're in an ancient city that was built in the time of horses and carts and carriages, not motor cars.'

'Well, mah dear friend, ah'm pleased tuh say we have more foresight in the good ol' Land of the Free,' he boasted.

'You are soooo raight, mah lil' honeybunch,' said Marilyn Monroe, replacing her mirror in her Italian handbag. 'Well, we mus' fly, 'cause it's York, England, today an' Paris, France, on Wednesday.' And, with a casual wave, they walked away to continue their tour of Europe, World.

I was a few minutes early and I strolled across the road and walked down High Petergate to the busy crossing between Stonegate and Minster Gates. I looked up at the familiar statue of Minerva. She was leaning on her pile of books as a reminder that this was once a street of book-sellers and bookbinders.

From out of the crowds, an unlikely figure approached me. 'Gorra light, mate?' He was dressed as a Viking and was wearing enough jewellery to make Danny La Rue jealous.

'Sorry, I don't smoke,' I replied.

'Never mind,' he said, untying the earflap of his hard leather skullcap and putting the cigarette behind his ear. 'Jason'll be 'ere in a minute.' He shivered and I stared down at his brown minidress tunic. The baggy green tights that covered his spindly legs provided little protection from the cold on this sharp April morning. 'It's Viking Day,' he said by way of explanation, 'in Coppergate.'

The Coppergate archaeological dig, destined to become the famous Jorvik Centre, was a popular meeting place each month for local historians and their re-enactments of famous battles provided great entertainment for the tourists.

He followed my gaze. 'It's a bit parky,' he said.

'Looks like your friend's here now,' I said, as a Viking on a Lambretta appeared suddenly and pulled up alongside.

''Ullo, Perce. Fancy a swift 'alf before t'battle?' asked

the new Viking. The bright buttons and sequins sewn on his leather skirt would have done credit to a finalist in *Come Dancing*. This was definitely an upmarket Viking.

Percy picked up his large round shield with a hemispherical iron boss protruding from its outer face. 'OK, Jase,' he said. 'Ah mus' say you've come up in t'world from last month. Ah see y'gorra new costume. Who you s'pposed t'be, then?'

Jason parked his Lambretta, dismounted and stared critically at his reflection in the shop window. 'Ah'm Erik Bloodaxe, the fearless an' bloodthirsty King o' Western Norway, son o' the magnificent King 'Arald Fine'air,' said Jason, adjusting the bow on his blond ponytail. 'An' ah'll tell y'summat f'nowt, this 'elmet's no fun. Ah've gone cross-eyed getting 'ere.'

We both stared at Jason's conical iron helmet with a thick bar protruding from the forehead to protect King Erik's nose.

'Why don't you turn it round the other way?' I suggested.

Jason pondered this for a moment. 'Good idea, mate,' he said. 'Y'not as daft as y'look.'

I took this as a compliment, especially as I was the only one not wearing a skirt.

King Erik Bloodaxe reversed his helmet. 'That's better,' he said with a relieved smile. He looked at Percy. 'So who are you, then?'

'Usual,' said Percy sadly. 'Ah'm still Sigurd the Mighty.'

''Ow's yer 'ands now wi' that rough shield?' asked King Erik, looking concerned.

'Lot better now, Jase,' said Sigurd the Mighty. 'Ah borrowed our Tracy's Aqua Manda Golden Body Rub.'

'Ah've 'eard it's really good,' said King Erik Bloodaxe.

'Y'spot-on there, Jase,' said Sigurd the Mighty. 'It meks yer 'ands lovely an' smooth. Jus' feel 'em.'

King Erik Bloodaxe leaned over and felt Sigurd the Mighty's soft hands. Then he sniffed them appreciatively. 'Lovely fragrance, Perce.'

Sigurd the Mighty gave his warrior-friend a gentle smile and climbed on to the back of the Lambretta.

'An', Perce, jus' watch where y'putting that pointy bit on y'shield,' added King Erik Bloodaxe.

They roared off to the Cross Keys public house on Goodramgate with memories of rape and pillage in the ninth and tenth centuries clearly far from their minds.

There was a tap on my shoulder. 'Hello, Jack,' said a familiar voice.

I turned round and there was Beth, looking relaxed in her fashionable beige coat with slightly padded shoulders and a yellow scarf that matched the sudden burst of April sunshine.

'Hello, Beth. Good to see you.'

Her honey-blonde hair was blowing in the breeze and the tiredness had gone from her eyes. She looked full of vitality and life. 'Come on, Jack: my treat,' she said and took my arm.

For a moment I felt that we were a couple again as we set off down Stonegate together. She had that excited purposeful air about her and walked quickly, her high-heeled leather boots clipping on the cobbles, into St

Helen's Square, the home of Betty's classic English Tea Rooms. It stood proudly opposite its great rival, Terry's Restaurant, which was about to close down.

'Perfect,' I said, looking up at the sign that read BETTY'S – EST 1919. This was Yorkshire's finest. The designers of the exquisite interiors of the Queen Mary transatlantic liner had created a perfect classical environment for the enjoyment of England's favourite beverage. We walked into the elegant ground-floor tea room and found one of the window tables, where you could watch the world go by. Beth ordered toasted Yorkshire teacakes and a pot of Earl Grey tea, which was served by a young lady in a starched white apron and cap.

'Shall I be mother?' she said whimsically and she picked up the delicate silver tea strainer and poured the tea from the elegant silver teapot. Then she smiled that familiar warm smile and nodded towards an old advertisement that stated boldly: *Eat Sweets and Grow Thin – Chocolate is a Cure for Weak Hearts.* At least that's what a certain German food expert, Dr Frederick Bosser, had believed.

It was a happy time and we chatted about her plans for her new school library and the momentum that seemed to be gathering in the new government for some form of common school curriculum. Then, right out of the blue, she mentioned Laura.

'Laura's going out with Desmond, her new boss.'

'Oh, good. I'm pleased for her,' I said.

Beth looked curiously at me for a moment. 'I'm sure she still thinks a lot about you, Jack.'

'She was always good company,' I replied.

Beth rotated the tiny bowl of assorted sugar cubes in front of her. 'Yes,' she said simply. We both stared out of the window deep in our own thoughts. 'I always dreamed of being a headteacher, Jack,' said Beth, suddenly changing the subject.

'I know,' I replied.

'But it's not everything . . .'

Then the spell was broken as a street busker across the street began playing the haunting theme from *Doctor Zhivago* on an ancient accordion. Fifteen minutes later, Beth paid the bill and we walked out into the sunshine.

After window-shopping in Stonegate, we wandered into York Minster and, immediately, gazed around us in awe at the sights within this wonderful building. Only the tap-tap of heels on the stone floor disturbed the hushed silence and we paused in front of the choir screen, carved with the figures of the Kings of England from William I to Henry VI. They looked down at us dispassionately and steadfastly, fixed in time, staring into the still air and silent spaces.

From the Minster we walked towards the great gateway of Bootham Bar and there, across the road, excited groups of children, with mothers and fathers in close attendance, were filing into the art gallery. Beth and I walked into the main hall, where a large crowd had gathered and an officious-looking local government officer stood up to introduce the main guest, who had flown in from America.

'It gives me great pleasure to welcome the distinguished artist from across the seas, the man who was described in the Arts section of the *Yorkshire Post* as "a post-Impressionist genius of shape and colour". So please welcome the American pop artist Mr Randy Finkleman III.'

We all clapped while a gangling figure ambled to the front and stood there in skin-tight blue, stonewashed Wrangler jeans and a New York Jets T-shirt. Then he flashed his perfect white teeth, shook his carefully permed Art Garfunkle hair and tossed the end of his pink silk scarf casually over his shoulder. Unfortunately it snagged on his pendulous and very sparkly single earring and there followed an embarrassing moment while the lady curator of the art gallery helped him to untangle it.

Then he stood feet astride in his high-heeled cowboy boots and addressed the audience. 'Mah good friends, it's a plee-sure t'be back in your pretty lil' town of York, England. Ah do declare mah exhibition well an' truly open.'

The first part of the collection was based on his early life that included fishing for his supper in a boat off New York harbour. I quickly concluded that Randy was not merely a fisherman but more a piscatorial artist.

Thirty-six of Randy's paintings were displayed on the first large wall of the gallery and the children's art exhibition followed on. Betsy Icklethwaite's painting had been mounted immediately next to the American legend's final piece of work, a colourful impression of Roy Rogers' horse, Trigger.

Beth and I met up with Sally, Anne and Jo and studied the list of exhibits printed on the programme. Number 37 was '"Daddy's Best Friend" by Betsy Icklethwaite, age 6'.

'I see what you mean, Sally,' said Beth. 'It really is a terrific painting.'

Suddenly Randy and his entourage arrived and began postulating with knowing looks and self-satisfied nods in front of us.

'This is quite wonderful,' said the art critic of the local paper. 'Such immediacy of line and colour.' He stroked his goatee beard, stared at Betsy Icklethwaite's painting and nodded with the assurance of an artistically superior human being.

'I agree,' said the lady curator, not to be outdone.

'Very, er . . . impressionistic,' said the local government officer.

The press photographer, in a hurry to get to his next appointment, a Max Bygraves sing-along at the local home for retired gentlefolk, captured the moment. The art critic smiled serenely, the lady curator was pleased she'd had her roots done and the local government officer assumed his 'I'm in charge' look. Randy was puzzled as he knew he had never painted a zebra watching television. However, as he lived his life in a transcendental parallel universe, it didn't seem to matter so long as people kept telling him he was the best thing since Picasso and sliced bread, preferably in that order.

So it was that little Betsy Icklethwaite's prize cow was immortalized and the newspaper cutting featured for the rest of the school year on the staff-room noticeboard.

Beth and I enjoyed our time together and she agreed to call into Bilbo Cottage on her way home. I bought a fish-and-chips supper and, at eight o'clock, we settled down to watch the *Eurovision Song Contest*, broadcast from The Hague, in the Netherlands. Beth laughed as Terry Wogan described the Luxembourg entry that featured a large man dressed as a penguin. Sadly, after the United Kingdom's success in 1976, when Brotherhood of Man won with 'Save All Your Kisses for Me', this year's entry, 'Love Enough for Two' by Prima Donna, was a disappointing third and the contest was won by Ireland's Johnny Logan with 'What's Another Year'. But it was a relaxing end to the day and Beth kissed me on the cheek as she left.

For the first time in many months, I washed the dishes with a smile on my face.

Three miles away in Ragley village, life was not progressing quite so smoothly for Billy Icklethwaite. At the recent North of England Show at Ryedale, Billy had won the coveted award for the finest cow in Yorkshire and was determined to share his success with his farming friends in the Pig and Ferret. When he arrived home, after several pints of Tetley's bitter, he clearly picked the wrong moment to present the engraved trophy to his wife with the words, 'Thish ish f'you, shweet'art.'

Betty read the inscription 'Best Beast 1980' and was not impressed, as Billy quickly found out. Little Betsy was tucked up in bed at the time and never did get the chance to paint a post-Impressionist masterpiece entitled, 'Where Mummy Put Daddy's Trophy'.

Chapter Seventeen

Who Shot JR?

School closed today for the annual May Day holiday and will reopen on Tuesday, 6 May. Children from Mrs Pringle's country dancing group will take part in a display of maypole dancing on the village green on Monday, 5 May.

> Extract from the Ragley School Logbook:
> Friday, 2 May 1980

Timothy Pratt carefully applied a small quantity of superglue to JR Ewing's left ear. With the infinite care of a surgeon he attached the small piece of plaster and leaned a cast-iron boot scraper against it to hold it in place. Then he stood back to admire his handiwork. 'Bloody vandals!' he muttered and walked back into his Hardware Emporium.

JR Ewing was by far his favourite *Dallas* character. Sue Ellen Ewing was too flashy for his taste and Bobby Ewing was just too good-looking. He liked the way JR's stetson was tilted at a jaunty angle over one eye, although that might have been caused by a slight fault in the plaster cast. Even so, he knew the *Dallas* range of garden gnomes, displayed on the forecourt of his Emporium, would prove even more popular than the seven dwarfs. If he could just find out who was damaging them, then life would be perfect.

It was lunchtime on Friday, 2 May, and the Revd Joseph Evans had walked into the staff-room at a critical moment in our discussion.

Jo was animated. 'But it has to be his wife, Sue Ellen,' she pleaded.

'It's too obvious,' I said.

'And she would be too drunk to pull the trigger,' added Anne decisively.

'It's probably Cliff Barnes who shot him,' I said. 'They were always arguing.'

'Goodness me, has someone been shot?' asked a confused Joseph.

'JR,' said Vera, without emotion, her head buried in her *Daily Telegraph.*

'JR?' said Joseph.

'Yes, Joseph. I'm afraid to say that JR Ewing has been shot,' said Vera stonily.

'Oh, I'm very sorry to hear that,' said Joseph, none the wiser. 'Let's hope he gets better soon.'

Vera was reading an article by Mary Whitehouse, the 'clean-up television' campaigner. After attending her 'Survival in the Eighties' lecture in the Tempest Anderson Hall in the Museum Gardens in York, chaired by the distinguished Michael Alison MP, Vera had added her name to the thirty thousand members of the National Listeners and Viewers Association. In Vera's opinion, violence on television should be banned. On the other hand, she thought it would be interesting to find out who shot JR.

Meanwhile, in the school hall, the merry sounds of English country dancing could be heard at full volume. Sally Pringle was hard at work preparing a performance of maypole dancing with the girls in her class. The May Day celebrations, to be held on the village green on Monday, 5 May, were always a very special attraction and the whole village turned out to enjoy their public holiday. This year's entertainment included the parade of the May queen, an exhibition of maypole dancing, a local group of morris dancers and Old Tommy Piercy's famous hog roast.

At the end of school, Ruby was polishing the office door handle, something she always did when she wanted a chat. 'Ah'm reight proud of our Natasha,' said Ruby. Her daughter Natasha had been selected by the village hall committee to be the May queen and Ruby remembered the day long ago when, in 1950, as a slim teenager, she had been queen for a day.

'I'm really pleased for you, Ruby, and we'll all be there to see the parade,' I said.

'And the Buttle twins are really excited to be her attendants,' said Jo. 'Mrs Buttle brought in their dresses to show my class.'

'Ah'm gonna press our Ronnie's suit,' said Ruby, polishing the handle with a sudden fierce determination. "E'll look smart . . . or 'e'll know what for,' she added menacingly.

On Saturday morning I pulled up outside Nora's Coffee Shop in bright May sunshine. I had half an hour to spare before driving on to Morton village to pick up Beth. All the local headteachers had been invited to look round the site of the Coppergate excavation. From there, we had decided, we would go to the Odeon cinema, so a good day was in store.

As I got out of my car I heard loud music. Clint Ramsbottom was walking down the other side of the High Street with his big brother, Shane. On his shoulder Clint carried his huge black plastic Hitachi ghetto-blaster. The name 3-D SUPER WOOFER was printed in large white letters on the front in between the stereo speakers, from which a deafening sound emerged.

Ominously, Shane was also carrying something over his shoulder. It was a rifle and I presumed he was going 'rabbiting'. Both men waved in acknowledgement and I waved back. Conversation was pointless because of the noise. However, as they strutted along, nodding their heads in time to 'Rat Trap' by the Boomtown Rats, unknown to Clint the new technology of the 1980s was about to cross his path.

The members of the Ragley Ladies Keep Fit Club were jogging towards them, including Petula Dudley-Palmer. Attached to her waist was a tiny portable cassette player, from which emerged a pair of wires culminating in tiny ear-pieces.

After looking longingly at a photograph of Omar Sharif in her *Daily Express*, Petula Dudley-Palmer had donned her lime-green Lycra jogging suit, scarlet ankle warmers and a fluorescent yellow headband. She was in a world of her own as she jogged in time to Abba's 'Mamma Mia'. Her husband, Geoffrey, had responded with a mixture of horror and astonishment when his wife began to fantasize about not only having a figure like Olivia Newton John but also a skin-tight outfit to match. Predictably, he decided he would do all he could to support her latest whim. His contribution was the revolutionary Sony Walkman. Although the early models were very expensive, with little change from one hundred pounds, he knew it would keep his wife happy for a short while.

It was a seminal moment in the life of Clint Ramsbottom, local farm labourer and would-be eighties fashion icon. As the ladies trundled past, he looked in astonishment at the wires that led to the tiny ear-pieces in Petula Dudley-Palmer's ears and then stared in dismay at his ghetto-blaster, which was the size of a small coffin. Clint knew, in that moment, his life had changed.

He had never heard of Akio Morita, Sony's Japanese co-founder and champion of the new technology, but Akio knew him . . . or, rather, people like Clint. He understood that the Clints of this world would go to great lengths to listen to their music in their cars and in the streets. So Akio's latest convert stared not at the shapely bottoms of the Lycra-clad ladies but at the small plastic box attached to Petula Dudley-Palmer's waistband. For Clint there was no turning back and, when Amelia Duff looked out of her Post Office doorway, little did she realize that it was the last time she would ever complain about Clint and his ghetto-blaster.

Meanwhile, in Pratt's Hardware Emporium, Timothy Pratt was washing glue off his hands. Tidy Tim had few luxuries in his life but he always bought good-quality soap from Prudence Golightly at the General Stores. Cussins Imperial Leather was his favourite. The smell was fragrant and the lather was rich. He washed his hands thoroughly and took care to replace the soap so that the lettering on its convex surface was the right way up. Then he dried his hands on a blue-and-white-striped towel and hung it back over the rail so that the stripes were exactly horizontal. When everything was in order he stepped back and nodded in satisfaction. Tidy Tim liked horizontal stripes.

Then, attracted by the noise of Clint's ghetto-blaster, he went to stand by the front door of his Emporium. Tidy Tim stared hard at Shane Ramsbottom's rifle, glanced down at his neat formation of garden gnomes and nodded knowingly. Shane was definitely a suspect.

The Three Degrees were singing 'My Simple Heart' on the jukebox when I walked into the Coffee Shop but, strangely, Dorothy wasn't swaying to the music as she usually did. I perched on a stool at the counter next to Little Malcolm.

"Ello, Mr Sheffield,' said Little Malcolm.

'Hello, Malcolm,' I said and then glanced towards the forlorn figure of Dorothy.

'How are you, Dorothy?' I asked.

'She's upset, Mr Sheffield,' said Malcolm quickly. 'Summat t'do wi' a freebie.'

'Norra freebie, Malcolm . . . it's called a phobia. Ah read it in *Smash 'Its*, so it mus' be true,' retorted Dorothy and absent-mindedly stirred another three spoonfuls of sugar into Little Malcolm's tea. 'It said a lorra creative people get 'em, these phobias . . . 'cept f'Lynda Carter o' course.'

I recalled that Lynda Carter, in her superhero guise of Wonder Woman, was Dorothy's idol. 'I'm sorry to hear that, Dorothy. So what's the phobia?' I asked.

'Dreams, Mister Sheffield. Ah jus' can't stop dreaming.'

Little Malcolm sipped his tea and winced but gallantly said nothing. I surveyed the display of jam doughnuts on the counter. They looked as depressed as Dorothy.

'It's just a coffee, please, Dorothy . . . Er, so what are your dreams about?' I asked somewhat reluctantly. Conversations with Dorothy rarely followed a logical path.

'Ah keep dreaming Wonder Woman's losing 'er powers an' she's waiting for a super'ero t'save 'er.'

Little Malcolm's neck blushed crimson under his council donkey jacket and, as he sipped his extra-sweet tea, he wondered if Dorothy would ever dream about a five-feet-four-inch bin man coming to her rescue.

Nora Pratt was sitting on a stool behind the counter and reading the *Yorkshire Evening Press*. 'This is intewesting,' she said: 'that weally good dancer, Fwed Astaire, is eighty an' it says 'e's gonna mawy a thirty-five-year-old, Miss Wobyn Smith, who wides wacehorses.'

'Ah think it's wonderful,' said Dorothy, fluttering her false eyelashes at Little Malcolm. 'Ah've always liked older men.'

In that moment, Little Malcolm vowed to buy a car so that on their next date they wouldn't have to go to a dance in a bin wagon.

As I waited for my coffee I looked up high on the wall, where the theatrical memories of Nora's time in the Ragley Amateur Dramatic Society were displayed. Nora was wearing the same Alpine leather corset in the posters of *Snow White*, *Aladdin* and *Puss in Boots*, but this did not detract from the overall impression that, in the firmament of thespian gems, Nora knew with absolute conviction that she was the jewel in the crown.

Finally, I sat down and enjoyed the usual hubbub of conversation. Today's topics included whom Prince Charles might marry, how to solve the Rubik Cube and, of course, who shot JR?

'Ah think it's Kwisten, Sue Ellen's sister,' said Nora.

'Y'mean 'er who wears Maxi-Moist Lipstick from Max Factor with eighty-three per cent moisturizer?' said Dorothy without looking up from filing her nails.

Nora stared at the five-feet-eleven-inch would-be

model and wondered why it was that Dorothy lived in a strange parallel universe.

Beth was waiting for me when I pulled up outside her house. Next to her front door, the Zephirine Drouhin climbing rose was bursting with vigorous shoots and new life. She smiled as she walked down the path in her fashionable light-beige mackintosh with button-down epaulettes. It flapped open in the breeze to reveal a floral-patterned dress that gave a first hint of summer days ahead.

We parked in the centre of York and, once again, it felt good to walk with Beth through the ancient streets of one of England's most cherished cities. Since the Roman settlement, known as 'Eboracum', was founded in AD 71, the Vikings had invaded and called it 'Jorvik' and finally the Normans had simply called it 'York'. Most of the schools in the area, including Hartingdale and Ragley, were currently doing projects based on the Coppergate excavation. We had been promised the chance to see some of the wonderful Viking artefacts that were being unearthed, so it looked like being an interesting visit.

After a sandwich in a snack bar in Goodramgate, Beth and I were sitting on a bench at the Coppergate dig with a group of other headteachers. A bearded man in a hand-woven sweater was playing a set of tenth-century panpipes, while a lady gave us a lecture on 'Dendrochronology', which we later discovered simply meant tree-ring dating. Then we studied a collection of amber and jet jewellery and Beth held up a tenth-century necklace and I smiled as she put it against her neck. It was good to meet other headteachers and Beth looked happy and relaxed as she swapped stories about life in our village schools.

In complete contrast, at half past seven, Beth and I were queuing outside the Odeon cinema to watch the latest James Bond film, *The Spy Who Loved Me*.

'You're quiet, Jack,' said Beth. 'Is everything all right?'

'I'm fine,' I said. It had just occurred to me that the last time I had been here was with Laura. Beth smiled and slipped her hand into mine.

Inside, we found two seats next to an aisle where I could stretch my long legs. *The Pink Panther Strikes Again* had just finished and we settled down for the main feature.

'Have a fruit gum,' said Beth. 'The film's starting.'

I soon relaxed and began to follow the plot. Roger Moore, with his whimsical disregard for danger, particularly when doing a free-fall parachute jump from a cliff, did much to lighten my mood. The exotic and beautiful Barbara Bach as a KGB agent reminded me that the best-looking woman in the cinema was sitting right next to me. When the wonderful villain, Richard Kiel as 'Jaws', threatened James Bond with his bear-trap steel teeth, Beth held my hand a little tighter and only relaxed it when Carly Simon sang 'Nobody Does It Better' through the final scene.

Back in my car on the return journey to Morton, Beth glanced up at me. 'So what's on your mind?' she asked.

'Tonight . . . in the cinema . . . it was good.'
Beth simply smiled and said nothing.

On Monday, after early-morning rain, sparkling sunshine burst through to welcome the May Day holiday. This was an important festival in the English county calendar and around two hundred people had gathered in Ragley to welcome the arrival of the May queen to the village green. On an open flat trailer, bedecked with garlands and flags, and towed up the High Street by Deke Ramsbottom on his tractor, Ruby's daughter arrived in style. Everyone cheered and clapped as Natasha, seated on her throne and flanked by the excited Buttle twins, waved a white-gloved hand to the crowd. She looked beautiful in a borrowed wedding dress with a bouquet of spring flowers and, on her head, a crown that glittered in the sunlight.

'She looks beautiful, Ruby,' said Vera.

'Thank you, Miss Evans,' said Ruby. 'Ah'm so proud ah could cry.'

John Grainger was taking photographs, destined for Ruby's mantelpiece. Anne and Vera stood on either side of Ruby and Ronnie, resplendent in his best suit and bobble hat, while Ruby couldn't hold back any longer and wept tears of joy into Vera's lacy handkerchief. As she watched her lovely daughter, she remembered the time, thirty years before, when it had been her special day. She hugged Ronnie, who was standing stiffly in his best suit and looking forward to his first pint of Tetley's bitter.

As the appetizing scent of Old Tommy Piercy's hog roast drifted across the green from the forecourt of The Royal Oak, the morris dancers were introduced over the loudspeaker by Albert Jenkins. The dancers were a local group and they wore white linen shirts with pleated fronts and sleeves, decked with bright rosettes, brooches and scarf pins. Their cord breeches had ribbons round the knees over long white woollen stockings and lightweight boots for dancing. The men wore black silk bowler hats with coloured streamers hanging down the back and the women had a circle of bright paper flowers intertwined in their hair.

Each performer held a pair of long handkerchiefs and danced to the sound of a penny whistle and an accordion. The gaiters of bells tied to their shins jingled as they danced the 'Cotswold Morris'. After half an hour of intricate steps and formations, there was warm applause and the troupers sat down, red-faced and perspiring, on the straw bales that had been arranged in a rough semicircle round the green. Their leader produced a collection of tall stoneware cider jars with the words HEY BROTHERS, OLD CHURCH, BOTANICAL BREWERY, PONTEFRACT stamped on the side and they relaxed and drank to their hearts' content in the warm May sunshine.

As Natasha sat on her throne, drinking from a goblet of mulled wine, and her attendants, Katrina and Rowena Buttle, sucked home-made Ribena lollies, we waited in anticipation for Sally's maypole dancers.

'Good luck!' shouted Jo to Sally.

In the centre of the village green, the maypole had

been topped in the traditional manner with eight bell garlands and, from each one, a long coloured ribbon, provided by Vera, drifted in the light breeze. Anne was helping with the preparations and Sally fussed about like a mother hen getting her group of girls in their correct places. Each girl wore a pretty dress and a headband of flowers.

'They look like little angels,' said a familiar voice. It was Beth, smiling at me.

'Glad you could make it,' I said.

We joined in the applause as the girls danced their patterns in and out until the ribbons were neatly plaited round the pole. Then they reversed the dance and, miraculously, the ribbons were unravelled. It was over and Sally breathed a sigh of relief as she was surrounded by parents expressing their thanks. Finally, looking hot and flushed, she came over to join us.

'Well done, Sally – that was terrific,' I said.

'The best maypole dancing we've ever seen in Ragley,' said Anne generously.

'How about a drink?' asked Jo.

Sally pulled a face. 'I'd rather have a cup of tea.'

'That's not like you,' said Jo.

'Come on,' said Sally, 'let's go in the Oak.'

'What about the ribbons on the maypole?' said Anne.

'I'll take them back to the vicarage,' said Vera.

'Good idea,' said Anne, knowing Vera wouldn't dream of setting foot in The Royal Oak or any other public house for that matter. 'Come on, John, we need your help.'

John Grainger followed on behind Vera and Anne and soon they were packing the ribbons into the back of Vera's Austin A40.

Beth and I were left standing on the village green, under the old oak tree.

'So, how about a drink?' I asked.

Beth looked anxiously at her wristwatch. 'Sorry, Jack, I can't stay. I promised Laura I would help her pack.'

'Pack?'

'Yes. She's going back to London. There's a new management job down there for her. She's renting out her flat in York and moving in with my parents in Little Chawton. Then she'll travel into the city on the train each day.'

'Oh, I see. Well . . . tell her good luck.'

Beth looked at me steadily. 'I will,' she said.

We stood there in silence for a few moments.

'Actually, I've got some lessons to prepare for this week,' I said, 'so I think I'll get off as well.'

Suddenly, John Grainger reappeared. 'Are you two coming in, then?'

'Sorry, John,' said Beth, 'I'm pushed for time and I have to get into York.'

'Same here, John,' I said. 'I've got some school work to do.'

Like a genial giant he placed his huge woodcarver's hands on our shoulders. 'Do you know what my mother used to say when I was always rushing about?' We both looked at his big, friendly, weatherbeaten face, flecks of sawdust in his curly beard and deep crow's feet round his eyes. 'She used to say, "Remember to stop a while to smell the flowers." It was good advice.'

'Perhaps one day we shall,' said Beth. She squeezed my hand and walked quickly down the High Street to her car.

'Think about it, Jack,' said John and he walked towards The Royal Oak, then stopped to talk to Old Tommy Piercy, who was carving delicious slices of crisp pork from his hog roast.

I watched Beth's Volkswagen Beetle pull out from the line of cars in the High Street and fork left on to the York Road. I found my car and climbed in. Norman Barraclough's fish van was parked in front of me and in the thick grime that covered the back doors someone had written, 'Shane Ramsbottom shot JR'. I smiled, set off down the High Street and took the right fork towards Kirkby Steepleton. As I drove on the back road to Bilbo Cottage I pondered John's words.

On Tuesday morning at eight o'clock, Jimmy Poole was walking down the High Street with his little Yorkshire terrier. Scargill loved his morning walk to collect Mr Poole's *Daily Express*. But now it was much more fun with all the strange little people sitting outside Pratt's Hardware Emporium, particularly the one that smelled strongly of glue. As they walked past, Scargill grabbed JR Ewing's white stetson hat in his strong teeth and bit off a chunk.

'So it's you, is it?'

Jimmy turned round in alarm. Timothy Pratt had just

emerged in the shop doorway, carrying his new supply of hedgehog-shaped boot scrapers.

'Ah'm thorry, Mr Pratt,' said Jimmy.

Deep down, Timothy had a kind heart and knew little Jimmy meant no harm. He crouched down and looked into Jimmy's black-button eyes. 'Just keep 'im on a lead in future!' he said softly.

Jimmy nodded, reattached the lead, much to Scargill's disgust, and they carried on their way. Timothy sighed and picked up the garden gnome and the broken piece of his hat and walked into his Emporium.

A mile away in Old Morton Manor, Major Rupert Forbes-Kitchener was sitting in his lounge drinking coffee and reading *The Times*.

In the outside world, the confrontation between Margaret Thatcher and Arthur Scargill, the left-wing leader of the Yorkshire National Union of Mineworkers, was becoming acrimonious. Arthur was reported to have said, 'I want to warn this woman at No. 10, who preaches on the altar of nuclear power, that the British miners will never again accept the butchery of pit closures.' Arthur didn't mince his words.

Opposite the major, his daughter was chuckling to herself. 'What is it, Virginia?' he asked, peering over his newspaper.

Virginia brushed the biscuit crumbs from her skin-tight jodhpurs, held up her copy of the *Daily Express* and pointed to the headline on page 7: WHO SHOT JR?

'It's obvious, isn't it?' he said, folding up his newspaper.

Virginia looked up in alarm. She had just put a five-pound bet on Sue Ellen at odds of five to one at William Hill's and wondered if her father knew more than she did. 'So who did shoot the fellow?' asked Virginia.

The major drank his coffee, stood up, buttoned up his waistcoat and muttered brusquely, 'Scargill . . . what?' and marched out.

Virginia stared lovingly after him and wondered why it was that older folk always seemed to be in another world.

Meanwhile, in the back room of Pratt's Hardware Emporium, Timothy Pratt opened his tube of super glue and picked up the broken piece of JR Ewing's stetson hat. He smiled to himself because at last he knew the answer.

Nobody had actually shot JR. He'd just been repeatedly chewed.

Chapter Eighteen

The Mystery of Life

The Parent–Teacher Association met this evening and decided to seek permission to extend the school entrance hall in order to accommodate a new school library, proposed building to commence in the autumn. We also agreed to hold a teddy bears' picnic on the last day of term.

Extract from the Ragley School Logbook:
Monday, 9 June 1980

'It's a mystery,' said Sally. 'They were here this morning.'

'What's a mystery?' I asked.

'My pineapple chunks,' said Sally. 'They've gone.'

'Sorry – haven't seen them,' I said, hurriedly gathering papers from my desk in the office. It was 7.30 p.m. on Monday, 9 June. Members of our Parent–Teacher Association were taking their seats in the school hall, the meeting was about to start and pineapple chunks were not on the agenda.

As usual, Staff Nurse Sue Phillips chaired the meeting superbly and had that wonderful skill of making everyone feel valued. Each person had the opportunity to make a contribution and clear decisions were made. I imagined she organized her nurses in the same way.

'So, to sum up,' said Sue, 'we've agreed that all PTA funds will go towards a major project to begin next academic year: namely, the building of a small extension to accommodate a new school library and resource centre. This will include books, maps, visual aids, slide projector . . . and perhaps even a computer.'

Jo Hunter's eyes lit up. For her, this would be a dream come true. She had always wanted a computer in school and firmly believed that, one day, every school would have one. Following our fund-raising activities of the past two years, our school library had grown considerably and it now filled a corner of the school hall on dozens of home-made shelves. It was a celebration of Contiboard. However, my dream was for the creation of a dedicated resource centre and, for this, we required more space.

It was my turn to provide a formal thank-you. 'On behalf of the school I'd like to thank Sue and all members of the Parent–Teacher Association for their wonderful support,' I said. 'This is a really exciting project and, if all goes to plan, this time next year the children of the village will have the opportunity to do independent research and become more effective learners.'

Anne gave me a wide-eyed smile as she recognized the 'education-speak'.

'Thanks, Jack,' said Sue, 'and, finally, we've agreed to organize a teddy bears' picnic on the school field next month, on the last afternoon of the summer term, and Shirley the cook has offered to make a party tea including honey sandwiches.'

On that happy note the hall slowly emptied of parents. Anne and Jo began to put away the chairs and dining tables and I set off to do my usual check of windows and doors. Sue Phillips and Sally volunteered to stay behind to wash the cups and saucers in the staff-room sink. Sue looked curiously at Sally, who appeared flushed as she put the tray of crockery on the worktop next to the sink.

'So how are you, Sally?' she asked as she ran the hot tap and squirted some Fairy liquid into the washing-up bowl.

'Fine, Sue,' said Sally, picking up a tea towel.

'You didn't seem quite your usual bubbly self tonight,' said Sue, staring down at the washing-up bowl. 'Are you OK?'

Sally picked up the first cup from the draining board and began to dry it. 'To be honest, Sue, I've been feeling a bit run-down and listless lately.'

'Maybe you need a tonic,' said Sue.

'Maybe I do,' said Sally. 'You know, it's strange. I've loved Weight Watchers and I've been sensible in what I have eaten, but my weight still seems to be the same.'

'These things take time, Sally,' said Sue as she immersed a pile of saucers.

310

'And I've begun to feel hungry at odd times.'

Sue dropped the teaspoons into the hot soapy water. 'What do you mean by odd times?'

Sally laughed. 'It's a good job my Colin is understanding. Two nights ago he made me mashed potatoes and beans at midnight and last night it was chocolate on toast.'

'I think you should go for a check-up.'

'Oh, I'll be fine,' said Sally.

Sue rinsed the bowl and dried her hands. Then she walked over to the staff-room door and closed it and turned to look at Sally more intently. 'Sally,' she said quietly, 'have you considered anything else?'

Sally stopped wiping the draining board and looked up in surprise. 'To be honest, I think I just feel a bit bloated. There could be lots of reasons.' She hung the tea towel over the radiator, then picked up her ethnic, open-weave shoulder bag and hunted in it for her packet of tissues.

Sue closed the cupboard doors and put on her coat. 'Look, Sally, why not call in tomorrow lunchtime to see Dr Davenport after his morning surgery?'

'Oh, I don't know,' said Sally, blowing her nose.

'It can't do any harm,' said Sue with a reassuring smile, 'and you're probably right. Maybe you're a bit run-down, in which case a tonic will be just the thing.' Then she buttoned her coat, picked up her bag and opened the door. As an afterthought, she walked back and squeezed Sally's arm. 'Ring me if you want to talk.'

A few minutes later, when Sally climbed into her car, she forgot to insert her cassette of the Carpenters into the cassette-player and drove off in silence.

Colin had prepared some bubble and squeak and a glass of white wine. Sally ate it quickly, picked up her wine and sipped it.

'You're quiet tonight,' he said.

'Busy day,' said Sally, kicking off her sandals and putting her feet up on the sofa.

Colin squeezed next to her and put his arm round her shoulder.

'You are a lovely man,' said Sally dreamily.

Five minutes later she was asleep.

On Tuesday morning, outside the leaded kitchen window of Bilbo Cottage bluebottles buzzed, while the fluffy seeds of willow drifted on the heavy still air. High summer was almost upon us and, as I walked out to my car, sunshine glinted on the yellow and chrome AA badge attached to the grill. The hedgerow was a riot of new life and bracken was uncurling in among the cow parsley and the first magenta bells of foxgloves. As I drove to school, sycamore and ash keys hung lazily above my head as the trees, now in heavy leaf, shaded the back road from Kirkby Steepleton into Ragley.

When I arrived, Anne was showing Sally and Jo a smart programme with a dark-blue cover. On the front it read,

> *York Festival & Mystery Plays*
> *6–30 June 1980*
> *Sponsored by the Midland Bank*
> *President: HRH The Duchess of Kent*
> *Vice-President: The Marquis of Normanby, CBE*

'My friend said it was absolutely wonderful and she gave me this programme,' said Anne. 'So how about it?'

'Count me in,' said Sally.

'I'll come, but Dan's working,' said Jo.

'How about you, Jack?' said Anne. 'We're going to the Mystery Plays on Thursday night.'

'Definitely,' I said. 'I've not been since I was a school-boy.'

Every four years the York mystery plays were performed open-air in the city and attracted huge audiences. Born in the Middle Ages, these 'mystery' or 'craft' plays flourished throughout the fourteenth and fifteenth centuries and the people of York had carried on the tradition.

'I see Christopher Timothy, the actor from *All Creatures Great and Small*, is in it,' said Sally, scanning the long list of actors.

'They usually have somebody famous as the lead part,' said Anne.

Sally looked at the back of the programme. 'It says here that the De Gray Rooms in Exhibition Square will be open from 6 p.m. to 2 a.m. throughout the festival and, if you have a meal, you get a concessionary ticket for 50p. So why don't we all meet there?' Everyone nodded in agreement. 'What about John?' asked Sally. 'Do you think he might go?'

'John's not one for watching plays,' said Anne sadly, 'but he might be interested in the scenery.'

'So are you organizing the tickets, Anne?' I asked.

'Yes. I'll check with Vera this afternoon and book them

tonight,' said Anne. 'I'll ring Beth, shall I, Jack? I'm sure she'd love to go.'

'Good idea,' I said, but I missed the smiles exchanged between the three women.

At lunchtime, Sally asked if she could slip out of school to go to Dr Davenport's surgery on the Morton Road. She explained she needed a pick-me-up and I asked her if she would get one for me as well. She seemed preoccupied and didn't get the joke.

The rest of us relaxed over a cup of tea in the staff-room when Vera arrived following a busy morning at her cross-stitch class in the village hall. She immediately began to replenish the black ink in the drum of the Gestetner duplicating machine and we all watched in admiration. Vera was the only person who could achieve this task without getting her hands covered in ink.

'I'm looking forward to the mystery plays,' she said, 'but I'm afraid Joseph won't be able to join us. He's involved in an ecclesiastical conference in York all this week and he says he won't be able to take his Religious Education lessons.'

I guessed Joseph was probably relieved.

I decided to do my Bible story during afternoon school and quickly understood Joseph's frustrations when I came to mark the children's exercise books. Eleven-year-old Frankie Kershaw had written 'Moses went up Mount Cyanide to get the Ten Commandments but he died before he got to Canada', while ten-year-old Cathy Cathcart informed me that 'the group who followed Jesus was called the twelve decibels'. I knew that to be a good teacher of young children you had to understand their world. As I put a small red question mark in the margin, I reflected that you also needed a sense of humour.

After school, I stayed late in the office to begin my end-of-year reports for the children in my class until seven o'clock, when I decided to call into The Royal Oak for a quick meal on my way home. I hadn't been shopping at the weekend and my kitchen cupboards were empty again.

At the bar, Sheila was in heated conversation with Stevie 'Supersub' Coleclough. 'What you on about?' shouted Sheila, pointing at the plate of food she had put on the bar. 'That's proper mince, that is, straight from Piercy's Butcher's in the 'Igh Street. There's none finer.'

Stevie looked dubiously at the mince-and-onion pie, chips and peas, covered in delicious gravy. It made my mouth water.

'It said in t'paper them scientists in London were mekking it from beans,' said Stevie. He pointed to a headline in a *Yorkshire Post* that had been left on the bar.

'Don't be daft, Stevie. 'Ow can y'mek mince from beans?' grumbled Sheila.

Stevie blushed scarlet, picked up his meal and wandered away to join the rest of the Ragley cricket team. Big Dave was the captain and was haranguing his followers about his latest concern. 'Handbags for men . . . they'll be wearing earrings next!'

Everyone agreed instantly and with equal contempt,

except for Clint Ramsbottom, who stared into the haze of cigarette smoke and thoughtfully fingered his left ear.

'Y'reight there, Dave,' agreed Little Malcolm somewhat belatedly. Malcolm's thoughts were elsewhere. He had his eye on a car. While the local council turned a blind eye to Big Dave and Little Malcolm using their bin wagon for personal business, Malcolm knew deep down in his heart that Dorothy Humpleby would be far from impressed if they turned up at their next dance in a three-ton refuse wagon. On Victor Pratt's forecourt, Malcolm had seen a 1250 cc. bright-green, two-door Deluxe 1973 Hillman Avenger with a sticker in the windscreen marked £795. This was a fortune to Little Malcolm but he thought his big cousin might chip in.

'An' what can ah do f'you, Mr Sheffield?' said Sheila. 'Yer looking tired.'

'Just a half of Chestnut and the same as Stevie, please, Sheila. It looked lovely.'

'Ah like a man wi' a good appetite,' said Sheila. 'Ah'll bring it t'yer table.' With a wiggle of her skin-tight leather miniskirt she disappeared into the kitchen.

I picked up the *Yorkshire Post*, found a quiet table away from the jukebox and began to read an article entitled 'Snap, Crackle and Stop'. It said that fifty Yorkshire folk had been asked if they wanted morning television and most of them had said no. Currently during the early morning there was nothing on television except for the Open University on BBC1 and BBC2 up to 7.55 a.m. and, on ITV, programmes for schools and colleges began at 9.30 a.m. So the idea of breakfast television seemed strange.

Sheila arrived with my meal and leaned over my shoulder to look at the newspaper. 'What y'readin', Mr Sheffield?' The smell of her scent was overpowering.

'It's about breakfast television, Sheila.'

'How d'you mean, breakfast television?'

'Well . . . it's television at breakfast time.'

'That'll never catch on, Mr Sheffield,' she said, 'unless y'put on *Hawaii Five-O* when ah'm slippin' out o' me negligée.'

'You're probably right, Sheila,' I said, quickly dispelling the image that had sprung into my mind.

I tucked into my meal and scanned the end of the article. 'Ah'm too busy mekkin' 'is breakfast,' a certain Mrs Cynthia Clack of Thirkby was reported to have said. It was clear that breakfast television would have a hard time catching on in Yorkshire.

On Thursday at six o'clock I pulled up outside Beth's house and she hurried down the path and jumped into my car.

'Thanks for the lift, Jack,' she said. 'It was difficult getting out of school so quickly.'

Beth was wearing an elegant floral-print, calf-length dress with a neat braid trim on the collar and looked stunning. She carried a fleece on her lap in anticipation of the temperature dropping as the night wore on. I was aware of the heady scent of Rive Gauche perfume as we sped into York and, once again, I knew contentment.

It was a perfect summer evening, warm and still, and the ruins of St Mary's Abbey were bathed in sunlight.

After meeting in the De Gray Rooms for a hasty summer salad, Anne, with a slightly bemused John Grainger in tow, gathered us together and we walked into the Museum Gardens.

Sally had brought a bag of sixpences and used them all to buy everyone an ice-cream cornet with a flake in it. The 'tanner', worth two and a half pence, was about to go out of circulation and Sally had collected a jarful of the small silver coins over the years.

'Isn't this the most perfect setting?' said Jo. We found our seats, enjoyed our ice creams and looked in admiration at the imposing stone walls and arched windows of the ruined abbey. Traditionally, it was against this dramatic setting that the mystery plays were performed.

'It used to be a Benedictine monastery,' said Sally, 'but in 1270 it was almost totally destroyed by fire.'

'Clever how they've built the scenery round it,' said John, 'and it's well-built: just look at those dovetail joints.'

'Pity Colin's not here – you could have compared notes,' said Sally with a grin.

I glanced at Beth. She had put her fleece over her shoulders. 'Are you warm enough?' I asked.

'I'm fine, Jack,' she said. 'It's good to be here.'

The summer sun was beginning to bleach her honey-blonde hair once again and, in the evening light, she looked beautiful.

To the accompaniment of the Rowntree Mackintosh band, the actors walked across the grass and the drama began. The plays were meant to represent the history of the world from God's creation to the Last Judgement. We watched, spellbound, as God created heaven, earth and hell and then witnessed the angel Lucifer's fall from grace. It was hard to believe that the ordinary artisans of the Middle Ages had the skill to create such wonderful plays along with beautiful stained-glass windows and the mighty cathedrals of England.

Eventually, all the audience were invited to sing 'Jerusalem' and, as the sun gradually sank behind the nearby St Olave's Church, the peacocks, wandering free in the grounds, screeched in accompaniment.

It was a tired but happy group who said goodnight and Beth and I set off for my car in Marygate. Far from the footfalls of the evening city, we walked hand in hand with calm conviction through the Museum Gardens.

On Friday morning, as I drove towards the school gates, I saw Heathcliffe Earnshaw sitting on the village green. He had filled an old Tizer bottle full of water and dropped in a liquorice shoelace. Then he screwed on the cap and shook it until his teeth rattled. Finally, he stared hard at the grubby-looking liquid. It had definitely changed colour. Then, he wiped the snot from his upper lip, unscrewed the bottle and lifted it to his lips. Like a connoisseur of fine wines he swirled it round his mouth and then, unlike a connoisseur, he swallowed it. With a satisfied nod of appreciation he screwed on the cap. Perfect, he thought. For Heathcliffe, this was a typical start to a day.

I parked my car, hurried across the playground and

bumped into Jimmy Poole. 'Hello, Jimmy. What are you doing?' I asked.

'Ah'm thuckin' a thweet, Mithter Theffield,' replied Jimmy. 'Ith a therbert lemon. Would you like one?'

I recalled my mother telling me never to refuse a present from a child. 'Yes, please, Jimmy.' I walked into the entrance hall, popped the sweet into my mouth and, in doing so, broke one of my own school rules.

Sally was using the phone in the school office. 'I'm just ringing to check the results and whether or not I need a prescription,' she said.

It sounded personal so I walked through to the staff-room.

''Morning, Jack,' said Anne, adding two more labels to the collection box on the staff-room table. The Ragley scout group was saving Golly labels from Robertson's jam and marmalade jars in order to provide camping equipment and we were all eating vast quantities to support the cause.

''Morning, Anne,' I said, but she had already gone.

There was clearly something going on in the school office, so I walked in. Sally was sitting at Vera's desk, staring at the telephone receiver. 'What's Colin going to say?' she murmured to herself.

'Life's a mystery,' said Vera with a smile. 'You never know how it will turn out.'

'Well . . . you've all guessed, I suppose,' said Sally.

'The pineapple chunks certainly got me thinking,' said Anne with a smile and she squeezed Sally's hand.

'Pineapple chunks?' I said.

'Oh, Sally!' exclaimed Jo and almost jumped over the desk to throw her arms round her.

'Pineapple chunks?' I repeated.

Vera gave Sally a hug. 'I'm so pleased for you,' she said.

'What's all the fuss about pineapple chunks?' I said. 'Oh, I remember now, Sally: you'd lost them.'

'Yes, I had, Jack, but it's not important now.'

'Personally, I prefer tinned pears, especially with vanilla and chocolate ice cream,' I said.

The three women stared at me as if I was from another planet.

'What?' I said.

'Jack, I think Sally might have some news for you,' said Vera.

Sally nodded and looked at me in the way women look at men when they genuinely feel sorry that their intuition and sensitivity were surgically removed at birth. 'Jack . . . I'm pregnant.'

'Pregnant!'

'Yes, Jack,' said Sally.

'Oh,' I said. 'Er, well . . . er, well done,' I spluttered.

'Thanks, Jack,' said Sally with a straight face. Then all four women burst into hoots of laughter.

It was a strange Friday. Colin left work as soon as he heard the news and rushed into school. After an emotional, tearful conversation with Sally he sped off back to work to take all his colleagues for a liquid lunch. Ruby professed to have known for the past month, owing to her vast experience in all things maternal, and Shirley the cook brought in a tray of home-made biscuits, still hot from the oven, at afternoon playtime. I volunteered to do playground duty and Vera, Anne, Jo, Ruby, Shirley and even Shirley's assistant, the fiercesome Mrs Critchley, could be heard laughing as Sally recounted the recent events in her life.

She told them she had read in an early edition of *Cosmopolitan* that Michael Parkinson had said that the most beautiful thing a man can do for a woman is have a vasectomy. Even the prim Vera laughed and was secretly pleased that Colin hadn't read that particular article in Sally's magazine.

That evening, driving home, I felt happy for Sally. She had found contentment and the gift of a child. As I walked into the hallway of Bilbo Cottage it occurred to me that life doesn't have to be a mystery. Perhaps you just have to ask the right questions.

Fortunately I knew Beth's telephone number off by heart.

Chapter Nineteen

Brass Bands and Butterflies

The Parent–Teacher Association has organized a day trip to Robin Hood's Bay on Saturday, 28 June, to support the Ragley and Morton Brass Band.
> Extract from the Ragley School Logbook:
> Friday, 27 June 1980

The butterfly hovered in the single shaft of sunlight and one pair of eyes followed its every movement. Amelia Duff gripped her programme tightly and stared at the flying insect. But there was no peace in the eyes that followed the beating of its multicoloured wings.

The village hall was full and, sitting in the row in front of me, the Revd Joseph Evans was nodding his head in time to the music. Next to him, Vera peered at the side of the stage and stared intently at Amelia. Then she followed Amelia's gaze until she saw the tiny butterfly, hovering with flickering wings by the open window.

Finally, a gentle smile of understanding crossed Vera's face. Then she turned back to the brass band and tapped her beautifully manicured nails on the side of her Marks & Spencer's handbag in time to 'We All Live in a Yellow Submarine'.

It was Thursday evening, 26 June, and the Ragley and Morton Brass Band were having their final practice before Saturday's annual Brass Band Festival at Robin Hood's Bay on the beautiful east coast of Yorkshire. This was a big event in the village calendar and the Parent–Teacher Association had organized a coach party to go and support them.

The band comprised a disparate group of villagers and a motley collection of cornets, tenor horns and trombones, as well as Ernie Morgetroyd's battered euphonium and the ancient flugelhorn played by his brother Wally. The youngest member of the band, thirteen-year-old Wayne Ramsbottom, who had been in my class two years ago, comprised the entire percussion section.

Sadly, their closing rendition of 'Abide With Me' lost some of its inherent beauty each time Wally sneezed and sprayed enough germs to infect the conductor and the entire front row. Peter Duddleston, the eloquent band leader and local bank manager, put down his baton on his elaborately decorated music stand with its brightly embroidered cover and turned to address the audience. 'Thank you for your support and let's hope for a sunny day on Saturday.'

*   *   *

It wasn't until Friday lunchtime that Saturday's trip to the seaside cropped up. Predictably, Joseph was looking downcast when he walked into the staff-room after his weekly Religious Education lesson. He put his pile of Class 1 notebooks on the coffee table, picked up Jodie Cuthbertson's book, opened it and read out loud, 'God must have big hands because Jesus sits on his right one.' He shook his head in dismay. 'Where am I going wrong?' he said.

'Don't worry, Joseph,' said Vera reassuringly, 'tomorrow we have a trip to your favourite seaside resort.' With that, she cleared her desk and gathered together the huge collection of letters and packages that had to be posted to County Hall in Northallerton. The official paperwork seemed to increase week by week but today the pile was larger than usual and Vera stacked the letters and packages in a large cardboard box.

'Come on, Vera,' I said, picking up the box, 'let me help. The fresh air will do me good.'

We walked out of the school gate, turned left under the avenue of horse-chestnut trees, skirted the corner of the village green and crossed the High Street. Next door to Diane's Hair Salon was the Post Office with a red telephone box outside. Blocking the Post Office doorway like a flying buttress was the huge frame of a very disgruntled Mrs Winifred Brown.

'Five pence f'telephone calls! It were only two pence las' year,' shouted Mrs Brown, rummaging in her purse for loose change.

'It's inflation, Mrs Brown,' came a tiny voice from inside the shop.

'Inflashun! Inflashun! More like daylight robbery!'

Mrs Brown glowered at me. However, I noticed she carefully avoided eye contact with Vera as she squeezed into the telephone box to ring her husband, Eddie, at his new place of work. Eddie Brown had just got a job at Portaloo in York, making mobile toilets. Alton Towers, Britain's first theme park in Staffordshire, built in the Disneyland tradition, had taken the executive decision to install a Portaloo Classic 480 Unit with a brown leather-ette finish to the cubicle doors. Eddie Brown's task was to attach the doors and he was proud of his work.

'Fit for t'Queen,' he said, as he screwed the final door in place. Then he visibly paled when he heard he was wanted on the telephone by Winifred. To Eddie, spending a working day in a portable toilet was sheer heaven when compared with spending ten minutes with his formidable wife.

'Get 'ome now, Eddie,' screamed Winifred down the phone.

'Y'what?' said Eddie.

'Ah sed, get 'ome.'

'OK, OK.'

'Frankenstein's gone missin'.'

'Y'what?'

'Jus' get 'ome.'

'OK, OK.'

Frankenstein was Eddie's emotionally disturbed ferret, who regularly sought out dark corners. Secretly, Eddie thought that Frankenstein had more sense than he was given credit for.

When Vera and I walked into the Post Office, the alarmed expression on Amelia Duff's face disappeared. 'Oh, hello, Vera. Lovely to see you,' she said, pushing a few strands of greying hair out of her eyes, 'and you too, Mr Sheffield.'

Amelia was a diminutive fifty-seven-year-old spinster and had been post mistress for the past fifteen years. She lived in the small rooms above the shop and, up to a few months ago, she had looked after her ailing father. When he died, Amelia had become introverted and forgetful. Her face was thin and pale and she gave us a strained smile from behind the counter. She took a quick sip of tea from her 1935 King George V Silver Jubilee mug.

'The school seems to have got more mail than usual, Vera,' said Amelia.

'It increases every week,' said Vera and she put the box on the counter and took out her purse. 'While I'm here, Amelia, I need a 25p television licence stamp, please, five 12p stamps and five 10p stamps.' Then she looked more closely at Amelia. 'What's the matter?' she asked gently. Vera had taken a great interest in Amelia's welfare and, recently, had encouraged her to become more involved in the Women's Institute. She stretched across the counter and put her hand on the post mistress's bony arm.

Amelia glanced down, responding to the touch. Then there was a hint of a warmer smile. 'They've asked me to play in the band on Saturday,' she said.

'But that's wonderful news,' said Vera encouragingly. 'You play beautifully.'

'Wally Morgetroyd's got a bad cold,' explained Amelia, 'so they need a flugelhorn.'

'And there's no one better than you, Amelia,' said Vera.

Amelia opened her big book of stamps. 'Well, there *was* one,' she said sadly. Her long fingers reached for the collar of her thick knitted cardigan and absent-mindedly rested on her delicate brooch, a beautiful enamel butterfly. Then she stared out of the shop window.

'Yes, and he would be so proud if he knew you were playing again,' said Vera.

'I don't think I'm ready yet, Vera,' said Amelia. 'Every time the shop door rings, I imagine him coming in.'

Vera glanced up at me and began to empty the box of school mail and put it on the counter. 'I'll see you back at school, Mr Sheffield,' she said.

I took the hint, walked out of the shop and left Vera and Amelia deep in conversation.

Shortly before five o'clock I was alone in the office, completing the school logbook, when Vera suddenly reappeared. 'Tea, Mr Sheffield?' she asked.

I put down my fountain pen. 'Yes, please, Vera.'

Minutes later Vera pulled up her chair next to my desk and we sat there sipping tea. Eventually, Vera put down her cup, took a deep breath and settled back. I knew there was something on her mind. 'I should like to tell you a story,' said Vera, 'because we all need to support my dear friend Amelia.'

'Of course,' I said, putting the top back on my fountain pen.

'First of all, you need to know a little about Amelia's father.' Vera paused. In the distance, the bells of St Mary's Church chimed and we both privately counted up to five. 'He was a Yorkshireman from Bradford called Athol Duff,' continued Vera. 'Amelia's mother died in childbirth, so it had always been just the two of them. They were inseparable and she has been inconsolable since her father's death in the summer.'

I nodded in understanding and repositioned my chair closer to the window to take advantage of the afternoon sunshine. It sounded as if this was going to be a long story and Vera poured the tea.

Vera told me that Athol Duff was a mill worker and had played the flugelhorn in the famous Black Dyke Mills Band. Helped by Athol's wonderful skill, they had won the prestigious *Daily Herald* National Championship Trophy three times in the 1940s. The tone of Athol's flugelhorn was mellow and haunting in contrast to the brightness of a trumpet or cornet and this had given the band its distinctive sound.

Then the mill hit difficult times with the decline of the textile industry. In the 1960s the United States imposed import tariffs and Black Dyke Mills had turned to Japan. Athol could see this was the beginning of the end of the life he loved and decided it was time for him to leave. So, with quiet finality, he packed his gleaming brass flugelhorn in its purple, velvet-lined case and took down his sepia photograph of Queensbury Mills, a Victorian colossus set against the smoky chimneys of Bradford and the bleak moors beyond.

He said goodbye to the factory ghosts, the chatter of mill girls and the silent echo of a million shuttles. On a freezing December morning, he climbed into his rusty Wolseley 14 and drove over the moors to his smoke-blackened, end-of-terrace cottage. By then, his paper-thin lungs convinced Amelia that they needed a new home in the fresh air of North Yorkshire and so she became the Ragley post mistress.

On the other side of the High Street, someone else was also drinking tea. Amelia was sipping a refreshing cup of Typhoo while staring thoughtfully at a pair of her father's old clogs in the corner of the back room. Next to them was a smaller pair that had been made for her by her father. She remembered them so well. A horse-shoe of iron protected the beech-wood sole and the stiff leather upper ensured both father and daughter would be protected from the huge machinery in the mill. She recalled sitting next to her father and tapping her feet to the rhythm of the giant looms – heel and toe, heel and toe – and her father would take pride in her ability to find music in the most unlikely places and the distant echoes still filled her mind.

But most of all she remembered the long winter nights of her childhood when she had practised on the flugel-horn until she was almost as proficient as her father.

Eventually, one Christmas, she stood on the old rag rug in front of a roaring coal fire in the front room and played 'Silent Night'.

Athol Duff put his arm round his daughter's shoulders and said gently, 'Amelia, you 'ave a gift.'

Amelia had looked round the room for a gaily wrapped parcel.

Her father had laughed out loud. 'No, my love, ah mean you 'ave the gift of music.' Then he had wiped away a tear and hugged his precious daughter. 'I've taught you all ah know, Amelia,' he said proudly.

On that special day, after searching in the old bureau, he gave her a brooch. It was in the shape of a butterfly.

'This was y'mother's,' said Athol. 'Likely as not, she'd want you to 'ave it.'

Amelia held it up to the light. 'It's beautiful, Dad,' she said.

'Whenever ah saw a butterfly, ah allus thought of 'er,' said Athol.

Then there was silence. There were no words between father and daughter. They both understood.

During 1979, the onset of illness told Athol that this Christmas would be his last. He was too weak to play 'In the Bleak Mid-Winter' on his flugelhorn, so Amelia played it for him. A few lucky souls were walking down the High Street on that snowy winter's night. They heard the sweet music drift up to the heavens and felt all the better for it before carrying on their way. A few months later Athol's vibrant life of hard graft and soft music came to its end.

Vera looked thoughtful as she collected the cups. 'So I've encouraged Amelia to bring her flugelhorn tomorrow, Mr Sheffield,' she said.

Saturday morning dawned bright and clear. Outside the village hall on Ragley High Street, the sun sparkled on William Featherstone's cream and green Reliance bus. William, in his brown bus driver's jacket, welcomed each passenger by doffing his peaked cap. It was the thirtieth time he had made this journey and he knew a good day was in store. Vera was standing next to him with a list of passengers on her clipboard.

'Good morning, Miss Henderson,' said Vera, ticking off her name. 'I've reserved you a seat just behind Joseph.'

'Thank you, Vera,' said Beth. She smiled as she climbed on to the bus. The spare seat was next to me.

'Morning, Jack. Lovely day.' She looked casual in her T-shirt, jeans and trainers and put her fleece and a bulky shoulder bag on the seat. I got up to put them on the luggage rack.

'Hello, Beth. What's in the bag?' I asked.

'My packed lunch,' said Beth, 'and if you're good I might share it with you.'

Her eyes twinkled and I relaxed back in my seat. This was a good start to the day.

Soon we were driving through the farmlands of the Vale of York, where the River Ouse and its tributaries drained the great agricultural region of the county. Out of the window, beyond the thorny hedgerows, tall stalks of green unripe barley swayed in the gentle breeze with a random, sinuous rhythm. It was as if whole fields had a life of their own, rippling with swirling shadows and reflecting the light of the new day.

Time passed slowly and we drove along a moorland road beneath a sky of wheeling starlings. The steepled line of distant villages huddled on the horizon and the green and grey of North Yorkshire stretched out before us, splashed with purple heather. The old coach chugged up winding roads and through pretty villages on to the tableland of the bare and windswept North Yorkshire Moors. After millions of years under primeval seas, the Ice Age had transformed this land. It seemed as if a giant claw had gouged the purple hills, leaving behind green valleys that ran in parallel lines into the Vale of Pickering. We were deep into grouse moor country, a natural home for bees and wildlife and one of England's greatest national parks.

In the seat in front of me, Vera stared out of the window in wonder at this wild land of moors and mosses. Next to her, Joseph frowned as he read his *Daily Telegraph*. Beyond the borders of our lives, the world continued to be dominated by those who searched for power and influence. During the recent trade union day of action, thousands of public-sector workers had demonstrated against the cuts in government spending and Arthur Scargill had addressed three thousand protesters at a rally in Sheffield. Meanwhile, it was reported that President Carter and a certain ex-movie star, Mr Ronald Reagan, had easily defeated their Democratic and

Republican rivals in the nominations for the presidency. Joseph chuckled and closed the newspaper.

Finally, the mighty cliffs and the North Sea could be seen in the far distance and we drove into Robin Hood's Bay. Many of the homes and cottages had been bought and renovated by 'incomers' and this had breathed new life into the area. However, the community remained humbled by the might of the sea and respectful of the giant forces of nature that had carved out this gem on the Yorkshire coastline.

In the car park at the top of the steeply sloping village street we disembarked and went our separate ways. We had an hour to spare before the concert began. The band made directly for the local public house, many of the villagers set off to explore the tiny gift shops and Beth and I walked down to the bay. The tide was out and sunlight reflected from a thousand rock pools.

'What a perfect place for lunch, Jack,' said Beth and we sat down on a rocky outcrop. It looked as though Beth had used her complete collection of Tupperware as she revealed a multitude of sandwiches, fresh tomatoes and fruit. There was space to breathe here and the cooling breeze was fresh in my face. Beth's face and arms were tanned again and emphasized her perfect English beauty as she leaned back against the rock and soaked up the view.

'Thanks for coming, Beth,' I said as I poured some more tea from her flask.

'Good to be here.'

'It wouldn't have been the same without you,' I said.

'Really?'

'Yes. I wouldn't have had any lunch!'

Beth threw a rolled-up tea towel at me and I fell backwards trying to avoid it. We both laughed and twenty minutes later we packed up her bag and set off to walk across the bay.

I felt like a child again as we took off our trainers and socks and paddled in the cooling sea water. Gentle wavelets caressed our feet and pebbles rolled with smooth erosion between our toes. Around us, sunlight played upon the natural beauty of the landscape and the blue-black waves stretched out to meet the awesome sky. In this vast amphitheatre of silence we walked together by the edge of the sea. I felt as though the driftwood of my life had been cast upon this lonely shore but I couldn't recall being happier. Then, suddenly, the loud cry of seagulls, salt sharp in the sea air, woke me from my dreams.

'Perhaps we should be making our way back now, Jack?' said Beth and she took my hand.

We walked back, both deep in our own thoughts. I looked up at the huddle of houses cascading down towards the rocky beach and wondered about the history of this unique place with its tales of smugglers in times gone by. Soon we reached the harbour and we leaned against a fishing boat and stared out to sea. It felt as if neither of us wanted to leave.

Then a long slim shadow appeared alongside us and I looked up, shielding my eyes from the sun. It was Joseph and he removed his straw hat and wiped his brow.

'Hello, you two. I just wanted one last view of this beautiful scene,' he said and, together, we looked across the bay. 'Born in fire, formed in ice,' said Joseph almost to himself. 'The breath of God has blessed this land.' I looked at him, at the ridge of his Roman nose reddened by the sun. 'That's what my father told me when I came here as a boy. I remember it as if it was yesterday.'

'Fine words, Joseph,' I said, 'and perfect for this lovely day.'

On a large flat grassy space at the top of the village, bands in their different-coloured jackets mingled casually, drinking beer and swapping stories with easy banter. Rivalry there may be, but comradeship and a shared love of music was the theme of the day. Vera had reserved two deck chairs next to her and Beth and I sat down. A brass band from Huddersfield began the proceedings with, fittingly, 'Land of Hope and Glory' and everyone tapped their feet. Above our heads, daring seagulls swooped from a cobalt-blue sky and brass trumpets flashed in the sunlight as we gloried in these magnificent surroundings.

The afternoon wore on until it was the turn of the Ragley and Morton Brass Band for the final performance of the day. They took their places and began their short programme. The final piece was the one we had all been waiting for.

'This is the one, Jack,' said Vera and she clenched her handkerchief and sat forward in her seat.

Peter Duddleston turned to face the audience. 'And

now, ladies and gentlemen, we finish with that wonderful hymn composed by Henry Francis Lyte in 1847. He wrote the words to his poem while he lay dying from tuberculosis. The lyrics are sung to William Monk's beautiful "Eventide" and it is, of course, considered to be England's national hymn.' He smiled gently at Amelia, who sat still as stone in her seat. She seemed to be staring at something just outside our range of vision. 'Ladies and gentlemen, we are proud to feature Miss Amelia Duff on the flugelhorn.' Then he tapped his baton on his music stand and a hush descended on the crowd.

Above our heads a butterfly hovered and, once again, Amelia's eyes followed its every movement. Then she stood up proudly, raised her flugelhorn to her lips and began to play. There was an intake of breath from the audience. Here was music the like of which they had never heard before. It was music blessed by angels.

Chapter Twenty

Dear Teacher

88 children were registered on roll on this last day of the school year. Thirteen fourth-year juniors left today and will start full-time education at Easington Comprehensive School in September. A teddy bears' picnic, organized by the PTA, was held on the school field.

Extract from the Ragley School Logbook:
Friday, 25 July 1980

It had been a restless night.

In the early hours there was no moon, only backlit clouds that scurried across the sky and covered the land with shadows of confusion. The night lay heavy on the sleeping earth and, even with the windows of Bilbo Cottage wide open, the heat was stifling. As I stared into the far distance, where the earth met the sky, the rugged hills were a pale violet against the distant glow of a new dawn. Finally, the first rays of daylight shimmered on the parched fields and bars of golden light invaded my dark bedroom.

It was Friday, 25 July, the last day of the school year. My third year as headmaster of Ragley School was about to come to an end. Scattered on the breakfast table were my notes for the final assembly and I sat down to put them in order. The problem was . . . all I could think about was Beth.

My drive to school was filled with thoughts of her and, after parking, I walked out of school to clear my thoughts. The village green was deserted and I leaned against the giant ancient oak tree. A thick tapestry of tendrils swarmed up the gnarled bark towards boughs heavy in leaf and acorn. There was peace and welcome shadow here in the shimmering heat haze of this breathless morning.

Then, in the stillness, the arrow of the old cast-iron weather vane on top of the village hall suddenly creaked in the first hint of a breeze. With a reluctant grinding of metal on metal, it slowly swung round towards the direction of the far distant clouds. The weather was turning.

Ragley was coming alive and I rejoiced that, year by year, I was becoming a part of the daily life of this beautiful Yorkshire village. Down the High Street, Prudence Golightly was watering a hanging basket outside the General Stores and Young Tommy Piercy was wheeling his delivery bicycle out of his grandad's butcher's shop. On the handlebars was a plastic bag containing a pair of pig's trotters destined for Maurice Tupham, the rhubarb champion. Natasha Smith was staring at the new range of lipsticks in the Pharmacy window and Timothy Pratt was setting out his aluminium cat-flaps in a perfectly straight line on the trestle table outside his Hardware Emporium. Little Malcolm Robinson, immensely proud of his new 1973 bright-green Hillman Avenger, had pulled up outside Nora's Coffee Shop. Instantly, the love of his life, Dorothy Humpleby, tottered out on her high heels to admire it, with Nora Pratt in close attendance. Big Dave Robinson clambered out of the passenger seat and gave his diminutive cousin a scathing 'big girl's blouse' look. He stopped to talk to Nora before they both shook their heads sadly and walked inside. Diane Wigglesworth was sticking a poster of Bo Derek in the window of her Hair Salon and Amelia Duff was telling Margery Ackroyd why every village in England would always need a post office.

Heading down the York Road towards Victor Pratt's garage came Deke Ramsbottom on his tractor, towing a trailer load of cow manure. With his stetson hat shielding his eyes from the sun, he appeared completely oblivious to the dreadful smell as he whistled the theme from *Rawhide* and waved to every passer-by. Finally, Stan Coe roared past the village green in his muddy Land-Rover and gave me an evil stare as he drove up the Easington Road.

The first children were arriving and Heathcliffe Earnshaw and his little brother Terry were walking towards school. They had just purchased two giant humbugs from Prudence Golightly's shop. The humbugs were so large their lips could no longer meet. Speech was rendered impossible, so they merely waved a cheerful hello with happy thoughts of six weeks of endless playtimes only one school day away.

When I walked back into school, Vera, Anne and Jo were standing in the car park in animated conversation with Sally. They all looked tired but happy and I guessed they were talking about holidays, babies or teddy bears or, possibly, all three. Each one of them carried a much-loved and well-worn teddy bear in preparation for the afternoon picnic on the school field. I glanced at the distant hills where clouds were gathering and hoped the weather would stay fine for our last day.

At a quarter past ten the hall was full of children, parents, grandparents, school governors and every member of staff. It was our 'Leavers' Assembly', when we said good-bye to the children in my class who were moving on to Easington Comprehensive School.

I welcomed our official guest, one of our school governors Major Rupert Forbes-Kitchener, military medals gleaming on the breast pocket of his smart grey suit. Our first hymn was 'All Things Bright and Beautiful'. The Revd Joseph Evans was sitting next to his fellow school governor and home-made wine connoisseur Albert Jenkins, resplendent in his new three-piece suit. They both sang with gusto.

After Sally's recorder group had played 'Morning Has Broken', we all enjoyed a rousing rendition of 'One More Step Along the World I Go'. Vera smiled at me as we sang the lines 'Give me courage when the world is rough, Keep me loving though the world is tough' . . . and I wondered what was going through her mind.

After Joseph had invited us to join him in the Lord's Prayer, ten-year-old Katy Ollerenshaw stood up and read our school prayer in a loud, clear voice.

'Dear Lord,
This is our school, let peace dwell here,
Let the room be full of contentment, let love
   abide here,
Love of one another, love of life itself,
And love of God.
Amen.'

The major made a wonderful speech about the good start in life provided by Ragley School during the past one hundred years and described it as the centre of our village community. With great ceremony, he presented a book to each of the thirteen school leavers. All the pupils were applauded as they walked out to receive their prizes, while their tearful parents craned their necks at the back of the hall.

Finally, it was my turn. I thanked the parents, the members of the PTA and the school governors for their support, but, before I could close the assembly, Staff Nurse Sue Phillips raised her hand politely and asked everyone to show their appreciation to all the teachers and the ancillary staff. There was a lump in my throat as I looked round at my colleagues.

Shirley Mapplebeck, Doreen Critchley and the dinner ladies, all in their best summer dresses, sat on a row of chairs in front of the kitchen door and smiled broadly. Vera Evans, immaculate in her pin-striped business suit and elegant cream blouse, looked at Ruby Smith, who was sitting next to her, and offered her a lace handkerchief. Ruby dabbed the tears from her eyes and pressed her favourite straw hat, covered in wild roses, further down on to her thick chestnut curls. Sally Pringle bowed her head thoughtfully and Jo Hunter's eyes sparkled with thoughts of a new computer.

I looked at my trusted deputy and Anne Grainger gave me that calm smile I knew so well. It was at times like this that I remembered why I had come into teaching.

Jodie Cuthbertson rang the bell for morning playtime and I wandered outside to talk to my school leavers, but it was a group of children in Jo's class who caught my eye. Elisabeth Amelia Dudley-Palmer had invited everyone in her class to her eighth-birthday party.

'We'll be playing Musical Chairs and Postman's Knock,' she announced to her assembled classmates.

'Ah'd rather play Star Wars,' said Heathcliffe.

'Well, it's my party and you'll play the games I choose,' said Elisabeth Amelia and walked away primly.

Heathcliffe stared after her. 'Yes, but when ah'm ruler o' G'lactic Empire you'll do what ah say then,' he added darkly.

At twelve o'clock Vera looked round my classroom door and beckoned me. 'It's Miss Henderson on the telephone,

Mr Sheffield. I'll send your class out to lunch if you wish.'

'Thanks, Vera,' I said and hurried into the empty school office. I picked up the receiver. 'Hello. Is that you, Beth?'

'Jack, sorry if this is a bad moment but it's hectic here and I didn't know when I might catch you.'

'It's fine, Beth. The lunch bell's just gone.'

'I just wanted to say I hope you have a great holiday and thanks for all your help this year, particularly with all the new documentation. I would have been lost without you.'

'It was a pleasure, Beth . . . and, by all accounts, you've had a really successful year. I've heard wonderful things about Hartingdale.'

'Thanks, Jack. It's been a good experience for me but there's a lot I would do differently next year.'

'That's what I said after my first year. I still don't know how I survived.'

'So what are your plans for the holiday?' asked Beth.

I sighed. 'Nothing certain as yet.'

'Oh, well . . .'

'Beth . . . how about meeting up, maybe over the weekend?'

There was a pause. 'I'm going down to Hampshire, Jack. My parents asked me to join them for a short break on the south coast.'

'Oh . . . so when are you leaving?'

'Tonight, around six.'

'So soon?'

'Yes.'

'Well, have a wonderful time. Perhaps you could call me when you get back.'

There was no reply.

Suddenly, Sally and Jo walked into the office.

'I'll have to go. 'Bye, Beth.'

''Bye, Jack.'

Sally and Jo glanced at me and hurried through to the staff-room and I was left alone with my thoughts.

At two o'clock it was time for the teddy bears' picnic and the whole school marched out with picnic rugs and teddy bears on to the school field.

The children in my class carried their chairs for the parents, governors and staff, while Shirley and Mrs Critchley set up a refreshments table that included a mountain of honey sandwiches and jugs of home-made lemonade. Mothers walked up the drive with their toddlers and a few with babies wheeled their prams and pushchairs into the shady area by the cycle shed. It was a great experience for the four-year-olds who were due to start school next September and they looked in awe as their big brothers and sisters showed them where they would be hanging their coats on their first day in six weeks' time.

Suddenly there was a huge cheer when Jeremy Bear arrived. In the back room of the General Stores, Prudence Golightly had dressed him in his party clothes and he looked quite magnificent. The major saluted him, Vera clapped her hands in delight and all the children rushed up to him to admire Ragley's best bear. Jeremy was wearing a neatly ironed, short-sleeved white shirt, chocolate-brown shorts with yellow gingham braces and a matching gingham bow tie. His socks were snowy white and his shiny brogues, much to the major's amusement, were similar to his. The ensemble was completed with an entirely appropriate straw hat and a pair of sunglasses for this hot sunny afternoon.

'Come and sit next to me,' said Vera.

'And me,' said the major.

Sally was soon surrounded by all the young mothers. Her news had spread round the village in the time it took Margery Ackroyd to visit each shop on the High Street. Meanwhile, Jo was moving from group to group, filling plastic beakers from a huge aluminium jug of lemonade, and my school leavers were handing out plates of sandwiches. The humidity was building up and I wished I didn't have to wear a tie. I removed my sports jacket and sat on a chair next to Anne.

'A perfect end to another year, Jack,' said Anne. 'We're lucky the weather has held out for us. In this heat, it has to break soon.'

I tugged at my collar and wiped the perspiration from my spectacles. 'I agree,' I said, 'and thanks again . . . for everything, Anne. It's been another busy year.'

Anne smiled and offered me a honey sandwich.

By five thirty the school was silent. Ruby had told me she would be in tomorrow to start her 'holiday polish' and, with a final clatter of her mop and bucket, she was gone. I sat at my desk in the office, opened the bottom drawer, and took out the school logbook. The academic year 1979–80 was over and I had just written '88 children were registered on roll on this last day of the school year' when, to my surprise, Vera's car pulled into the car park. I had already said goodbye to her.

She walked into the office and began to fill the kettle.

'Hello, Vera. Have you left something behind?'

'Yes. I forgot my camera, but I'll make you a cup of tea while I'm here.'

'Oh, thank you.'

Vera took my mug off the shelf. 'I saw Miss Henderson shopping in the village,' said Vera.

'Yes. She's going down to Hampshire.'

I stood up and stared through the office window. The school field was silent and still in the oppressive heat of this humid day. Suddenly, the whistle of the kettle broke the silence. Vera poured the tea and placed the mug on the coaster on my desk.

Then she did something she had never done before. It took a few moments for me to realize it. She put her hand on my shoulder and stared at me in a knowing way. It was as if she had been waiting for an eternity to say exactly what was on her mind. Then, very quietly, she said, 'Jack . . . Jack, listen to me.'

It was the first time she had ever called me by my first name. After almost three years of working together Vera had never, ever, called me anything but Mr Sheffield.

'Jack,' she repeated softly. 'You are a dear teacher.'

I looked up in surprise.

'You are also a dear man . . . but sometimes I wonder

if you know the first thing about women.' Her eyes crinkled into a smile tinged with sadness. Then she stood up and walked to the window. Outside, the countryside shimmered and dark, ominous clouds had begun to gather. 'Go and find her, Jack . . . don't let her go. That happened to me once. I wouldn't want you to let it happen to Beth.'

I didn't know what to say, so I closed the logbook and returned it to the drawer in the desk. At the bottom of the drawer was a photograph and I took it out and handed it to Vera.

Three people . . . two sisters . . . one problem.

Vera looked at it for a moment, smiled and put it back on my desk. Then she walked to the office door, opened it and turned to face me. 'Jack, there are many doors to the heart and not all of them are closed.'

Then she walked away.

I looked at the photograph again. There were many pathways to love but mine felt like a labyrinth in a maze of secrets. Once again, the school was silent apart from the tick-tock of the school clock.

I glanced at my watch. It was a quarter to six.

I made my decision. There was no time to lose.

The weather looked ominous as I locked the school door, hurried down the worn steps and across the playground. The sky was getting darker and the oppressive heat was almost unbearable. I wrenched off my tie and unbuttoned my collar. When I reached the car park, I glanced across towards the Hambleton hills, where rain squalls like grey lace curtains were gathering over the dark slopes and the patchwork quilt of fields and forests.

The countryside around me was still, waiting for the onslaught. The hedgerows, thick with bracken and wild blackberries, harebells and the tall crowns of cow parsley, shimmered in the heat haze. Threatening clouds, like celestial chariots of war, began to fill the sky. Any second now the storm would arrive . . . a big storm.

The light turned to dusk. I switched on my headlights and drove down the school drive, past the village green and up the Morton Road. I prayed I would get to Beth's house before it was too late.

And then suddenly it happened.

The sky was broken.

The world became dark as night, crushed beneath the iron fist of a cloudburst, then lit with the searing flash of lightning strikes. It was as if the heavens were being ripped apart. All round me, the vast plain of York was being hammered by the deafening drumbeat of a summer thunderstorm of massive ferocity. In seconds the road before me was awash with black running water and I peered through narrowed eyes as I tried to steer my car through the deluge.

The heat that had built up during the strawberries-and-cream days of Wimbledon had finally exploded in a withering hail of tumultuous rainfall. My windscreen wipers couldn't cope and I slowed down, unable to see. On a sharp bend there was a dip in the road and, as I splashed into a huge pool of standing water, my engine cut out. I remembered reading about water in the carburettor in a car-maintenance manual long ago but it was of little use to me now. My car was well and truly stranded!

I knew every yard of the journey to Beth's house. It was only a few minutes away. There seemed to be no alternative. I couldn't push the car out of the dip in the road and a jump-start was out of the question. After a few futile turns of the ignition key, I took a deep breath and jumped out into the torrential downpour. In seconds I was soaked to the skin. I tried to push the car into a safer position but it was to no avail. Then I removed my spectacles, stuffed them in my pocket, put my jacket over my head and began to walk.

Beth's car was still outside her house and I dashed up the path and rattled the door knocker. The door opened and Beth looked at me in amazement.

'Jack . . . What on earth! . . . Come in quickly.' I stepped on to the Welcome mat, water dripping from me, and Beth closed the door. 'Come into the sitting room. I'll get a towel.'

'No, please wait, Beth. I'm sorry about this. My car broke down just down the road. I needed to speak to you before you left.' The words came out in a torrent.

Beth looked at me curiously. 'What's the matter?'

'There's something I want to ask you, Beth.'

'Yes?'

'It's been on my mind for a long time.'

Beth just stared at me and didn't reply.

I struggled to find the right words. 'You must know how I feel about you.'

Beth's gaze softened. 'Do I?'

'From the first moment I saw you.'

She smiled. 'You mean when you were dressed in your old overalls, sweeping the school drive?'

'Well, not exactly . . . but certainly since we went on holiday two years ago.'

'What is it, Jack?'

I took a step forward and held her hand. Then I took a deep breath. 'Beth, will you marry me?'

The door of her lounge was open and she glanced at a faded photograph propped on her old upright piano. It showed Beth and Laura as children, holding hands on a sandy beach during a long-ago holiday.

I looked at her face.

There was silence between us.

It seemed like a lifetime.

Then her soft green eyes stared back at me like mirrors of experienced past.

And in a heartbeat I knew what her answer would be.